Macmillan   A Study in Ambiguity

by Anthony Sampson

Allen Lane The Penguin Press London 1967

Allen Lane The Penguin Press   Vigo Street   London w1

Printed by Western Printing Services Ltd, Bristol

Photogravure plates printed by D. H. Greaves Ltd, Scarborough

CONTENTS

By the same author:

Drum: A Venture into the New Africa
The Treason Cage
Commonsense about Africa
Anatomy of Britain
Anatomy of Britain Today

ACKNOWLEDGEMENTS

The author and publisher wish to thank the following for permission to reproduce photographs: Syndication International; the Press Association; Fox Photos; the Camera Press; the Radio Times Hulton Picture Library; Keystone; Loomis Dean; *The Observer* and *The Times*.

In this book I have tried to put the political career of Harold Macmillan into some kind of perspective, and to assess his achievement against the problems of his age. Macmillan had the longest unbroken term as prime minister – six years and nine months – of any man since Asquith; and that period was long enough, and defined enough, to have some meaning as 'the age of Macmillan'. It began, dramatically, with the collapse of the Suez adventure; and it ended, equally dramatically, with the aftermath of the Profumo affair and the prime minister's sudden disappearance. His premiership coincided with the penultimate stage of the retreat from Empire, and with unprecedented domestic affluence, both of which came to be closely associated with his presence: and Macmillan's style and methods stamped themselves so firmly on the country, that when he resigned Britain seemed a noticeably different place.

I have not attempted to write a comprehensive biography. For many important facts – both public and private – we must wait another twenty years. My method has been to pick up the important threads in his character, to trace them through his career, and to dwell on significant moments. I have interspersed contemporary evidence with my own recollections of him during his premiership, when I spent some happy times observing him, particularly on his tours abroad; I have also drawn heavily on the impressions and recollections of his colleagues, to whom I am indebted for their helpful candour. For information about Mrs Helen Macmillan I am much indebted to Mr James Eldridge, himself from Indiana, who is writing her biography.

In assembling this book, I have owed much to Mrs Mollie

Philipps, for her great help in research and advice; and also to my secretary, Miss Alexa Wilson, for her patient assistance, typing and re-typing. I must specially thank Tony Godwin, of Allen Lane The Penguin Press, for asking me to write it.

MACMILLAN: A STUDY IN AMBIGUITY

1. Four Macmillans

Pure English blood does not seem capable of producing
a really strong man.
— DE GAULLE; TALKING TO KENNEDY ABOUT THE MIXED
ANCESTRY OF MACMILLAN,
CHURCHILL, LLOYD GEORGE AND DISRAELI[1]

There are several different Harold Macmillans. All politicians are actors, and prime ministers play a variety of roles. Any man who has both to preside over a cabinet and to make electioneering speeches must have some kind of split personality. But Macmillan's special complexity is made up, not only of subtlety and theatricality, but of the tangled roots which appear and reappear throughout his career. I have traced four particular roots: the Scottish publisher; the radical intellectual; the Guards officer; the duke's son-in-law. Each of them goes quite deep, and each has a remarkable history. The contrast between these backgrounds gives the key to Macmillan's character, but it also accounts for the flaws.

The Publisher

The deepest, and the most enduring, heritage belongs to Macmillan the publisher; and it is certainly the memory and the experience of this family tradition which helped to give Macmillan his special confidence and toughness. His family background went far into the nineteenth century. His grandfather Daniel, who founded the Macmillan fortunes, was born in 1813; and in his short lifetime – he died at forty-four – he thrust into the midst of Victorian religious, intellectual and commercial life, and forged a powerful tradition.

Harold Macmillan often referred to himself as 'a crofter's grandson'; but Daniel, though never a crofter, was one of the most remarkable of the Victorian self-made men. The Macmillan family had settled on the island of Arran, at the mouth of the Clyde, in the early eighteenth century; they were poor proud people of Covenanting stock. Daniel's father, Duncan Macmillan, had migrated to the small town of Irvine on the mainland, and Daniel was brought up in great poverty, the misery of which he never forgot. He was educated at the local Common School, and at eleven was apprenticed to an eccentric Irvine bookseller. At the age of twenty, in spite of bad health, he came to London. He could find no bookselling work – he was refused a job by Longmans – and finally went to Cambridge where he found a place at £30 a year, and worked twelve hours a day. He read prodigiously – including Jeremy Taylor, Landor, Carlyle and Leighton – and suffered from religious doubts about 'Calvinistic cobwebs'. He became a Baptist, and started a diary full of his spiritual experiences as well as rules on study, 'fixing the attention' and 'improving the memory'.

Later Daniel moved to London, with his brother Alexander, started his own shop in Aldersgate Street, and in the same year bought another shop in Cambridge – with the help of a loan of £500 from Archdeacon Hare, whom Daniel had met following a correspondence. Soon afterwards the brothers published their first book, called *The Philosophy of Training*.

So began the publishing house of Macmillan. Like other Victorian publishers – Thomas Nelson, Collins, Hodder and Stoughton – it was founded on a mixture of Christian zeal and commercial shrewdness. Its success was based on the surging desire for self-improvement, the growth of schools and the need for educational books; but Daniel and his brother always emphasized their high ideals.

In selling books [Daniel wrote to his friend Maclehose], you never, surely, thought you were merely working for bread . . . if the business should prosper, we shall, both of us, do our best to realise some of our ideals . . . we feel however, that the world can go on without us, or our ideals; and, in the meantime, we shall strive to do the work that lies nearest us in the best manner we can.

The Macmillans prospered. Archdeacon Hare introduced them to Cambridge figures, liberal churchmen and social reformers, who not only bought their books, but also brought them their own work to be published. They had met Charles Kingsley and in 1855 published *Westward Ho!*, their first bestseller. Two years later they published Thomas Hughes's *Tom Brown's Schooldays*.

Daniel's correspondence with Archdeacon Hare led to, among other things, his involvement with the Christian Socialist Movement, which had a large influence on the family. Before their first meeting Daniel had written to Hare,

It may be as well to let you know that I am only one of the Clerkly species whose singular and unfortunate position with regard to spiritual culture was the first cause of my writing to you. I have no learning, can speak no language except English, speak none except a partly intelligible Scotch-English dialect.

Hare introduced him to his brother-in-law, F. D. Maurice, whose book *The Kingdom of Christ* had already impressed Daniel – 'A book I could not live without'. Maurice was an Anglican theologian, who had been shocked by the year of revolutions of 1848. He agreed with the Chartists and radicals on the necessity for reform, but felt that Christianity should take the place of socialist doctrines in the reconstruction of society. He was the spiritual leader of 'the Christian Socialist Movement', irreverently called 'muscular Christianity', of which Charles Kingsley was a leader. Maurice became a close friend of the Macmillans, they called him 'The Prophet', published his numerous books and were indefatigable in promoting his beliefs. Largely due to Maurice's influence Daniel left the Baptist Church for the Church of England.

The Christian Socialists believed that 'politics for the people cannot be separated from religion'. They made contact with working-class leaders and encouraged cooperative production.

3

They were called Christian Socialists 'to commit us to the conflict which we must engage in sooner or later with the unsocial Christian and the unChristian socialists'. Their curious slogan was 'consumption is the merely human element in life – production is the divine'. Alexander Macmillan helped to found the Cambridge Working Men's College and wrote a tract called 'British Industry and Socialism' which foreshadowed some of his great-nephew's thoughts in the 1930s. In the end Christian Socialism faded away, and the cooperative associations failed, but its leaders had helped to develop the working-class movements, and to stimulate the social interest of the churches. The influence of Christian Socialism endured in the Macmillan family: the Calvinist element in his upbringing contributed to Harold's sense of being one of the elect – which was to be reinforced by Balliol. But it also left him without that common touch so precious to politicians.

Daniel died in 1857, leaving a widow with four children, of whom Maurice (Harold's father) was the second son. 'You will see so much of me come out in the children, dear,' he said in his last words to his wife, 'it will be a great comfort to you . . . but you will see the impetuosity.' Daniel left the firm, and the family, with his personality deeply embedded in it. He was an extraordinary combination – a scholar more than a businessman, an ambitious man who kept his detachment and idealism – and his achievement fascinated his grandson.

Daniel's memory inspired his brother Alexander, who brought up his children as his own, and built up the firm. Alexander was a more vigorous character, a born publisher who handled his authors with skill, and became a friend of fashionable intellectuals. He moved the business back to London and held what he called 'Tobacco Parliaments' once a week after the shop was closed, where such figures as Tom Hughes, Holman Hunt, Tennyson, Huxley and Norman Lockyer would meet. Alexander started a magazine to attract new authors, became publisher to Oxford University, gave a new policy to the Clarendon Press, started an American branch in 1869 and founded the scientific journal *Nature* (which the firm still publish very successfully). By the 1880s Macmillans were publishing philosophers and logicians, psychologists and economists. Macmillans, said H. G. Wells in 1915, were 'solid and sane and sound'.

Daniel's and Alexander's sons were all brought up together in a large house in Upper Tooting. Maurice inherited his father's studious bent: he was a classical scholar under the great Dr Thring, headmaster of Uppingham, and at Christ's College, Cambridge. He became a classical master at St Paul's for five years (Harold Macmillan, like de Gaulle, was very much a schoolmaster's son). He then joined the family firm, where he was responsible for the large educational side. He was withdrawn, shy, but hard-headed: he had a great capacity for detail, and built up the enormous Macmillan business in India. ('It was a foible of his,' wrote Charles Morgan, in his history of the company, 'to pretend that his hard-headedness had been given to the world as a check upon his elder brother's enthusiasms.'[2]) Maurice was a director, with his elder brother Frederick and his cousin George. The three directors were a law to themselves, and board meetings were often heated. Lovat Dickson described them as 'bluff Christian gentlemen dispensing good and making a satisfactory profit out of it'.[3] A 'Macmillan book' came to have a special connotation of solidity and endurability: their authors included Tennyson, Hardy, Gladstone, Henry James, Kipling and Lewis Carroll. By the time Harold Macmillan was a young man, Macmillans was an institution.

On to this strong Scots growth there was grafted, in 1883, an American addition: when he was thirty, Maurice Macmillan met in Paris an American music student, called Helen Belles. She was a powerful woman, and was to have a dominating influence on Harold's life. Her father was a modest country doctor in Indiana, and she had been brought up as a Methodist at the local village school, and at a finishing school at Indianapolis. She had married a painter, who died soon afterwards, and she boldly decided, as a widow of nineteen, to go to Paris, to study music and sculpture on the left bank. Maurice Macmillan sang duets with her, married her, and brought her to London.

Helen Macmillan – or Nellie as she was called – was handsome, efficient and very energetic, while her husband was shy and self-effacing. Her impact on the family firm was formidable: she had none of the aristocratic aloofness from 'trade'. She took a close interest in the business, and helped to start the textbook side: she ran a charity school for orphaned boys, which provided staff, including several managers, for the firm. She had great business sense, and it was she who insisted that her sons bought the rights of *Gone with the Wind*, which turned out to be their greatest best-seller. At home, she ruled the household firmly and meticulously, laying in enormous stocks of commodities, and like many American matriarchs regarded housekeeping as a kind of heavy industry. It was Nellie Macmillan who decided to buy Birch Grove, the spacious country estate in Sussex where the Macmillans went to live in 1906. Her two other sons, Daniel and Arthur, both escaped from her overpowering influence when they grew up; but Harold remained close to her. When he became engaged, his mother decided to build a new house – a big neo-Georgian villa, which she thought would be suitable for a future prime minister. She went on living there, much of the time with Harold and his family, until she died in 1937.

It was Helen Macmillan, much more than Maurice, who spurred Harold's ambition; she wanted him to be prime minister, and she urged him and protected him through every stage. 'No one who has not experienced it,' her son wrote, 'can realise the determination of an American mother defending one of her children.' Her influence on Harold was so lasting that when he regained consciousness after being bombed in Algiers in 1943, six years after she had died, his first words were, 'Tell my mother I'm alive and well.'

Harold Macmillan was always intensely aware of his family tradition, his Scottish ancestors and their Victorian achievement: this doubtless encouraged him to see himself as the last of the Victorians – a role he enjoyed more as the years went by. He took a picture of his grandfather's cottage from ministry to ministry and finally to Downing Street: it was his version of the log-cabin story of American politics. He believed that the Scots people had a more rooted and solid background than the great mass of suburban people in the south, whom he always despised. But he was not as genuinely Scottish as he boasted; he was vulnerable to the peculiar snobberies that expatriate Scots develop in England, and he did not seek after the company of Scotsmen. Yet much of his strength certainly came from his grandfather's stern tradition.

The Scholar

Harold's education followed a family pattern: the Macmillans were scholars as well as businessmen, and they instilled a respect for scholarship in their children. When he was nine, in 1903, Harold was sent to Summer Fields, an exclusive prep school in Oxford, which already had a strong family connection: it had been founded by Mrs Maclaren, who was married to the founder of the Oxford University Gymnasium. Inevitably, the school motto was *Mens Sana in Corpore Sano*. But, in the words of the school's present headmaster,

what really gave the school impetus was the enthusiasm of Alexander Macmillan, the founder of the publishing firm. He met the Maclarens when they were holidaying at Sandown in the Isle of Wight in August 1864. He decided to put his nephew and son in her charge. They later became respectively her first scholar and her first Eton scholar in 1866 and 1868. They started not only the tradition of scholarship but also the dynastic tradition on which Summer Fields so much relies. They still have fourth-generation descendants in the school. Perhaps it was this literary and artistic background that kept this school safe from the philistine athletic excesses that overcame so many others in the last century. It has always been the brains rather than the brawns that have earned the extra half-holidays. [4]

Harold thus found himself in a very competitive world. As he argued sixty years later:

We did somehow get it into our heads that if a thing was worth doing at all it was worth doing well. Today, when many people

7

deplore any form of competitive effort or emulation among the young as anti-social and even immoral, I am happy to see that the pride of the school in scholarship and games remains undimmed.

He was a promising scholar. He was the best classic in his form,[5] and played the part of the Prime Minister in the school play, *Rumpelstiltzkin*. A photograph of him at the time shows him looking angelic, with big soulful eyes and a very sensitive mouth. 'I cannot remember anything particular about him except that he was extremely pleasant when one met him,' recalls one contemporary, Major-General Sir Miles Graham. Admiral Sir Edward Parry says, 'I do just remember Harold Macmillan as a little boy who always wore Norfolk jackets.' A. D. Finney remembers that

Macmillan liked the type of story in which one man produces a garbled version of what was said by another with ludicrous results, e.g. 'Moses was an oyster (austere) man and made toe ointment (atonement) for the people's shins (sins). . . .'[6]

Summer Fields concentrated on Eton, and particularly Eton scholarships (of the 2,800 boys who had been through the school by 1960, 951 had gone to Eton, of whom 343 were scholars). And from Summer Fields Harold went, like his uncle George and his elder brother Daniel, to Eton as a scholar. His career at Eton was undistinguished – the only mention of him in the *Eton College Chronicle* was in the autumn half in 1909, when he played in the College side in the Wall Game. In scholarship he was eclipsed by Daniel, two years his senior, who was a brilliant classicist, a close friend of Maynard Keynes, and won the Newcastle prize and a scholarship to Balliol. Daniel – who later became head of the publishing firm – was wittier and more relaxed than his young brother. Harold was always aware of his brother's superior intellect, and often referred to it in later life.

Harold was a bookish, introverted boy: he said later, 'I learnt books before I learnt people'. His home life, in Cadogan Place, was quite austere: he looked with envy at Lord Cadogan's big house at the end of the street, and longed to go to country houses in the summer. Eton reinforced the family austerity: 'It was plain living and high thinking – at least in those days. But I was brought up in both.'[7]

He left Eton early, with a weak heart, and we have a glimpse at this time of the sensitive and anguished boy. While staying at home as an invalid he was given private tutoring by one of Daniel's friends, Ronald Knox, who was then a High Anglican, and one of the most brilliant young men of his generation: at Oxford he had been president of the Union, and the centre of a group of bright undergraduates who included the legendary Grenfells, Patrick Shaw-Stewart, etc. He taught them the ritual of Anglo-Catholicism, and wrote them long letters full of theology and gossip. Knox's influence on Harold was considerable, and in his autobiography, *The Spiritual Aeneid*, he describes his friendship with a boy called C, who can be clearly identified as Macmillan. Knox's tutoring post was not, he explains, of a religious nature, but he felt that C was 'in need of spiritual assistance'. When one of Knox's friends wrote asking whether he was making Harold an Anglo-Catholic he replied, 'I'm not making him anything yet, but biding my time. I trust I may be sent some opportunity.'[8] Harold was greatly impressed by a High Church service to which Knox took him, and enthralled by Knox himself. His mother, who was a Methodist, disapproved of this growing fascination and Mrs Macmillan asked Knox to promise not to mention religion to her son. Knox refused and left. He wrote to his sister, 'The only thing which complicates the situation is that I'm by now extremely and (not quite unreturnedly) fond of the boy and it's been a horrid wrench to go without saying a word to him of what I wanted to say.'[9]

In the autumn of 1912 Macmillan went up to Balliol, with an exhibition; and the brilliance of Balliol clearly came as a sudden contrast to the austerity of his home and school life. Balliol at that time was described (as Canteloup) by Aldous Huxley:

There is an equal profusion of Firsts and Blues; there are Union orators of every shade of opinion and young men so languidly well

9

bred as to take no interest in politics of any kind; there are drinkers of cocoa and drinkers of champagne. Canteloup is a microcosm, a whole world in miniature; and whatever your temperament or habits may be . . . Canteloup will provide you with congenial companions and a spiritual home.[10]

Balliol was no longer the intellectual forcing house of Jowett's day, but Balliol men still had what Asquith called a 'tranquil consciousness of effortless superiority'. As Ronald Knox described it:

At Balliol we came in for a tradition bequeathed by earlier generations of Balliol men and some of us I must say developed it: its atmosphere was one of energetic rowing, hard drinking, plain dressing, occasional gambling and unexpected because apparently unmerited academic triumphs.[11]

Asquith himself, 'the epitome of the Balliol man' and the first Balliol prime minister, was then at his peak.

The Balliol dons were dedicated to the college, and known by their Christian names or by nicknames like 'Fluffy' Davis or 'Sligger' Urquhart. Macmillan saw much of Urquhart, who was very popular and had cosy and varied gatherings of undergraduates in his rooms: he helped to change the Balliol ethos from preoccupation with intellect to concern with more personal relationships. In the summer he would take carefully selected reading parties – which included Macmillan and Walter Monckton – to his chalet in the Alps. Another of Macmillan's tutors was A. D. Lindsay, later Master of Balliol, a high-minded Scot, reformer and egalitarian, who much impressed his pupil: twenty-five years later Macmillan supported him in the famous Oxford by-election.

Macmillan enthusiastically adopted the affected nonchalance of the 'Balliol manner', and was known as an aesthete. One of his contemporaries Colin Coote described him as being 'tall, willowy and languid', and suspected him of modelling himself on Arthur Balfour.[12] He was still a shy man, and quite early established the protective theatrical façade, which he took into politics. His first recorded involvement with politics was in the

Union (Oxford-educated prime ministers can be divided into those who didn't use the Union, like Rosebery, Attlee, Eden, Home and Wilson, and those who did, like Gladstone, Salisbury, Asquith and Macmillan). The Union favours a formal mandarin style, and Macmillan's speeches already showed the love of epigram, the careful preparation and the histrionics which showed themselves all through his political career. He was elected secretary of the Union 'as expected' in November 1913, and junior treasurer in March 1914. (Had it not been for the war he would probably have been president.) Party politics were bitter at the time and this was reflected in the Union. Macmillan's allegiances veered between Liberal and Labour. In October 1912 he supported Harry Strauss (now the High Tory Lord Conesford) on the motion 'That this House approves the main principles of Socialism'. In 1913 he again supported Strauss in a pro-socialist motion ('Mr H. Macmillan made a really good effort,' said *Isis*, the Oxford undergraduate magazine, 'He added distinctly to the discussion by dissecting the economic tendency of the age'), and also supported Asquith ('he was hardly logical and rambled badly').

His first speech 'on the paper' at the Union was in February 1913, on a motion *against* Public Schools.

Mr M. H. Macmillan in a brilliant maiden speech did not attack the public school man, but argued that a public school education did not produce active citizens [according to *Isis*]: but why this extravagant laudation of more and often misplaced energy? The prime and peaceful repose of the protoplasm, which he understood to be the chief ideal of the Tory mind, could be rudely shaken by this new doctrine.

After this Macmillan often spoke and was reported frequently – 'Mr Macmillan was decidedly amusing. He concluded *inter alia* with quotations from F. E. Smith, John Bright, G.O.M. and Macaulay' . . . 'Mr M. H. Macmillan was quite brilliant in his way. His phraseology was wonderful and except for a tendency to become inaudible at the end of his sentences his delivery was nearly perfect'. He kept to his literary, mandarin style all through his political career, and later lamented how in Parliament the 'rapier' had given way to the 'bludgeon'.

One report calls him 'One of the most polished orators in the Union – perhaps just a little too polished', and he is already criticized for his artificial style and lack of originality. Though he is mentioned as being one of the three good exponents of the 'Oxford Manner' and 'the most polished of the mere epigrammatists', this was not altogether popular. (The best speakers of his day were A. P. Herbert and Victor Gollancz.) Macmillan always delivered 'prepared speeches', and showed no skill at debating. The Union at this time was much criticized for the dullness of its speakers. While Macmillan was secretary, the leading members were called 'miniature tyrants': 'They approach the despatch box with the appearance of a parson approaching the pulpit or a lecturer his desk.'

Macmillan's involvement with Ronald Knox continued, more intensely; and we see more of the emotional and quite vulnerable young Macmillan, who was later to retreat into a shell. In 1912 Knox had taken up his new post as Chaplain at Trinity, where he was 'at home' to a circle of undergraduates. Knox wrote: 'I have never met conversation so brilliant – with the brilliance of humour not of wit. It was among these that I first began to make proselytes.'[13] To the undergraduates Knox was a connection with the golden age of Balliol. Macmillan joined this group, as did Guy Lawrence, whom Knox refers to as 'B' in his *Spiritual Aeneid*. Knox, writing of the two of them, said they had adopted 'Ronnie Knox's religion' (he shuddered at the name), and that his friendship with them 'did much at the time to make me comfortable in my then position'.[14]

In vacations Knox arranged reading parties, and he planned one for the summer of 1914, to which Lawrence was going, and to which Macmillan was invited; but his mother disapproved. 'Why should "C" give any reason whatever for his whereabouts?' wrote Lawrence: 'It's all silly nonsense this truckling onto the old-fashioned ignorance of his parents, hanging on to his mother's apron strings. I should like five minutes' conversation with her on the point.'[15] But war broke out, the reading party never came off, and Macmillan and Guy Lawrence both went off to enlist. They came to Knox to ask his advice on becoming Roman Catholics, as they thought the Anglican position was becoming impossible. Knox could only tell them to do as they thought best, whereupon Lawrence went straight to Farm Street and in an hour came out a Roman Catholic. (He wrote to Knox, 'Come and be happy. "C" will, I think, follow very soon.'[16]) However, on 22 July 1915 'C' wrote to Knox,

I'm going to be rather odd. I'm *not* going to 'Pope' until after the War (if I'm alive).

(1) My people. Not at all a good reason which weighs . . .

(2) My whole brain is in a whirl. I don't think God will mind. . . . But I believe now that I may have to *relearn* everything. . . . We go to France Sunday.[17]

When Knox became a Roman Catholic in 1917, Macmillan wrote that he and Lawrence had reached the end of the journey 'while I am still lagging, timidly cowardly and faint. I feel sure you are right.' He feels 'horribly like a deserter' but hopes they will think of him as a 'conscientious objector'. Although their ways will diverge, 'There is left in me at any rate a memory; an experience never forgotten or, I hope, a turn of mind, which but for you I should never have had, remains to me – "for information and necessary action" if God wills.'[18]

Knox remained a life-long friend of Macmillan, and there remained something of the monk *manqué* inside the politician. In 1957 when Knox was dying of cancer, Macmillan invited him to stay at 10 Downing Street when he came to see his doctor. The next day the prime minister took him in his car to Paddington.

Macmillan, like most Balliol men, loves to commemorate its splendour. He never showed much enthusiasm for other kinds of education. Its sophistication, and *la douceur de vivre* became a much sharper memory after the war: of the scholars and exhibitioners of his year, only he and one other – Humphrey Sumner, later Warden of All Souls – survived. In later years, Macmillan seemed at his happiest when revisiting Oxford, culminating in his extraordinary election to the Chancellorship of Oxford. In a speech to the Balliol society in 1957 he said:

Balliol still retains its unique character among all Oxford colleges and, I was going to say, among all human institutions. . . . And so, because in spite of all the affected cynicism, the passion for epigram, the very natural cult of extreme views, sometimes on the right, sometimes on the left – that youth properly pursues, because after all Balliol is something greater than can be described except in very simple words, I will – greatly daring – go back to Belloc:

> *'Balliol made me, Balliol fed me,*
> *Whatever I had she gave me again;*
> *And the best of Balliol loved and led me.*
> *God be with you Balliol men.'*

As for many men of his background, Oxford was probably the emotional high-point of his life, to which he never ceased to look back with nostalgia. In the summer of 1914 he took a first-class degree in Honour Moderations. Balliol had also given him an exceptionally well-trained mind, which could see through very difficult problems and which he knew to be better than most people's. As with Asquith before him, it was this cool intellectual mastery, more than anything else, that gave him the key to the top.

The Soldier

Then came the war, and a third Macmillan emerged – the disciplined Guards officer. He first joined the King's Royal Rifle Corps and then, through his mother's influence, was allowed into the Grenadier Guards. He has described how he came to admire the qualities of the regular officers: 'I learnt to be a little ashamed of the intolerance and impudence with which the intellectual classes (to which I belonged) were apt to sweep on one side as of no account men who had not learnt their particular jargon or been brought up with their prejudices.'[19] He envied them their contact with ordinary men, and he became fascinated by the discipline. He saw himself acquiring confidence and humility, and having been by nature a 'gownsman', acquiring some qualities of the 'swordsman'.

He had a gruelling and painful war, but – as his letters to his mother show – he found fulfilment and a new self-confidence.

He showed great courage and stamina, and it is surprising that, unlike most of his political contemporaries – Duff Cooper, Eden, Lyttelton, Monckton – he was not decorated. He was wounded three times – first in the head, at the Battle of Loos, another time only slightly, and the third time on the Somme in September 1916. This put him out of action for the rest of the war. He has often described how he lay in no-man's-land with a shattered pelvis for a whole day, surrounded by the dead, and distracting himself by reading Aeschylus between the shelling, and feigning dead when German soldiers passed. After his rescue, he was taken back to England, and spent months in hospital, reading classics and political biographies, re-thinking his beliefs (as his correspondence with Knox shows) and speculating about the political future. He did not finally leave hospital until after the armistice: it was not till 1920 that the wound was healed, and it gave him pain and a shuffling walk for the rest of his life.

The war had a lasting effect on Captain Macmillan's outlook. He talked about it so much afterwards, and in such a stylized way, that his soldier image often seemed artificial. Certainly he could use his military background as a kind of weapon. 'I have always felt a certain contempt for those "gentlemen of England now abed", whether in the First War or the Second, who voluntarily missed their chance or chose to avoid danger by seeking positions of security':[20] and this contempt was apparent in his relations with cabinet colleagues and with Hugh Gaitskell as leader of the opposition. He seemed anxious to compensate for his rarefied academic upbringing with an exaggerated assumption of a military manner, symbolized by that large moustache over the sensitive mouth, which tallied well with High Tory manners.

But beneath the mannerisms, the war had changed his perspective. He had seen the full horrors of mass slaughter – 70,000 men killed in one day on the Somme. He had acquired a political concern for the lives of ordinary men. He had become tougher, more pessimistic, more practical, and a great deal more confident.

The Duke's Son-in-law

After the war, Captain Macmillan, not wanting to go straight into the family firm, stayed on for a year in the Guards and – again through his mother's influence – was offered the job of A.D.C. to the Governor-General of Canada, the Duke of Devonshire. And so a fourth Macmillan made its appearance.

The Cavendish family, of whom the Duke was the head, at that time led a regal, separate existence; they were thought to be richer than the king. They had enormous estates in Ireland and Yorkshire as well as their vast house, Chatsworth, in Derbyshire, and their London mansion, Devonshire House in Piccadilly (where the Rootes showrooms now stand). The family, fortified by their ancient wealth, had a tradition of independence and eccentricity. One Cavendish discovered the composition of water, another built the Cavendish Laboratory at Cambridge. The first duke was one of the seven peers responsible for inviting William of Orange to England, and got a dukedom as a reward; he also built Chatsworth and was fined £30,000 for brawling at Court. Since the sixteenth century the Cavendishes had been knee-deep in politics: they were prominent Whigs, until the eighth duke parted with Gladstone on Home Rule and became head of the small new Liberal Unionist party.

It was his son, the ninth duke – a big walrus-like man – who was now governor-general of Canada. He had been an M.P. for nearly twenty years, and financial secretary to the Treasury until he succeeded to the title. As a popular and conscientious governor-general, he toured the whole country. Later he became colonial secretary in Bonar Law's aristocratic cabinet, worked hard for the Wembley Exhibition of 1924 (he was the anonymous guarantor of its success), and opened Chatsworth to the public. His son, the tenth duke (Lady Dorothy's brother) held minor office in three successive Tory governments, and was head of the British Freemasons.

Macmillan loved his time in Canada – 'In many ways the happiest in my life'. The shy scholar and the serious-minded soldier were both fascinated by the splendour and Whiggish independence of the Devonshires. Macmillan talked politics with the duke, admired him greatly, and got on well with the other A.D.C.s, nearly all sons of peers. There, too, he met the duke's daughter, Lady Dorothy, a warm and attractive girl who had the outspokenness of her family, and who put the intellectual captain at his ease. They became engaged, and in January 1920 came back to England together. After their marriage in April, at St Margaret's, Westminster, their reception was one of the last great social events held at Lansdowne House, the mansion of the bride's grandfather Lord Lansdowne – which was soon afterwards let to Gordon Selfridge, and later demolished: Devonshire House, which was next door, had been sold the week before. The bride's family had invited a huge number of guests, including Queen Alexandra and Princess Victoria, the future King George VI and the Duke of Connaught. The Macmillans, not to be outdone, invited a string of famous authors, led by Thomas Hardy, wearing his O.M. on his last visit to London. A wedding photograph shows the tall stiff figure of Macmillan, in the Groucho moustache, surrounded by young Cavendish bridesmaids.

It is not easy to assess the influence of the Devonshire family on Macmillan's political career. He was never very directly indebted to the Devonshires for his political advancement, and as it turned out, perhaps the most advantageous family connection was with President Kennedy (whose sister was married to Lady Dorothy's nephew). In his early married years, relationships with the Devonshires were never very easy: the family patronized him, and were bored by his intellectual talk. There is a contemporary story that the old duke – one of whose daughters had already married a brewer, Cobbold – muttered gloomily on hearing the news of Lady Dorothy's engagement: 'Well, books is better than beer.' Macmillan enjoyed shooting and loved country houses, but was always bored by the Devonshires' passion, racing. His new ducal *persona* was sometimes at odds with the Balliol scholar.

17

But the connection with the Cavendishes, who had politics in every vein, gave Macmillan a quite new perspective, and soon spurred him into Parliament. In 1922 the Duke became Colonial Secretary, and Macmillan thus heard a lot of High Tory politics: he became friendly, too, with the Duke's son and heir, the Marquess of Hartington, who entered parliament the next year; and with another son-in-law, James Stuart, who became an M.P. in the same year. By this time he was already related by his marriage to sixteen M.P.s. Macmillan, with his natural bent for politics, was determined to do better than those around him: his marriage into a powerful family, as with many other sons-in-law, gave a spur to ambition and a new stage for it, not a resting-place.

Perhaps most important, the Cavendish connection increased Macmillan's fascination with the life of the great country-houses – a life which cut across his own austere family background, and his intellectual discipline. He loved the aristocratic style of their politics, and the atmosphere of Whiggish independence: 'My wife's family had a traditional indulgence for eccentrics,' he wrote later; 'If I had held odd views on politics and economics, so, many years ago, had Lord Shelburne – and more recently, his descendant, Lord Lansdowne – so had Uncle this and Cousin that. It was all in the Whig tradition.'[21] He appreciated the privileged aloofness, and *la douceur de vivre*. It was a fondness which grew on him, with national repercussions, in his premiership.

*

These, then, were four strands of the young Macmillan. Many contemporaries, emerging with moustaches and social indignation from the first war, had similar cross-pulls and varied backgrounds; but Macmillan's mixture, emphasized by his sense of drama, was more extreme than most; and it was not easy to guess which strand, in the end, would be dominant.

NOTES

1. Theodore Sorensen, *Kennedy* (New York: Harper & Row, 1965; London: Hodder & Stoughton), p. 560
2. Charles Morgan, *The House of Macmillan* (London: Macmillan, 1944), p. 185
3. Lovat Dickson, *The House of Words* (London: Macmillan, 1963), p. 204
4. R. Usborne, *A Century of Summer Fields* (London: Methuen, 1964), p. 4
5. Ibid., p. 62   6. Ibid., p. 62
7. Harold Macmillan, *Winds of Change*, vol. I (London: Macmillan, 1966), p. 41
8. Evelyn Waugh, *The Life of Ronald Knox* (London: Chapman & Hall, 1959), p. 106
9. Ibid., p. 106
10. Aldous Huxley, *Limbo* (London: Chatto & Windus, 1946), p. 28
11. Ronald Knox, *A Spiritual Aeneid* (London: Burns & Oates, 1958), p. 53
12. Colin Coote, *Editorial* (London: Eyre & Spottiswoode, 1965), p. 35
13. Ronald Knox, *A Spiritual Aeneid*, p. 117
14. Ibid., p. 118
15. Evelyn Waugh, *The Life of Ronald Knox*, p. 128
16. Ibid., p. 139   17. Ibid., p. 142   18. Ibid., p. 160
19. Harold Macmillan, *Winds of Change*, p. 99
20. Ibid., p. 99   21. Ibid., p. 369

2. Stockton and Parliament

The dual character of the Macmillan experience, namely the soft heart for and the strong determination to help the underdog, and the social habit to associate happily with the overdog.
LORD BUTLER[1]

In 1923, at the age of twenty-nine, Captain Macmillan – who was now working in the family firm – decided to try for Parliament, and went to see the Conservative Central Office. He was asked to stand for a constituency which he had never seen, but which, as it turned out, was to affect his outlook and policies for the rest of his life. Stockton-on-Tees was a town which was feeling the full misery of the gathering slump. Macmillan, like most men of his class, had never seen at close quarters the wretched conditions in the north of England; and the discovery of Stockton had (as he liked to put it) the same kind of impact as going to the front line of the trenches after living in headquarters. He viewed the people of Stockton with the same paternal eyes as he saw his troops in the war.

Stockton was an extreme example of the industrial chaos of Britain in the 1920s. In the early nineteenth century it had been almost the first boom town of the industrial revolution, the port for the rich Durham coalfields, and the casual originator of the first railway in the world: the River Tees in the early nineteenth century was the lifeline of industry, and Stockton itself became a proud and prosperous town, with a magnificent town hall and one of the widest high streets in the north. The shipbuilding yards along the river gave work to thousands of men. Then, after the war, trade collapsed, the yards gradually closed down, the shops were boarded up: the old ware-houses remained crumbling down by the river, as they remain today, a reminder of past prosperity. At the worst point of the slump almost half the male population of Stockton was out of work. Only across the river was there a glimpse of a more hopeful future where, in the new ammonia town of Billingham, the Imperial Chemical Industries were soon building up a well-planned plant.

For Macmillan, the discovery of the desolation of Stockton gave a focal point to his vague radicalism. No place could have been more of a contrast to the world of Chatsworth or Lans-downe House. Stockton at that time was a constituency where most of the working classes voted Tory, and the middle classes voted Liberal: the Labour party was only beginning to make itself felt. Macmillan thus oddly found himself the workers' candidate. In the 1923 election, which he didn't expect to win, he lost to the Liberal candidate by seventy-three votes.

Electioneering was an alarming experience.

I have never liked the rougher side of politics [Macmillan once said]; often I have been repelled in starting off for some meeting at the thought of the heckling and din and the having to attack and defend and all the rest of it. But I used to think to myself – 'My mother would know how to do this, or she would approve of my doing it, and that would make it much easier.'[2]

He was nervous, and had difficulty in making himself heard. His agent told him he would never make a speaker, but his manner gradually improved. The next year the Labour Government fell, and in the general election of October 1924 Macmillan won Stockton by over 3,000 votes. He was then thirty years old.

When Macmillan entered Parliament in October 1924, Baldwin had been elected, in strong contrast to the erratic brilliance of Lloyd George, to give the country 'a period of tranquillity and prosperity in which to recuperate from the war and its aftermath'. The young Macmillan had considerable admiration for Baldwin, learnt much from him, and the two men shared some characteristics. He saw Baldwin as a decent man with a real concern for industrial problems; as a latter-day Disraeli, determined to bridge the Two Nations and to bring peace to the class war. He was impressed by Baldwin's moderation and 'steadying process', and his perception of the tides of history. He noted Baldwin's own nervousness, behind his outward tranquillity, and his ability to rise, calmly and strongly, to face a crisis. He reckoned that he was, for many years, 'the most powerful prime minister since Walpole'.[3] It was some time before Macmillan became convinced that Baldwin was not doing as much as he could to solve industrial problems, and that he had, in fact, no policy.

In Parliament, Macmillan soon grouped himself with other young Tories, many of whom had also just come into the House, and who had served in the trenches. Some of them represented industrial towns in the north or midlands: they had come out of the war with a sense of mission towards their soldiers, and they were increasingly shocked by the unemployment of their electorate. The group included Oliver Stanley, R. S. Hudson, Robert Boothby, John Loder and Terence O'Connor, together with Anthony Eden and Duff Cooper, who were more concerned with foreign than home affairs. Their leader was Noel Skelton, the M.P. for Perth, who provided some of the theory of industry and employment. They were nicknamed the Y.M.C.A., in contrast to the right-wing capitalist Conservatives, who were the 'Forty Thieves'. They campaigned, from the beginning, for government intervention to revive industry and bring work to the unemployed. 'We had little influence on the course of events,' wrote Boothby, 'but we did our best – and no one asked us to leave the Conservative Party.'[4] Macmillan was much less brilliant than the fascinating Boothby, his rival in many fields; but he was more consistent. Most of the 'Y.M.C.A.' got office in 1931 or earlier, and adapted their public policies accordingly. Macmillan became the lone wolf.

He began his parliamentary career as a fairly loyal Tory. His maiden speech, five months after entering Parliament, was

23

in support of the budget of the chancellor, Winston Churchill, which introduced contributory old-age pensions and reduced income tax to 4s. in the pound. The speech was in Macmillan's over-polished Union manner, echoing (as so often) Disraeli. He elaborately attacked the Socialists: 'They are not quite certain whether to take the line that we have been stealing their clothing while they incontinently went to bathe in the muddy waters of Russian intrigue or whether they are to say that the clothes were no good anyway.' He replied rather priggishly to Ramsay MacDonald's appeal to young progressive Conservatives to join the Socialists:

I can assure him that I belong very much to that body of the younger members of the Party and if he thinks we are either so young or so inexperienced as to be caught by a trap as clumsy as his, it shows that he totally misunderstands the moral principles and ideals of democratic Toryism. If all he and his party have to offer us as true socialism is a sort of horrible political cocktail consisting partly of the dregs of exploded economic views of Karl Marx, mixed up with a little flavour of Cobdenism, well iced by the late Chancellor of the Exchequer . . . if he thinks that this is to be the draught given to our parched throats and that we are ready to accept it, he is very much mistaken.

But as the Parliament wore on and unemployment went up, Macmillan – like other of his contemporaries – became aware that Baldwin had not grasped the seriousness of the crisis. From the vantage-point of Stockton, the state of Britain looked very different. Macmillan was a later convert to Keynes than, for instance, Boothby; but he was moved as much by moral indignation as by economic reasoning, and before long came strongly under Keynes's influence: he knew him through his brother Daniel, who was an old school friend of Keynes's and his publisher. Macmillan became increasingly convinced that the economic structure of Britain must be changed, if a breakdown and even revolution were to be averted. He began to define his views on the relationship between government and industry, the need for government intervention, and how capitalism should develop in answer to the new problems. He rejected socialism because 'the remedy would be worse than the disease' but he believed that on the solution of the problem of State control 'the continued certainty of a capitalist society and, as I think, almost the whole of our civilization will depend'.

The General Strike, and the bitter deadlock between miners and coal-owners, increased the unease of the younger Tories. Macmillan (who helped pack copies of *The Times* during the strike) was impressed by Baldwin's handling of the dispute but felt more certain than ever of the need for the reorganization of industry, and for unity between managers and labour, so that 'industry may find its own cure for its own ills'. After the strike, when the Government introduced the Trade Disputes Bill to make illegal any strike 'designed or calculated to coerce the Government', Macmillan made a speech on 2 May 1927 generally supporting it, but warning that the psychological effect on industry could be harmful, and that the Bill must not be 'an attempt to set the clock back'.

In the meantime, in April 1927, Macmillan and three other members of the 'Y.M.C.A.' – Boothby, Oliver Stanley and John Loder – published a book called *Industry and the State*, which was Macmillan's first step towards a 'middle way'. The authors emphasized that they were anti-socialist, because socialist remedies would spell economic disaster and deprive the individual of his independence. But they were also against *laissez-faire*, and they offered a compromise Conservative solution, through 'economic opportunism'. They recommended government intervention to encourage mergers of industries for modernization, to provide an overall guide for the development of finance and industry, and to influence the credit system and the Bank of England, so as to be able to regulate prices. They advocated the cooperative approach in industry – 'the hyphen' between the individualist and collective theories. They wanted an extension of ownership of property and diversification of shares. In public industries the Government should introduce employee shares and labour co-partnership, and set up compulsory arbitration machinery. Other industries would have a system of Trade Boards with delegates from employers and workers, which would fix hours of work and overtime and would take action in disputes. They summed up with a warning:

If conservatives will realize the urgency of the position, if they will take their courage in their hands and decide upon the adoption of bold and comprehensive measures, the country may be spared not only the follies of reaction today but also the devastation of revolutions and counter revolution in the future.

The book not surprisingly came under attack from right-wing conservatives, including *The Daily Mail* and *The Sunday Pictorial*. But though this programme was a Tory heresy, it was the kind of solution that many intellectuals were thinking about: even Neville Chamberlain sent Macmillan a letter of congratulation. It was becoming clear that free-for-all capitalism, insofar that it existed, was breaking down. Soon after *Industry and the State*, a group of Liberals, including Maynard Keynes, produced a book called *Britain's Industrial Future*, known as the Liberal Yellow Book, which produced many similar ideas. Macmillan commented on the resemblance, harking back again to Disraeli's old joke about clothes: he hoped 'that the good Tory tradition of taking the Whigs' clothes while they are bathing may be continued to its full extent if these garments are found of a satisfactory nature. I for one will watch with complete equanimity the electoral nudity which may follow in the Liberal party.' In fact, a lot of the clothes for both books came from Maynard Keynes: Macmillan was never himself a very original thinker.

In Parliament, Macmillan gave his colleagues the impression at this time of being an idealistic don, who had accidentally strayed into the jungle of politics. His appearance corroborated that view; with his wide eyes, his rather toothy smile and his stiff walk he seemed altogether too lofty for the political fray. For most of the time he was right outside the world of government; but in the argument on rating reform between Chamberlain and Churchill he had his first glimpse of the inner workings, and in particular the fascination of Churchill. Churchill had planned a bold scheme for relieving industry of rates, and Macmillan was specially interested in the subject: he even wrote an article on local taxation in *The Banker*. Macmillan exchanged views with Churchill (who was fostering the support of young Tories) and went on to a deputation to Chamberlain, then Minister of Health, to urge the de-rating of railways, to which Chamberlain was opposed. Chamberlain eventually gave in, Churchill's de-rating Bill was passed, and Macmillan felt that he had played some part in a measure that would lift the burden from industry.

After four years as an M.P. Macmillan had made some mark. He was regarded as one of the most promising of the young Tories, but not as promising, for instance, as Boothby or Oliver Stanley. His approach was not very original and – it had to be said – rather boring. In a book by a journalist James Johnstone, called *A Hundred Commoners*, which described M.P.s between 1924 and 1931 he is given a goodish report: Johnstone says that of 'the young enthusiasts in the Conservative Party who have devoted themselves to the advocacy of social reform' (the 'Y.M.C.A.'), the most prominent and the most efficient speaker was Harold Macmillan.

He is a model Y.M.C.A. man. His correctness of manner and bearing, his moderation of speech, the suggestion of the 'good boy' which he carries about with him are all typical . . . his fresh youthful face predispose the House in his favour. He has charm, marred perhaps by a touch of smugness. Smugness, however, with him is free from the slightest taint of insincerity. He is sincere in the fullest sense, earnest with the earnestness of devoted youth . . . an enthusiast who does not enthuse. . . . He holds his ideas and is not held by them.

Johnstone considered that though Macmillan was not an inspired speaker, he was a practical planner as well as an enthusiast, 'a master of Blue Book knowledge and in personal contact with the realities of life'. He found Macmillan representative of the new economic era in politics and concluded

He is one of the few promising men whom this Parliament has produced. He has the affinity with the spirit of the age and understanding of Parliamentary ways which guarantee success in the political life of the future. Some day he will be one of the guiding forces of the Conservative Party, a capable and persuasive Minister.[5]

His hopes were soon dashed. In May 1929, Baldwin went to the country, with the slogan 'Safety First', against a background of high unemployment and lingering industrial unrest. Macmillan fought Stockton again, but the odds were now against him: partly because the Liberals were pulling back voters from the Tories; partly, ironically, because navvies had come to build the I.C.I. works at Billingham, and were voting Labour. In the country, the Conservatives were defeated, and Ramsay MacDonald's Labour Government took over. Several of the progressive young Tories lost their seats, and at Stockton, Macmillan lost his seat to Labour by 2,389 votes. It was a great blow, as he had already come to regard himself as the special guardian of Stockton's unemployed. Hugh Dalton, who had been elected as Labour member for the Durham constituency of Bishop Auckland, recalled seeing Macmillan at Darlington station after the election, among the waving and cheering Labour members. As the train to London was moving out, Macmillan came to a window 'and waving his Tory colours all alone, and with tears streaming down his cheeks, called for "three cheers for Baldwin".' 'In politics,' Dalton said to him afterwards, 'there are ebbs and flows.'[6]

Macmillan's two years out of Parliament were an unhappy time. He was depressed by the state of politics and the inertia of Baldwin and MacDonald. The Tory defeat had been ascribed by some to the 'socialist' elements of the party, and *The Daily Mail* complained 'it was the semi-socialist policy that went down in the great defeat'. He complained to Earl Winterton in 1931: 'I don't see much future for people like you and me, people of independent minds, while the present set-up exists.'[7] But he missed the involvement with day-to-day politics, and longed to get back. He was invited to be prospective candidate for Hitchin, and accepted; but the by-election did not happen, and he switched back as candidate for Stockton.

Like many other young politicians at the time, Macmillan

was perplexed and frustrated by the apparent irrelevance of the parties, and became increasingly restless, and dreamy. He told Harold Nicolson, in July 1930, that

the old party machines are worn out and that the modern electorate thinks more of personalities and programmes than of the pressure put on them by an electoral agent. He thinks that the economic situation is so serious that it will lead to a breakdown of the whole party system. He foresees that the Tories may return with a majority of twenty and then be swept away on a snap vote. No other single party will form a Government and there will be a Cabinet of young men. He was kind enough to include me in this Pitt-like Ministry. [8]

At one time, Macmillan considered openly supporting Lord Beaverbrook in his move to get rid of Baldwin, but was dissuaded by Beaverbrook himself. [9] Then, for a time, he came under the spell of Sir Oswald Mosley. When Mosley presented his memorandum to the Labour Government, urging bold methods to combat unemployment, Macmillan went as far as to write to *The Times* in Mosley's defence, in 'a letter of singular courage' (as Mosley described it) pointing out that Mosley was simply proposing to carry out election promises:

I confess, Sir, that I do not understand the reasons which have led you and non-Socialist commentators generally to such an unappreciative attitude towards Sir Oswald Mosley's position. Is it to be the accepted rule in our politics that a political programme is to be discarded as soon as it has served its electoral purpose?

The next day a supercilious letter appeared in reply, from four Tory M.P.s. It said:

Sir, we have read with much interest and some surprise Mr Harold Macmillan's letter published in your issue of today. When a player starts complaining that 'it's hardly worth bothering to play' the game at all, it is usually the player and not the game who is at fault. It is then usually advisable for the player to seek a new field for his recreation, and a pastime more suited to his talents.

Three signatories were Lord Lymington (later Lord Portsmouth), Harold Balfour (later Lord Balfour) and M. Beaumont.

The last was R. A. Butler, then twenty-seven. It was the first thrust in a life-long duel.

When Mosley resigned from the Labour party, and founded his 'New Party', with proposals for a planned economy, Macmillan was one of many who were tempted to join forces with him. Many Tories, most notably Oliver Stanley,[10] had serious talks with Mosley, and Macmillan went often to Mosley's house. Mosley was surprised by the interest of this aloof young publisher: he has been credited with saying that 'shaking hands with Harold Macmillan is like shaking hands with the fin of the cod':[11] but Macmillan was impressed by the intellectual grasp of Mosley and his circle, who included John Strachey and Allan Young, a brilliant young ex-Marxist from the Clyde who had helped Mosley in his election campaigns and contributed many ideas to Mosley's manifesto. Macmillan was tempted by this group, who shared his own impatience with the old parties, and his interest in economic planning; but he stayed inside the Tory party.

He takes the usual young Tory view [recorded Harold Nicolson in May 1931], that his heart is entirely with the New Party but he feels he can help us better by remaining in the Conservative ranks. . . . He anticipates the present Government being in power for another two years, followed by a Tory administration lasting some three years. He feels that five years from now, the New Party will have its great opportunity.[12]

But the opportunity did not come, and when Mosley turned towards Fascist policies they drifted apart. Allan Young left Mosley, to become Macmillan's economic adviser, bringing with him a detailed grasp of economic problems, which showed itself in Macmillan's later books: as Macmillan himself recalled, 'I was able to make use of Young's experience and keen intelligence'.

In this time out of Parliament, Macmillan seemed tense and personally unhappy; he worked hard at publishing as well as politics, and was preoccupied with his work: he seemed increasingly reserved, and shut into himself. He had periodic pains from his war-time wounds, and also suffered from neurasthenia; in 1931 he went for two months to a clinic in Germany, to recuperate.

In the meantime the future prospects of the Tories had been dramatically transformed. The economic crisis had broken on the Labour Government: Ramsay MacDonald had formed his National Government to save the pound; and in October, facing a continuing crisis, MacDonald went to the country, asking for 'a doctor's mandate' for the National Government. Macmillan hurried back from his clinic, still walking with sticks, to fight at Stockton. His campaign was noisy, but the result was assured: there was no Liberal candidate, and the Liberal vote went, almost solidly, to Macmillan as the National candidate. There was a landslide throughout the country, and the Conservatives held 473 seats: Macmillan came in with a spectacular majority of 11,031. He met Hugh Dalton, once again, at the station, and Dalton reminded him about the ebbs and flows. Macmillan said that electors tended to vote Left in prosperous days and Right in days of depression; and Dalton recalled Keynes's words: 'It is prosperity not adversity that makes the slave shake his chains.'[13]

NOTES

1. *Town*, October 1966
2. *The Star*, 29 October 1959
3. Harold Macmillan, *Winds of Change*, vol. I (London: Macmillan, 1966), p. 514
4. Robert Boothby, *My Yesterday Your Tomorrow* (London: Hutchinson, 1962), p. 31
5. James Johnstone, *A Hundred Commoners* (London: Michael Joseph, 1931), pp. 52–4
6. Hugh Dalton, *Call Back Yesterday* (London: Muller, 1953), p. 212
7. A. H. Brodrick, *Near to Greatness* (London: Hutchinson, 1965), p. 228
8. Harold Nicolson, *Diaries and Letters 1930–39* (London: Collins, 1966), p. 51
9. Harold Macmillan, *Winds of Change*, p. 256
10. See Mosley's review in *New Outlook*, October 1966
11. According to Hugh Massingham, but denied by Mosley. See *The Sunday Telegraph*, 21 and 28 August 1966
12. Harold Nicolson, *Diaries and Letters 1930–39*, p. 76
13. Hugh Dalton, *Call Back Yesterday*, p. 279

3. Rebellion

Toryism has always been a form of paternal socialism.
HAROLD MACMILLAN, 1936

In the new Parliament of 1931, Macmillan was certainly one of the most hopeful of the young Conservatives. When Tom Jones, Baldwin's intimate private secretary, was asked in 1931 by an American to suggest a speaker for America he wrote: 'If I were suggesting a speaker to represent the point of view of the young Conservative I should choose from the following list: Walter Elliot, Robert Boothby, Oliver Stanley, Duff Cooper, Harold Macmillan, Terence O'Connor.' He thought that Walter Elliot would be the most authoritative as well as being a 'brilliant and witty speaker'; Boothby was also intelligent and eloquent, Stanley had 'an impressive House of Commons manner' and Duff Cooper was 'first-rate on the platform'. Macmillan 'belongs to the famous publishing firm and is married to a daughter of the Duke of Devonshire, is quite able, but I think rather pedestrian'.[1] It was a description he would have hated.

Many of Macmillan's contemporaries were to get junior jobs in 1931 or later, and he was one of the few intellectual young Tories left out. He was now thirty-seven, and other men younger than he were already in office: by 1932 Eden, who was three years younger, was under-secretary at the Foreign Office, while young Rab Butler – five years younger still – was an under secretary at the India Office. Macmillan was aware of being left behind: speaking on 26 November 1931 about unemployment, he congratulated one of his contemporaries, Rob Hudson, on becoming parliamentary secretary at the Ministry of Labour, and being poacher turned keeper. But he did not despair of 'being able to recruit others to carry on the good work of the guerrilla warfare against the Ministry of Labour'. He wryly watched the new respectability of his contemporaries, like Leslie Hore-Belisha at the Board of Trade, who showed the 'morbid enthusiasm of the recent convert'.[2]

The misery of unemployment was his constant, and magnificent, preoccupation. He was not afraid to be thorough, and tirelessly recited and published statistics and evidence – in a way that was very unlike his later style. Early in the new Parliament Macmillan realized that the Government was not prepared to fulfil its election promises; and he became its self-appointed conscience on the hardships of unemployment policy. He unearthed one letter addressed to the Public Assistance Committee which did not agree with election promises and which 'reposed for a time in the prim obscurity of the Library, but was eventually published at the insistence of myself and other honourable Members'.

As the 1930s wore on, Macmillan wrote and spoke more and more, with missionary zeal, about planning. In March 1932 he circulated to all M.P.s a pamphlet called 'The State and Industry in 1932' which discussed the recent Import Duties Act and proposed an Industrial Council to enable the Government to plan ahead. Three months later he published 'The Next Step', which advocated selective protection for the home market, and the formation of National Councils for Industry and an Industrial Development Board to co-ordinate the plans of government, industry and finance. The pamphlets were not much noticed, but John Strachey, then a prominent Marxist, attacked 'The State and Industry' in his book *The Coming Struggle for Power*. Macmillan's proposals, wrote Strachey,

contain, the reader will observe, all those elements which we have mentioned as essentially characteristic of the drive for monopoly. 'The necessary degree of centralization of control' is to be achieved, in other words each industry is to be consolidated by the great banks and trusts, the independent producers are to be squeezed out; trade-union officials are to be 'associated' with the councils controlling these increasingly monopolistic industries; and finally the apparatus of the State is to meet and fuse with the apparatus of consolidated industry at the designated point, at the point of the imposition of tariffs by which external competition is to be progressively eliminated.[3]

The arguments between the two kinds of planners, Marxist and capitalist, foreshadowed many of the problems of Western society after the war.

In 1933 Macmillan published his first book under his sole name, called *Reconstruction*, which continued the case for planning. The choice was between 'orderly capitalism and economic and social disorder'. To ensure price stability, he advocated giving controlled monopoly powers to industry; each industry, through a National Industrial Council, would be self-governing and the changes would come from within the industry itself. A Central Economic Council would sit under the chairmanship of a member of the cabinet. Macmillan ended by warning that Fascism or Communism would overthrow the capitalist system if it did not reform itself.

The New Statesman called *Reconstruction* 'this bold and thoughtful scheme of national economic planning': and *The Times* said it 'does not err on the side of timidity'. But *The Economist* called it an 'oddly half-baked book', and accused it of 'major fallacies', and 'glaring errors' – notably the author's belief that it was the price system rather than the monetary system which had produced the crisis. (Macmillan replied in a letter to *The Economist* that he had *not* rejected monetary causes.) Macmillan's advocacy of boards was to become a by-word: some years later (on 2 March 1936) Ernest Brown, the Minister of Labour, complained that when faced with knotty problems Macmillan specialized in 'boards and then more boards. . . . I think he has an unlimited faith in the possibilities of what boards can do to solve the great problems with which we are confronted.'

In his writings and speeches, Macmillan was powerfully influenced by Maynard Keynes. He insisted that Government expenditure should be increased to stimulate demand, and that this expenditure should be used to build houses, bridges, roads and for agricultural development – anything that would take people off the dole. He asked Chamberlain, the Chancellor of the Exchequer, to increase demand by reducing taxation and unbalancing the budget. He insisted that the Government must intervene in the north: redundant industries must be closed down, special inducements offered to firms to move elsewhere, and the Government must 'cease to work in the dark'.[4]

In fact, behind the old dogmas of the parties, the Tory party was slowly moving towards State intervention, in the direction that Macmillan was advocating. The *laissez-faire* philosophy had become untenable, with the need to rationalize industry, and the new acceptance of protection. Influenced by Neville Chamberlain the Tories were accepting the 'managed economy':

In their reassertion of State power over the operation of the economic system as a whole [wrote Professor Beer], they not only broke with fundamentals of British policy in the previous hundred years, but also created many patterns of government action which, in spite of important modifications, have been followed since that time.[5]

Some Tory theorists welcomed the new role of the State and the 'corporatism' of industry as a return to medieval or Elizabethan society. Arthur Bryant, writing in 1929, explained that 'in place of the extreme rivalry of the nineteenth century, industry is returning to the ancient medieval practice of co-operation and mutual agreement'.[6] And Macmillan in *Reconstruction* talked about 'the organic conception of society which was the distinct contribution of medieval thought'.

Macmillan was specially qualified to be a Tory prophet: for he was one of the few men who combined a practical acquaintance of conditions of the north with a sufficient grasp of economic theory. He welcomed the appointment of the two commissioners for 'the distressed areas' in 1934 and in a speech on 21 November said: 'War is not the only operation in which it is sometimes an advantage to have a visitation from general H.Q. to the front line trenches. I am glad there has been on this occasion a visit from Whitehall to the Passchendaele of Durham and South Wales.' But he went on:

Lord Beaconsfield used this famous phrase 'The keys of India are not in Herat or Kandahar; the keys of India are in London!' So it is with unemployment. The key lies, not in South Wales or Durham, but in Downing Street and Threadneedle Street.

Part of the trouble was a boom with two million unemployed and not enough capital invested at home or abroad; 'money is all dressed up and nowhere to go. . . . The cheaper we make it the less of it we use. . . . Mr Disraeli once said he saw before him a bench of extinct volcanoes . . . now there are a few disused slagheaps which might well be tidied up.' When the ineffectual Depressed Areas Bill was eventually produced as a result of the commissioners' report, he complained on 13 December 1934 'the mountains have been in labour and there has been born a mouse . . . a nice mouse, a good little mouse, a profitable and helpful little mouse, but a ridiculous microscopic, Lilliputian mouse'.

Macmillan by now had the settled reputation of being a clever but impractical idealist: a fellow M.P. commented: 'I think there is something very heroic in this persistence in being the midwife for a new world which stubbornly refuses to be born.'[7] He was a dull and still nervous speaker, still with his mandarin 'Oxford manner', and with a fondness for overpolished epigrams: and he was aware that he often bored his audience. 'I am afraid it has been said of my contributions to these debates,' he said sadly in the debate on the depression on 9 July 1935, 'that they are too dry, too academic and too precise; but that is not because either in private or public affairs those who speak most readily and babble most freely necessarily feel most deeply. I am much concerned about the political future of this country.'

Macmillan was really more effective outside Parliament than in it, and as his deadlock with the Tories became fixed, he spent more time with non-party groups which, in the general atmosphere of scepticism of Parliament, were growing up. Macmillan's house became a meeting-place for dons, economists and industrialists: at one such meeting Tom Jones described how Macmillan 'talks very much like a Professor of Economics'. He became quite deeply involved in the movement of progressive businessmen to try to work out a saner economic system: he helped to launch (with Henry Mond) the 'Industrial Reorganization League', with an impressive body of tycoons, which studied the problems of each industry and promoted a bill to allow for the reorganization of fifteen major industries. He also – surprising though it would seem later – became interested in the science of management, and actually became president of the Institute of Industrial Administration.

Most important, he was one of the prime movers of 'The Next Five Years Group', originating from a meeting at All Souls. The group was inspired by Lord Allen of Hurtwood, a courageous Labour idealist who was, said Macmillan, 'one of the most remarkable men whom I have known and one of the most attractive'. The group was made up of radical-minded people from all parties and professions, who urged a 'new deal' for Britain. They planned a book to put forward their policy, and Macmillan joined the drafting committee for the section on home affairs, which met at his house in London: other prominent members were Geoffrey Crowther, Arthur Salter and Hugh Molson. The book, called *The Next Five Years*, came out in July 1935. It aimed hopefully to attract 'overwhelming public support' for a policy based on planning and collective action, and stated that old political divisions were now irrelevant. Its detailed plans included a government planning committee of cabinet ministers, an economic general staff, public control of utilities and a nationalized Bank of England. It advocated reducing hours of work, abolishing the means test, raising the school-leaving age, increasing death duties. *The New Statesman* welcomed the book as showing that 'socialistic' views are now widely held among leading men of various political affiliations, and regarded the programme as more socialistic than Lloyd George's. G. D. H. Cole, writing in *The Economic Journal*, found the book significant, but 'too democratic for the conservatives and too unsocialistic for Labour'. It was a kind of premature 'Butskellism'.

The movement towards a planned economy cut across existing parties, and was shared by many economists and businessmen. The plan of *The Next Five Years* had close resemblances with Lloyd George's 'New Deal', which appeared soon after, and which likewise proposed a large programme of public works, and a non-departmental cabinet. As with the Yellow Book, Macmillan was embarrassed by the resemblance. He pointed out that he and his friends had been preaching this policy for four years and 'even if we have fallen under the wiles of the wizard, he had not been able to ante-date his magic by that time. We have done this on our own account.' He told *The Yorkshire Post* (9 November 1935) that Lloyd George's plan was so like his, 'indeed taken from my book – that it is impossible for me to say I don't agree with it'.

But Macmillan had come quite close to the wizard at this time. He had always been fascinated by Lloyd George, ever since he had first met him at an Oxford breakfast. When Lloyd George formed his 'Council of Action' in 1935, Macmillan said it was 'a political event of the first importance'; he went down to see him at Churt, and sat on the platform of the first meeting at the Central Hall. Macmillan complained that the manifesto might have given more credit to the Government, but (he said) he supported this all-party group because he was concerned about the political future; the Left, he believed, was tied to shibboleths, and the only governments which could be formed depended on support from the Right – a situation which he considered dangerous because it gave too much responsibility to the prime minister. He warned that if people couldn't get what they wanted through parliamentary methods, they might try other means – 'and the prime minister and his colleagues will be the true begetters of revolution'.

But these non-party manoeuvres were soon eclipsed by the coming election, and Macmillan had to fall back into some kind of line. In October 1935 Baldwin (who had taken over from MacDonald four months before) went to the country, and Macmillan campaigned in Stockton in an independent mood. He told his constituents that he stood by *The Next Five Years*, and that he would, if necessary, support any government that would carry it out. Lord Allen gave him strong support and even tried unsuccessfully to persuade the Liberal to stand down. Allen came up to Stockton to speak, and told a meeting that 'he had seen Mr Macmillan at pretty close quarters during the past three or four years': to which someone in the audience replied: 'We haven't seen him since the last election.'[8] The election was three-cornered, and Macmillan had the noisiest time, with a great deal of heckling and cross-questioning. The Conservatives came back victoriously, with an overall majority of 247: and Macmillan held his seat with a gratifying majority of four thousand.

The National Government continued as usual, and Macmillan remained a backbencher with growing disillusion. Five months after the election, on 8 April 1936, he voted against the Government on the Unemployment Insurance Bill, which he regarded as 'the message of a Government which is fading away'. A month later, speaking in the debate on the Special Areas Reconstruction Bill (the unemployed areas had by now graduated from 'depressed', to 'distressed' to 'special'),* he said (7 May 1936): 'It made me feel rather sad and old, and it recalled the enthusiasm with which twelve years ago my then friends and myself used to address themselves to this problem. I'm afraid we have made little headway.'

As he became more depressed about the state of the parties, Macmillan became still more interested in the Next Five Years Group, to which he devoted much of his time. But between the figures in the group there soon developed acrimonious arguments, such as occur between idealists without prospects

---

* Compare the progress achieved by backward countries, *via* undeveloped and underdeveloped, to developing.

of power. From the beginning there were differences about the group's function, and particularly on how to deal with Lloyd George and his *New Deal*. Lord Allen was against joining forces with Lloyd George, because he distrusted him, and because he thought the group should not become directly involved in electoral activities; but Macmillan was more interested in actual power, and gave a foretaste of his political toughness. After the election, Macmillan proposed meeting with other groups, including Lloyd George. Lord Allen wrote to a member of the executive warning him:

The fact is that when Macmillan was a supporter of the National Government he took X view of the functions of the 'Next Five Years' Group. Now that he has cut his traces and has no political home, he looks at the work and function of our Group in a new way, which is largely influenced by his own personal position. My own feeling is that the functions of the Group remain inter-party just as much today as they were originally, and that our influence will be destroyed if we slip into the Popular Front Movement because of the personal troubles of certain individuals amongst us.[9]

Allen wrote to Macmillan saying 'do let me beg you to keep absolutely clear of LG until after the group has met. He is now a discredited man. Do be careful of getting entangled with him and forgive me for venturing to say this. I only do so because I care so much about your future.' Allen was determined that the group should not be a political conspiracy against the Government, but a constructive academic pressure group. When the group planned its own newspaper *New Outlook* – with which Macmillan and Allan Young were both closely involved – there was much argument about the form and prospectus of the periodical. Macmillan, to Allen's indignation, virtually took control of the paper, relegating Allen to a back seat: the paper then became officially separated from the group itself:

I am compelled now to see [wrote Lord Allen in June 1936], that much of the trouble during the last 2½ months has been due to one man, Mr Macmillan, functioning on every committee and attempting the guidance of practically all our activities.[10]

Macmillan proceeded to use *New Outlook* as a vehicle for his own ideas, and particularly for a popular front, based on a five-point programme of collective security, abolition of the means test, steps to help distressed areas, willingness to reduce tariffs and extension of public control over industry. There was growing conflict between Allen and Macmillan, who wrote afterwards 'I have no doubt that he was right and that I was impatient'. Macmillan was certainly quite ruthless and overbearing in his conduct; but there was a strong case for some kind of popular front at that time, and the academic tactics of the group did not achieve much. Eventually, by the end of 1937, the group could no longer contain its conflicting elements, and it was formally wound up in November.

Macmillan was moving towards some kind of vague centre party. In a revealing interview in *The Star*, who were running a series about the possibility of a 'popular front', Macmillan said on 25 June 1936 that he thought the Government would fall very soon and 'the longer it takes the more inglorious will its end be'. He did not think it was yet the right moment for a popular front: the man in the street emphasized responsibilities more than rights. Toryism, he said, has always been a form of paternal socialism: the trouble with the Conservative party now was that it had become too Liberal in the *laissez-faire* sense of the word, and had become dominated by money and the City. 'A party dominated by second-class brewers and company promoters – a Casino capitalism – is not likely to represent anybody but itself.' But there was not much confidence in the Left either: 'after ten years of no imagination, no drive, all we are left with is men like Attlee and Lansbury who are quite incompetent to govern an Empire'. Macmillan felt that progress could be made in creating a centre party but it would have to be done slowly. What was needed was the formation of a great popular political party – he suggested Herbert Morrison as leader – which would be Labour stripped of its extremes, 'but he would have to achieve a fusion of all that is best in the Left and the Right and it would have to be a Left Centre rather than a Right Centre'. 'Make no mistake about it,' he concluded, 'the great centre vote of this country must find its new philosophy if democracy is to be saved not only here but in the world.'

By 1936 Macmillan was a man of forty-two, no longer a promising young Tory, but apparently a settled rebel, regarded as too left-wing and too impractical for office in his own party, and too capitalist and paternalist to be linked with the socialists. Although he had identified himself closely with the electors of Stockton, he was always aware that he was himself a wealthy and privileged man, with a special position to maintain. He found it hard to understand those rich young men who had turned socialist, and who advocated equality. He was proud to think of himself as a successful businessman. He believed in the 'paternal socialism' of his father and grandfather, but never in egalitarian socialism.

All through the 1930s he worked as a publisher as well as a politician: he was a director of the firm, with his brother Daniel, and looked after the editing of general books, with a particular interest in books on economics, politics and social problems. Among many other authors he published Keynes, Lewis Namier, E. H. Carr, G. D. H. Cole, W. B. Yeats, Sean O'Casey, Charles Morgan and Hugh Walpole; and his contact with this literary and intellectual world gave him far wider horizons than most of his fellow-Tories. He was a very able businessman, capable of taking bold risks as well as driving hard bargains. He did not, like Gollancz on the Left, regard publishing as a form of propaganda; when asked why Macmillans were publishing a pro-German book, he said 'We are publishers, not policemen'. Lovat Dickson, a Canadian who joined Macmillans just before the second war, describes in *The House of Words* how Macmillan seemed at first remote and absent-minded in the office; but he soon discovered 'beneath the bland appearance of a typical young conservative politician of the thirties, he had an extremely keen and incisive brain'.[11]

In politics, Macmillan had until now been primarily concerned with home economic matters. But by 1936 he was turning more to foreign affairs, and particularly to the danger of Italy and Germany. He had committed himself at the 1935 election to support of the League of Nations, and he had warned in London on 24 June that the removal of sanctions against Italy might cause him to leave the Conservative party.

Conflict of opinion between myself and the government separates me strongly – it may prove permanently – from the political party of which I have been a keen, if not very satisfactory, member for fourteen years and in whose support I have taken part in five contested elections.[12]

In June 1936 Baldwin abandoned the sanctions against Italy, which had been imposed after the invasion of Abyssinia. The Labour party, led by Clement Attlee, moved a vote of censure. Only two Conservatives voted against their party. One was Vyvyan Adams, M.P. for West Leeds: the other was Harold Macmillan. He defied the dreaded chief whip, Captain Margesson and, six days later, wrote to Baldwin saying that, although he would 'probably be found in the great majority of cases in the Government lobby', he would like to resign the whip, and no longer to be 'regarded as among the official supporters of the Government'. Baldwin replied formally, saying 'I regret this decision'. He was more upset about Adams.

Soon afterwards, Macmillan met his constituents at Stockton, and spoke in emotional terms about the future of civilized society. He promised that 'I shall give my allegiance only to those whom I represent in Parliament and to the policy to which I am pledged'. He said that he had led the agitation against Hoare after the Hoare–Laval pact, and called the Government policy 'weak, constantly changing and vacillating'. There was a unanimous vote of confidence. *The Morning Post*, commenting on his resignation, said that he was one of those intellectuals who should never be in politics. *The Sunday Times* said that Macmillan had joined 'that small group of untouchables found in every Parliament', but that his isolated position would not be out of keeping with his general political outlook. He had seemed a promising candidate for office when he first entered politics, and had zeal and courage. But unfortunately 'he is a rebel at heart, a theorist at war with facts, a passionate humanitarian whose sympathies are with those who live in the shadows, an incorrigible satirist'.

Macmillan now became a junior member of a group of students of foreign affairs, which had been formed by Arthur Salter (M.P. for Oxford University) and which included Liddell Hart, Harold Nicolson, Lord Allen, H. A. L. Fisher, A. L. Rowse, Arnold Toynbee and Gilbert Murray. Ultra-Conservatives dubbed them 'Salter's Soviet', though they included no Marxists. They met for week-end conferences at All Souls', or at Nicolson's chambers in the Temple, and sometimes sent memoranda about their conclusions to the Foreign Office. Macmillan was industrious but inconspicuous: Liddell Hart describes how when he enquired among the other members about Macmillan none of them remembered him being one: later Nicolson unearthed the minutes and found his name. Liddell Hart remembered Macmillan partly for his combination of forward thinking with carefully balanced views, and partly for the extraordinary contrast between the self-effacing personality of that time and the actor-like air he displayed after the war.[13]

Macmillan spoke with growing pessimism: he adopted the tone of an unheeded prophet, expected to repeat familiar warnings. He became gloomier about the future of politics, and accurately foresaw that by 1945, a right-wing government would have been so long in office that there would be a violent swing to the Left: 'I should be much happier about that movement if the party of the Left was one that could rely upon a great tradition in English politics and drew its strength from a much more varied part of our community.' He reiterated the need for a centre party in a speech in Birmingham on 6 October 1936, to 'carry out a programme of reform in the traditional English spirit of a reasonable, practical and attainable programme'. In the same month he wrote in *New Outlook* that if the Government refused to act decisively abroad, 'We shall have proved to the satisfaction of the British worker that even the liberal-minded and progressive sections of capitalist society are concerned only with the preservation of their property rights'; and that this would invite revolution.

He voted against the Government again on 27 November 1936, when they took inadequate measures for the distressed areas. 'At every stage there is a delaying action fought,' he said: 'We who pleaded for this policy were treated as a kind of pariah hardly decent to speak to five years ago.' He compared Baldwin to the Duke of Plaza-Toro in *The Gondoliers*, who led his regiment from behind: 'This is not new Toryism or old Toryism or Disraelian Toryism, it is "Plaza-Toro-ism".' He complained again in a debate on the special areas on 6 April 1937.

For about ten or twelve years I have taken part in Debates – perhaps I have bored the House – on the Special Areas . . . if we bargain and chop logic and think in these petty terms of this great problem, then not those who have tried to raise their voice will be the authors of revolution but those who have shut their ears and sought with niggling futile peddling methods to deal with vast and overwhelming issues.

Macmillan was torn between his repugnance for the National Government, and his dread of a socialist alternative. He was embarrassed by his isolation, and a year after his original defiance, he returned reluctantly to the Tory ranks. In a contorted letter, dated 27 July 1937, to Chamberlain, who had now succeeded Baldwin as prime minister, he explained:

I think that I may perhaps be of greater service if I am once more in the ranks, since I feel convinced that a National Government under your Leadership, is the only effective instrument now available to serve the cause of peace and progress.

But his return to the fold made little difference, and his plaintive advice continued: 'I am tempted by the opportunity to do what I have not done for more than two years, that is to present some observations to the House of Commons.' He found solace in the fact that though suggestions might not immediately be taken up 'what was the epigram, the paradox of one period becomes the truism of four or five years hence'. When he spoke on the budget on 27 April 1938, a Labour speaker commented 'I sometimes wonder how long it will be before the hon. member finds his spiritual home. He roams about the home a good deal. The door is open and whenever he has the courage to cross the threshold I can offer him a warm welcome inside.'

In June 1938 Macmillan published the book that he was to regard as his political testament, with the bleak title of *The Middle Way*, sub-titled 'a study of the problem of economic and social progress in a free and democratic society'. It was a daunting volume – four hundred pages of analysis and statistics, presented with uncompromising gravity and detail, assembled with the help of Allan Young. It began by describing the economic situation since the depression, went on to analyse the present extent of government intervention, and then expounded in greater detail than before the proposed reconstruction of industry. As with its predecessors, it foreshadows some of the institutions which came into being thirty years later – most notably the 'Neddy' of 1961. It recommended, among many other things, the nationalization of coal and other essential industries, and the setting up of a 'national nutrition board', to deal with the delivery of milk, butter, cheese and other basic foods. In financial policy it quoted extensively from Keynes and advocated once again a nationalized Bank of England. It was in many ways revolutionary, but in an early chapter Macmillan stressed that the transference of wealth from the rich to the poor was no longer an important question: 'We have reached the end of radical reformism . . . a new age of radicalism would not be able to rely upon the negative method of meeting social obligations out of the transference of wealth.' This was his kind of 'paternal socialism' which was to reach its ambivalent triumph in the 'never had it so good' of twenty years later.

The dynamic of social change, the driving power towards the achievement of these ends, resides in our discontent with things as they are. If that discontent is shared by the comfortable as well as the unfortunate, then these changes can be accomplished by a process of peaceful evolution throughout which we shall continue to preserve the heritage of our liberty. If, however, it is not shared by all classes in society, if our political views are merely the reflection of the money in our pockets, if the poor are to do the driving, and the rich stubbornly to resist, if at this critical moment, we hesitate to be guided by the British tradition of peaceful change, then we shall move stage by stage towards the embitterment of class antagonism and the decay and destruction of our democratic institutions.

The *Middle Way* caused a small stir, and among the young Tories at Oxford, like Hugh Fraser or Edward Heath, it became a kind of revolutionary bible. *The Times* said, 'Mr Macmillan grapples positively and hopefully with large problems of reform which are immediately important': E. A. G. Robinson in *The Economic Journal* said that, 'so long as he is concerned with the machinery of industrial government, Mr Macmillan is always cogent and persuasive', but also that 'Mr Macmillan's attitude to the surplus producers of an industry is a little too reminiscent of the healthy man who regards his sick neighbours as sources of infection rather than as objects of solicitude'. G. D. H. Cole in *The New Statesman* said: 'This is much from a Conservative member of parliament. It has indeed a great deal in common with the actual policy which a Labour Government might be expected to pursue during its first year of office.'

Meanwhile Macmillan was much more concerned by the greater crisis, the threat of Nazi Germany. He had been aware of the dangers of Hitler as soon as he marched into the Rhineland in 1936. It was at this time that he first came to know Churchill well, and he was awed by his personality and vision. 'I should doubtless have shared the general complacency,' he records with frankness, 'had I not by now have come to be more frequently in Churchill's company.'[14] Just after the invasion of the Rhineland, Macmillan – influenced by Churchill's views – wrote a perceptive article in *The Star* (20 March 1937), describing the current 'uneasy conscience' about Germany: 'Much as we abominate many aspects of the Nazi mentality, we ask ourselves how far we are responsible.' He accused Baldwin and MacDonald of having shirked the foreign problem, and having 'elevated inactivity into a principle and feebleness into a virtue'. He concluded 'let us either settle with Germany now, or coerce her now. But don't let us purchase an uncertain peace at a terrible price to be paid later.'

When Baldwin resigned, Macmillan for a time had some confidence in Neville Chamberlain: he was impressed by his progressive social record, and his logical mind. But he soon perceived Chamberlain's weakness in foreign affairs. When Anthony Eden resigned as foreign secretary in 1937, Macmillan, encouraged by Churchill, joined twenty other members in abstaining in the subsequent debate. From this time on, he followed Churchill's lead – though he was not quite as close to Churchill as he later made out. After the annexation of Austria, he talked to the Stockton women Conservatives about the dangers of war, and said 'I should also like to see the inclusion of a great outside figure like Winston Churchill'. In the summer of 1938, when the Tory dissidents became more organized, forming into a 'Churchill Group' and an 'Eden Group', Macmillan became loosely attached to both of them and was (by his own account) a link between the two: 'I found myself, by my connexion with both these groups, far better instructed in the inner significance of what was happening than ever before.'[15] But he was still very much a lone wolf, compared to Churchill's gang – Bracken, Sandys, Boothby, Lindemann – and to the more gregarious members of Eden's group: he carried less political weight than most of them, and was still regarded as rather impractical, and often maddeningly smug. Though he described himself later as 'something of a national figure', he features very little in the recollections of these times.

By the time of Munich, Macmillan was totally disillusioned with Chamberlain. In the debate after Munich he abstained, together with the rest of Churchill's and Eden's groups. On the last day of the debate he made a speech, saying that, 'The situation with which we are faced today in this country is . . . more dangerous and more formidable, more terrible than at any time since the beginning of Christian civilization.' He was much involved in the plotting between parties which surrounded the Munich debate. Three days before the debate, with Churchill's approval, he warned Hugh Dalton, one of the tougher Labour members, that there was a plan to hold a general election so that Chamberlain, as the hero of the hour, might sweep the country: and that because of this the vote on the Munich debate might be regarded as a test of loyalty. Macmillan took Dalton, with Attlee, to meet Churchill and members of the Eden group at Brendan Bracken's house in Lord North Street. Various meetings and plots followed, based on the idea that the Labour leaders and the rebel Tories should join forces to oust Chamberlain, and touching the sub-plot that Morrison should replace Attlee as leader of the Labour party. Macmillan and others advocated a new kind of National Government – with Labour, Liberals and Tory rebels – 'a kind of 1931 in reverse'.[16] But while Churchill would join with anyone to oust Chamberlain, Eden demurred; and it was not to be until eighteen months later that Chamberlain was pushed out. Macmillan's attitude in these talks was bold and far-sighted, and undoubtedly made a strong impression on Churchill.

Macmillan's most extreme act of open rebellion came the same month, in the by-election at Oxford. Quintin Hogg, the official Conservative candidate, was opposed by A. D. Lindsay, Master of Balliol and Macmillan's old tutor, who ran as an independent popular front candidate, or 'progressive independent' with the slogan 'A vote for Hogg is a vote for Hitler'. Macmillan, after his abstention in the Munich debate, wrote a letter supporting Lindsay and helped in his campaign – in common with other dissident Tories, including Edward Heath, then a Balliol organ scholar, who met Macmillan at a Gaudy dinner. In his letter to Lindsay Macmillan said

I feel myself honour bound to say that if I were a voter in an Oxford constituency I should unhesitatingly vote and work for your return to Parliament at this election. The times are too grave and the issue too vital for progressive Conservative opinion to allow itself to be influenced by party loyalties or to tolerate the present uncertainty regarding the principles governing our foreign policy.

Macmillan went to Oxford to speak for Lindsay, and delivered a forthright attack on appeasement: 'One could always appease lions by throwing them Christians.' (Yet he did not later resent the appeasers: his own favourites for the succession to the premiership in 1963, first Hogg and then Douglas-Home, were both appeasers.)

Soon afterwards, Macmillan set out his own views on Munich in a pamphlet called 'The Price of Peace', in which he said that what had been achieved was 'an armed truce for a temporary period with a prospect of war under conditions less favourable to us in the future'. He lashed out at the Government who

gave away the substance voluntarily . . . and from that date onwards everything that has happened belongs to the realms of hysteria and unbelievable fantasy . . . I believe with Mr Duff Cooper that a member of Parliament has a higher duty to perform than to become a voting machine in favour of the Party 'right' or 'wrong'. The action I have taken is in accordance with the mandate I sought from my constituency at the last election. It is not I who have to answer for a dereliction of duty.

Macmillan's interest in economics began to shift from the problems of unemployment to the problems of rearmament; but the basic solution he offered was the same – a system of planning which could combine democracy with efficiency. On 18 November 1938 he voted against the Government, with Churchill and Bracken, when they refused to set up a Ministry of Supply. In February 1939 he produced yet another pamphlet, with the help of Thomas Balogh and Paul Einzig, called 'Economic Aspects of Defence', which showed Britain's backwardness compared to Germany, gave an outline of the Nazi economic system, and advocated the same kind of institutions as in *The Middle Way*, plus a Ministry of Supply to build State armament factories and control profits. Macmillan expounded these views in several debates on defence: 'Curiously enough, I have been trying, rather unsuccessfully perhaps, to promote many of these policies by speeches in the House and writings outside for a different purpose, namely to cure the problems of poverty.' It was the final irony of the pre-war years – that the eventual cure for unemployment was to be war.

Macmillan was now insistent on Chamberlain's resignation, and was regarded by many colleagues as a hothead. Leo Amery, before he himself became an anti-Chamberlainite, recorded 'I found some of these young men, particularly Harold Macmillan, very wild, clamouring for an immediate pogrom to get rid of Neville and make Winston Churchill prime minister'.[17] Harold Nicolson described in April 1939:

Harold Macmillan is enraged that Chamberlain should remain on. He thinks that all we Edenites have been too soft and gentlemanlike. That we should have clamoured for Chamberlain's removal. That no man in history has made such persistent and bone-headed mistakes, and that we shall go on pretending that all is well.[18]

He made little secret of his rebellion. When in March 1939 he was attacked at Stockton for his 'revolutionary' policy, he replied: 'You may hear that I am a bit of a "Bolshie" and sometimes make myself a bit of a nuisance in the House. Frankly, I feel it is a role that must be played by someone in the party.' In a debate on 8 June, after Chamberlain had eventually agreed to a Ministry of Supply, Macmillan said he was glad that the Government had been converted and commented superciliously: 'There must be a traffic problem on the road to Damascus'; but he angrily attacked Chamberlain's domination of his party, after being so consistently proved wrong: he quoted Joseph Chamberlain on Gladstone: 'The Prime Minister calls "black" and they say "it is good". The Prime Minister calls "white" and they say "it is better". It is always the same voice of God.'

So Macmillan watched Europe move towards war, and the Government belatedly taking the actions which he and his colleagues had advocated for so long. He watched them with detachment, and a touch of bitterness, as if he had long ceased to hope that he might be fully engaged in the great events. Six weeks after the war broke out, he said on 18 October 1939: 'I have now for some fifteen years advanced a number of proposals on economic and other questions . . . and if the supreme test of sincerity is that they have brought me neither any kind of profit, advancement nor preferment, it is in that spirit that I propose to make a few observations. . . .' At the age of forty-five he had little reason to hope that he would ever achieve political power.

NOTES

1. Thomas Jones, *A Diary With Letters, 1931–50* (Oxford: O.U.P., 1954), p. 2
2. House of Commons, 18 February 1932
3. John Strachey, *The Coming Struggle for Power* (London: Gollancz, 1932), pp. 240–41
4. *British Weekly*, 13 January 1934
5. S. H. Beer, *Modern British Politics* (London: Faber & Faber, 1965), p. 277
6. Ibid., p. 277
7. House of Commons, 12 April 1935
8. Arthur Marwick, *Clifford Allen* (Edinburgh: Oliver & Boyd, 1964), p. 133
9. Quoted in Martin Gilbert, *Plough My Own Furrow* (London: Longmans, 1965), p. 323
10. Quoted in ibid., p. 317
11. Lovat Dickson, *The House of Words* (London: Macmillan, 1963), p. 191
12. *North Mail*, 8 July 1936
13. Liddell Hart, *Memoirs*, vol. II (London: Cassell, 1965), p. 150
14. Harold Macmillan, *Winds of Change*, vol. I (London: Macmillan, 1966), p. 465
15. Ibid., p. 549
16. Hugh Dalton, *The Fateful Years* (London: Muller, 1957), p. 202
17. Harold Macmillan, *Winds of Change*, p. 585.
18. Harold Nicolson, *Diaries and Letters 1930–39* (London: Collins, 1966), p. 397

4. War

*If it hadn't been for Hitler you wouldn't be prime minister
and I wouldn't have become an under secretary.*
MACMILLAN TO CHURCHILL, 1943[1]

In 1939 Macmillan was a frustrated and little-known member
of parliament. Five years later he was to emerge as a confident
man of power, who was even talked of by some as a future
prime minister. The discrepancy between the pre-war and the
post-war Macmillan struck many of his contemporaries – the
switch from the 'gownsman' to the 'swordsman' that we noted
twenty years before, in the First World War. Behind the intel-
lectualizing, the man of action had been longing to get out.

His war began dully enough. He went on making speeches
about planning, and attacking Chamberlain's complacency. He
complained about the lack of coordination between government departments, and accused Chamberlain of trying to
'muddle through'. He advocated planning to absorb the unemployed, to divert men from non-essential tasks into vital
war work, to recruit women into industry, to mobilize foreign
investment and currency, and to stimulate exports. He was
shocked by Chamberlain's casual conduct of the war.

His contempt for Chamberlain grew when the Russians
invaded Finland in November 1939. Macmillan saw the
tragedy at first hand: while the Russians were massing troops
for their major attack, a committee was formed in London,
under Leo Amery, to organize a small international force to
help the Finns. Macmillan was one of its members, and he went

out with the volunteers to Finland (equipped with white overalls for snow warfare by Marks and Spencer, and left-over non-intervention badges from the Spanish Civil War), to find out what was happening. Soon after he arrived, the Russians had made their massive attack, breaking the Finns' 'Mannerheim Line'; and the Finns, despairing of direct help from Britain or France, had negotiated an armistice. Macmillan was shocked by the duplicity and meanness of the British attitude; he kept a diary of his visit, and when he came back sent it to Geoffrey Dawson, editor of *The Times*, who read it in bed 'till a late hour absorbed in it'.[2]

When he got back, Macmillan made a strong speech in Parliament on 19 March 1940, attacking the Government's attitude to the Finns. He did not criticize the Government for their failure to rescue Finland – a difficult and hazardous enterprise: he considered that Finland should never have been considered part of our strategic front. But he insisted that, having decided to intervene, the Government should have acted with speed instead of hovering between two policies. He gave a moving account of the heroism of the Finnish soldiers and civilians, and castigated the Government for authorizing misleading statements about how much we had given to them. He had discovered that materials had always been too few and too late; and the armaments were not gifts, but paid for. If we had supplied more men, the Finns might have held out until the thaw. The whole affair, he concluded, had pinpointed the dangers of Government irresolution.

Macmillan, with the rest of the 'Eden group', had been working for the removal of Chamberlain since before the war. By May 1940 – after the disastrous British campaign in Norway – their opportunity finally came. In the historic debate of 7 and 8 May, when Herbert Morrison asked for a vote of censure, sixty Conservatives abstained and thirty voted against Chamberlain, including Macmillan. When the figures were announced Macmillan – who did not speak in the debate – said, 'We ought to sing something'; and the rebel Tories struck up with 'Rule Britannia'. Two days later Chamberlain had resigned and Churchill was prime minister of a coalition Government. Churchill did not forget his friends: he told Amery that of the rebel Tories he could find posts for Macmillan, Richard Law, Boothby and Cranborne (later Lord Salisbury). Soon afterwards Churchill summoned Macmillan and offered him the modest job of parliamentary secretary to the Ministry of Supply.

So, at last, Macmillan found himself in the Government, at the most crucial and exciting time. His two years at the ministry gave him his first experience of practical power after sixteen years in Parliament. He worked first under Herbert Morrison, whom he had admired in the pre-war years as a man of exceptional political courage. Morrison, on his side, was much impressed by Macmillan's ability, and realized for the first time the extent of his ambition – both for himself and his boss: 'Indeed in his loyalty to me,' wrote Morrison snidely in his autobiography, 'his advice for my advancement tended to occupy his mind to such an extent that I had to remind him that we had a war job to do and that personal careers were not important.'[3]

Macmillan was not outwardly a great success at Supply: for the first time he had to answer questions in the House, concerned with salvage, scrap-metal, collection of waste or removal of iron railings. He hated question time, then and ever after, and his way of answering questions irritated other M.P.s. But inside the department Macmillan was very effective, and he was able to put into practice at last the planning ideas which had been rotating in his mind over the last decade. The boards and committees which had been so mocked before now took shape. He helped to reorganize the ministry, to give closer contact between government, industrialists and labour: neat new Area Boards were set up, with representatives from different ministries, which were responsible to the 'Industrial Capacity Committee' with Macmillan as chairman. It was a planners' paradise. He lovingly explained the new system in a speech on 7 August 1940, and jokingly remarked that he would try to introduce State Socialism in the country if he did not have to put up with the tremendous resistance of the Labour movement. Later, on 9 July 1941, he spoke about the problems of planning in wartime: 'I have thought it wise to attempt to convey an impression of the vast organization that is required for production. It is a subject which I tried in the old days to study in theory. During the past year I have learnt something of the difficulties of putting it in practice.' He was worried by the problem of democratically converting the economy from one regulated by the price system to one on a wartime basis, but he felt that it was being built in England 'upon the solid rock of democratic consent'.

In July 1941, after a few months under Sir Andrew Duncan, the Ministry of Supply was taken over by Lord Beaverbrook, with almost dictatorial powers, and Macmillan was his second-in-command. He was fascinated by Beaverbrook's ruthless drive, his mastery of power and his dramatic style: he would ring up his parliamentary secretary from Washington at three or four in the morning, and Macmillan found himself working all round the clock until 'you could not call your soul your own'. Some of Macmillan's Liberal colleagues suspected that Beaverbrook had had a coarsening influence on him; certainly Macmillan – in his own words – 'learnt to appreciate the extraordinary gifts of this strange and wayward genius' and made use of the experience ten years later, in the Ministry of Housing.[4]

After eight months under Beaverbrook, and three months again under Duncan, Macmillan was shifted to the Colonial Office, where he was appointed under secretary in June 1942, under Lord Cranborne, who had been an old friend and colleague in the Eden group. The two men were the same age, at Eton and Oxford together; Macmillan said on 26 November 1942 that they had had a long and intimate personal friendship for more than thirty years: 'both through shadow and sunshine, unclouded and unbroken' – though the friendship was to become thickly clouded after Macmillan became prime minister. The Colonial Office gave Macmillan new opportunities for practical planning, and for thinking about imperial policy.

He made a speech just after he had moved into the job, on 24 June 1942, in which he enthusiastically explained the problems of colonial food production, and showed an unshaken confidence in the continuation of the Empire which was to take another twenty years to wear itself out. He pointed to the loyalty of colonial peoples, and their offers of help ('These offers include, for instance, that of one chief and his three sons who proposed they should be dropped by parachute on Berlin to slay Hitler with bows and arrows, an ambitious but alas an impracticable plan'). He went on to give his views on the future of the colonies. 'The Empires of the past have died because they were rigid. By contrast our Empire has had the great quality of adaptation. It lives.' He did not share the view that when the colonies have grown to their full stature they would 'drop off like ripe fruit': he believed that the future of the world lay in large organizations, and that Britain should think of her future relationship with the colonies as a permanent thing. The colonies should be treated as a whole: 'We want no depressed areas in the Colonial Empire.' There would have to be long-term capital expenditures for development. The colonies 'are four or five centuries behind. Our job is to move them, to hustle them across this great interval of time as rapidly as we can.' Closing the debate, he explained that his plan was not a revolutionary one, but a middle way.

These two ministries gave Macmillan useful experience; but it was not until November 1942, when the war was half-way through, that he had his real opportunity, and felt himself to be, as he put it, 'In the big stuff'. Churchill sent for him, and asked him to go out to French North Africa, which the Americans and British had just invaded, to be Minister Resident in Algiers. It was a job which two people had already turned down, and Macmillan suspected would be a 'political Siberia'. But he accepted, and the job proved to be the turning point of his career. For the first time he had independent power, and could act on his own initiative. He was able to display his administrative gifts and his daring. Above all, he could show his diplomatic skill in a sphere of war where, for the first time, Anglo-American relations were crucial and very difficult.

French North Africa was an American sphere of influence, with an American political adviser, Robert Murphy: but Churchill insisted that Britain should be represented there politically. As he said in a telegram to Roosevelt:

We feel quite unrepresented there yet our fortunes are deeply involved and we are trying to make a solid contribution to your enterprise. Murphy's appointment has already been announced and I hope you will agree to my publishing Macmillan's. He will be, I am sure, a help. He is animated by the friendliest feelings towards the United States and his mother hails from Kentucky.*

Roosevelt agreed and Macmillan was sent out with instructions that the final authority rested with General Eisenhower, who commanded the Anglo-American forces. Churchill at first wanted Macmillan to go in uniform, but Macmillan explained that he didn't feel that a Grenadier captain on the reserve would carry much weight in Eisenhower's headquarters. Churchill replied 'I quite understand. You mean there's no place between the Baton and the Bowler.' So Macmillan went out as a plain politician. *The Times* commented that 'the appointment of Mr Macmillan meets a want which has been increasingly felt since American and British forces occupied French North Africa. In no theatre of war has there been more apparent the need for some high-ranking political representative.'

Macmillan succeeded, quickly and quietly, in gaining the confidence of Eisenhower and of Robert Murphy, who had a rather naïve and old-fashioned view of French politics. Macmillan set himself up in a big villa ('desirably vulgar', according to Lady Diana Duff Cooper) and patiently set about influencing the American administrators at their headquarters in the Hotel St George. He gave British officers quiet pep-talks about the importance of tact with the Americans. One of them was Richard Crossman, who arrived in Algiers as Director of

* He was wrong. She hailed from Indiana.

Psychological Warfare, and who later described his memorable encounter with Macmillan:

> Macmillan sent for me straight away. No doubt the speech he made to me was made to every other arrival, but it impressed itself indelibly on my memory. 'Remember,' he said, 'when you go to the Hotel St George, you will regularly enter a room and see an American colonel, his cigar in his mouth and his feet on the table. When your eyes get used to the darkness, you will see in a corner an English captain, his feet down, his shoulders hunched, writing like mad, with a full in-tray and a full out-tray, and no cigar.
>
> 'Mr Crossman, you will never call attention to this discrepancy. When you install a similar arrangement in your own office, you will always permit your American colleague not only to have a superior rank to yourself and much higher pay, but also the feeling that he is running the show. This will enable you to run it yourself.
>
> 'We, my dear Crossman, are Greeks in this American empire. You will find the Americans much as the Greeks found the Romans – great big, vulgar, bustling people, more vigorous than we are and also more idle, with more unspoiled virtues but also more corrupt. We must run A.F.H.Q. as the Greek slaves ran the operations of the Emperor Claudius.'[5]

The idea of being Greeks in the American empire was to fascinate Macmillan, too much: but here it seemed to work. Murphy said in his memoirs that Macmillan was an expert in not appearing to influence the Americans but that in fact 'he did indeed exercise greater influence upon Anglo-American affairs in the Mediterranean than was generally realized'.[6] Although they were endlessly involved in controversial policies, said Murphy, 'we got on famously together'. The American State Department and War Department were suspicious of political 'advisers' and the Assistant Secretary for War complained, 'You simply cannot have a Cabinet Minister on the ground, particularly one of Macmillan's character and ability, without his taking part in the play.'[7] But the suspicions eased and, in the words of the official history, 'in the creation of this Anglo-American instrument of government, much was owed to the efforts of General Eisenhower and Mr Macmillan'.[8]

Algiers was not only politically exciting. It had also an atmosphere of gaiety and eccentricity which Macmillan loved. It was full of surprising characters, and it was here that he first encountered John Wyndham, the explosive young aristocrat who was to be his devoted secretary and companion in future years.

Macmillan faced a tangled relationship between the Americans and the French. First there was the difficulty of Darlan, the right-wing French admiral with whom the Americans did a deal, who was assassinated on Christmas Eve. Then there were the rival French generals, Giraud and de Gaulle. The Americans, wanting to rally the Algerian French behind them while they prepared for the invasion of Sicily, had smuggled Giraud out of France, and were committed to back him. But Giraud, although a distinguished general, was politically a child. The British, meanwhile, had (as Macmillan explained to Murphy) invested £70 million in de Gaulle.

Macmillan could master the intrigue of French politics, and could speak French – which few of Eisenhower's staff could. The British delegation enjoyed jokes about the rivalries of Giraud and de Gaulle, and concocted sophisticated reports to London: when Macmillan told Churchill that de Gaulle had sent Giraud an ultimatum that unless he resigned, de Gaulle would, Churchill telegraphed back

You are quite right to play for time and let de Gaulle have every chance to come to his senses and realize the forces round him. See St Matthew, Chapter vii, verse 17; 'Ye shall know them by their fruits. Do men gather grapes of thorns or figs of thistles?' Indeed the whole chapter is instructive.

Macmillan replied, 'Doing my best. See Revelations 2, verses 2–5.' ('I know thy works and thy toil and patience and that thou canst not bear evil men . . . but I have this against thee, that thou didst leave thy first love.')[9]

Macmillan's relationship with de Gaulle was thorny, but they respected each other, and Macmillan could sometimes protect de Gaulle from the Americans: when Roosevelt told

Eisenhower to get rid of de Gaulle, Macmillan persuaded Eisenhower not to, on the grounds that it would delay the conduct of the war. De Gaulle often refers to Macmillan in his memoirs, sometimes with irritation but on the whole with admiration. He says that though

[Macmillan was] originally directed by Churchill to associate himself, although with some reservations, with the political actions of the Americans in North Africa, Macmillan had gradually realized he had better things to do. His independent spirit and lucid intelligence had found themselves in sympathy with the French group that desired a France without fetters. As our relations developed I sensed that the prejudices he had nursed towards us were dissolving. In return he had all my esteem.[10]

In a telegram to the London Committee of Liberation in June 1943, after his arrival in Algiers, de Gaulle, said 'Macmillan, whom I see often, seems to have seen the light. Murphy remains aloof.'[11] Macmillan could, however, be tough with de Gaulle and his supporters, and never allowed them to perceive any rift in Anglo-American relations: he once shouted at a meeting with de Gaulle's emissary in Algiers, 'If General de Gaulle refuses the hand stretched out towards him, let him know that Britain and the United States will abandon him completely – and he will be nothing any more.'

Macmillan's first involvement with big-time diplomacy came at the Casablanca Conference, with Churchill and Roosevelt, in January 1943. Macmillan and Murphy had evolved a plan giving de Gaulle joint political leadership with Giraud, which had been approved by Giraud and also, with difficulty, by Roosevelt; and a telegram was sent to de Gaulle asking him to join the conference. De Gaulle refused: he felt it an insult to meet Giraud under the auspices of the allies. Roosevelt telegraphed to Eden 'I have got the bridegroom but where is the bride?' Finally de Gaulle was persuaded to come, and Macmillan had to break the news of the plan to de Gaulle. The general crushingly replied that a 'Giraud–de Gaulle *entente* could only be realized by Frenchmen'. He refused to associate himself with the arrangements, and had a stormy meeting with Churchill. Eventually Roosevelt managed to persuade him to be photographed shaking hands with Giraud, after which the two Frenchmen stalked away, followed by Macmillan and Murphy 'exactly as nursemaids following wandering children'.[12]

Gradually it became obvious how much of a liability Giraud was to the allies, and how strong was support for de Gaulle in Africa. Macmillan had to deal with the problems created by Giraud's Vichy legislation and prison camps, and made an effort to 'democratize' him. His staff wrote a liberal speech for him and, as Giraud said afterwards, 'I made the first democratic speech of my life'. But it became obvious that a joint administration between Giraud and de Gaulle was needed, and Macmillan worked hard for it. By May 1943 agreement was near and Macmillan flew to London for consultations, playing a large part in the final settlement. Macmillan told Vincent Massey, the Canadian High Commissioner in London (and an old Balliol friend), that at the last minute the Americans were unhappy about the union but that luckily things had gone too far to be disturbed, and the 'best man', General Catroux, was going to Algiers with him the next day, followed by the 'bridegroom', de Gaulle.[13] The 'bride', Giraud, was waiting and an 'indissoluble marriage' would take place shortly with great pomp'. The joint Committee of National Liberation, with de Gaulle and Giraud as joint presidents, was set up in June 1943: the British delegation gave a 'victory lunch' for the French.

But the honeymoon was soon over, and Macmillan had to cope with still wider differences between the two generals. At one point, before King George VI was due to visit Algiers, both generals had resigned: Macmillan managed to get them back in office just in time for the royal visit. Churchill became increasingly concerned about de Gaulle's power in the new French Committee. He warned de Gaulle against devouring Giraud 'in one mouthful' and was pressed by Roosevelt to 'get rid of our mutual headache'. Macmillan helped to smooth over the conflict. Churchill, determined to preserve American friendship at any cost, was cautious about officially recognizing the new joint committee and hoped that de Gaulle would gradually merge unobtrusively into it. But eventually Macmillan persuaded Churchill, and Churchill persuaded the Americans, to join a general declaration of recognition. Then a new rumpus occurred, when de Gaulle was not brought into the discussions about the Italian armistice: Macmillan had the tricky task of telling de Gaulle that it had been agreed without him. He told Massigli (who was on de Gaulle's staff) in confidence 'that he was afraid the contacts between us were not always as intimate as they should be: General Bedell Smith did not know French and General Dewinck did not know English. This state of affairs did not facilitate conversations.'[14] Gradually Giraud's position in the committee weakened. In November 1943 he resigned, leaving de Gaulle sole president.

In all the negotiations, Macmillan showed that, when London and Washington were dilatory, he could take decisions into his own hands; and even on one occasion, when Churchill telegraphed an order to arrest a leading resident, which Macmillan thought might result in civil war, he completely ignored his instructions, and burnt the telegram. Throughout these awkward operations, Macmillan maintained a gaiety and resilience which impressed nearly all his colleagues. To quote Crossman again:

I have a feeling that I worked under Macmillan when he was at his peak – a dashing man of action, self-confidently poised in his behaviour, gambling on his hunches and, when we lost, as we sometimes did, loyal to his subordinates. . . . What I remember chiefly about Macmillan as a boss at this time was his buoyancy. And no wonder. Not even the Prime Minister in Britain enjoyed quite such unquestioned prestige as Harold Macmillan had earned for himself both in his own British staff and in Ike's entourage. As a Conservative politician he had had to conceal for years the fact that he is not merely a supremely intelligent man but an intellectual who was prepared to stake everything on an idea. Among the soldiers in A.F.H.Q. these qualities brought him not suspicion but admiration, and the more he dazzled the Americans, the more fertile his mind became. I suspect it was in Algiers, where he could do all the thinking and take all the decisions while Ike took all the credit, that Harold Macmillan first realized his own capacity for supreme leadership, and developed that streak of intellectual recklessness which was to be the cause both of his success and of his failure when he finally reached No. 10.

By November 1943, the allies had successfully occupied Sicily and southern Italy, and concluded an armistice with the Italians. Macmillan was appointed United Kingdom High Commissioner in Italy, while remaining Resident Minister to Allied Headquarters, which had moved to Naples. He no longer had to deal with the French generals, and Churchill sent out Duff Cooper, another old political crony, to be Ambassador to the French Government in Africa. Duff Cooper was impressed by how far Macmillan had gained Eisenhower's trust, and even de Gaulle's. His wife, Lady Diana, commented in her diary on Macmillan: 'He's a splendid man. He feeds us and warms and washes us. One day he'll be prime minister.'[15]

For the next year Macmillan was preoccupied with Italy, and the setting up of an Italian government. He had already played a prominent part in the negotiations for the Italian armistice, which began after the successful invasion of Sicily in August 1943. The Italians proposed that the allies should land near Rome, cutting off the Germans near Naples and rallying the Italian armed forces to their side. Macmillan was enthusiastic about this cooperation, both for military reasons and for the sake of the future political situation in Italy and the Balkans. The allied leaders met the Italians in Sicily to discuss armistice terms. Macmillan agreed with Alexander that speedy Italian cooperation was necessary, and was deeply concerned lest an allied defeat in Italy might discourage the exhausted British people. He pointed out to the hesitant Italian delegation that this was their last chance and should be taken quickly: if they refused to sign the king would be discredited and there would be heavy bombing of Italian cities. Finally after a long struggle the military armistice terms were signed on 3 September 1943.

Later Macmillan and Murphy discovered that General Ridgeway, who commanded the American air force division, had doubts about landing near Rome – doubts which would ruin any chance of organized Italian opposition to the Germans. Macmillan felt that if the allies did not support the Italians, their prestige would suffer. Ridgeway said he would agree to the landings only if 'the two double-damned political advisers went in the first plane'. This dashing plan was proposed to Eisenhower who agreed saying, 'There's nothing in the regulations which says diplomats are not expendable.'[16] But owing to the delay in signing the armistice, the Germans moved reinforcements to Rome and the landings were called off. On 8 September Macmillan told the Italian delegation on his own initiative that 'It was too late for us to arrive in the rear and that at 18.30 as arranged, General Eisenhower's declaration would be broadcast', from Algiers.[17] Marshal Badoglio hesitated another two hours before making his announcement from Rome: as a result the Germans entered Rome, and Badoglio and the king had to flee to Brindisi.

Macmillan was then sent to Brindisi as political adviser to the American General Mason Macfarlane, who was head of a diplomatic mission, and became increasingly involved in Italian politics. More Anglo-American arguments ensued. Macfarlane had nothing but contempt for the Italians and called Badoglio a 'has-been', and Macmillan tried to convince him that Italian cooperation was essential. (When he was criticized later for making a deal with Badoglio, Macmillan said: 'I would have signed a treaty with the devil himself to get our boys ashore.') Macmillan and Murphy had talks with Badoglio, and Macmillan reported to Churchill that Badoglio was now prepared to sign the second armistice document, which gave effective control to the allies over all aspects of Italian affairs. Macmillan found himself a kind of unofficial kingmaker for the Italians: Churchill asked him to vet the king's speech if there was not time for the British Government to see it. The allies decided to retain military government for Italy, and Macmillan spent much of his time at Allied Force Headquarters near Naples. By the spring of 1943 there was increasing pressure, particularly from the Americans, for the abdication of the king. Macmillan supported Murphy in this, though Churchill believed the monarchy should be retained as a stabilizing influence and felt that any replacement of Badoglio would lead to Communism. Eventually, in April 1944, by a constitutional compromise, the king handed over his powers to his son, until a plebiscite could be held.

In December 1943 Macmillan was appointed Resident Minister for the Central Mediterranean, to give political advice to General Maitland Wilson (the new Supreme Commander for the Mediterranean who had taken over from Eisenhower) and to work alongside General Alexander who was in command of the campaign in Italy. Churchill, Macmillan and others had wanted Alexander to be supreme commander but had been dissuaded by Alan Brooke and Eisenhower. Brooke indicated Macmillan's influence in his diary for 8 December 1943:[18]

[Churchill] is now back again wanting Alexander as Supreme Commander for the Mediterranean. I shall have heavy work ahead. The trouble has been caused by Macmillan, who has had a long talk with the Prime Minister suggesting Alex as the man for the job and that he, Macmillan, can take the political load off him. He, Macmillan, came round to see me for an hour this evening and evidently does not understand what the functions of a supreme commander should be.

Brooke continued to resent Macmillan's influence, and a year later – after Alexander had become Supreme Commander – he recorded

I had a long and useful interview with Alex. Finally told him that some of us had doubts as to whether Macmillan or Alexander was Supreme Commander of the Mediterranean. This had, I think, the required effect . . . I had the highest regard and affection for Alexander both as a soldier and man but felt that in his absorption in Greece he was being too much influenced by his very able political partner, the Resident Minister of State.

Alexander and Macmillan were certainly very close: they had known each other since the First World War, and Alexander was very content to leave political decisions to Macmillan.

For a time in Italy Mr Macmillan shared my mess at Caserta [Alexander recalled], and during this period he and I would go to the front in my open desert car to visit the troops. Those were happy days for me. I had a delightful companion who was both wise in advice and always amusing; a man of great intellect, morally and physically brave, but far too reserved to show these admirable qualities outwardly.[19]

Macmillan had plenty of scope for political advice, and soon found himself involved in the rebuilding of Europe. After the fall of Rome in 1944, the American Government more or less opted out of Italian politics, but the British had definite plans for the country, and took over the administration with competition only from the Communists. Churchill took a close interest, paid several visits to Italy, and in November 1944 appointed Macmillan as head of the Allied Commission in Italy, which became a more civilian organization to give constructive assistance, and a 'New Deal' for Italy. Macmillan had been scathing about the military Control Commission which operated after the invasion. After seeing it in action for two months he said

Planning of the Allied Control Commission by academic methods, thousands of miles from the scene of operation without comprehension of the situation likely to exist in conquered and largely devastated territory has produced an organization ill-conceived, ill-staffed and ill-equipped for its purpose.[20]

Macmillan's views on Italy carried great weight in London and Washington, and he took the most important part in implementing the 'New Deal', which gave many political concessions: Allied Commission officers were withdrawn from Italian Government territory, and regional control was given back to the Italians. Macmillan reorganized the commission, decided that its staff should be mainly concerned with consultation and advice to the Italian Government, and demobilized the Allied Commission regional officers. He later described sardonically how the Italians had had to undergo 'for nearly two years the double experience of being occupied by the Germans and liberated by the allies. . . . It was hard to know which process was the more painful or devastating.' The Allied Commission, he said, had done its best to assist Italian reconstruction. 'We were very keen, we had lots of experts, we made a great quantity of plans, we imported a lot of food and materials; we set up all sorts of commissions and boards and committees. We started to govern (or try to govern) and regulate (or try to regulate) every aspect of Italian life.' The Italians had listened and appeared grateful, 'but were waiting for us to leave. Since then they have made a constitution, held free elections and reduced Fascism to a tiny minority. They had resisted Communism. They had raised living standards and done great work of reconstruction.' This had been possible, Macmillan maintained afterwards, because the Italian Government had recognized the fact that Italians were individuals.[21]

Macmillan's power at the time, however temporary, was colossal – perhaps more absolute than ever again. His responsibilities stretched way beyond Italy: he had to deal with the supersession of Mikhailovich by Tito in Yugoslavia, and was involved in the crisis in Lebanon and Syria, during 1943, which brought him back to Anglo-French disputes.

By the end of August 1944 his territory had extended to Greece, and his extraordinary experiences there certainly strengthened and justified his determination to get tough with Communists. 'He was always looking ahead,' wrote Sir Reginald Leeper, who became Ambassador in Athens, 'foreseeing the next difficulty and taking steps to forestall it.'[22] Macmillan was the principal architect of the Caserta Agreement signed at Allied Headquarters in September 1944, when the guerrilla leaders Seraphis and Zervas agreed that their forces would be subject to the orders of General Scobie, the commander of allied forces in Greece. When the Greek Government under Papandreou returned to Greece in October 1944 Macmillan went with them, and soon found himself with a Greek Civil War on his hands. It became obvious that Papandreou's Government had little influence outside Athens. Eden and Macmillan advised Churchill to support the king and Papandreou. Civil war broke out with guerrilla forces fighting in the streets. Macmillan and General Alexander (who had just been made Supreme Commander in the Mediterranean) flew to Athens. Leeper had previously protested that if a cabinet minister was sent to take charge in Athens he would resign but added 'if Mr Macmillan were chosen there would be no difficulty whatever and nobody would be more pleased than I to have his sagacious counsel'. When Macmillan arrived the firing was so fierce that he and Alexander had to drive to Athens in an armoured car driven through a hail of bullets.

By now Papandreou had lost his authority, and the Communist-controlled guerrillas were in control of most of Athens. Churchill, with support from Macmillan, gave firm instructions to General Scobie, in charge of British troops in Athens, to neutralize or destroy the rebel bands approaching the city, which was done with a good deal of bloodshed. It was a highly controversial instruction, for the Greek king was not a democrat, and Britain's relations with Russia were still, officially very close. Churchill was under heavy criticism from the American State Department, *The Times* and the House of Commons, for supporting a reactionary regime against democrats. Macmillan was confirmed in his distrust of *The Times*, 'pitifully ignorant and dangerously pedantic'.[23] He said later:

Has there ever been a more dramatic reversal of policy than that of the United States towards Greece? . . . Has there ever been a more sensational justification of the wisdom of what we did then? The revolutionary communist fire [he went on], was lit in Athens in the winter of 1944 and, but for us, that conflagration might have spread through what was left of free and democratic Europe.[24]

It was a lesson in 'going it alone' which certainly influenced him twelve years later.

Macmillan then found himself rebuilding another country: he and Alexander were instructed to end the fighting as soon as possible with the assurance of future peace and cooperation of all Greek political parties. 'I know that you have sent Macmillan there with broad powers to find a solution,' cabled Roosevelt to Churchill. Macmillan was strongly in favour of a regency, under Archbishop Damaskinos, the Archbishop of Athens, who was a very controversial figure. He was mistrusted by both Papandreou and the king; Churchill was convinced that he was a Quisling and a Communist, and called him a 'scheming medieval prelate'. Macmillan on the other hand talked of 'the noble personality of the Regent' and was convinced that the only hope of peace lay with him. Macmillan and Churchill were at loggerheads, and Churchill referred to Macmillan and Leeper as. 'our two fuzzy wuzzies'. Finally Churchill decided, just before Christmas, that he must come and see for himself. The situation was ideally suited to Macmillan's temperament. Bullets were flying everywhere: the British embassy was painted pink and was a favourite target. When Churchill arrived he was met by Macmillan who suggested calling a conference of all the political leaders including E.L.A.S., the Communist-controlled 'National Army of Liberation'. Churchill agreed, and Damaskinos was chosen to preside over the conference, which eventually led to an armistice being signed and Damaskinos becoming regent.

Macmillan stayed in Athens for the peace-making conference between the different factions, which took place at Varkisa, outside Athens. The conference met for several days, and the Greek leaders reached a deadlock. Macmillan was then invited to join it, and he and Leeper set off at five in the afternoon. They sat at the conference all night with nothing to eat while the Greeks argued: 'Macmillan enjoyed this more than I did,' said Leeper. The Greeks reached agreement at about four in the morning. Macmillan made a speech, and the peace treaty was signed.

Macmillan returned to Italy, where in the meantime the Eighth Army had broken through the Gothic Line, and had been delayed by the winter south of Bologna. Then in the spring they moved on, crossed the Po and forced the Germans to unconditional surrender. Macmillan had slipped away for a day or two of quiet in Assisi, 'before facing the new problems peace would bring'. At Assisi he received telegrams to report that the Germans, on 29 April, had signed the surrender documents. 'Many of us remember,' he said later, 'that curious sense of emptiness and even flatness.'

Macmillan's wartime experiences could hardly have been more opposite to his pre-war life. After all the theorizing, the pleading and waiting, he had found himself in a succession of situations where he could influence whole populations, and convert political theories, on the spot, into battles and constitutions. He could no longer be regarded as absurd or ineffectual. Among flying bullets his impassive moustache and classical manner acquired a new splendour: he was able to be the soldier–philosopher, tempering his intellect to action. He was still not a major public figure when the war ended, for his political sphere of influence had always been lesser-known, and more confused, than the epic battles of the desert, or Burma, or Normandy. In political life, he was still eclipsed by the more glamorous figures of Eden, Duff Cooper or Stanley. But to those who worked with him, the wartime Macmillan was quite a dazzling phenomenon; and for himself, it was probably the most fulfilling time of his life.

Power had certainly changed him and his attitudes since his pre-war days as a spectator. But perhaps a greater influence was Churchill. Many of his colleagues noticed how much he had adopted the mannerisms, style and postures of his boss; but the influence went deeper than that. The two men were strikingly different; Macmillan was much more introverted, more intellectual and analytical, more in conflict with himself. But he was bowled over by the magnitude and romance of the leader. Here was the complete man of action, the embodiment of history, with a vast vision of the world and destiny, with himself in the middle. Macmillan was not the only intellectual who suspended his critical judgement in the presence of Churchill. But Churchill's influence on him was to have a special historical importance.

MACMILLAN

NOTES

1. Quoted in *The Listener*, 8 September 1966
2. Evelyn Wrench, *Geoffrey Dawson and his Times* (London: Hutchinson, 1955), p. 409
3. Herbert Morrison, *An Autobiography* (London: Odhams, 1960), p. 300
4. Harold Macmillan, *Winds of Change*, vol. I (London: Macmillan, 1966), p. 256
5. *The Sunday Telegraph*, 9 February 1964
6. Robert Murphy, *Diplomat Among Warriors* (New York: Doubleday, 1964; London: Collins), p. 207
7. Quoted in F. S. V. Donnison, *History of Second World War: Civil Affairs and Military Government* (London: H.M.S.O., 1966), p. 57
8. Ibid., p. 59
9. Quoted in Nora Beloff, *The General Says No* (Harmondsworth: Penguin, 1963), p. 34
10. Charles de Gaulle, *War Memoirs*, vol. II (London: Weidenfeld & Nicolson, 1960), p. 213
11. Charles de Gaulle, *War Memoirs (Documents)*, vol. II (London: Weidenfeld & Nicolson, 1960), p. 187
12. Quoted from Drew Middleton in Peter Tompkins, *The Murder of Admiral Darlan* (London: Weidenfeld & Nicolson, 1965), p. 237
13. Vincent Massey, *What's Past is Prologue* (London: Macmillan, 1963), p. 370
14. Charles de Gaulle, *War Memoirs (Documents)*, vol. II, p. 221
15. Diana Duff Cooper, *Trumpets from the Steep* (London: Hart-Davis, 1960), p. 174
16. Robert Murphy, *Diplomat Among Warriors*, p. 242
17. Charles de Gaulle, *War Memoirs (Documents)*, vol. II, p. 219
18. Arthur Bryant, *Triumph of the West* (London: Collins, 1959), p. 111
19. Earl Alexander of Tunis, *Memoirs, 1940–45* (London: Cassell, 1962), p. 110
20. C. R. S. Harris, *Allied Military Administration of Italy, 1943–1945* (London: H.M.S.O., 1958), p. 115
21. 'Bevin's astonishing blunder in Italy', *The Sunday Chronicle*, 12 December 1948
22. Reginald Leeper, *When Greek Meets Greek* (London: Chatto & Windus, 1950), p. 70
23. Harold Macmillan, *Winds of Change*, p. 131
24. House of Commons, 16 May 1947

74

5. Opposition, 1945-51

By noon it was clear that the Socialists would have
a majority. At luncheon, my wife said to me, 'It may well
be a blessing in disguise'. I replied,
'At the moment it seems quite effectively disguised'.
WINSTON CHURCHILL[1]

Back in England after victory in Europe, Macmillan – like other war leaders – saw total anti-climax. He was quickly back in party politics, for the first time for five-and-a-half years. In May 1945 Churchill disbanded the coalition and formed his 'caretaker Government' before the general election. For six weeks, Macmillan found himself a cabinet minister, with the job of Secretary for Air. At the same time he began once again electioneering. He had been offered a safe seat, for St George's, Westminster, but he had told the Stockton Conservative Association that he would offer himself for re-election there (he had been their member all through the war years).

He might have expected to emerge from his wartime successes with new political inspiration. But he did not: the sword was back in its sheath. He spoke in a familiar vein, as if nothing had happened in the meantime. He stressed to the electors of Stockton that the Conservatives would carry out schemes for social reform; but he still preached the same Middle Way:

In the realm of national economic planning we shall hold a wise balance between the field suited for private enterprise and that allocated to public ownership or control . . . the Government will follow the national characteristic – a middle course avoiding equally the extreme of *laissez-faire* and that of collectivist control for its own sake.

But the Middle Way no longer stirred the voters of Stockton. Macmillan was the first cabinet minister to fall in the general election of 5 July: he lost his seat to the Labour candidate, George Chetwynd, by 8,664 votes. The Conservatives were out of power, and he was out of Parliament: after the exhilarating experience of running the Mediterranean, in the centre of great events, he returned to unwanted theories and blue-prints. It was a bitter moment. As *The New Statesman* later described it:

At this precise moment, when Macmillan had finally come to full maturity as a politician, the catastrophe he had prophesied occurred. In the election of 1945, Macmillan lost not only his seat, but his faith. His own decimated generation had been betrayed by its ruthless, corrupt elders; now, in its place, was a new generation – and it had chosen the other side. When Macmillan returned to the House in November, he found idealist youth crowding the Labour benches – and clamouring for policies which to him were anathema. He abandoned himself to a mood of unrestrained pessimism.[2]

Soon after the general election, a safe seat had fallen vacant at Bromley, Kent, a solidly conservative middle-class suburb in south London, with none of the romantic challenge of Stockton. Among the Tory candidates for the nomination were Harold Macmillan and one of his fans, Randolph Churchill; but when Churchill heard that Macmillan was up for it, he wrote to Bromley Conservative Association: 'He's a great friend of mine and I think that no-one has a greater claim. Will you please, therefore, withdraw my name.'

Macmillan was chosen, and went rather sadly into the fray. In his adoption speech, in August 1945, he attacked the Socialists, in the familiar style of his weary metaphors twenty years before: he talked about their

high pressure salesmanship skilfully applied to a gullible, war-weary and suffering population. There was a refined appeal to youth. . . . A most heady and intoxicating drink was made and freely distributed. It was a powerful political cocktail, part bitter and part sweet.*

* Compare his maiden speech, p. 24.

He said that Conservative foreign policy was based on the honest facing of realities. It was foolish to attack America; the dominions and colonies should be strengthened, the alliance with Russia should be maintained: 'we must be loyal to the world security system and work for closer cooperation of Western Europe as inheritors of the great European tradition.' Winston Churchill sent Macmillan an election message mentioning his war work which was 'important, difficult and delicate'.

It required qualities of an exceptional order, and it must have given you an acquaintance with the affairs of the Mediterranean States and the Middle East which few can rival . . . moreover in the social field at home you are distinguished for your constructive and progressive outlook. We need you very much on the Opposition Front Bench in the Commons.

On 16 November 1945, Macmillan won Bromley in a three-cornered fight with a majority of 5,557, and was back again in Parliament.

To some of Macmillan's wartime colleagues, his reappearance in party politics, with a rather fusty air, came as a shock. Richard Crossman described his impressions:

The studied Edwardian elegance of his despatch-box manner, the mannered witticisms and the whole style of professional party polemics which he so consciously adopted – everything about him disconcerted me. But one evening we got into conversation and I walked home with him to have a drink. For an hour he complained to me about the decadence of Britain, and talked at length about his First World War experience as a Guards officer. 'All my friends were killed,' he said. 'The Somme drained off what should have been the leadership, and now our country is in irreparable decline – under your gang.' I do not think I have ever spoken to him since then, mainly because I preferred to remember the man I knew for a few months in Algiers.[3]

For many of the wartime ministers, the change to the ineffectuality of peacetime opposition induced acute depression. For Macmillan who had waited so long for power, and excelled at

77

it, the rejection seemed almost unbearable. He was back to his defensive, unconvincing rhetoric; and he had acquired, too, a rather embarrassing heartiness of manner, which seemed designed to attract the more right-wing Conservatives; and he was observed making expansive gestures in the House of Commons smoking room. In the words of a contemporary observer:

A casual meeting with him makes him appear pompous, but actually he is shy, and this shyness is both a weakness and a strength. Though he can display emotion and even intelligence on political issues, in personal relationships he is unemotional and does not court friendship. He has humour and wit, and though rhetorical in speech, is brief in committee . . . for Macmillan personalities would never influence principles, and though he would seek a compromise over method, he would not over principle.[4]

His biographer and left-wing sparring-partner, Emrys Hughes, has described how

Macmillan soon became the Tory Front Bench speaker who could most easily raise the temperature of the House. He cultivated an oratorical style of the Gladstonian period. He would put his hands on the lapels of his coat and turn to the back benches behind him for approval and support. He would raise and lower his voice and speak as if he were on the stage. . . . His polished phrases reeked of midnight oil. He delighted in jibes at the benches opposite and the taunts that invited retort. To those opposite he seemed the political actor and poseur, the cynic, the knock-about artiste of the Parliamentary stage.[5]

He made a speech on 5 December 1945, and said: 'I feel like a kind of political Rip van Winkle. Everything is so changed . . . on the benches opposite sit many old colleagues. . . . Side by side with them sit their old enemies. Ebbw Vale (Bevan) and Limehouse (Attlee) together.' He advocated a short-term plan for reconstruction, the 'unleashing' of production, and true partnership between the State and private enterprise. He insisted that long-term schemes of public control and ownership were now irrelevant: 'Let sleeping dogmas lie.'

His position in the party was now quite important: he was a member of the shadow cabinet, and chairman of the Conservative Fuel and Power Committee. He opened the opposition case against coal nationalization, though with a parodoxical attack – not surprisingly, since he had advocated coal nationalization before the war. *The Observer* commented (20 January 1946) that since his return to Westminster Macmillan had increased in parliamentary stature and was qualifying for the leadership. He set himself up as the scourge of the Socialists, and as a planner himself continually attacked them for their lack of a real plan – 'they preached planning and practised confusion' – and for their food and housing programmes. He kept special venom for a few Socialist intellectuals (such as Laski), 'those clever men who in every age were always wrong', and who were dragging the party 'down the slippery slope to Communism'.[6]

Like other Conservatives at the time, he was worried that the Labour party might never be ousted, and he was looking round for new kinds of political alliance. In September 1946 he made a speech referring to a 'new democratic party' which would cling to all the sound traditions of the past while seeking true economic and political freedom – which was interpreted by the Press as meaning that Macmillan had joined Eden and Churchill in a plan to abandon the name Conservative in the hope of attracting the Liberals. Macmillan told a reporter later that he didn't know whether any moves were yet being made to combine the 'democratic' elements in the Conservative, Liberal and Socialist parties who were opposed to the Government, but that he wanted 'to start people talking'. The suggestion received much publicity. Later Macmillan wrote an article for *The Daily Telegraph* on the 'Anti-Socialist Parties' Task – the Case for Alliance or Fusion', in which he developed his theme for the integration of anti-socialist parties. But the idea soon fizzled out.

Macmillan became the Conservatives' expert on industrial policy, and on 20 November 1946 made a big speech in the House of Commons: Herbert Morrison suggested that it might have been unpopular with some Conservatives, but Churchill patted Macmillan warmly on the back. He said:

In the various phases of our long political and social history there seems to emerge through each succeeding generation one dominating theme on which are concentrated, for the time being, men's hopes and fears, satisfactions or disappointments, struggles, controversies, failures, triumphs. During all my political and business life, that is during almost the whole period between the two wars, the question of unemployment has in the field of home politics played the major role. . . . I believe that in this period on which we are now embarking the problem of unemployment will be replaced by the problem of production . . . in overcoming scarcity, in increasing both visible and invisible exports. . . . We shall need a new and more imaginative approach.

He already talked of the need for a wages policy – which was to loom so much larger: 'We cannot close our eyes to the necessity for some form of voluntary self-discipline to replace the harsh and cruel discipline of the days of unemployment.'

Macmillan had become much involved in the long and painful process of reforming and modernizing Conservative policy. After the party conference in 1946 at Blackpool, Churchill set up an Industrial Policy Committee, with Butler as chairman, of which Macmillan was a member, which met with industrialists, managers and trade unionists, and drafted the 'Industrial Charter'. The charter was the most important of the Conservative post-war policy statements, and it went beyond industrial relations, to outline a whole philosophy. It showed a final break with pre-war policies, and the beginning of the common ground between Conservatives and Socialists which came to be known as 'Butskellism'.[7] It marked the triumph of the 'Middle Way', though Butler took the credit. As Macmillan put it: 'Between the wars there was always a progressive element in the Party. Now it has seized control, not by force of palace revolution, but by the vigour of its intellectual and spiritual power.' Macmillan was able to claim with justice that it marked a victory over the forces of reaction. The charter in fact combined traditional Tory private enterprise, with many features of centralized control advocated by Macmillan before the war, and now introduced by the Labour Government.

The charter, in Macmillanish style, accused the socialists of 'confusing the real meaning of central planning, by all-round meddlesome interference without a proper sense of general direction'. It advocated decentralization, but with 'strong central guidance': 'the strategy of a campaign is conducted by the general staff, the tactics by the Commander in the field.' It outlined in some detail the proposed methods of 'National Housekeeping' – the new word for planning. It was opposed to nationalization in principle, but now accepted the nationalization of coal, railways and the Bank of England. It proposed to 'review the scope of the nationalized industries', submit them to the 'test of the highest standards of commercial efficiency' and to 'humanize even when an industry has been nationalized'. It concluded with the 'Workers' Charter', which laid down three general rights for workers – security of employment, incentive to do the job well, and status as an individual, however big the firm.

After its approval, Macmillan was its main salesman. 'The Industrial Charter had a wonderful welcome,' he said at the Constitutional Club in May 1947: 'The Socialists are afraid of it. Lord Beaverbrook dislikes it. And the Liberals say it is too liberal to be fair. What more can one want? Was ever a child born under such a lucky star? It is of course a challenge as well as a charter. It is the true doctrine of the Middle Way.'

The attacks from the right were not, in fact, very deadly. The eccentric magazine *Truth*, which had already complained that Macmillan's opposition to Socialism was half-hearted,[8] protested in June 1947:

Mr Harold Macmillan takes too much for granted. Because a few eminent Conservative politicians concocted a pamphlet termed 'The Industrial Charter', Mr Macmillan blandly assumed that this eclectic document, which draws so freely on Fabian and other Left-wing sources, automatically becomes the policy of the Conservative Party.

The Economist commented on 21 June that the struggle was

81

between those in the Tory party who thought that what the Socialists did was wrong, and those who thought that they could do it better. But after the next party conference at Brighton, Macmillan was able to congratulate the party workers on 'the triumphant adoption of the inspiring and progressive principles of the Industrial Charter'.

The Industrial Charter was re-echoed more faintly in 1949, in 'The Right Road for Britain', in which Macmillan was also involved. As power came closer the Conservatives became more conservative. As J. D. Hoffman put it:

The hot white light of free enterprise was present in The Industrial Charter, but it was blurred by a reddish filter – a filter which balanced support for free enterprise with the determination to apply strong central guidance over the operation of the economy. In the 'Right Road' the white light burned as before, but, to extend the analogy, the reddish filter was replaced with one of a fainter hue.[9]

In fact, soon after the charter had appeared, the attitudes of corporatism and State intervention in industry which it represented were already beginning to pass out of favour. The resentment against socialist controls and bureaucracy, and the reaction against planning, was encouraging a new mood of *laissez-faire* liberalism, which gathered weight in the following years:[10] so that when the Tories came into power, 'planning' was once more a bogy-word. It was not until 1961 and 1962 that the notion of planning again became respectable.

In the meantime, in Parliament, Macmillan continued to attack the Socialists with a studied rhetoric, and a maddening cynicism which was doubtless made more bitter by his watching the systems he had himself advocated, being carried out by the opposite side. His manner, as Emrys Hughes described it, was 'flippant, superficial, supercilious and arrogant'.[11] He still specialized in artificial epigrams. 'The Government if not altogether airworthy are still in the air.' 'Perhaps it would be truer to say they are suspended like Mahomet's coffin between heaven and earth by the operation of a kind of political helicopter.' 'The second Daltonian period was succeeded by the beginning of the Cripps era. After the warm almost tropical luxuriance of the former dispensation came the new ice age, with arctic austerity, the wage freeze and all that.' The Festival of Britain in 1951 gave him a special opportunity for studied scorn. He talked about 'a little gem of mismanagement, a cameo of incompetence, a perfect little miniature of muddle'. His style was still laboured: 'The Brave New World has turned into nothing but a Fish and Cripps age after all.' 'Socialists attacking monopolies are rather like Satan rebuking sin.' Morrison was 'the Artful Dodger' and Bevan 'the fat boy in Pickwick'. Attlee, 'seems born to doodle while Europe burns'. Cripps 'was like an inverted Balaam: he begins with a blessing and ends with a curse'.

Macmillan's stature in Parliament gradually increased. Though not regarded as a future prime minister – he was still eclipsed by such men as Eden, Oliver Stanley and Oliver Lyttelton – he had emerged as a much more confident and convincing speaker. 'Every trace of his old diffidence and shyness has gone,' said *The Observer* on 15 October 1950. *The Sunday Times* (22 January 1950) included him in their portrait gallery, ending with a gratifying Churchillian reference:

Harold Macmillan is a political philosopher as well as a practical statesman. And he is an able administrator . . . he talks convincingly in the language of an intellectual, yet an intellectual with much practical experience of national and international affairs, of public office and private commerce, and a sympathetic understanding of the life and difficulties of the ordinary man. . . . If he is sometimes a shade impulsive and individualistic in his approach to political problems, he is in that respect in distinguished company.

Opposition was perhaps 'a blessing in disguise'. The political correspondent of *The Liverpool Daily Post* wrote (19 February 1950): 'The situation of the Conservative Party after the defeat of 1945 exactly suited his talents. It was not only that he himself had long been impatient with the old Conservatism, he also possesses a brilliantly speculative mind.' Macmillan in a speech to the 1900 Club on 27 June 1949 said that the defeat of 1945 had saved the Tory party. They had now revived and reconstituted the party machine 'and it was surprising how good it had become'. They had made more real progress during the past four years, he said, than at any time since he had been in the party.

But in spite of this kind of talk, Macmillan gave many people the impression of deep disillusion during his time in opposition. He seemed personally despondent, almost despairing, and for much of the time he saw no prospects of a return to power. He seemed to see little future for Britain, or for Europe.

His pessimism embraced foreign affairs. Like many others, including Churchill, Macmillan immediately after the war believed that Russia was more concerned with security than domination. In his first post-war speech on foreign affairs, in February 1946, he said that Russia had formed a new kind of *cordon sanitaire* of satellite and dependent States, and was becoming isolationist, so that the Great Powers should therefore be reconciled at the points where they met: with Russia 'I believe that this can only be done by direct and personal negotiation'. But the following month Churchill made his Fulton speech about the 'iron curtain' and the menace of Russia. Macmillan, whose view of Russia was always liable to swing from one extreme to another, quickly changed.

By May 1947, Macmillan had abandoned the idea of Britain becoming an 'honest broker' between Russia and America, and was castigating the Socialists for ever having thought that 'Left would be able to speak to Left'. In a speech on 16 May, he warned that Europe must be defended against Russia: at the moment the situation was 'only a war of nerves, but a war of nerves may be very dangerous' ... 'All over central and eastern Europe the struggle has begun.'

Like Churchill, Macmillan saw the fight against Communism in dramatic, almost religious terms. In an interview with *The Recorder* (26 February 1949) Macmillan said that materialism had now supplanted moral values.

What then have we to do? Surely we must go back to the broad principles on which Western Christendom is based. . . . Today the position of the Christian World is not unlike that of the fifth century A.D. at the time when the invasions of the Goths ultimately led to the break-up of the Roman Empire. What saved civilization then was the conversion of the conquerors to Christianity.

He went on to explain how 'with the fervour of a Crusade we must make active inroads for ourselves into the enemy's own territory. With spiritual as well as material instruments we must seek the reconversion of the world.'

He transferred much of his pre-war zeal as an anti-appeaser to the post-war situation, and attacked the Berlin airlift as 'an act of political appeasement'. He argued (23 March 1949) against trading with Eastern Europe:

With Communists we cannot say it with flowers . . . do not give away guns in order to get butter. Go elsewhere. Go to the Colonies. Make the world on our side of the Iron Curtain a demonstrably better place to live in and then ultimately the news of this success will filter through. . . . The cold war must be fought with as much energy and single-mindedness as the shooting war. . . . Step by step the cold war must be won. If the way be long and weary let us have courage and faith. It is perhaps the last Crusade.

Macmillan, who had always been much influenced by Churchill, now faithfully echoed his world attitudes and saw Britain's role in the centre of those three interlocking circles – America, Europe and the Commonwealth – a comforting but misleading image. He was on fitful personal terms with Churchill, and suffered like many others from his rudeness. ('Do you know what he called me this morning,' he said to Dalton in Strasbourg, after Dalton himself had been insulted by Churchill: 'a lily-livered hare'.) But he was under Churchill's spell, and increasingly adopted his rhetorical tricks. In a speech in October 1948 Macmillan said, with extravagant Churchillian rhetoric: 'The storms and gatherings against East and West, under a darkening sky. Shall we turn this time, before they break, to the old and trusted pilot? Or shall we wait until it is too late?'

It was his growing fear of Communist expansion that led

Macmillan, like many other Conservatives, to turn his attention to United Europe – which was to prove the climax and the tragedy of his career. Like Churchill, he wanted to believe that Britain could become further involved in Europe while being primarily dependent on the Commonwealth as a 'pillar of world power'. He was quoted in 1944, as saying that Britain would maintain its historic attitude of aloofness from the continent.[13] But when Churchill launched the United Europe Movement in June 1947, Macmillan (with Duncan Sandys and Maxwell Fyfe) was one of its most prominent members. 'Incomparably one of the vital issues of the day is the survival or decay of Europe,' he said at Bromley in June 1947.

In May 1948 Macmillan attended the Congress of Europe at the Hague – 'This somewhat amateur and rather disorderly Congress', as he called it later[14] – at which the central figure was Churchill. For the next three years Macmillan was closely involved in the European movement. 'Europe is poised at the crisis of her fate. She waits between hope and despair and above all she waits for a lead,' he said in Parliament on 17 September 1948. He foresaw some kind of common market: 'Europe needs a common currency, a free movement of goods with due regard to existing obligations and preferential arrangements of the participating countries.'

When the Council of Europe was established at Strasbourg, Macmillan became in 1949 one of the British delegation to the Consultative Assembly; he was deputy leader of the Conservative section, which included Eccles, Boothby and Maxwell Fyfe (but significantly not Eden). On 17 August he tabled an amendment boldly suggesting to the Consultative Assembly that 'the Committee of Ministers shall be an executive authority with supranational powers. The Committee shall have its own permanent secretariat of European officials' – a proposal which *The News Chronicle* described as a 'political bombshell'. He seemed very serious, and was one of the most ardent of the British delegates at Strasbourg: John Beavan, the political commentator, recalls meeting him at Strasbourg: 'Macmillan put an arm on my shoulder and spoke with a fervour which

I thought embarrassing about his belief in the European idea.'[15]

Despite this embarrassing enthusiasm, Macmillan – like most other Conservatives – put the unity of Commonwealth and Empire above European unity. But he was deeply anxious to find a way of having both. In September 1949 he even called for a Commonwealth Conference to prepare a plan of action to put before the Council of Europe, in a speech that proved all too true: 'But we must act swiftly. Now is the moment of destiny. If we let this chance slip it will not return. Already there is deep resentment in Europe at the British Government's double dealing.' He described his conflicting priorities in *The Manchester Dispatch*, on 11 October 1949:

The Empire must always have first preference for us: Europe must come second in a specially-favoured position. Politically, strategically and economically, Britain is part of Europe, though she is also head of the Empire. We cannot isolate ourselves from Europe.

Macmillan's main concern with Europe, as for others at that time, was to save it from imminent collapse – with the help of the British Empire. It was Britain that was to save Europe, not vice versa. He thought that Europe without Britain could not 'overcome the dual menace of her own economic sickness and the perpetual ceaseless moral disintegration to which Communist agitation and infiltration subject her'.[16] In a speech in Central Hall, Westminster, on 29 September 1949, he described how the Empire should be 'the centre and pivot of the grand design. The new structure must include the countries of Europe which still remain free before they are themselves engulfed either by a new Nazi Germany or an irresistible Russian Communism – or worse still a combination of the two.'

His vision of Europe fitted in with his personal pessimism. Hugh Dalton described an extraordinary meeting in Strasbourg in March 1950

Macmillan took little part in the discussions of the Committee and did not seem to be following its work with very close attention. He said to me at the end of one of the meetings 'I think Europe is finished; it is sinking. It is like Greece after the second Peloponnesian war. Athens and Sparta are quarrelling and Philip of Macedon is watching and waiting to strike. I have been reading Thucydides lately and it is just like our times. If I were a younger man, I should emigrate from Europe to the United States.'[17]

He seemed very serious about European unity. When in 1950 the French proposed the 'Schuman plan' for an Iron and Steel Community – the first step towards a Common Market – Macmillan said in May 'I hope that British statesmanship will at least be equal to the new opportunity. If the plan is pursued and implemented it will mean a wonderful step forwards. But if it fails . . . it will be a disaster.' When Bevin in June 1950 said that the Labour Government felt unable to take part in talks on the Schuman plan, Macmillan said that it had been 'a black week for Britain, for the Empire, for Europe and for the peace of the world'. He used almost identical words twelve years later.

But Macmillan already had fears about the powers of the new authority; on 16 August 1950 Macmillan told the assembly at Strasbourg

One thing is certain and we may as well face it. Our people are not going to hand to any supranational authority the right to close down our pits or steelworks. We will allow no supranational authority to put large masses of our people out of work in Durham, in the Midlands, in South Wales or in Scotland.

The idea of technical administrators, he said in this characteristic speech, did not appeal to Britain:

Fearing the weakness of democracy, men have often sought safety in technocrats. There is nothing new in this. It is as old as Plato. But frankly the idea is not attractive to the British. . . . We have not overthrown the divine right of kings to fall down before the divine right of experts.

In the same speech he pleaded for a more pragmatic approach, saying that in time of crisis 'we British will certainly be prepared to accept merger of sovereignty in practice if not in principle'. In the tradition of 'muddling through', he analysed the difference between the Anglo-Saxon and continental views:

The difference is temperamental and intellectual. It is based on a long divergence of two states of mind and methods of argumentation. The continental tradition likes to reason *a priori* from the top downwards, from the general principles to the practical application. It is the tradition of St Thomas of Aquinas, of the schoolmen, and of the great continental scholars and thinkers. The Anglo-Saxon likes to argue *a posteriori* from the bottom upwards, from practical experience. It is the tradition of Bacon and Newton.

He added slyly, 'Of course, the Scottish people, who are the intellectuals of Britain, know that there is nothing to be frightened of: one should accept everything *en principe*, get around the table and start the talks.' ('Nobody had a better grasp of the Anglo-Continental misunderstandings', commented Nora Beloff.[18])

In September 1951, he summed up his view of Britain and Europe in an article in *World Review*. He quoted the recent words of Spaak: 'You British have in all this a great responsibility. Why do you refuse, after having been Europe's leader in war, to be her leader in peace?' He thought that although progress had been made through Franco-German reconciliation and through the Schuman plan, there was a feeling of frustration – partly due to traditional British cautiousness, partly to Socialist mistrust of a non-socialist Europe. The fear of endangering links with the Commonwealth, existed only in Britain and was not shared by the Dominions.

But very soon after the Conservatives came back into power, they showed that they cared little for Europe. The issue was a European army. The idea of an army under unified command had first been mooted by Churchill in Strasbourg in 1950, and gathered weight with the Korean War. The motion to set up a European Defence Community (E.D.C.) was passed at Strasbourg in 1950 by eighty-nine to five, and Macmillan said that the resolution 'might well be a turning point in history. . . . We have taken our stand irrevocably on this issue.' The Labour party had been against the plan, but when Churchill came back into power in October 1951, the Europeans looked forward to British support. A month later Sir David Maxwell Fyfe, who had become Home Secretary, told the Council in Strasbourg that his Government welcomed 'this imaginative plan'. But on the same day Anthony Eden, attending a NATO meeting in Rome, made it clear that Britain could not join the E.D.C. It was, said Maxwell Fyfe bitterly afterwards, 'the single act which above all others destroyed Britain's name on the continent', and he explained:

No doubt, we few pro-Europeans in the Cabinet, Macmillan and myself, should have done more at the time. But against us there were senior ministers of the stature and authority of Eden and Salisbury, supported hesitantly but inevitably by Churchill . . . in foreign affairs, I and those who thought like me were powerless in the face of the enormous authority of Eden and Churchill.[19]

Macmillan, too, now Minister of Housing, was fully aware of the mistake, and Foreign Office men remember his insistent memoranda about Europe.

About Europe, regrets still haunt me [he wrote twenty years later]; I was so fully occupied with my own office, which combined the conduct of complicated legislation with the largest administrative job I had ever undertaken, that although I wrote to Churchill to protest, I did not press the issue. The considerations I have stated are, alas, excuses, not valid reasons. I can only comfort myself that I could not, even with the help of the few colleagues who shared my view, have had any hope of getting my way. I could only have contented myself with the sense of rectitude following a resignation on a matter of principle.[20]

The attitude of the new Government to the E.D.C., and its subsequent ambiguity towards European unity, disillusioned many continental enthusiasts: in the words of Paul Reynaud, the former French prime minister, 'The trouble is, I know, that in England statesmen are pro-European when they belong to the opposition and anti-European when they are in power.'[21]

*

Throughout these opposition years one is struck by the tone of determined, almost Cassandra-like pessimism which Macmillan adopted in his assessments of foreign as well as home policy. It was a personal pessimism by no means shared for instance by all in his party and it seems worth enquiring whether it might have a cause beyond his evident private unhappiness at that time. After the First World War the gallant young soldier found himself in a phase of retreat and withdrawal. And now when he once again puts up the sword with which he served his country so remarkably effectively in the early 1940s he retires into a period of private anguish. This seems like the very natural frustrations of a gifted and many-sided man denied by the exigencies of political life the full exercise of his talents. When all four of the Macmillan aspects I have described at the beginning of the book are in full operating order (1940–45, 1951–4, 1957–60) Macmillan can be seen as a fulfilled, happy, confident, witty, brave and brilliant man. When one or more are silenced – particularly when the man of action, the swordsman, has been paid off and the limitations of peacetime politicking are starkly revealed – then comes this gloomy figure, projecting on to a far from perfect world the backed-down, frustrated energies of an enigmatic man. That he was at this time sincere in his assessment, for instance, of the over-running of Europe by Communist hordes is not to be doubted. But the cause, or part cause for the extreme attitude he took (along with his master Churchill and many on the right wing of the party who were not his natural allies) might arguably lie in the unconscious anger of a world statesman faced with loss of power, who could not do the work for which his combination of talents fitted him. It is not, after all, uncommon for future prime ministers to have wilderness periods in which personal and public frustrations somehow mirror each other. This seemed to be the case with Macmillan.

NOTES

1. Winston Churchill, *The Second World War*, vol. 6 (London: Cassell, 1954), p. 583
2. *The New Statesman*, 5 November 1955
3. *The Sunday Telegraph*, 9 February 1964
4. *The Observer*, 19 May 1946
5. Emrys Hughes, *Macmillan: Portrait of a Politician* (London: Allen & Unwin, 1962), p. 66
6. Speech at Hatfield, 1 September 1946
7. See S. H. Beer, *Modern British Politics* (London: Faber & Faber, 1965), p. 317
8. *Truth*, 1 November 1946
9. J. D. Hoffman, *The Conservative Party in Opposition* (London: MacGibbon & Kee, 1964), p. 192
10. See Nigel Harris, *Conservatism: State and Society, with special reference to industrial policy since 1945* (unpublished thesis)
11. Emrys Hughes, *Macmillan: Portrait of a Politician*, p. 70
12. Hugh Dalton, *High Tide and After* (London: Muller, 1962), p. 328
13. Max Beloff, *United States and the Unity of Europe* (London: Faber & Faber, 1963), p. 100
14. *The Spectator*, 16 September 1949
15. *The Statist*, 18 October 1963
16. House of Commons, 28 January 1949
17. Hugh Dalton, *High Tide and After*, p. 327
18. Nora Beloff, *The General Says No* (Harmondsworth: Penguin, 1963), p. 59
19. Viscount Kilmuir, *Political Adventure* (London: Weidenfeld & Nicolson, 1964), p. 189
20. Harold Macmillan, *Winds of Change*, vol. I (London: Macmillan, 1966), p. 24
21. Quoted in Nora Beloff, *The General Says No*, p. 63

6. Cabinet, 1951-6

He is both the most brilliant and the least assured of the present triumvirate, and this, perhaps, explains why the more thoughtful Tories would like to see him as its leader. But there is little chance that their wishes will come true.[1]

In October 1951 the Labour Government finally fell, and Churchill was back in power. Macmillan, not surprisingly after his close wartime experience with Churchill, had hopes of very high office, but Churchill (apparently on the advice of Beaverbrook) offered him only the Ministry of Housing – crucial, but not prestigious. It was a heavy disappointment, and he asked to think about it. Butler, nine years his junior, the pre-war appeaser, was to be Chancellor of the Exchequer; Eden, three years his junior, was of course Foreign Secretary; and Lyttelton was Colonial Secretary. Eventually Macmillan accepted. As he put it later:

> Winston asked me if I could build 300,000 houses in a year, and if so, would I be Minister of Housing. I agreed on condition that I could run it my way. We ran it in fact like a war department. You see I'd learnt a thing or two at the Ministry of Supply working with tycoons.[2]

Macmillan admitted that he knew nothing about housing. 'The Parliamentary system is one of government by amateurs advised by experts,' he said to Parliament on 13 November, 'I must frankly admit that the tasks now entrusted to me are not ones which have hitherto fallen within my experience.' But he was bold and ingenious in his choice of experts; he enlisted two self-made businessmen, very much outside the Whitehall tradition. As his junior minister he chose Ernest Marples, a cocky and talkative accountant of forty-five, who had built up a fortune with a construction company, and had come into Parliament in 1945, bursting with ambition. Marples was eager for any opportunity to show how hard he could work, and had the specialized knowledge for the job. Between Macmillan, with his languid style and Marples, with his boasting efficiency, there existed an alliance of mutual advantage, between the amateur and the professional.

The other expert was a Birmingham businessman from outside Parliament, Sir Percy Mills, as an 'unpaid adviser' on the housing programme. Mills was managing director of W. and T. Avery, the weighing-machine people, and Macmillan had met him in the Ministry of Production during the war, when he had been controller-general of machine tools; he was a down-to-earth Midlander, and Macmillan trusted him thoroughly. He became Macmillan's confidant as well as his colleague. He brought new methods and common sense to the Ministry of Housing: not surprisingly his intrusion aroused the antagonism of the senior civil servants, so that at one time the Head of the Civil Service, Sir Edward Bridges, even complained to the prime minister.

Inside the Ministry of Housing, Macmillan had the help of Evelyn Sharp, a dedicated civil servant of alarming efficiency, who was later promoted to permanent secretary. 'She was brilliant,' wrote Macmillan's predecessor as minister, Hugh Dalton: 'Often she would come rushing into my room with a flashing new idea or she would pull some tiresome old problem to pieces and put it together again in a quite new shape, ripe for a Ministerial decision':³ and in later years, as ministers came and went, Dame Evelyn (as she became) dominated the department.⁴ As his parliamentary private secretary, Macmillan recruited Reginald Bevins, an ambitious Liverpudlian who had worked his way up through the party organization, and who watched Macmillan's operations with unconcealed admiration. He described how Macmillan successfully won round his civil servants: 'Ministers are the kings against the civil servants who are the modern barons', he told Bevins, with a characteristic fondness for romantic historical parallels: 'Your job is not to accept what they say, but to criticise them and go on criticising.'[5] He held weekly discussion meetings with politicians and civil servants, allowing very free discussions but always keeping the decisions to himself. 'He exuded enthusiasm – his zeal was infectious . . .' recorded Bevins. 'He was really superb at handling people', 'tactful, courteous, never giving much away'.[6]

Macmillan drew heavily on his war-time experience with Beaverbrook.[7] In a statement of housing policy at Nottingham (22 January 1952) he quoted Beaverbrook's remark in the war that 'the duty of a Production Minister is to create a vacuum and then fill it, to make bottlenecks and break them'. Macmillan continued

I think he was right. Naturally we must not go to the other extreme of complete disorder. But in my experience there is no form of production or business enterprise which can be successfully conducted except by a continual pressure upon every department which is lagging behind to catch up the lead of those who are most effective.

Macmillan's achievement in housing was not quite as spectacular as it looked. Housing was second only to defence in the Government's priorities. There were two million on the waiting list for houses: and in cabinet Churchill backed Macmillan's demands against Butler, the Chancellor of the Exchequer, who felt, with some justification, that Macmillan's housing programme put too great a strain on the economy. Yet Macmillan, still with his passion for planning, brought a special energy and ingenuity to the problem. He said that he wanted to 'create throughout the whole country the spirit of a housing crusade' and called for a 1940 spirit.

He did not conceal his indebtedness to his Labour predecessor, Hugh Dalton, whom he liked and admired for his pre-war record: 'A fine, robust, and hearty fellow, who combined Socialism and patriotism in a good old-fashioned English way.'[8] He had inherited from Dalton plans for a simplified smaller standard house, with minimum passages and stairs coming out of the dining hall. Dalton, Macmillan admitted, 'is the pioneer of simplification, he has shown the way and I am merely following humbly in his track'. On 29 November 1951, he announced the designs for the 'People's House', each of which would save £150, and could be built more quickly. The People's House quickly helped to speed the flow of new housing: by May 1952 sixty per cent of the new houses were People's Houses, which saved ten per cent on building materials.

He also set about decentralizing – a favourite theme for twenty years – and this was an ideal opportunity to experiment. He explained (*The Daily Graphic*, May 1952) that he was making the housing ministry a production ministry, not merely an administrative one. With the help of Mills, he set up local Housing Production Boards, like his Area Boards in Supply in the war, with members from the ministries, from employers, and from trades unions. He also gave local authorities more discretion to grant licences for private building which, since it used more expensive materials, would relieve some of the demand on cheaper ones.

By May 1952 Macmillan could announce that 1,000 more houses a week were being built than under the Socialists, and by August he announced a big reduction in the time of construction and in cost. At the Conservative Conference at Scarborough in October 1952, Macmillan was greeted 'like a conquering hero'. He, Marples and Eccles (Minister of Works) stood up to be applauded, and he restated his pledge to build 300,000 houses. He made a sentimental speech in which he talked about the home as 'the basis of the family' and said he had tried to 'make housing a great national crusade'. With his penchant for music-halls, he quoted the song 'ours is a nice house, ours is'.

He was now considered to be one of the outstanding successes of the Government. In May 1953 he was chosen to give the first-ever party political broadcast on TV, and this began his chequered relationship with the new medium. With

Marples he appeared to give a congratulatory account of progress in housing. One paper reported that 'Macmillan was firm and friendly and at moments might have deputised for "Uncle Mac" of Children's Hour he was so patiently informative'. Another said that Macmillan 'with all his ease, could not hide the hunted look, as he seemed to wonder if the figures would flash on at the right moment'.

By the end of 1953 the target had been reached. In 1953, 318,779 new houses were built – 249,884 for letting and the rest for sale. Macmillan said he now intended to keep the number of new houses built at around 300,000 (though he confessed that too many houses had been started in the summer of 1953) to allow for repair work, and for more industrial and commercial building.

At the next Tory conference, in Margate, in October 1953, Macmillan announced a campaign for repairing old houses, called 'Operation rescue', and proposed to start dealing with rent restriction. 'In a cupboard in my office I have skeletons marked "local government reforms", "housing subsidies", "rating and valuation" and "rent restriction" which are dusted and paraded before every minister when he takes office.' The Housing Repairs and Rent Bill (which had its second reading in December 1953) allowed rents to be raised in certain cases, where they were too low to enable the landlord to keep his houses in good repair. Macmillan said that this bill marked the beginning of the biggest comprehensive attack on the housing problem for fifteen years. But in fact it did not have much effect on the millions of dilapidated houses, and most landlords preferred to leave their crumbling properties unrepaired. Aneurin Bevan remarked in the debate that the landlords were getting 'a mouldy old turnip'. The skeletons had not really been brought out of the cupboards, and it was left to Macmillan's successor, Duncan Sandys, to grapple with rents and subsidies.

But after three years in the Ministry of Housing, Macmillan had established his reputation as a man who could get things done. Hugh Dalton had to admit that the Tory housing record was much better than the Socialists', 'though some which they built had lower standards than most of ours. But this, I am afraid, was only a secondary debating point. It was the totals of new houses which counted with public opinion and public comfort, and led the way towards the "affluent society".[9]

Macmillan had great advantages. He had the support of the prime minister in cabinet, and he was able to run his programme on a war footing. But he moved with a speed and efficiency which surprised his colleagues. (Eden said afterwards that he had 'brilliantly fulfilled a programme which I had considered over-ambitious when it was announced'.[10]) He worked hard, inspired his juniors and never lost sight of the main problem. He had regained some of his wartime verve, and he was again putting into practice his favourite theories of cooperation between government and industry, of following 'the middle way'. He could see intellectual schemes take shape in terms of people.

But he was sixty, and still a very long way from the top. He was more effective in Housing than in his subsequent ministries, but it was not how he saw himself. To the general public he was still an aloof, unglamorous figure: in the summer of 1954 *The Daily Mirror* held a popularity poll on Churchill's likely successor: Eden had fifty-two per cent; Macmillan had under two per cent. Beside Eden's glittering reputation he seemed unheroic and dull. His close colleagues in Algiers or in Housing knew his effectiveness: but in Parliament and among his cabinet colleagues he still seemed a rather musty and obscure figure.

In October 1954 Churchill reshuffled his cabinet, and Macmillan moved to become Minister of Defence. In the next two-and-a-half years he was to occupy three different cabinet posts, in none of which he left a strong mark. He seemed to many people to be tired, bored and ready for retirement. Yet he emerged in the end at the top, with hidden energies released.

His six months at Defence were not notable. The job helped to bring Macmillan closer to his greatest love, international affairs; but he had much less scope than in Housing.[11] A large difficulty was Churchill, who was becoming obviously senile. 'You know, Moran,' Macmillan said to Churchill's doctor, 'Winston ought to resign. He didn't interfere in my housing, just left it all to me. But since I became Minister of Defence I have found that he can no longer handle these complicated matters properly.'[12] And, as even Eden explained, 'Sir Winston, whatever his head ordained, never accepted in his heart the position of a Minister of Defence divorced from his own authority. In impatient moments he would sometimes murmur that the post did not exist.' A contemporary cartoon shows an ebullient Macmillan as Minister of Housing, and a drooping figure as Minister of Defence.

Macmillan's new job brought him back into the discussions on a European army. Since 1951, when Churchill and Eden had decided to stay out of the European Defence Community, the Europeans had gone ahead on their own: but as the threat of Russia became less, so the danger of German rearmament – particularly without Britain as a counter-weight – seemed greater; and in August 1954 the French Assembly had voted against the European army. Churchill's Government set about trying to patch up some kind of alliance to keep Europe together. It was agreed that Britain should keep four divisions and an appropriate fighter force on the Continent until the end of the century, and the French in return, agreed to German rearmament. A new body, the 'Western European Union', was set up to coordinate the national armies. Macmillan, speaking on 18 November 1954, tried to put the best face on an unsatisfactory compromise.

After all these years and all this talk, this long way from Strasbourg to London and Paris, here it is at last – the European Army in the NATO frame.... After many heart-searchings, after many false starts, hesitations and disappointments, a way has now been found which enables Great Britain to play her full part, both as a great Imperial and a great European power.

Four months after Macmillan moved to Defence, an historic white paper, which had been brewing up for the past year,

expounded Britain's philosophy of the deterrent. It opened
with the sentence, 'overshadowing all else in the year 1954 has
been the emergence of the thermo-nuclear bomb', and went on
to announce Britain's intention to make hydrogen bombs
which, it argued, would reduce the risk of major war. A major
debate on the white paper, on 2 March 1955, was opened with
a sonorous speech by Churchill, and closed by Macmillan.
Macmillan talked about the slaughter of two world wars, and
the possibilities of disarmament, which was to be a major preoccupation in following years. It should, he said, be based on
two simple principles – it must be comprehensive and it must
allow a proper system of control, which would provide
'effective international, or if we like, supra-national authority
invested with real power. . . . Hon. members may say that this
is elevating the U.N., or whatever may be the authority, into
something like world government. Be it so, it is none the
worse for that. In the long run, this is the only way out for
mankind.'

Meanwhile, he insisted, 'we have to prevent the hot war and
to win the cold war', and he went on to state his belief in the
independent deterrent, which was to dominate his thinking on
defence for the next nine years. To rely on an American deterrent would surrender our power to influence American policy,
and deprive us of any influence over the selection of targets.

In the meantime, behind the scenes, Macmillan was involved
with the problem of the aging and failing prime minister.
Churchill clearly liked him and respected him; and for some
time Macmillan had seemed anxious for Churchill to stay on,
against the growing demands for his departure. (Did he feel
that a senile Churchill was preferable to an indecisive Eden?)
When at Whitsun 1954 Churchill had temporarily decided that
he should resign, Macmillan protested that 'it would be very
inconvenient for members who had Bills to put through the
House'.[13] Churchill regarded Macmillan as a staunch ally, and
'Captain of the Praetorian Guard'. But by January 1955 Macmillan, too, had decided that Churchill should go. He told
Moran 'he can't do his job as it ought to be done. He does not

direct', and bravely he told Churchill himself. 'Plainly there is a growing feeling among Winston's friends that the time has come for him to go,' recorded Moran on 24 January: 'But only Harold Macmillan has had the guts to say so. I am beginning to have second thoughts. If I did not dread the future I might agree with Macmillan. Anyway he did what he thought was right, and he must have hated doing it.'[14] 'It was only when Harold Macmillan made his position untenable,' concluded Moran, 'that Winston recognised that he must go.'[15]

At last, in April 1955 – in the middle of a newspaper strike – Churchill resigned, at the age of eighty. There was no doubt about the succession: Eden had been his dauphin for the past fifteen years and though Churchill had had doubts about his capacities, he felt that the premiership was Eden's due. The succession was applauded by the Tory Press, and by many Labour papers, for Eden was a semi-legendary figure, glowing with reflected glory. But for many of the cabinet the prospect of a long spell with Eden was not welcome – not simply for reasons of rivalry, but because Eden was suspected of being vain and vacillating. Macmillan, in particular, had made little secret of his doubts about Eden: he had seen how Churchill had dominated Eden, and reduced him to nervous indecision,[16] and he had watched Eden's insular attitude to European unity. During the war, when Macmillan had been in the thick of things and Eden had been in London, he had been aware of Eden's jealous and difficult temperament.

Eden had wanted to choose Salisbury to succeed him at the Foreign Office, but decided he could not have a foreign secretary in the Lords. 'Having reluctantly decided that I could not offer this post to Lord Salisbury,' he recounts pointedly in his memoirs, 'I was sure that Mr Macmillan should be my choice. I felt that his active and fertile mind would team well with the high quality of Foreign Office leadership under Sir Ivone Kirkpatrick.'[17]

The foreign secretaryship was something that Macmillan had always wanted, but it was his least successful appointment. Eden had been foreign secretary, with one interval, for nine years, and still regarded it as his private preserve. Macmillan's views were often divergent from Eden's – in particular over the Russians. Macmillan was clearly infuriated by Eden's interference; and he also seemed worn out by the exacting conditions of work – the travelling, the bombardment of telegrams, the phone calls from America in the middle of the night.

In the meantime, the political picture in England seemed quite rosy: the financial crisis was over for the time being, Butler had reduced taxes, Macmillan had achieved his housing target and there was industrial peace. Eden had settled the crisis over the nationalization of the Abadan oil wells, and resolved the Egyptian crisis by agreeing to withdraw British troops from the Suez Canal base. The war in Korea was ended. Stalin had died. In these happy circumstances on 14 April Eden announced a general election. It was the first election in which TV was used extensively, and Macmillan was one of the Tories' star performers (a special Gallup poll after one appearance in May 1955, gave Macmillan's performance forty-one marks out of 100: Attlee got twenty-eight out of 100). In the election, the Conservatives for the first time since 1935 got more votes than Labour, with 345 seats to Labour's 277, and an overall majority of fifty-nine. Macmillan increased his majority at Bromley by 1,014.

Back as foreign secretary, Macmillan was soon rushing round Europe. In May he flew to Paris to meet the French Foreign Minister, Pinay, and Dulles. He got on very well with Dulles – the only British foreign secretary who did – and helped to persuade him to invite the Russians to join summit talks on Germany. From Paris he went on to Vienna for the signing of the Austrian treaty, an emotional occasion, where he spoke with Molotov about Vietnam, and about the proposed summit. Back in England Macmillan explained that a summit meeting would 'lay down a structure of negotiation by which we shall be able to proceed from step to step'. In *The Spectator* (20 May 1955) Macmillan explained that Britain, because of her diplomatic skill and political stability 'can establish for herself in the nuclear age a position of authority as the chief source of moral inspiration for the whole free world'. In June he went to the United Nations in New York, to celebrate the tenth anniversary, and make a speech about 'this unique instrument for international cooperation'.

Soon afterwards he went to Geneva to attend the four-power summit conference, mainly to discuss German reunification. He was inevitably overshadowed by Eden: in the words of *The News Chronicle*, he 'loyally played Tenzing to Eden's Hillary'. It was Macmillan's first experience of the summitry that was to fascinate him in the following years, and the outcome showed the dangers. The basic difference between East and West was unresolved. The West insisted on free elections in East Germany and put forward the 'Eden Plan' for a demilitarized zone. Not much was achieved or agreed, but the good humour became prematurely known as 'the Geneva spirit'. Returning to England, Macmillan, in another vague burst of music-hall *bonhomie*, said 'there ain't gonna be any war'. Eden, more sedately, said 'Geneva has given this simple message to the whole world: it has reduced the dangers of war'.

But both remarks were premature. The Geneva spirit soon weakened at the Foreign Ministers' conference three months later, also at Geneva, at which Macmillan clashed directly with Molotov. He emphasized that the West would not dissolve NATO and described the Russian proposal for an all-German Council as 'an unparalleled *diktat*'. Macmillan reported to Eden that the Soviet attitude had now hardened. In his closing speech on 9 November 1955 Macmillan said that 'instead of taking another step forward, at the best we are locked in stalemate, at the worst we have taken a step backward . . . once more we are back in the strange nightmare where men use the same words to mean different things'. But he still felt that new forces were beginning to emerge in the Communist world: 'The Geneva spirit if it is anything is an inward spirit. Its light is not bright today. It burns low. But it burns.'

In the middle of the conference Macmillan returned to London to cope with another fiasco: he had to explain the two defected diplomats, Burgess and Maclean. As *The Daily Telegraph* remarked (8 November 1955), Macmillan 'though there was almost nothing to be said, said it with that blend of humility and moral fervour which will always disarm a hostile house'. 'Few Ministers could get away with murder as Macmillan did,' commented Henry Fairlie.

Macmillan's greatest difficulties in the Foreign Office, and probably his greatest mistakes, were in the Middle East, which (as he told the Commons on 12 December), had leapt into the foreground as a trouble-spot. The position was immensely intricate, complicated by the agreement to balance arms between Israel and Egypt, and the divergence between American policy – determined not to offend Israel – and British policy – preoccupied with defending oil interests. Macmillan, more than Eden, was against appeasing the Russians; he was largely responsible for the Baghdad Pact, with Iraq as its centrepiece, which was intended both to fend off Russian incursions and to build up Iraq as a counter-weight to Egypt and Syria. It may well have incited, rather than prevented, Russian intrusion:[18] soon after its formation, Egypt bought Russian arms via Czechoslovakia. When Macmillan heard the news in New York, he was still more convinced of the need for tough defence against Russia; the 'Geneva spirit' had now totally evaporated.

Macmillan went out to Baghdad in November, to attend the first meeting of the Baghdad Pact powers: he insisted that the Egyptian arms deal had been planned long before the Pact, and that the economic activities were much more important than the military. Back in London he explained that 'the Pact is not intended to split the Arab World . . . I believe in the long run it will unite it'. Macmillan was so well pleased with the Pact, and so alarmed by the activities of Communist agents, that he had decided that Jordan should be invited to join, too: Jordan was offered ten Vampires as part of the reward for joining, and Macmillan advised Eden – in what has been described as 'one of the supremely foolish decisions of post-war British policy'[19] – to send out General Sir Gerald Templer, who had gained his reputation for toughness in Malaya, to persuade the Jordan

Government to join. It was certainly a disastrous idea; Templer's visit not only failed to persuade Jordan, but was followed by a cabinet crisis in Amman, succeeded by riots, threats by Saudi Arabia and dismissal of King Hussein's adviser, General Glubb. It began the succession of cross-purposes which was to culminate a year later, in Suez.

The foreign secretary was also much occupied with another calamitous situation – Cyprus, which was then still regarded as a crucial Mediterranean link. Terrorism had broken out early in 1955, and the maintenance of Cyprus as a British base had become a point of principle with the right wing of the Tory party. In August 1955 Macmillan presided over a tripartite conference in London between Britain, Greece and Turkey – with the strong opposition of Archbishop Makarios, who called the conference a 'trap'. At the conference Macmillan described Cyprus as 'the hinge of the North Atlantic and Middle Eastern defence systems' and put forward new proposals for self-government: 'We are a very empirical people,' he said, 'we try to deal with facts as we see them. Nothing is permanent in the world.' But the conference was abortive, and the Greeks and Turks were still further at deadlock: the murders in Cyprus increased, and rioting broke out in Istanbul and Izmir. By October Macmillan and the cabinet had turned to a policy of tougher military repression, and sent out Sir John Harding, the veteran field-marshal, to direct operations – while insisting that the only solution would be a political settlement. But three months later, in March 1956, the only means to a settlement was abandoned, when Makarios was exiled to the Seychelles.

Macmillan was hardly more successful in his perception of Western Europe, which was now already moving towards a common market. In his first speech as foreign secretary (on 15 June 1955), after referring once again to the triple partnership of the Commonwealth, America and free Europe, he talked about Europe:

If we have not always been able to accept the path of full federation, we have been anxious to promote the true unity of Europe by every practicable means. I am convinced that the European idea is one by which, and perhaps by which alone, the German people can be kept within the European fold, the Western fold.

The next month he went back to Strasbourg for the first time for four years, and told the assembly on 6 July that he was impressed by the progress and was not sure that 'they had not been making Europe without knowing it'. He called the Western European Union 'the fulfilment of a dream', said that the West must learn 'a certain flexibility of manoeuvre in dealing with the Communists', and suggested Yugoslavia, for instance, might have an observer there.

But while Macmillan was making these vague and unhelpful generalizations, the Europeans had been planning the 're-launching' of the European idea, which neither Macmillan nor the Foreign Office took seriously, but which proved to be the foundation of the Common Market. When a conference was held at Messina in June 1955, including foreign ministers of the 'six' and a team of experts, Britain was invited to join the conference; but only an under secretary from the Board of Trade, Mr Bretherton, was sent out there, and though he was much impressed by the seriousness and enthusiasm of the Europeans, he did not persuade the Foreign Office, who were convinced by their embassy in Paris that the French would not ratify a customs treaty. The Messina conference was followed by the Spaak committee, which planned the first stages of the Treaty of Rome: the British again were invited, but though they again sent Mr Bretherton, they stressed he was not a delegate but a 'representative', and Mr Macmillan (perhaps influenced by Eden) replied to the invitation with a piece of classic cold Foreign Office prose. He pointed out that the work of O.E.E.C. should not be duplicated, and went on:

There are, as you are no doubt aware, special difficulties for this country in any proposal for a 'European common market'. They [the British government] will be happy to examine, without prior commitment and on their merits, the many problems which are likely to emerge from the studies and in doing so will be guided by the hope of reaching solutions which are in the best interests of all parties concerned.[20]

Altogether, Macmillan was not a success at the Foreign Office. Diplomacy, unlike housing, began to bring out the romantic and misty side of his character – as he demonstrated in his long speech on the Middle East in December, which began with a succession of nostalgic references, to Lord Grey and the lights going out over Europe, to the Antonine Age, to the Austro-Hungarian empire. *The Times*, in an editorial on 16 December said that the public had no idea either of foreign policy in several vital fields, or of Macmillan himself. Because of the murkiness and confusion of the situation, thought *The Times*, Macmillan was not much better known than when he went to the Foreign Office. 'He was one of the worst foreign secretaries in our history', wrote the editor of *The National and English Review* in 1958.

The New Statesman, in a knowing profile on 5 November 1955, summed up his reputation:

Not surprisingly, the personality of the new Foreign Secretary is puzzling his colleagues at the Foreign Office. Their views on his predecessors are quite clear-cut: Bevin they adored, Morrison they despised, Eden they regarded with a sharp dislike occasionally tinged with professional admiration. On Macmillan, they seem to have no views at all. But among those few who have grasped the essential truth that the end of the cold war has brought fresh dangers, and that we are moving, with increasing speed, into an era of open diplomacy, opinion is hardening. Last week, an official who had just read through a telegram from Macmillan in Paris, and who failed to place – poor man – the lengthy quotation from Virgil it contained, permitted himself a small sigh of exasperation. 'I never thought,' he said, 'that the time would come when I should say "thank God we have Mr Dulles".'

But it would be rash to write Macmillan off as a failure. When he appeared on the platform at Bournemouth, the roars of the Tory delegates were only a shade less strident than those which greeted Sir Anthony himself. Nor have his limitations as a Minister been grasped, as yet, by the exultant gentlemen on the benches behind him. Macmillan is, in many ways, a formidable House of Commons man.

His arrogance, his rudeness to Labour members – due, in part, to shyness, but also to his conscious sense of membership of a ruling class – are not necessarily liabilities in the Tory Party. In an age when every Tory minister tries, more or less successfully, to ape Sir Walter Monckton, Macmillan has done himself no harm by going to the opposite extreme. Indeed, now that Mr Butler has become a political liability, and Sir Anthony has demonstrated beyond doubt his pathological reluctance to take decisions, Macmillan's stock is inevitably rising.

And yet [the profile concluded], the forces which made him a Tory rebel for twenty years still lie beneath the surface. Macmillan's pessimism, his disenchantment with politics, spring primarily from his own integrity. . . . Those who keep the Tory conscience are respected by their colleagues and praised by future generations; but they never head the Tory Party.

These contemporary judgements of his foreign secretaryship are severe, and certainly Macmillan's nine months' stint was a failure. But his position was acutely difficult: and it was not easy to disentangle how much policy was his, and how much Eden's. Eden was certainly anxious to run his own foreign affairs, and Macmillan, three years older and more detached than his master, was well aware of the tension. It was an almost impossible relationship.

At the end of 1955, Eden reshuffled his awkward pack. Butler, who had been at the Treasury for four years, was visibly tired, and dispirited by the death of his wife. Eden thought of moving Heathcoat Amory, the self-effacing Minister of Agriculture, to the Treasury, but decided that he lacked the necessary authority, and so asked Macmillan, whom he didn't really want at the Foreign Office. Macmillan said he was 'rather sad about that because I enjoyed the Foreign Office'. But he reluctantly agreed: it was the second time he was Eden's second choice. According to Lord Kilmuir he 'accepted the Treasury on the strict understanding that this was to be regarded as a step towards and not away from the Premiership', which amused his colleagues.[21]

The move may have been away from Macmillan's favourite field, but it gave him greater independence, as well as more leisure: 'Being Foreign Secretary is like editing a daily paper,' he said later, 'being Chancellor is more like a weekly paper.' By now Eden's Government's prestige was already beginning to wane, with the deteriorating economic situation and Britain's declining position abroad. According to the Gallup poll, the support among electors for Eden's Government dropped from seventy per cent in the autumn of 1955 to forty per cent in the spring of 1956. By the summer of 1956, in a by-election at Tonbridge, the Conservative majority was reduced from 10,196 to 1,602.

Macmillan moved to the Treasury during one of the periodic economic crises. Up to 1955 Butler had been on the wave of the new economic liberalism, lifting controls and giving the market free play: the 1955 election slogan was 'Conservative Freedom Works', in a mood of anti-planning. Then in mid-1955, world prices turned against Britain, home prices rose further, and there was a big demand for higher wages. There was an inflationary crisis, which had been helped on by Macmillan's own housing programme. Butler was forced to bring in a special autumn budget and a credit squeeze.

Macmillan arrived in the Treasury without obvious pleasure: he commented in his budget speech that Churchill was surprised to find himself in the Treasury in 1924, 'but not half so surprised as I was, thirty-one years later'. But he brought in some fresh air. He refreshed many Treasury officials by his lack of doctrinal commitments and his interest in planning. In private he proclaimed un-conservative views about the excessive cost of defence, and the dangers of *laissez-faire*. His economic secretary was Sir Edward Boyle, the radical young intellectual, who shared Macmillan's interest in 'purposive planning' and was a kind of junior Macmillan.

This Macmillan–Boyle team at the Treasury [wrote Andrew Shonfield], was rather demonstrative about its lack of doctrinal inhibitions on matters like the reimposition of building licensing, which filled many of the party faithful with almost religious horror. They were even it seems prepared to defy the party's strong feelings on the subject of income tax.[22]

In public Macmillan took a strong stand against inflation. 'It is really a matter of the most desperate urgency,' he said in February 1956, 'that the whole country should realize what is wrong and combine to stop the progressive debasement of our currency.' He told the House of Commons that he would attack the roots of the problem; he pushed up the bank rate to $5\frac{1}{2}$ per cent (the highest since 1931), tightened hire purchase, cut subsidies on bread and milk, cut back spending on the nationalized industries, and cancelled the investment allowance which Butler had introduced. Harold Wilson described it as 'selling the seed corn'.

But while he was arguing the dangers of inflation, he was much more emotional about deflation and unemployment. He was still thinking about the 1930s. In a debate on 20 February he reminisced in a way that was to become very familiar in the next seven years: 'I cannot forget the twenty-five years when I sat for a Tees-side constituency. I cannot forget those terrible times when some 17,000 out of 25,000 able bodied men in my constituency walked the streets unemployed.' With candour he added: 'To people of my generation who have seen the ups and downs of our economic fortunes for more than thirty years, it is rather confusing to have to accommodate oneself to the present situation.' He embarked on the first of many attempts at a voluntary incomes policy. The next month he produced a white paper, advocating restraint in wage claims and fixing profit margins, and then asked both sides of industry (as so many chancellors have asked since) to cooperate in the fight against inflation.

While Eden's weaknesses were arousing criticism, Macmillan's stock went up. *The Observer* (4 March) commented that Conservative backbenchers were thinking of Macmillan as the man to provide leadership. Henry Fairlie in *The Spectator* (24 February) said, 'No one now doubts he is this Government's potential leader, the best Prime Minister we don't have.'

In April Macmillan introduced his only budget, in a cheerful and reflective speech – 'by far the most entertaining of the whole post-war series', as Samuel Brittan described it.[23] He described the inflationary crisis, but repeated that deflation was out of the question. 'We must all be expansionists of real wealth. The problem of inflation cannot be dealt with by cutting down demand; the other side of the picture is the need for increasing production.' He quoted Macaulay, to show how Britain thrived in the eighteenth century despite the growing national debt, in a passage concluding: 'On what principle is it that, when we see nothing but improvement behind us we are to expect nothing but deterioration before us?'

The Budget was not spectacular. He put 2*d*. on cigarettes, and increased taxation of profits. He promised to cut government expenditure by £100 million and referred to the picture of Gladstone at 11 Downing Street; 'I am told that some former chancellors – I will not specify them – could not stand those eyes looking at them day by day, reproachful and nostalgic. The picture was therefore during certain periods removed. Anyway it is there now.' The bizarre innovation was Premium Bonds: 'Let me say at once this is not a pool or a lottery where you spend your money', he explained: but the Bonds gave a new glimpse of the more raffish and adventurous Macmillan.

It went down quite well. *The Observer*'s political correspondent, Hugh Massingham, commented on the speech, 'There were the genuinely funny jokes, the flashes of wit, and on the other side the rather dull passages and the lapses into slightly bad taste. It was a typically Macmillan speech.' Some Conservatives thought that the budget should have been fiercer; Gaitskell described it as a standstill budget. The Premium Bonds caused a furore in some non-conformist circles. Harold Wilson said, in the debate, 'In 1951 they promised us Britain Strong and Free. Now Britain's strength, freedom and solvency apparently depend on the proceeds of a squalid raffle.'

Apart from his budget, Macmillan brought some new thinking to the Treasury. He introduced a new system of statistics to give earlier information: 'We are always, as it were, looking up trains in last year's Bradshaw' – he remarked in a much-repeated phrase. He referred to his old idea of an Economic General Staff, which he had put forward in 'Industry and the State' twenty years before. At one time he seriously considered a capital gains tax, against the objections of his party and the Inland Revenue.

He spent a good deal of time exhorting trades unionists and industrialists to stem inflation, in homely phrases: he talked about 'overloading the electrical circuit', a 'price plateau', 'this ruinous spiral of wages', 'you cannot take more than a pint out of a pint pot'. During the summer he went to a series of meetings with Eden and Iain Macleod, then Minister of Labour, to appeal to both sides, without much effect: 'this was the government that whispered wolf', said one commentator. But Macmillan's budget began to have some effect: savings increased, and the balance of payments – helped by the sale of the Trinidad Oil Company – began to improve. By July Macmillan could announce a surplus of £144 million: and he told the House of Commons – as he was to reiterate so often – 'the general position of the mass of our people – and they all know it – has been better almost than ever within living memory'.

Macmillan at the Treasury had gained some stature. He seemed less exhausted than at the Foreign Office, but in spite of his pre-war interest in economic reorganization, he did not seem excited by his new role: he talked about retirement, and indeed seemed ready for it. He was still visibly impatient with Eden, his next-door neighbour in Downing Street; and though there was growing talk of 'Eden must go', there was very little prospect of Eden going.

NOTES

1. *The New Statesman*, November 1955
2. *Queen*, May 1963
3. Hugh Dalton, *High Tide and After* (London: Muller, 1962), p. 351
4. Charles Hill, *Both Sides of the Hill* (London: Heinemann, 1964), p. 230
5. Reginald Bevins, *The Greasy Pole* (London: Hodder & Stoughton, 1965), p. 35
6. Ibid., p. 29
7. See A. J. Cummings, *The News Chronicle*, 25 January 1952
8. Harold Macmillan, *Winds of Change*, vol. I (London: Macmillan, 1966), p. 550
9. Hugh Dalton, *High Tide and After*, p. 358

10. Anthony Eden, *Full Circle* (London: Cassell, 1962), p. 274
11. Ibid., p. 274
12. Lord Moran, *Winston Churchill, The Struggle for Survival* (London: Constable, 1966), p. 627
13. Ibid., p. 554   14. Ibid., pp. 627-8   15. Ibid., p. 788
16. See, for instance, ibid., p. 627
17. Anthony Eden, *Full Circle*, p. 274
18. 'It cannot be certain whether the Baghdad Pact provoked or mitigated the shock of Soviet intervention' – C. M. Woodhouse, *British Foreign Policy Since the Second World War* (London: Hutchinson, 1961), p. 56
19. Paul Johnson, *The Suez War* (London: MacGibbon & Kee, 1957), p. 22
20. Cmd 9525 (London: H.M.S.O., 1955)
21. Viscount Kilmuir, *Political Adventure* (London: Weidenfeld & Nicolson, 1964), p. 256
22. Andrew Shonfield, *British Economic Policy Since the War* (Harmondsworth: Penguin, 1958), p. 228
23. Samuel Brittan, *The Treasury Under The Tories, 1951-1964* (Harmondsworth: Penguin, 1964), p. 182

7. Suez

*It is all very familiar. It is exactly the same
that we encountered from Mussolini and Hitler
in those years before the war.*
HUGH GAITSKELL, AUGUST 1956

On 26 July 1956, President Nasser nationalized the Suez
Canal, and there followed the most intricate phase of Macmillan's career. The question seems more baffling after ten years,
with all the new evidence. How was it that a man of such intelligence, such apparent detachment, such awareness of America,
could have urged on so ill-judged and incompetent an adventure? Macmillan was the most consistently ardent advocate of
the Suez invasion – not excepting Eden. However skilful his
subsequent retreat, the fact has to be faced that without his
consistent support as chancellor, the invasion would probably
never have happened.

The case of Eden, with some help from hindsight, is more
explicable. By early 1956, after only a few months as prime
minister, Eden was facing ugly Tory discontent: he was
accused of weak government by *The Daily Telegraph*; he was
infuriating his colleagues with his fussiness and interferences;
and, more dangerous – in spite of his old fame as an anti-
appeaser – he was coming under heavy fire for appeasing both
the Russians (over Indo-China) and the Arabs. It was a time
heavy with humiliation for the Conservative right wing, particularly in the Middle East. The arch-enemy was Nasser, who
seemed at that time to many people in both parties to be part of
a great Russian plot to sweep into the Persian Gulf and Africa.

Eden was very vulnerable to criticism. It was he who had negotiated the 'scuttle' (as Churchill called it) from the Suez base in 1954 – with the help of Selwyn Lloyd – and who had assured the Tories that Nasser could be trusted. By 1956 there were a series of setbacks: Nasser was building up arms, bought from the Russians; the king of Jordan sacked his old British mentor, General Glubb, just when Selwyn Lloyd, now Foreign Secretary, was having talks with Nasser; and Cyprus, the next base after Suez, was harassed by sabotage and terrorism. Eden was taunted, by his party and the Press, to 'get tough' with Egypt; and, more important for a man of Eden's rather brittle vanity, he felt personally betrayed by Nasser.

Macmillan was now much more detached. As Chancellor of the Exchequer there was no reason why he should be closely concerned with Suez at all: indeed, on the surface he was not involved, and in the height of the crisis he was to be seen in Trafalgar Square with the Dagenham Girl Pipers, launching the Premium Bonds. If the chancellor had to be involved he would be expected to be on the side of caution, carefully questioning the balance-sheet. He took pride in his broad historical perspectives; he had the reputation of being – in the Tory language of the time – more 'robust'. He was not in political danger: the right wing preferred him to Eden, and were encouraged by his Churchillian style. He was never, like some of the cabinet, 'vamped' by Eden's reputation and glitter. In contrast to Eden's tenseness, Macmillan was always studiously calm (he had a habit of arriving at cabinet meetings rather late, from his house next door).

In fact he was from the beginning in the thick of it, and from the moment when Nasser nationalized the Suez Canal, he made little secret of his determination to use force. He was part of Eden's secret 'inner cabinet' or 'Suez committee' who planned the operation, and found an occasion for it; he advised on the cost of it, and on the American reaction. He spoke with high emotion in cabinet, and there is reason to believe that his advocacy was crucial. He was opposed to the Suez dispute being taken to the United Nations, and when Eden was

tempted to accept a settlement in early October – a better
settlement than was eventually achieved – he insisted in
cabinet that the invasion should go ahead. The fact that the
chancellor, of all people, was playing this role certainly helped
to confuse the cabinet. His colleagues saw him as the Lady
Macbeth of Suez: 'Infirm of purpose! Give me the daggers!'
(*Macbeth* was much in the air at the time, and a lot of people
were saying 'If it were done when 'tis done, then 'twere well
it were done quickly.')

Macmillan did not (amazingly) seem to have worked out the
consequences, or to have any clear idea of how Britain would
stay in Egypt, having invaded: when questioned by one of his
colleagues he talked vaguely about 'not going back to the old
ways', 'not being like Napoleon in Italy'. During the three
months of the Suez crisis he seemed to younger colleagues,
with whom he normally enjoyed intellectual discussion, to be
closed to any reasonable argument, and to retreat into an older,
more blimpish *persona*.

Macmillan was intimate with the American administration,
and his advice thus had a special authority in cabinet. He was an
old friend of Eisenhower's, he was much closer to Dulles than
Eden was (Dulles never really forgave Eden for his diplomacy
over Indo-China), and he was in direct communication with
both. As soon as the crisis broke out, Eisenhower sent Robert
Murphy, Macmillan's old colleague in Algiers, 'to see what it's
all about'. Macmillan invited Murphy to a stag dinner, with
Field-Marshal Lord Alexander, his wartime comrade, and
Murphy wrote later that he 'sensed that although Macmillan
was well pleased with No 11 Downing Street, he had aspirations to move some day to No 10'.[1]

At the dinner Macmillan talked about Britain becoming
'another Netherlands', and made it plain that force would have
to be used at Suez, and that 'Nasser has to be chased out of
Egypt'. Macmillan and Alexander explained that the military
operation would be quite easy, needing only one or two divisions, and ten days. They conveyed the impression to Murphy
'of men who have made a great decision and are serene in the

belief that they have decided wisely'. Macmillan and Eden sent messages through Murphy to Eisenhower, stressing that the decision to use force was 'firm and irrevocable'.

As a result Dulles hastened to London, on 1 August. He had less strained conversations with Macmillan than with Eden. Macmillan insisted to Dulles that Britain would be finished as a world power if Nasser got away with it, and exclaimed 'this is Munich all over again'. When Dulles returned to Washington, he told the Canadian ambassador that Eden, Lloyd and Macmillan had reached 'the calm and deliberate decision that they cannot accept having Britain at the mercy of a man like Nasser . . . even though the calculated risk of their decision is nuclear war'.[2]

Dulles tried to restrain the British, through the ambiguous device of the Suez Canal Users' Association; but Macmillan still believed that force would have to be used. While S.C.U.A. was meeting in London, Macmillan went to Washington to the World Bank meetings, and on the way visited his mother's home in Indiana. Speaking 'off the record' at a lunch, he warned that if Nasser were not stopped, the oil would fall into his hands, the strength of the Western European economy would be sapped, and N A T O might collapse. If Nasser controlled the canal, he went on, 'it would mean war in a matter of months'.[3]

In Washington Macmillan saw George Humphrey, the Secretary of the Treasury, and discussed the possibility of a loan, to offset speculation against sterling which was already mounting. He also talked with Dulles and with Eisenhower. Washington was absorbed in the presidential elections, and attitudes to Suez were confused by the political conflict; many Democrats urged the British to strong action. But it is hard to see how Macmillan can have been left in doubt about Eisenhower's attitude. Nevertheless he returned to London to reassure Eden of American support, and to press ahead with the secret plans for invasion.

How did Macmillan remain so convinced? There was, of course, an extraordinary public mood in Britain. There was some hysteria on both sides. Few public figures made alto-gether balanced judgements, and Hugh Gaitskell, in the first debate on Suez, made a rash and bellicose speech. There was a fog of misinformation – about the inability of Egyptians to run the canal, about Nasser's perilous political position, about Russian plots, about the efficiency of the army, and the ease of an invasion. There was, moreover, a current wave of nostal-gia for the last war, a sense of the boredom and fatuousness of contemporary Britain: it was the year of *Look Back in Anger*, Colin Wilson and rock 'n' roll. Nearly everyone seemed touchy, and when the canal was seized there was an instinctive feeling that something must be done. There was a mood of almost tribal recidivism, like the moods that sweep through a school, which was not easy to resist. There was a sound of sabre-rattling, which Macmillan readily joined.

Among many politicians there were stirrings of wartime daring, and Macmillan, in spite of his impassive looks, was easily stirred. Like Eden, he remembered a heroic past, and looked back to the horrors of the First World War, and to the dangers of appeasement; like Eden, he constantly, and almost longingly, compared Nasser to Hitler, and Suez to Munich. Macmillan no doubt, too, remembered his own undoubted triumphs in the Second World War, with his skill in handling the Americans and his 'intellectual recklessness', as Crossman called it (he was, in the words of one colleague 'a kind of Tory Crossman' – easily carried away by ideas). Perhaps most important, he remembered his time in Greece, when he insisted on British intervention against the Communists, in spite of bitter American criticism, and was vindicated by history.

For Macmillan, perhaps even more than for Eden, the giant example of Churchill was dominant, reminding him of how one man could change the course of history. 'There are times in a man's life when he has to make bold decisions,' Macmillan explained afterwards. 'History alone will prove whether what we did was right or wrong.'[4] He had often talked about the weakening of Britain's will after the two world wars, and for some time before Suez he had felt the need for action in the

Middle East: when Mossadeq had seized the Abadan oil refinery in 1951, he was already talking about the need for force. He saw – in one of his favourite images – the Russians moving in from the East as the barbarians at the gates of Constantinople. He was often addressing himself to history. 'I hope when history judges the matter,' he said at the height of the campaign on 2 November, 'it will be said: "These men have made mistakes, but they have had the courage to act instead of slinking into the easy way of passing the buck to someone else."'

And he had, too, a Greek sense of tragedy, which made him inclined to exaggerate disaster. 'It's ruin either way; but it's better the quick way,' he was reported to have said at one point in the Suez crisis; he talked often about the end of civilization, the fate of grandchildren, and the Third World War. It was partly the characteristic of his age: he was to admit some time later that his generation was perhaps over-obsessed by its experience of war and appeasement. It was partly his old feeling of imminent doom, which showed itself all through his political career, from his talk about revolution in the 1920s, to his talk about socialism in the 1960s. But, more simply, it was the swordsman, the aggressive man of action, longing to get out again after years of frustration. After the invasion had begun, Macmillan seemed relieved and rejuvenated, and one cabinet colleague said 'it was the young Macmillan of the Thirties again, hat thrown in the air'.[5]

It is possible to visualize how Macmillan, in a mood of wartime was tempted to bold adventure. But how could he have so misjudged, or ignored, the American reaction? He did not (as Robert Murphy noticed) have illusions about Britain's post-war power, as many Tories including Eden had, and he had first-hand opportunities for hearing American attitudes. Macmillan made it known that Dulles had promised support, while Eisenhower had prevented him. It is true that Dulles was devious, sometimes ambiguous and maddening; in his first talks he said that 'a way had to be found to make Nasser disgorge what he was attempting to swallow' – a remark which stuck in the minds of Eden and Lloyd – and his protracted negotiations over S.C.U.A. helped finally to exasperate the British. But there is still no published evidence of Dulles sanctioning invasion, and much evidence to the contrary.

As for Eisenhower, his patient correspondence, published in 1966, leaves no room for ambiguity. 'I personally feel sure that the American reaction would be severe,' he wrote to Eden on 31 July.[6] 'Permit me to suggest,' he said in a very courteous letter on 8 September, 'that when you use phrases in connection with the Suez affair, like "ignoble end to our long history" in describing the possible future of your great country, you are making of Nasser a much more important figure than he is.'[7] It was clear from the beginning that Eisenhower saw the canal, not as a bastion of the West, but (in his own flat words) as 'the world's foremost public utility'.

There can be no doubt, from the black-out of news before the invasion, that Eden and Macmillan knew that the Americans would oppose it. They expected that once the British had taken Suez, and the American elections were over, Eisenhower and Dulles would accept it, if not with enthusiasm, at least with neutrality. Macmillan, in spite of his old friendship with Eisenhower, quite underrated his determination and intelligence, and was unprepared for his eventual reaction: 'I've never seen great powers make such a complete mess and botch of things,' Eisenhower said to his speech-writer, Emmet John Hughes, when he learnt of the British invasion.[8]

There remains the 'Macchiavellian' explanation of Macmillan's advocacy of Suez, which is sometimes put forward. It is that Macmillan urged Eden on to the Suez adventure, well knowing that it was a gamble; that he foresaw that, if it failed, Eden was likely to fall; but that he, Macmillan, could survive and succeed him. It is difficult to follow this far-fetched explanation. Macmillan certainly had no great respect for Eden, and was well aware that he was under great strain. He certainly thought (rightly) that he would make a better prime minister. He knew the dangers for Eden: he was reported to have said to his son-in-law, Julian Amery: 'I think Anthony's going to have a rough ride for the next few weeks. In fact, I shouldn't be surprised if he lost his seat.'⁹ But it is not conceivable that he should foment a war to achieve this result.

Macmillan was clearly genuinely carried away by Suez, and shared Eden's defensive emotions. He certainly saw the operation as a gamble; but he was convinced that the danger was as great if Britain did nothing. The actual outcome of the Suez war could not have been predicted by anyone, for the situation was confused and criss-crossed with emotion and miscalculation. It was not, in the end, the failure of Suez which brought Eden down, but his illness: to some extent Suez actually strengthened his support. Macmillan seemed determined to be loyal to Eden – even to be leaning over backwards – the more so, perhaps, because he knew Eden's jealousy of him.

As it happened, Macmillan was decisive not only in urging the invasion, but in stopping it. On the fateful Tuesday, 6 November, when British troops were advancing from Port Said, there were many reasons pressing on Eden for a cease-fire. Not much notice was taken of the Russian threat of 'volunteers', or the danger of revolt from Tory M.P.s; much more important was the uncompromising American opposition at the U.N. But the last straw came from the Chancellor of the Exchequer. Macmillan had originally advised that the whole cost of Suez would only be £100 million, and that sterling could survive. But early on the Tuesday morning Macmillan was told at the Treasury that the run on the pound from American selling was so great that an immediate loan of £300 million was needed to avoid devaluation. Macmillan had to ask Washington for an urgent loan from the International Monetary Fund, and the reply eventually came, that a loan could only be granted if Britain accepted a cease-fire. Faced with this condition, Eden was forced to accept. At midnight the Suez war came to an end.

At this point Macmillan appeared in his most remarkable role. Faced with the abrupt humiliation, he – much more successfully than Eden – emerged as the unshaken warrior. He had not spoken publicly during the prelude to the war, but now in a series of speeches he doggedly defended the adventure, in the style of Dunkirk. 'Have we in this age, when young and old demand security, forgotten what risks mean?' he asked on 6 November; and explained that the Government 'had stopped at least temporarily a war which looked as if it might have been the beginning of a great war'. He spoke in his devil-may-care, buccaneering vein:

We do live of course at rather a difficult time, but we have done that before. At the moment we seem rather isolated, but we have been that before. Nothing matters as long as we think what we have done is right and that what we do will lead to something better coming out of it. That I think will happen.

On 12 November, in a fiery debate in Parliament, Harold Wilson asked him why the chancellor, whose traditional duty was to oppose defence expenditure, did not oppose this. Macmillan replied:

I want to say quite frankly to the House that it was a great temptation to me to take exactly that course. . . . I could also look forward, if I may introduce a purely personal note, if these events had not taken place and when I had reached what is the end of, normally, the last decade of one's life, political life at any rate, to retirement from many of these troubles. . . . All my interests would have been to follow what we used to call appeasement . . . why have I not followed that? I will tell the House frankly and sincerely. It is because I have seen it all happen before.

(Was this a telling thrust at Butler?) He compared the situation once again to Hitler in 1936, and gave Britain credit for the presence of a U.N. force: 'We have perhaps created for the first time a United Nations.' (Bevan retorted later that this was like giving Hitler and Mussolini credit for the U.N.)

By now it was becoming unlikely Eden would continue as prime minister: he was unwell, haggard and pale, and had recurring fevers. On 23 November he flew to Ian Fleming's house in Jamaica, for a three-week holiday, leaving Butler in charge. He came back before Christmas, but the fever returned.

On Boxing Day he asked the Lord Chancellor, Kilmuir, whether he thought he should stay: Kilmuir said yes (Eden's resignation, he thought, would be taken as a triumph for Nasser). But on 7 January Eden's doctors advised him to give up, and two days later he tendered his resignation and held his last cabinet.

There were only two possible successors – Macmillan and Butler – and so began the next engagement in the duel between these two contrasting and ambitious rivals. Macmillan was far from ideal: to many Tories his Edwardian manner seemed faintly ridiculous, and his record over Suez was not really satisfactory, to either wing of the party. The left knew that he had helped to start the Suez war, the right wing knew that he had helped to stop it; and words like 'political acrobat' were in the air. But Macmillan in the previous weeks had managed brilliantly to give the impression that the war had been a kind of victory, and that nothing much had happened. Talking to the 1922 Committee he was (unlike Butler) able to calm the backbenchers by claiming that the U.N. force was Britain's achievement, and by suggesting in heroic style that its success was 'the great challenge facing Western civilization'. He seemed undeterred by the Suez furore.

Butler, on the other hand, had been consistently sceptical about Suez. He was not privy to Eden's plans, as Macmillan was, and he had let it be known that he thought that the cabinet was going a little mad. In the heroic atmosphere of the time, Butler's ambiguities were unwelcome. A number of Tory M.P.s, led from the right wing, made it clear that Butler's appointment would split the party. Lord Lambton recollected afterwards when he had become a bitter critic of Macmillan: 'the campaign against Mr Butler was singularly effective. It was also the most squalid political manoeuvre that I have ever been aware of and one which went to an inch of shocking me out of politics.'[10] But, even without this lobbying, Butler could hardly have won: he had a peculiar flair for arousing Tory hostility, and – as he showed again some years later – for not rising to the occasion.

The Press was almost unanimous in predicting Butler for prime minister: the *Express*, *Mail*, *Chronicle* and *Herald* all plumped for Butler on the morning of 10 January: *The Times* was more doubtful. Only Randolph Churchill, reporting from Suffolk for *The Evening Standard*, predicted the actual outcome.

Meanwhile those mysterious customary processes of the Conservative party were at work. Lords Kilmuir and Salisbury considered the constitutional position and decided that the Queen 'need and ought not to wait for a party meeting' before choosing the prime minister. They consulted all the cabinet ministers, one by one, in Lord Salisbury's rooms in the Privy Council offices. Salisbury (as Kilmuir recounts it) asked each one the question: 'Well, which is it, Wab or Hawold?' Kilmuir reported that 'an overwhelming majority' favoured Macmillan.'[11]

The two peers talked to Oliver Poole, the chairman of the party, and rang up Major John Morrison, the chairman of the backbenchers' 1922 Committee, on his island in Scotland. They talked to the chief whip, Ted Heath, who had had several letters from M.P.s against Butler, and who strongly advised choosing Macmillan.

Armed with advice, Lord Salisbury went to see the Queen at about eleven o'clock on 10 January, and recommended Macmillan. The Queen also saw Churchill, who (as he said two years later) gave the same advice. There is no evidence that Eden was asked his advice. At 1.45 P.M. the Queen sent for Macmillan, and asked him to form a Government. That evening, Macmillan invited Ted Heath to champagne and oysters at the Turf Club. It was widely assumed that Macmillan's premiership would be a stopgap to tide the Tory party over the crisis. No one imagined that it would last nearly seven years.

MACMILLAN

NOTES

1. Robert Murphy, *Diplomat Among Warriors* (New York: Doubleday, 1964; London: Collins), p. 462
2. Terence Robertson, *Crisis* (London: Hutchinson, 1965), p. 82
3. Herman Finer, *Dulles Over Suez* (Chicago, Ill.: Quadrangle, 1964; London: Heinemann), p. 276
4. House of Commons, 12 November 1956
5. Hugh Thomas, *Suez Affair* (London: Weidenfeld & Nicolson, 1967), p. 126
6. Dwight D. Eisenhower, *Waging Peace* (New York: Doubleday, 1966; London: Heinemann), p. 665
7. Ibid., p. 669
8. E. J. Hughes, *The Ordeal of Power* (London: Macmillan, 1963), p. 217
9. See Hugh Thomas, *Suez Affair*, p. 126
10. Lord Lambton, *The Evening Standard*, 6 May 1959
11. Viscount Kilmuir, *Political Adventure* (London: Weidenfeld & Nicolson, 1964), p. 285

8. Prime Minister

NIGEL LAWSON: *Would you say it is easier for a Prime Minister in this country to do one thing if he says he is doing something else?*

HAROLD MACMILLAN: *It is a very common method, yes.*[1]

The condition of the Tory party when Macmillan took over was worse than at any time since 1940. To many M.P.s it seemed that it was only a matter of weeks or months before the Government collapsed, and Macmillan was talked of – and perhaps saw himself – as simply a stopgap. Suez, however much ministers continued to defend it, was (whether politically or militarily) an acknowledged disaster. The Gallup polls were consistently against the Tories, as was, for the next eighteen months, every by-election. But this depressed state had, for Macmillan, a great advantage: it could hardly be worse, and the predicament itself had united the Tories. 'The crucial political fact about the Suez crisis,' wrote one commentator afterwards, 'was the support of the Government by Conservative M.P.s including some who never wanted to go into Egypt and some who never wanted to come out.'[2] Any show of confidence would be better than the dithering of Eden, and the party was longing to acclaim a new leader.

And from the moment he took over, Macmillan made it clear that he was enjoying the job. Only a few months before, many colleagues thought that he was ready for retirement, exhausted by the rigours of the Foreign Office and the Treasury. Now, as prime minister, he suddenly seemed younger and stronger. The atmosphere of national crisis was one that suited his temperament and his theatrical style, and it enabled him to show off his *sang-froid* – which in more normal times, in more junior posts, could look merely dull or absurd – to sudden advantage. In his first public broadcast as prime minister, on 17 January, he called for an end to defeatist talk about Britain being a second-class power: 'What nonsense. This is a great country and do not let us be ashamed to say so . . . there is no reason to quiver before temporary difficulties.'

Macmillan moved next door, to No 10, with a deliberate show of calmness. It was not difficult to present a contrast: in the last few months, quite apart from the worries of Suez, Eden had increasingly irritated his colleagues by his tenseness, his interference in departments and his unpredictability. Macmillan was not naturally a phlegmatic man: he was nearly always nervous before speeches, and very self-conscious. But he had great self-control, patience and a capacity to retreat from pressing problems into a world of books. The acting talent that he had first shown at Oxford now at last came into its own. On becoming prime minister, he carefully let it be known that he was reading Trollope; he insisted that the klaxon on the official prime minister's car – which Churchill had installed and Eden had much used – should stop sounding; he hung up a notice inside Downing Street quoting from *The Gondoliers*: 'Quiet Calm Deliberation Disentangles Every Knot.' He made a point of appearing in the smoking room of the House of Commons, or in Tory clubs, and talking relaxedly to back-benchers. At week-ends he arranged informal gatherings of senior ministers at the official country house, Chequers.

He chose his cabinet with subtlety, not seeming to disown the Suez expedition, while introducing some new blood. He kept Selwyn Lloyd, the most obvious scapegoat, at the Foreign Office, where he returned, as *The Economist* put it, 'down a long, cold arch of raised eyebrows'. To take over his own place as Chancellor he chose Peter Thorneycroft, whom he had respected as President of the Board of Trade. He put three cabinet ministers (Walter Monckton, Lloyd George and Buchan Hepburn) into the Lords, and sacked Antony Head, the Minister of Defence. He dropped his own brother-in-law, James Stuart, from the Secretaryship for Scotland. He promoted his two old businessmen colleagues from Housing: he made Percy Mills a baron and brought him into the cabinet as Minister of Power; he made Marples Postmaster-General. Among junior ministers he kept a careful mixture of right and left: he brought back Edward Boyle, the young intellectual who had resigned over Suez, and whom he rather admired, to be number two in Education; and he simultaneously brought in his son-in-law Julian Amery, a vociferous supporter of Suez, to be number two in the War Office. When talking about his own politics he said, on 7 February,

I am slightly amused by the fact that during the early part of my life I was accused of leaning too much to the Left. I have seen recently accusations that I have leaned to the Right. I propose, as I have always, to follow the Middle Way.

He very soon established an easy dominance over his rattled cabinet. He was ten years older than most of them (their average age was fifty-three, Macmillan was now sixty-three); they knew the dangers of rocking the boat; and he knew how to run the cabinet in a quick, businesslike way. 'It is impossible,' wrote Lord Kilmuir, 'to over-emphasize the personal contribution of the Prime Minister to the renaissance'.[3] Another member of the cabinet, Charles Hill, wrote afterwards that he thought his

chairmanship of the Cabinet to be superb by any standards. If he dominated it (he usually did) it was done by sheer superiority of mind and of judgement. He encouraged genuine discussion provided it kept to the point. If he found himself in a minority he accepted the fact with grace and humour.[4]

'Our first objective,' he told his friend Lord Swinton, 'must be to keep the party together, at all costs united. It's like keeping five balls in the air simultaneously, knowing that we are doomed if we drop one.'[5] He quickly set about, on the one hand, hotly defending the Suez action in public, and on the other hand repairing the damage and preparing the retreat from Suez. It was a tricky combination for which he was ideally equipped: he had the Churchillian manner to assure the right wing, and a sufficiently agile intellect to come to terms with the harsh facts. It may seem odd, looking back on it, that the Conservative right wing could be deceived for so long about Macmillan. But the fact is, they *wanted* to be deceived. There was no real alternative to the retreat from Suez: they wanted the retreat to look like a victory, and Macmillan obliged.

His first major step was to visit Eisenhower (with Lloyd and Dulles) in Bermuda in March. He thought that Eisenhower had let Eden down over Suez, but he knew that the American alliance was crucial. He made much of his old friendship with Eisenhower in Algiers, and the visit seemed to go well: they talked about the Middle East and Cyprus, and nuclear tests. When someone asked Macmillan afterwards what it was like meeting Eisenhower, he is reported to have said: 'What was it like? Why, very pleasant, very friendly, very encouraging, but not at all like an experience in the modern world. More like meeting George III at Brighton.'[6] Eisenhower, on his side, was anxious to patch up the quarrel. When Macmillan had first become prime minister, he had sent a breezy letter, saying 'Welcome . . . to your new headaches. Of course you have had your share in the past, but I assure you that the new ones will be to the old as a broken leg is to a scratched finger. . . . Knowing you so long and well I predict that your journey will be a great one. But you must remember the old adage, "now abideth faith, hope and charity – and greater than these is a sense of humour".'[7] At Bermuda Eisenhower talked calmly about Suez but (as he recounts it) Macmillan still hoped to topple Nasser.

Foster and I at first found it difficult to talk constructively with our British colleagues about Suez because of the blinding bitterness they felt toward Nasser. Prime Minister Harold Macmillan and Foreign Minister Selwyn Lloyd were so obsessed with the possibilities of getting rid of Nasser that they were handicapped in searching, objectively, for any realistic method of operating the Canal.[8]

One matter on which Eisenhower pressed Macmillan was Cyprus – the next sticking point in the Middle East. Eisenhower said that he thought there was no point in keeping Archbishop Makarios a prisoner in the Seychelles. Macmillan seemed impressed: in any case, Cyprus as a base had now become less important, and soon after he returned to London on 27 March, it was announced that Makarios would be allowed to return to Cyprus.

It was the first major step in the retreat from Suez, and it had a dramatic effect: Lord Salisbury resigned from the cabinet. To the public it seemed barely possible that Macmillan could withstand the shock: less than three months before, Salisbury had been hailed as the 'kingmaker' who had put Macmillan into power, and romantic newspaper articles had extolled the power of the Cecils. Salisbury was related to half the old Tory families and, by marriage, to Macmillan himself. His political record had been impressive: he had resigned in protest against appeasement in 1938, and during the war he had actually stood up to Churchill in cabinet. He was a symbol of aristocratic independence, and a father-figure to the right wing.

But within the Government, Salisbury's position did not appear so magical. In the election of the prime minister, he had been little more than a head-counter, and in Macmillan's cabinet he was visibly out of sympathy with the younger members: he was testy and seemed often on the brink of resignation. He did not have an adaptable mind; and in many contemporary problems he seemed merely confused.

Macmillan handled Salisbury's departure with a handy technique; he made it merely seem trivial. He announced it just before the week-end, to let the news simmer down: and when he made a statement on the Bermuda talks the next week it was elaborately boring, very carefully avoiding the subject of Cyprus and concentrating on the importance of H-bomb tests – a subject more reassuring to the right wing, and more disconcerting to the Labour party. He replied to Salisbury's letter of resignation with calm courtesy: 'We have been together now for so many years in politics and are linked by so close a

friendship that I cannot hide from you the personal loss. . . .'
But the loss seemed hardly to be noticed; cabinet worked more
smoothly, the retreat from Empire became less bumpy, and
the magic of the Cecils seemed to go up in smoke. Lord
Salisbury had disappeared into Macmillan's *oubliette*. As one
cabinet minister put it: 'Harold understands power.'

Macmillan was well aware that for satisfying British pride
his most useful asset was the H-bomb, which lurked behind all
his premiership. How far he really believed in its real effectiveness as an independent deterrent is uncertain, but Suez had
shown the inadequacy of Britain's conventional forces, and the
country was in no mood for continuing conscription. Macmillan had made Duncan Sandys – the tireless hatchet man of
successive governments – the most powerful Minister of
Defence since Churchill, and in April he published the most
drastic of post-war white papers on defence. The notorious
'Sandys white paper' announced the end of conscription, the
reduction of armed forces from 690,000 to 375,000 in five years,
and the reliance on nuclear forces as the main means of defence
– the policy of 'big bangs and small forces', which was later
largely discredited. The new policy caused alarm among
Britain's allies and fury among admirals and generals, but in
the defence debate Sandys and Macmillan sailed over their
critics. Macmillan proclaimed that there could be no middle
way in defence policy, and, 'We must rely on the power of the
nuclear deterrent or we must throw up the sponge'. The first
British H-bomb was exploded the following month.

The long trail back from Suez continued, as it were, under
the smokescreen of a mushroom cloud. The final ignominious
come-uppance was in May, the same month as the H-bomb
explosion, when the British Government were finally forced
to accept Nasser's terms for operating the canal – terms worse
(as Gaitskell pointed out) than were available before the British
invasion. On 13 May Macmillan said that, although the terms
could not be regarded as permanent or satisfactory, he could
no longer advise ship-owners to boycott the canal. Emrys
Hughes remarked that 'this was the greatest and most spec-

tacular retreat from Suez since the time of Moses'. On the same day as Macmillan's statement, Salisbury spoke in the Lords, protesting about the giving in to Nasser and Makarios. He admitted that Macmillan's approach was 'practical and businesslike', but advocated a partial boycott of Nasser for the moral effect: 'By doing so we would have regained the moral leadership of the world.' He insisted that foreign policy should be above all firm and consistent, and that a truly great nation 'must always be ready to risk severe material sacrifices, if that be required, in defence of the principles in which it believes'. But no one else was much interested in making sacrifices to boycott Nasser, or in the moral leadership question.

A debate followed, in which Macmillan reasserted: 'We are a great world power and we intend to remain so', but went on

We are not foolish enough to think we can live in this modern world without partners. That is why we stand by our alliance with NATO, SEATO and the Baghdad Pact, and that is why I have laboured to try to get our American friends to understand the hard facts and co-operate with us facing them. . . . But [he went on], we in Britain must not be afraid of making our position clear and defending our own interests. That is why, in spite of all the pressure and agitation against me, I am determined that this country should be and remain a great nuclear power.

The debate marked the last and futile stand of the Suez die-hards. The original 'Suez rebels' who had begun their protest three years ago when the Suez base had been evacuated, were already depleted: Captain Waterhouse, their leader, had stumped off to Rhodesia, to become chairman of Tanganyika concessions. Julian Amery, their Young Turk, had joined father-in-law's Government. In the vote of 16 May, fourteen of the Suez rebels abstained, and eight resigned the Government whip. But they were not an effectual force: of the eight, one, Victor Raikes, left soon afterwards for Rhodesia; another, Angus Maude, left for Australia; one, William Maitland, took the whip back soon afterwards, and the rest formed a little troupe under Lord Hinchingbrooke (later Lord Sandwich, later Mr Montagu) which only lasted a year.

The Suez crisis was over and, as *The Spectator* (17 May) remarked, 'The real surprise is how little effect Suez and its repercussions have had on the British political scene': one reason, as *The Spectator* went on to explain, was that rebellion from the right was possible but ineffective, while rebellion from the left would be effective but was impossible. Macmillan knew that he was in a position of great strength, with no real alternative Tory leader or policy. He knew that the party would follow him, remarked Taper (Bernard Levin), 'if he were to lead them smack into the River Weser, and he is not going to let a well-connected Marquess get into the way of his meticulously rehearsed bonvivary'.

Next month Macmillan continued his patching-up at the Commonwealth Prime Ministers' Conference; he made a strong personal impression on most of them. Welensky described how he 'went back to Salisbury saying that England had found the man to provide her in peacetime with the kind of leadership that Churchill had given in war'. A polite communiqué emphasized the 'broad similarity of approach' and Macmillan proclaimed that if at any time there should be a conflict of calls upon Britain 'the Commonwealth came first in our hearts and mind'. Macmillan also continued his *rapprochement* with America. He went to see Eisenhower again in October, 'to study ways in which our two countries can be of greater service to the free world', and when he came back he managed to give the impression that it was Britain who had brought America back into the fold, rather than vice versa: 'The President,' he said, 'accepted whole-heartedly what he and I called the doctrine of interdependence.'

There were still complications in the Middle East. A new crisis came in July 1958. After massacres in Iraq, which cut out the lynch-pin of the old Baghdad Pact, the Lebanon and Jordan appealed for help: the Americans sent troops to the Lebanon, and then Macmillan, after a three-hour cabinet discussion, sent 2,000 parachutists to Jordan, to protect King Hussein. It was, Macmillan told the House on 17 July, 'the most difficult decision that I personally remember having to take . . .'. The landings in Jordan and Lebanon were welcomed by some Tories as showing that the Americans had come round to the tougher British attitude towards revolutionaries in the Middle East, and that the Suez-type intervention was found to be justified. But there was a huge distinction, both of scale and of motive; for both the Americans in Lebanon, and the British in Jordan, had been invited by the ruling government. The landings were really the tail-end of the Suez policy, and the troops left at the end of the year.

In the meantime, Macmillan was slowly changing his line over Cyprus. Ever since Makarios had returned in March 1957, it was clear that the British were trying to disentangle themselves from the island. New bases were being established in Aden and Kenya, and in December 1957 Macmillan sent out Sir Hugh Foot to become governor – an ingenious appointment. Foot was a much more conciliatory and liberal figure than his predecessor, Sir John Harding: at conferences Macmillan would turn to Foot and say: 'Now wheel on the idealist.'[9] On his way back from Australia, in February 1958, Macmillan stopped in Cyprus to see Foot, and began to work out a new constitutional programme. In June 1958 Macmillan and Foot launched their new 'Partnership plan' for Cyprus, with an elaborate dual constitution, designed to satisfy Greek and Turkish Cypriots, and to safeguard remaining British bases. Macmillan made it clear that Cyprus was now seen not as a colonial problem, but as an international one: it was a drastic switch from the attitude of Macmillan as foreign secretary three years before, when he said at the Tripartite Conference of August 1955, 'The internal affairs of Her Majesty's possessions cannot be discussed with foreign powers.'

When the plan was announced there was ten days of peace on the island, and then a new outbreak of terrorism: Macmillan flew out to Athens and Ankara to try to get the two governments to accept a modified plan, but the Greeks and Makarios refused the amendments, and the terrorism went on. It was not till February 1959 in a meeting in Zurich, that the

Greek and Turkish Governments finally, exhausted by the quarrel, reached agreement, on the basis of an independent Cyprus, incorporating elements of the Macmillan–Foot plan. The delegations flew on to London for a formal Cyprus conference, the Greeks and Turks agreed to safeguard the British bases, and the treaties were signed. Macmillan said: 'I regard the agreement as a victory for reason and cooperation. No party to it has suffered defeat. It is a victory for all.' In the debate in the House of Commons Gaitskell said that the Government deserved 'particular credit for eating so many words'; Macmillan characteristically replied in his most offensive style that Gaitskell 'never had been and never will be able to rise to the level of great events'. ('Failing to rise to the level of events' was a favourite Macmillan condemnation.)

In the meantime, the most remarkable stage in Macmillan's progress had come with his Commonwealth tour, early in 1958. The tour not only helped to change the image of the Tory party abroad; it also increased Macmillan's stature and self-confidence at home, and marked a turning-point in his fortune. When he left, just as all three Treasury ministers had resigned,* it seemed doubtful whether he would have a Government behind him at all; the journey seemed in danger of becoming ridiculous. But his calm dismissal of the 'little local difficulties' managed to make the resigners look merely mean, while he was attending to the new shape of the world. When he returned six weeks later, he seemed distinctly bigger.

He set out on the tour, as he explained, to learn rather than to teach, to put across the idea of the multi-racial commonwealth, and to show to the Asian countries that the Conservative Government welcomed them as independent members. It was – as he never hesitated to point out – the first time that a British prime minister had ever visited any of the countries of the tour – India, Pakistan, Ceylon, Australia or New Zealand: and the fact remained astonishing, however many times he repeated it.

He did not, on the face of it, seem the man best equipped to

* See p. 160.

inspire the Commonwealth. He arrived in India, looking old, stiff and uncompromisingly English. He stepped down from the plane at Delhi airport, straight from the English mid-winter into the tropical sun, wearing a dark blue suit, the usual Old Etonian tie, and an expression of nervous confusion: he looked shy as the customary garland was hung round his neck, and anxiously aloof from the hubbub around him. He walked, with his slow stiff shuffle as if half in a daze; and he spoke in each country with the same rehearsed phrases: 'my wife and I are indeed delighted' . . . 'this is the first time that a British prime minister' . . . 'this is a unique occasion '. . . , with the same lack of expression. He was often nervous – clutching at the bottom of his coat, or tapping with his fingers. In the active, hospitable atmosphere of India, he seemed an apparition from the imperial past.

But as the tour progressed, his nervousness eased. Nehru received him with warmth and informality, while arranging receptions of almost Viceregal proportions, and Macmillan was stirred by the friendly echoes of the Raj: he was delighted when, at one banquet, Nehru turned to him and said, 'I wonder if the Romans ever went back to visit Britain?' He was clearly surprised by the responsiveness of the Indian crowds, and came to regard them much as floating voters at an English election: 'You've only got to raise your hands and say "my friends!",' he said one evening, 'and you get an immediate response.' In Pakistan, which was in a precarious state under its dictator, Iskander Mirza, he found it less easy to get through to the people; but he was driven up to the North West Frontier, had lunch at the officers' mess still draped with imperial trophies, and chatted up the old soldiers about their campaigns under the British. In Karachi he made a private speech to bewildered British residents on a favourite theme – of how the Victorian age was only a brief interruption of Britain's more humble and practical role in the world, as a vigorous trading nation.

He showed extraordinary stamina on the journey: he was able to spend day after day travelling, speech-making, talking and listening: he had the politician's ability to switch on to an overdrive – to listen without fully listening. In the evenings he would work at business from London with his private secretaries and the cabinet secretary, Sir Norman Brook, often till the small hours: the entourage made up a new kind of airborne government.

The Australian part of the tour was awaited with some dread – particularly because an Australian diplomat had been accidentally snubbed on the way through Singapore: there were visions of catcalls for the stuffy pommy. But it was in fact the most triumphant sector. Macmillan, helped by the breezy high commissioner, Lord Carrington, managed to put himself over to the Australians more effectively than he had ever done in Britain. The extroversion and noise seemed to break down his reserve, and away from sceptical Britishers he became suddenly almost jolly: he drove in a jeep, set off on a 'meet-the-people' campaign, and rushed up to startled onlookers with phrases like 'how *are* you', 'very nice of you to come!'. He had long talks with his host, Robert Menzies (who advised him, among many other things, to televise Parliament), and made tactful speeches stressing the importance of the multi-racial Commonwealth. There was no doubt that Australia had a therapeutic effect on Macmillan. As he said in Melbourne: 'Everybody's so much nicer to you in other countries than they are at home. At home you always have to be a politician: when you're abroad you almost feel yourself a statesman.'

The new Macmillan was noticed when he returned to England in February: he talked quite movingly about the tour on television, and a spate of successful television interviews seemed to show a loosening-up after Australia. After he was interviewed by Robin Day on *Tell the People*, *The Yorkshire Post* commented: 'Certainly he is no longer just a House of Commons man.' He made a speech in a foreign affairs debate on 19 February:

I must say that I found it profoundly moving to feel that these great countries with their immense populations, so different in creed, colour, tradition and history, should now be free and willing partners with the old Commonwealth countries . . . the best of the old Empire is continuing into the new Commonwealth.

The Times commented that Macmillan, on his tour, had succeeded in removing the impression that the Conservative party was indifferent to India, and Angus Maude wrote in *The Spectator* on 28 February that he appeared a new man: 'He spoke with the attractive diffidence of a schoolboy who had been abroad for the first time, desperately eager to communicate something of the vision he had seen.'

Macmillan the prophet of the multi-racial Commonwealth seemed a long way from Macmillan the bellicose champion of Suez. Partly perhaps there had been a change of heart: from his new eminence, Macmillan seemed less easily moved by national pride, more fascinated by the world picture. The issues which used to sway the Tory party – Suez, Cyprus, Makarios – now seemed quite small and boring. But Macmillan, also had an adaptable mind – more so than Eden: he saw the attraction of the Commonwealth, particularly *vis-à-vis* America, in enhancing Britain's prestige; he saw himself as a broker between the two parts of it, the black and the white; and, since he still saw Britain as the centre of three interlocking circles, the Commonwealth circle had to be kept together.

Of all the phases of Macmillan's political life these post-Suez years are perhaps the most bizarre and revealing. How the ambivalent Suez champion and the failed foreign secretary suddenly became the only man the Conservative party had to lead the country remains in many ways a mystery, but two factors in these years, which may be overlooked, seem to me extremely relevant. One is the inhibiting fact of his next-door neighbour Sir Anthony Eden, his junior by three years but his senior in office all through the thirties, forties and fifties, and a man who had been naturally and unquestionably at the centre of great events since the rise of fascism. To have such a daunting neighbour breathing down one's neck would not encourage one to do a good job. But in addition Macmillan had the natural leader's inabilities and hopelessness at the prospect of tackling any number two job. Except in a personal way with Churchill, he had never been a good lieutenant. He knew that he would be a better leader, and could not conceal the fact: his failure as a lieutenant led him to fail in the jobs that Eden had, with some reluctance, pushed in his way.

With Eden out of the way and Butler on the retreat, Macmillan at last had a clear field. We should not be deceived by the histrionics, the casual air, the reading of Trollope, the determined unflappability. Here was a man at the height of his powers of extreme ambition who had waited thirty years for this opportunity. He seized it with both hands. It was a pity that it came ten years too late.

NOTES

1. *The Listener*, 8 September 1966 (interview)
2. Leonard D. Epstein, *British Politics Since Suez* (Urbana, Ill.: University of Illinois Press, 1964; London: Pall Mall Press), p. 87
3. Viscount Kilmuir, *Political Adventure* (London: Weidenfeld & Nicolson, 1964), p. 308
4. Charles Hill, *Both Sides of the Hill* (London: Heinemann, 1964), p. 235
5. Lord Swinton, *Sixty Years of Power* (London: Hutchinson, 1966), p. 183
6. Quoted in Joseph Stewart Alsop, *The Reporter's Trade* (London: Bodley Head, 1960), p. 332
7. Dwight D. Eisenhower, *Waging Peace* (New York: Doubleday, 1966; London: Heinemann), p. 121
8. Ibid., p. 122
9. Hugh Foot, *A Start in Freedom* (London: Hodder & Stoughton, 1964), p. 57

9. On to the Summit

It's no use crying over spilt summits.
HAROLD MACMILLAN, OCTOBER 1960

Very early in Macmillan's premiership, it became clear to his colleagues that his real passion was foreign affairs. He was virtually his own foreign secretary, with Selwyn Lloyd as his deputy, until Lord Home moved into the Foreign Office in 1960, with greater independence. Macmillan was always working on his vocation as a mediator between East and West. A vast amount of his time and thought was spent in trying to convene summit meetings, and from his many statements it was clear that it was in this role that he would like to appear to posterity. He saw himself as the heir to Churchill, who had been 'the author of the concept of the summit meeting' in 1953:[1] and he never ceased groping towards summits throughout the seven years of his premiership. The proposals for summits came under heavy criticism from the professional diplomats – who saw them as muddling the orthodox diplomatic channels, giving dangerous opportunities for exhibitionism, cross-purposes or breakdown, or resembling the pre-war tactics of Chamberlain. The only summit that Macmillan in fact achieved was an almost total fiasco.

Macmillan's showmanlike attempts at summits had elements both of farce and wartime nostalgia. They diverted attention from the unpleasant facts of Britain's declining importance in the world, and her economic predicament. They continually aroused the suspicions of Paris and Bonn, and often of Washington too. But there were some occasions when mediation between America and Russia was necessary, and Macmillan was well qualified to provide it. He was constantly steering a course between the American Government, who suspected him of appeasement towards Russia, and the British left wing, who saw him as needlessly hanging on to the British bomb. In a speech on 19 February 1958, he admitted that the older generation in Britain were 'perhaps too much obsessed by the danger of falling into the same errors which misled us in the thirties', while the younger generation were appalled by the prospect of nuclear armament: a balance had to be struck.

The whole atmosphere of diplomacy had been changed in October 1957, when the first Russian sputnik astonished the West, and induced a feeling, first in Europe, then in America, that some kind of negotiation towards disarmament was essential. Before he left for his Commonwealth tour, Macmillan made a broadcast suggesting a non-aggression pact, which had some publicity: and when he got back, speaking to the House of Commons (19 February), he re-stated the need for disarmament and a summit meeting, and asked 'What then can we do? . . . Are we to live forever in this sort of twilight between peace and war?'

The prospects of a summit ebbed and flowed: Khrushchev was keen on one, but Dulles was determined not to negotiate from weakness, and to close the 'missile gap' before anything. Throughout 1958 the Russians blew hot and cold. There seemed a prospect of a summit early in 1958, but it had evaporated by the time of the NATO meeting in May. The Middle East crisis of July 1958 revived the possibility: Khrushchev proposed a meeting of Russia, America and Britain, together with France and India, at 'any day or any hour': Britain and America were then reluctant, but Macmillan later wrote to Khrushchev, suggesting a meeting in the United Nations. Khrushchev replied agreeably, Macmillan suggested August, but soon afterwards Khrushchev made a three-day visit to Peking, and the idea was dropped.

Then, in November 1958, Khrushchev appalled the Western allies by announcing that he was soon going to sign a peace treaty with East Germany, and thus to bring to an end allied rights in West Berlin. The allies rallied anxiously to the defence of Berlin, while privately wondering how it *could* be defended; and soon afterwards Khrushchev gave a six months' deadline for an agreement to be worked out.

For the next six months, as the deadline came closer, Berlin dominated diplomacy, and produced a flurry of activity. Mikoyan visited America, assured Eisenhower that there was no question of an ultimatum, and explained that Moscow wanted 'a conference at the highest level': Moscow put forward proposals of a summit conference on Berlin, but Eisenhower, who was always afraid that summits meant concessions, was still insisting on a foreign ministers' meeting first. Western attitudes to the Berlin crisis differed alarmingly: de Gaulle and Adenauer insisted on stern terms for any Berlin settlement, including free all-German elections and a reunified Germany, to be allowed to join NATO: Macmillan was willing to discuss some form of confederation, and advocated a thinning-out of forces in Central Europe: Eisenhower and Dulles stood somewhere, rather anxiously, between the two. Confronted with this disunity, Dulles flew to London, to try (with some success) to bridge the gap: it was decided that the Western foreign ministers should meet in March.

In the meantime, on 5 February, Macmillan dropped a bombshell: he intended to take up a long-standing invitation to visit Moscow. He would be going, not to negotiate on behalf of the West, but 'to have an exploratory exchange of views on world problems'. 'I informed, though I cannot honestly say I consulted, our allies,' he recalled later:[2] 'President Eisenhower did not much like it, but wished me good luck; President de Gaulle was sceptical; Chancellor Adenauer was offended.' The expedition was greeted with scepticism, both by the allies, and by the Labour party, for it smacked of electioneering. Macmillan, in a speech before leaving on 19 February 1959, insisted that it was the result of long plans and negotiations:

'The truth is that for some time I have been making really strenuous efforts to get to the summit, but it has seemed a very difficult and disappointing journey . . . I cannot help feeling that a visit of this kind can do no harm. I trust it may do some good.' The allies, particularly Adenauer, were clearly alarmed that Macmillan might be 'soft' towards Moscow, and that he was trying to take over the leadership of the West – not least because Dulles was now in hospital.

Macmillan arrived in Moscow on 21 February, accompanied by luxuriant publicity from the British Press: the fact of a British prime minister travelling to Moscow, for the first time since the war, was itself a booster to national pride, and symbolized openly Britain's bid to be the world's peacemaker. He was wearing a white fur hat, twelve inches high, which he had fished out from an old drawer, which gave to his visit a dangerous panache. He was accompanied by a huge entourage, ranging from Selwyn Lloyd and Sir Norman Brook to a bevy of Foreign Office advisers. Khrushchev's welcome was cordial, without being spectacular: Macmillan made a safe speech emphasizing that Britain was not 'the Britain of Dickens', and got down to talks about Berlin and disarmament. At a dinner at the Kremlin Macmillan praised the new building in Russia, and wished 'with all his heart' that competition over nuclear weapons would stop: Khrushchev replied that Macmillan's visit was a thaw in the cold war. The next day an elk shoot was cancelled to make more time for discussions.

But the thaw did not last, and Khrushchev began to play an elaborate hot-and-cold game. As soon as Macmillan showed support for Adenauer, Khrushchev's tone changed. While Macmillan was visiting a nuclear research station Khrushchev made an 'election speech' in Moscow, saying that the Western idea for four-power foreign ministers' meeting was a 'bog with no way out', and that only Germany could discuss German reunification: but he offered Britain a non-aggression pact, and insisted that the Russians wanted a full summit meeting. Macmillan, distressed by this outburst, asked Khrushchev to lunch at a *dacha* the next day; but the atmosphere was chilly. Khrushchev conceded nothing on Berlin, and again demanded a summit: Macmillan is reported[3] to have replied: 'If you go on like this there will only be a war, and where shall we all be?' Khrushchev leapt to his feet and shouted, 'You have insulted me!'

Discussions collapsed. Khrushchev announced that he had toothache, which was clearly a diplomatic ailment, and could not accompany Macmillan on the rest of his tour. He came to a gloomy reception at the British Embassy, but characteristically escaped from Macmillan and the ambassadors and circulated through the other rooms, pursued by the ambassador's wife; I watched him talking gaily to Malcolm Muggeridge about Russian humour in *Krokodil*, and to Mikoyan about whisky. The following day Macmillan, looking wan and dejected, continued the tour without Khrushchev, to Kiev and Leningrad, while Mikoyan in a Moscow speech accused him of being too tough on Berlin, and ignoring the non-aggression pact. It was a Russian custom, Mikoyan said, 'to begin a meal with tart dishes and end with sweets', and Macmillan had done the opposite. Macmillan was being made a fool of; the American correspondents looked smug.

Then, when Macmillan arrived at Leningrad, there was the cryptic and smiling figure of Mikoyan, together with Gromyko, waiting for him at the airport; and a telephone call came from Khrushchev, to say that the toothache was cured, and that 'a British drill had cured it'. Mikoyan put foward a modified Soviet proposal, agreeing to a limited foreign ministers' conference, and proposing a summit for broader questions of disarmament and disengagement. Macmillan travelled back on the night train to Moscow with Mikoyan, and was greeted with a brass band at the station, and a renewed cordiality. He went to a vast reception at the Kremlin, and spoke stiffly on Russian television about British achievements. He and Khrushchev signed a joint declaration which admitted disagreement over Berlin, but agreed on the possibility of negotiation, and an investigation into arms limitation in part of Europe. The Russians admitted that Macmillan had put forward constructive ideas on nuclear tests* – which was in fact the most fruitful part of the visit. In his farewell broadcast Macmillan said that 'each side needs concrete reassurances . . . let us see if we can make a start and go forward step by step'.

Macmillan was received back in London with qualified praise. He explained to Parliament that it was 'a great gain that we have reached agreement on the principle that differences between nations should be resolved by negotiation'. In Paris and Washington there was renewed resentment that he was trying to lead the alliance. *The Times* said – very tactlessly – 'with the American Head of State a declining force, the German Chancellor an old unhappy man, and the French President fully preoccupied with other problems, the responsibility falling on the British Prime Minister to lead the alliance sensibly and yet strongly in the weeks ahead is paramount'.

After Moscow, Macmillan toured the allies to tell them what had happened, and to work towards a *détente*. He went to Paris, to try to convince de Gaulle of the necessity for flexibility and disengagement, without much success; and then to Bonn, where he had some success in persuading Adenauer of the case for partial disarmament in Germany, and gained the impression that Adenauer was becoming less rigid in refusing to deal with East Germany.

Then he went to Washington. He visited, with Eisenhower, the ailing Dulles, who gave the usual warnings of the dangers of appearing afraid of the Russians; and then he settled down to long talks with Eisenhower in Aspen Cottage at Camp David, with American advisers flying in and out all day by helicopter. Macmillan reported on his progress in Moscow, and Eisenhower was cordial:

I thought again of how good it was to have as the leader of our closest and strongest ally a man with whom my acquaintance had been cordial and intimate since the days when we were together in North Africa in 1942.[4]

But when they came to talk about summits, there was the

* See p. 228.

inevitable conflict. Macmillan made an emotional speech, and argued that 'World War One – the war which nobody wanted – came because of the failure of the leaders at that time to meet at the summit. Grey went fishing, and the war came in which the United Kingdom lost two million young men.'[5] Eisenhower replied that the Second World War happened soon after a summit meeting with Chamberlain and Hitler, 'and I intended to be associated with nothing of the kind'. Macmillan said that he could not take Britain to war without first trying a summit: Eisenhower, always suspecting that a summit would mean concessions, said he would not 'be dragooned into a summit meeting'. The next day, Macmillan suggested a compromise formula for a letter to the Russians, proposing a foreign ministers' meeting, followed by a summit 'as soon as developments justify'. Surprisingly, Eisenhower accepted the formula, Macmillan had achieved what he wanted, and once again a summit was in sight.

The Americans seemed to be moving towards a more flexible position, and with the resignation of Dulles in April – succeeded by Christian Herter, a lesser personality – there seemed to be a growing prospect of compromise.

On 11 May 1959 the four foreign ministers – Herter, Gromyko, Lloyd and Couve de Murville – met in Geneva. Lloyd, backed by Macmillan, thought that agreement on Berlin was within reach, and went on coaxing his colleagues. Gromyko said that Macmillan's conversations with Khrushchev had produced a 'noticeable thaw' in the cold war. And in the meantime conferences were continued on nuclear test suspension, and Khrushchev, Eisenhower and Macmillan were having a lengthy and quite hopeful private correspondence on methods of verification, which showed that Macmillan's suggestions in Moscow had taken some effect. But at Geneva, Herter reported to Eisenhower that he suspected that Macmillan was going to press for a summit, whatever the outcome, and that this was why the Russians were making no concessions. Soon afterwards, Macmillan told Eisenhower that he thought the conference would soon break up, but that Eisenhower should propose an 'informal' meeting of the four Heads of State. Eisenhower was very upset,[6] summoned the British ambassador, and wrote Macmillan in characteristically homely style, saying that if he agreed to a summit without progress at Geneva, Khrushchev would consider him a 'pushover'.

The Geneva conference was clearly doomed; but before it broke up, there was a new surprise. Khrushchev suddenly announced to some American governors that he would very much like to visit the United States, and suggested that Eisenhower might come to Russia. Eisenhower, rather muddled about the implications, agreed to invite Khrushchev. Adenauer and de Gaulle showed consternation, and Macmillan was delighted, suggesting – predictably – a summit conference soon afterwards. Eisenhower made a quick journey to the allies, and visited London just before the election. Macmillan had private talks with Eisenhower about Berlin and disarmament, which were inconclusive, and – making full use of electoral opportunities – had a cosy conversation with Eisenhower on TV, in which their disagreement on summits was politely aired: Macmillan said 'I have always wanted a summit meeting', and Eisenhower said 'I will not be a party of a meeting that is going to depress and discourage people'.

Khrushchev's visit to America – the climax to this extraordinary year of 'personal diplomacy' – went off quite well, and the Russians seemed to be modifying their attitude to Berlin. When the British general election came up in October, Macmillan was able to appear convincingly in the role of the world's peacemaker.

With the election behind him, Macmillan – to the disappointment of many of his colleagues – seemed more than ever preoccupied with foreign affairs: he left the home ministers very much to themselves. 'As he gets older he thinks mainly about three things,' said one of his colleagues, 'the cold war, the Common Market and the Atlantic alliance.' His mind was set on a summit, and he was hopeful again: 'the general situation has improved', he said in the debate after the Queen's speech in November: 'we do not want it to slip back again'.

The year 1960 marked the peak of Macmillan's activity as a statesman. It was a year of great tension for the West: Dulles was dead, Eisenhower was bewildered, his new Secretary of State, Christian Herter, was not strong. The American administration was visibly running down. De Gaulle was already beginning to strain the Western alliance, and Khrushchev was looking for every opportunity to press his advantage. In this situation, Macmillan's calm and patience were precious, and for a short time he seemed to be the one steady element in the wobbly alliance.

A summit was at last agreed by the Western allies in December 1959: there followed long wrangling about the timing and the agenda, though there were modifications after pressure from de Gaulle and Adenauer, including the dropping of what had come to be called the 'Macmillan plan' for a controlled arms zone in Western Europe. But at last the date was fixed for 16 May 1960 in Paris. Khrushchev was invited and accepted. Macmillan's future ambitions revolved round this date: for him it was not just a summit meeting, but a great opening-up into a new era of trade and exchange, with Russia coming closer and closer to Europe, and Britain in the central position, the indispensable broker. He envisaged whole vistas of summits, and a whole new diplomatic secretariat to make closer contacts with Moscow. It was on this, above all, that he staked his place in history – the final achievement of Churchill's ambition.

Then, ten days before the date, disaster fell from the skies. An American high-altitude U-2 plane was missing over Russia. The American Government issued an elaborately mendacious explanation: Khrushchev triumphantly retorted with the sensational news that the pilot, with the equipment, had been captured intact, and that he had confessed he was spying. Eisenhower promptly and bravely admitted that the plane was spying, took the responsibility himself, and set off, undeterred, for the summit.

Macmillan spoke in the House on 12 May just before he left, still with apparent optimism: he explained 'to this new meeting the path has been slow, painful . . . some crevasses have opened right at the last minute': but he hoped that 'if the summit comes in a bit like a lion perhaps it will go out like a lamb'. He hoped that the summit might produce a three-power agreement on nuclear testing: on Berlin he hoped that, even if agreement was not reached, the decision might be postponed, 'and something which was menacing and dangerous, by the mere fact of being put off for a period, can begin to lose its importance'. He went on to say: 'I have striven also very long for the concept that the summit should not be one single ascent of one single mountain, but rather a chain and that we should have a series of meetings, make a little progress at the first, and then go on to another.'

The Heads of State finally gathered in Paris, in an atmosphere of foreboding. Macmillan arrived in an old suit and suede shoes, and established himself with a large entourage at the Embassy; he talked characteristically about the 'possible extinction of civilization'. He was visibly tense and irritable: it was the occasion for which he had worked and waited for two years, and it was soon clear that it was doomed. Macmillan and de Gaulle had both received angry letters from Khrushchev, explaining that he could not possibly attend a summit unless Eisenhower denounced all U-2 flights, and promised that they would stop. Macmillan privately, without success, tried to persuade Eisenhower to announce publicly that U-2 flights would stop, which he would not agree to: but publicly both he and de Gaulle were loyal allies.

The next day the conference began. Khrushchev, with a show of fury, called for an apology from Eisenhower. Macmillan and de Gaulle tried to mollify him, and to begin negotiations. Khrushchev insisted that he would publish his personal attack on Eisenhower, and eventually stomped out of the conference. Macmillan was sunk in gloom. He tried a last bid to rescue the conference: that evening he called on de Gaulle, Eisenhower and Khrushchev – 'pub-crawling' as he called it – and sat talking with Khrushchev until nearly midnight: he appealed to Khrushchev to continue with the negotiations 'on which all our hopes depended'. But to no avail: the next day

Khrushchev said that, unless Eisenhower apologized, he would leave Paris immediately. Another meeting was called by de Gaulle but Khrushchev did not turn up. The summit was over. The Western leaders issued a melancholy communiqué saying that they were ready to meet 'at any suitable time in the future'.

Eisenhower was not much upset: he had thought the summit would be a failure anyway. But for Macmillan it was a personal disaster. The critics of 'summit diplomacy' – including a large part of the Foreign Office – were full of 'I told you so'. The breakdown left an atmosphere of crisis: Khrushchev gave a furious Press conference, pouring abuse on Eisenhower's 'subterfuges and half-confessions': only the Geneva disarmament conferences continued to give some hope, which flickered when the Russian delegation walked out in June.

Macmillan seemed close to collapse. He did not believe that the U-2 incident was the cause of the breakdown of the summit, but rather that Khrushchev was under strong pressure to stop Eisenhower coming to Moscow, and this was an easy way to break it off. But that was no consolation. His foreign policy was shattered overnight, and there was no obvious new turning.

His views of the Russians always seemed to oscillate between extremes of gloom and optimism: now he was talking about them as incorrigible barbarians, and comparing them to the Goths and Vandals. He spoke about having to face a kind of religious war with Russia and China for the next two or three generations, and often referred to the miserable fate of grandchildren. He saw the position in Roman terms: America was an extension of Europe – Byzantium to Rome – and the Commonwealth was a kind of intermediary, a potential civilizer of barbarians, to stave off the barbarian hordes: Europe would be overrun, for a few hundred years, as it was in the fifth century – only the Western allies could hold them off.

Macmillan seemed to be almost revelling in doom. Yet it was in the next six months that he was in some respects most useful to the Western alliance. The American administration was confused and alarmed, and to the Berlin crisis was added, in July, a Cuba crisis and a Congo crisis: 'it was the peculiar service of the British prime minister', said the 1960 Survey of International Affairs, 'to have stepped into the breach and restored some element of balance, coherence and sang-froid to the badly rattled Western alliance'.

After the summit, Macmillan told the House of Commons 'I cannot conceal from the House that there may be grave implications in what has happened. . . . We must be prepared for the international outlook to be more stern.' He advocated patience and keeping in touch. His diplomatic difficulties were offset by his political popularity: after the collapse of the summit, the Gallup poll showed the popularity rating of the prime minister as seventy-nine per cent – the highest ever recorded for a peacetime prime minister.

Macmillan now took to a franker style of communication with Khrushchev. When the disarmament conference broke down in Geneva in June, he wrote saying that, just as the West were about to put new proposals 'you chose to break off the negotiations as if you did not want to know what we were going to propose'. When, next month, an American RB-47, operating from a British base, was shot down over the Barents sea, he wrote again 'about my anxieties about the way the world situation is developing': he summed up with his most celebrated diplomatic phrase: 'I simply do not know what your purpose is today.'

At the end of July the Americans were made still more jumpy by the threatened disruption of N A T O: de Gaulle was already quarrelling over American bomber bases in France, and had an ominous meeting with Adenauer at Rambouillet which was regarded as a demonstration of independence from America and Britain. Macmillan promptly flew to Bonn (on 10 August) to try to convince Adenauer of the dangers of splitting the Western alliance, and then on to Rome to enlist the support of the Italians.

Macmillan did attend a summit of a kind. At the climax of this tempestuous year, a collection of Heads of State assembled in September at the United Nations in New York. After

the disarmament meeting at Geneva had collapsed, Khrushchev proposed that he should discuss the subject at the U.N.
In a year when new States were reaching independence almost
every month, he wanted to woo the uncommitted countries,
and other Heads of State followed suit. The Americans could
not stop him, so Eisenhower, too, joined in. Macmillan hesitated, but then decided to go, emphasizing that he wanted to
discourage the two big blocs from lining up the uncommitted
countries, and to sound out the Russians about future negotiations. He had quick talks with the Commonwealth leaders,
emphasized his respect for non-commitment, and said that
(unlike Eisenhower) he was quite ready to meet Khrushchev.

He made an eloquent speech at the General Assembly,
playing the part of a wise old Greek, trying to lower the temperature: he talked about the tragedy of mutual fear – the
American fear of Russia, and the Russian fear of America – and
the pointlessness of propaganda: he said that the 'sponge of public opinion' was so 'saturated with the persistent flood of propaganda' that it could pick up no more, and insisted that 'ordinary
people, all over the world, in their present mood, are beginning
to tire of the same conventional slogans and catchwords . . .
obsessed by our own ideologies we are becoming prisoners of
our own arguments'. It was, as *The Guardian* described it, 'the
speech of a civilised, cultivated gentleman, honourably reflect-
ing the aspirations of decent people everywhere', and it did
something to offset the shock-tactics of Khrushchev, who had
rather crudely denounced the West to the uncommitted nations.

On the same afternoon as the speech, Macmillan met
Khrushchev, who was reported to be calm and reasonable, and
that evening appeared on TV, saying that there was hope of
going back to the mood before the summit: it was, he said 'a
question of a little generosity on everybody's side'; it needed
'a little good sense . . . a little loss of face . . . but I think it's
what the people of the world want'. Khrushchev returned
Macmillan's visit a few days later. He was in a genial mood and
had 'very productive' talks: it was cautiously emphasized that,
though Macmillan was firmly on the Western side, and did not

see himself as a broker, he was determined to keep discussions with the Russians going, with the hope of a new summit. Macmillan came back to London with some of his optimism apparently restored: at the Conservative party conference in October, he remarked cheerfully: 'It's no use crying over spilt summits.'

In fact, there were already signs of a steady thaw, and the *détente* had begun: the Berlin ultimatum had been forgotten, and the emergence of China as a rival power was changing the perspective. The breakdown of the summit had not, in retrospect, affected the pattern of East–West relations, which depended on factors other than the meetings of top men. Macmillan's public shows, on which he set so much store, had added up to very little. It was not his flamboyant, Churchillian movements, but his more pedestrian behind-the-scenes activities – as we shall note in Chapter 15 – which left a real contribution to peace.

In November, Kennedy defeated Nixon in the American elections, and Macmillan wrote a farewell to Eisenhower, concluding 'I cannot of course ever hope to have anything to replace the sort of relations that we have had': in fact, his relations with the new President were to be closer, though perhaps less influential.

NOTES

1. Harold Macmillan, *Winds of Change*, vol. I (London: Macmillan, 1966), p. 25
2. Ibid., p. 26
3. See Desmond Donnelly, *Struggle for the World* (London: Collins, 1965), p. 415
4. Dwight D. Eisenhower, *Waging Peace* (New York: Doubleday, 1966; London: Heinemann), p. 352
5. Ibid., p. 354   6. Ibid., p. 402

10. 'Never had it so good'

Man lives with his eyes on the future. He wastes little
time in congratulating himself
or his benefactors because his present conditions of life are better
than the conditions of his predecessors.
HAROLD MACMILLAN, 1938

From soon after the resignation of Churchill and the 1955 credit squeeze, until 1958, the opinion polls had registered a preference for Labour: for over three years the Tories were governing with the majority of the public against them. Then, in the summer of 1958, the Gallup poll began to register a swing towards the Tories: and by the middle of 1959 – in spite of two shattering condemnations of colonial policy – the Devlin report and the Hola report – the Tory lead seemed established.

There were many factors behind this remarkable shift. The opposition was certainly weak, and Hugh Gaitskell could not present a united front or a bold personal image. But most Conservatives thought that the chief factor was the prime minister himself.

Macmillan's achievement since Suez was certainly spectacular. At a time when the party – and the whole country – were defensive and jumpy, he had carried on as if nothing had happened, and shown a confident showmanship which had reinvigorated the Tories. He had ignored differences and blunders within his party by putting loyalty above everything; and it was loyalty which was the master key – and eventually the broken key – to Macmillan's technique. He defended his colleagues through thick and thin, over Suez, over Nyasaland, over Hola. It infuriated the opposition and the academic students of politics, and it fortified the cabinet and the party: as Arthur Butler wrote in *The Political Quarterly* in October 1959:

Despite four troubled years in office, ministers retained their aggressive and resilient front until the last – buoyed up by the confident expectation that the generalship of Harold Macmillan had assured them victory at the polls and a further term of office. It probably did not matter to them much that their successes had at times been founded on contempt for the best in the British political tradition.

Macmillan's scope for showmanship had been greatly increased by two inventions which made themselves fully felt during his premiership – jet planes and television. Jet planes speeded up the process of 'personal diplomacy', to the advantage, not only of Macmillan, but of Eisenhower, Kennedy, de Gaulle and Harold Wilson. These excursions increased the prime minister's prominence, compared to the opposition or to his own colleagues. They ensured dramatic headlines and patriotic reporting; and they made it harder for the opposition to attack the prime minister honourably, when he was representing his country abroad.

Television added to the personal predominance. In the four years since 1955, the proportion of homes with TV sets had increased from forty per cent to seventy per cent and, after the beginning of commercial TV in September 1955, television reporting became more intense and dramatic: the old 'fourteen-day rule' which limited topical discussions had been discarded, and both channels wanted big names with big news: they welcomed a peripatetic prime minister, and were contemptuous of little-known opposition spokesmen. Apart from the official party broadcasts, politicians were dependent on the invitations of news-minded producers; and the prime minister could always make news. Macmillan was well aware, as Baldwin had been with the wireless thirty years before, that the new medium gave him a unique chance to by-pass the Press lords and project himself – and nobody else – to the nation. His own television technique had steadily improved – particularly after his Australian tour – and had been acclaimed after an impromptu interview with Ed Murrow in May 1958, in which he appeared (said *The Spectator*) 'relaxed, easy and genial, every inch the favourite fireside politician': it was followed by a Gallup poll showing a greatly increased popularity. Macmillan spoke fondly of the new medium: he saw television as a way of bringing a more theatrical, nineteenth-century approach to politics to the whole electorate as a new development in 'Tory democracy'.

The helplessness of the opposition in this blaze of showmanship was illustrated by the rebounding of the two supposedly-ironic slogans – 'Macwonder', coined by Bevan, and 'Supermac', coined by the cartoonist Vicky. The irony was soon blown off, and the slogans became part of Macmillan's image. They underlined the importance for a prime minister in the television age, as for a film star, of keeping in the news; always to do something, to go somewhere. It was a lesson which Harold Wilson was painfully, but thoroughly, learning.

The popular appeal of Macwonder or Supermac was not so much due to his attempts at summits, as to his association with the new prosperity. It was as the prime minister of affluence that Macmillan established his mass popularity. Much of this association was accidental; whoever had been prime minister at this juncture would have benefited from the prevailing economic climate. But Macmillan had shown himself, from the 1930s as being a cheerful expansionist, determined to avoid deflation and unemployment, and wanting whenever possible to increase spending on social services.

His dread of slumps had, from the beginning, brought him into conflict with colleagues. His first chancellor, Peter Thorneycroft, had begun his stint in the same optimistic mood as Macmillan. The economic aftermath of Suez had been less serious than had been expected. Thorneycroft reduced the bank rate, and in April 1957 produced an optimistic budget with some relief of taxation. In his budget speech, in keeping with Macmillan's known views, he said

There are some who say that the answer lies in savage deflationary policies resulting in high levels of unemployment. They say that we should depress demand to a point at which employers cannot afford to pay and workers are in no position to ask for higher wages. If this be the only way in which to contain the wage–price spiral it is indeed a sorry reflection upon our modern society.

However precarious, the economic boom was spectacular to ordinary people, and was most visible in the rush of spending on cars, refrigerators, washing machines or TV sets, accelerated by TV advertising and hire purchase; after the long stagnation of the post-war years, this affluence was still a novelty. On 20 July 1957 Macmillan made a speech at Bedford, which seemed harmless enough at the time, but was to reverberate throughout the rest of his career. He began by saying that the general economic prospects were good, that dollar and gold reserves had risen by £88 million in the first half of the year, and that increased earnings came from increased production. He went on:

Indeed let us be frank about it: most of our people have never had it so good. Go round the country, go to the industrial towns, go to the farms and you will see a state of prosperity such as we have never had in my life-time – nor indeed ever in the history of this country.

Macmillan boldly repeated the boast in a major debate on 25 July, in a passage which, in view of later turns, deserves careful examination.

I confess that I find it rather a strange experience to sit here day after day and listen to the arguments and problems presented by high prices and over-full employment. When I first stood for the House of Commons in 1923, soon after the post-war boom broke, and for the next twelve or fifteen years, including four general elections, one problem and one problem only held the political field. It was the problem of deflation, violently and rapidly falling prices, and massive unemployment. We debated it, as many of the older Members here remember, week by week and day by day. We put forward all kinds of rival views as to how it should be solved. . . .

Today, it has somehow solved itself, but this new trouble has come which seems to dog our footsteps. Having solved one problem we have now the one we are discussing, that of rising prices. Every hon.

Member knows, and every man and woman in the country knows, that for the mass of the people – I would say for the great mass of the people – there has never been such a good time or such a high standard of living as at the present day. I repeat what I said at Bedford, they have 'never had it so good'. Curiously enough, that is what *The Daily Herald* says, under its revised management. It has chosen today to put an advertisement into the capitalist Press, *The Financial Times*, urging capitalist employers to use *The Daily Herald* as an advertising medium. This is the reason it gives, together with a little picture of young children and a car: 'Thousands of *Daily Herald* families already enjoy a car, but many more will be planning one in the near future if their standard of living continues to rise at the present rate.'

I can only repeat that I have been grateful to see the change. I believe that all of us in the House, certainly the older Members, feel grateful that there has been this great change. When I am told by some people, some rather academic writers, that inflation can be cured or arrested only by returning to substantial or even massive unemployment, I reject that utterly.

He repeated the words 'they've never had it so good' in a speech on 15 November, but went on to say: 'The luxuries of the rich have become the necessities of the poor, but people are asking "what is it all for?".'

This first Macmillan boom was precarious. During the summer of 1957 there was a sudden run on gold reserves – partly as a result of the devaluation of the French franc and the threatened revaluation of the mark – and by the autumn there was again an economic crisis. Thorneycroft quickly changed his line, and determined on deflation: he was backed by the Bank of England and by his two intimidating lieutenants in the Treasury, Enoch Powell and Nigel Birch, who between them raised the campaign against inflation into a kind of austerity crusade. With some difficulty, and with the help of the *eminence grise* outside the Treasury, Professor Robbins, Thorneycroft persuaded Macmillan and the cabinet to agree to some 'September measures' – which included cutting back on Government spending, and raising the bank rate to seven per cent.

In the following months the pound began to recover, and

Macmillan resumed his expansionist plans: but Thorneycroft's trio were still crusading against further inflation, and against the cabinet. The argument reached a head over the next budget estimates, which Thorneycroft, like other chancellors before and after him, wanted to hold at the same total figure as the previous year; which, since prices had risen, would mean cuts in social services. Deadlock followed. On 7 January all three Treasury ministers resigned. Thorneycroft, in his letter to Macmillan, said that he regarded the limitation of Government expenditure as 'a prerequisite to the stability of the pound, the stabilisation of prices and the prestige and standing of our country in the world'. Nigel Birch – the chief conspirator – said that, in the battle of inflation 'We were fighting to win and they were not'.

It might have been a more devastating blow than Salisbury's resignation nine months before. But Macmillan had the cabinet behind him, and he knew that politically deflation would not attract much support. He described the amount of money at issue – £50 million – as 'chickenfeed', and was able to appear to the public as the guardian of social services: 'Your resignation at the present time,' he replied angrily to Thorneycroft, 'cannot help to sustain and can only damage the interests which we have all been trying to preserve.' He put on his great show of calmness: he appointed Derick Heathcoat Amory to succeed Thorneycroft, referred casually to 'little local difficulties', and left the next day for his six-week tour of the Commonwealth.

By the time he got back, the 'little local difficulties' had apparently evaporated. The new chancellor was avoiding too much inflation, without tears; and Macmillan loftily congratulated himself in March:

The day I left for my Commonwealth tour I had a feeling that the strict puritanical application of deflation was in danger of being developed into a sort of creed. When I got back six weeks later I found quite a different atmosphere; people were beginning to talk about quite different problems. The real truth is that both a brake and an accelerator are essential for a motor car. . . .

Soon afterwards, on 12 March, he took the opportunity to set out his political philosophy in a long speech to the Conservative Political Centre called '*The Middle Way* – 20 years after', which celebrated the twentieth anniversary of his pre-war book. The two works make an odd contrast. The original book, with its charts about milk distribution and marketing schemes, was dull, honest and massively serious, like the work of a professor of economics. The speech twenty years later was mannered, exaggerated and very political. It began with a long attack on the menace of socialism:

I have been rather amused sometimes by the suggestion I see in the Press that I carry about with me some aura of Edwardian days; but at any rate I do not, like the leaders of the Labour party, spend my time peddling political panaceas that were already 'old hat' when Aristophanes was ridiculing Socrates.

It went on to a ponderous denunciation of egalitarianism:

Human beings, widely various in their capacity, character, talent and ambition, tend to differentiate at all times and in all places. To deny them the right to differ, to enforce economic and social uniformity upon them, is to throttle one of the most powerful and creative of human appetites. It is wrong, and it is three times wrong. It is wrong morally; because to deny the bold, the strong, the prudent and the clever, the rewards and privileges of exercising their qualities is to enthrone in society the worst and basest of human attributes: envy, jealousy and spite. It is wrong practically – I have said this before but do not hesitate to repeat it – because it is only by giving their heads to the strong and to the able that we shall ever have the means to provide real protection for the weak and for the old. Finally it is wrong politically; because I do not see how Britain, with all its rich diversity and vitality, could be turned into an egalitarian society without, as we have seen in Eastern Europe, a gigantic exercise in despotism.

In the rest of the speech, he re-stated his old view, that the Conservatives should always 'occupy the middle ground'. He had certainly kept his party shrewdly in the centre: but it was not long before he would find the middle ground had shifted.

In the following months, Macmillan continued to urge

expansion. Heathcoat Amory's budget in April 1958 was cautious and neutral, fearing to lose the confidence of the 'gnomes of Zurich' who had already made their entrance into British mythology. But soon afterwards there were signs of slump, and Amory began making large concessions, removing all controls from bank lending and hire purchase. Macmillan chaired a committee to set about reflation, and urged a bumper budget for next year. He got one, and the budget of 1959 was 'the most generous budget ever introduced in normal peace-time conditions'.[1] Macmillan himself insisted that 9*d.* should come off income tax, instead of 6*d.* which the Treasury wanted: and although Amory explained 'this is no spending spree budget', it was exactly that. It made 1959 the most spectacular boom year of Macmillan's premiership.

The stage was now set. Macmillan flew to see the Queen on 5 September, and announced a general election to be held on 8 October 1959. It was widely expected: the Parliament was over four years old, the Conservatives were riding high. A hot summer and the prospects of a summit completed the rosy scene. The Conservative party had been preparing for an election since June 1957, under the chairmanship of Oliver Poole, the banker and director of *The Financial Times*. He had launched a campaign of advertising and public relations which was to make history as the most elaborate and expensive of its kind: according to the calculations of Butler and Rose, £468,000 was spent between June 1957 and September 1959 on Press and poster advertising,[2] organized with the help of Colman, Prentis and Varley, and using such slogans as 'Life's Better Under the Conservatives. Don't let Labour Ruin It'. In September 1957 Macmillan rashly asked Lord Hailsham, his pre-war rival, to become chairman; he thought that Hailsham was capable of exciting the party's rank-and-file, and Hailsham and Poole – the showman and the technocrat – organized the election campaign together.

They let out an unprecedented bombardment of advertising and pamphleteering, ranging from a series of Press advertisements headed 'You're looking at a Conservative', to one-and-a-half million copies of a very comic pamphlet of strip-cartoons called *Form*, presenting the success stories of Tory leaders to the masses. It depicted Lord Hailsham as a young man wearing bright sweaters at Oxford, and Heathcoat Amory bronco-busting in the Argentine. The vulgarity of the campaign horrified many old-school Conservatives, and aroused both contempt and envy among Socialists: Richard Crossman said that Macmillan was being sold 'as though he were a detergent'.

Behind much of the Conservative campaign lay the theme of 'They've never had it so good' (though the phrase was not actually used), and the emphasis on the increasing standards of living. The evidence was striking for, as elsewhere, the consumer boom had transformed family life: in the four years since 1955, stimulated by the new goad of commercial television, refrigerators, washing-machines, lawn-mowers, as well as television sets, had come into millions of homes for the first time: the hire-purchase debt for durable goods had risen by £300 million in eighteen months. The number of cars had gone up from three-and-a-half million to nearly five million. For the three million investors in shares, the improvement was still more spectacular. The austerity of the post-war years had ended with a sudden spree, and the Labour party was still stuck with the image of ration-books and shortages. The Conservatives proclaimed 'You've had it good. Have it better. Vote Conservative.' The posters emphasized cars, new houses and grinning young people, in the classless world of the affluent suburbia, which Macmillan personally so much disliked.

The Conservative manifesto was called 'The Next Five Years' – an echo of Macmillan's group in the 1930s – and it began with Macmillan asking two leading questions: 'Do you want to go ahead on the lines which have brought prosperity at home?'; and 'Do you want your present leaders to represent you abroad?' Macmillan's statesman image had been reinforced by the arrival of Eisenhower a few days before the campaign opened, greeted by cheering crowds all the way from the airport: he and Macmillan appeared in a television conversation, on 31 August, sitting in Downing Street wearing dinner jackets (Macmillan's black tie as usual tucked under his collar): they talked about the pound, the prospects of a summit, and Anglo-American relations, which Eisenhower said 'have never been stronger and better than they are now'. Macmillan tried to make a summit part of the campaign, and on 30 September he said that a summit conference would be announced in 'a few days'; but he was quickly contradicted from the White House.

Macmillan was clearly enjoying himself: he travelled 2,500 miles on his election tour, spoke at seventy-four meetings, and seemed confident and relaxed. The party leaders were most anxious about his television image, and he did not appear in any party broadcast until the end. Eventually they asked Norman Collins, the tycoon-novelist, to advise them: Macmillan pre-recorded a careful talk, with a map and a globe, to emphasize his statesmanship, which he patted like a dog. The whole act failed and was later parodied in *Beyond the Fringe*.

The election result was by no means foregone. The Labour party excelled in jaunty television broadcasts, supervised by Anthony Wedgwood Benn, which projected a young lively party of the future. Morgan Phillips presided over vigorous Press conferences each morning, which made bold headlines. In addition to the committed Labour Press, *The Guardian*, *The Observer* and *The Spectator* – all disgusted by Macmillan's covering up of Suez and the Devlin report* – advised their readers to vote against the Government. A fortnight before the polls, Gaitskell was confident of winning, and the Conservatives seemed worried. Then Gaitskell made a rash statement, promising at Newcastle that 'there would be no increased income tax under a Labour Government'. Macmillan immediately pounced, and poured patronizing scorn on Gaitskell: 'Elections are a very severe test,' he said on 1 October, 'and Mr Gaitskell has managed to destroy in a week a reputation he had built up over a number of years. Mr Gaitskell has brought himself down to the level of Mr Harold Wilson.'

A few days before polling the big investors began buying

* See p. 182.

shares, particularly steel shares, and Stock Exchange prices began rising. Many cabinet ministers seemed unsure of the outcome, but Macmillan kept up the appearance of optimism. At the end of polling day, the result was very soon clear: the Conservatives were gaining marginal seats, and by one in the morning Gaitskell, depressed and exhausted, had conceded defeat. The eventual result gave the Tories a lead over Labour of 107, as against sixty-seven in the previous election. The Stock Exchange was in a frenzy of amazed delight. Some steel shares went up by as much as 10s., and all shares reached a new peak: 'Members of the Stock Exchange with up to forty years' experience had never witnessed such scenes,' said *The Times*. Since the 1955 election *The Financial Times* Share Index had risen from 199·4 to 268·6. It looked like 'casino capitalism'.

Macmillan took the news with studied calm: he said on television 'it has gone off rather well', and explained that the result showed that 'the class war is obsolete'. The Labour party, having lost for the third time in succession, began a period of gloomy self-analysis. 'The simple fact is,' said Patrick Gordon-Walker, 'that the Tories identified themselves with the new working class rather better than we did.' Many Labour leaders could not see the way out of opposition. If the workers no longer wished for social revolution, how could Labour compete with the Conservatives? And if they preferred a proud, patrician leader, how could Gaitskell outplay Macmillan? 'Tory democracy' had made an astonishing come-back, and to those who – like Macmillan – remembered the Tory gloom in the first post-war years, the revival was astonishing.

In a feat unprecedented in British political history [wrote Professor Beer], at each of the four succeeding general elections the party increased its share of the major two-party vote, and from 1951 remained in power with growing majorities in the House. It almost seemed as if that 'pendulum' on which writers on British politics had so long depended for a regular alternation of parties in power had ceased to swing against conservatism.[3]

But the success had a powerful backlash. At the time the election campaign did not arouse much open Tory criticism.

When Lord Altrincham (later John Grigg) attacked the campaign in the October issue of *The National and English Review*, he had no support from Tory M.P.s. Most Conservatives were too dazed by the recovery of their fortunes and too grateful for Macmillan's performance, to complain about the methods, and it seemed that their position was now unshakeable. But later, particularly after the Tory defeats in the 1964 and 1966 elections, many Conservatives came to blame the cynicism and opportunism of the 1959 election for their later demoralization: their view was summed up by William Rees-Mogg in *The Sunday Times*, who wrote in 1966:

Everyone knows now that Mr Macmillan's real contributions . . . are overshadowed by the failures of his last years, and the 'never had it so good' election which prepared the way for those failures. The record of history is that the short cut to a big election victory is to offer false reassurance; the record also is that when the reassurance is found to be false, it destroys the credit of a Prime Minister in a way nothing else can do, and destroys it for good.[4]

The phrase 'you've never had it so good', became in the following years a sour reminder of the materialism of the campaign: it was the phrase of Macmillan's which stuck most in the national memory. Why did it sound so hollow? It was quite true; it was said by a man who had seen the sufferings of the 1930s, and was happy to see the new prosperity; and it was accompanied by proper warnings of the new dangers of inflation. But it stuck out, not only because of its vulgarity – the same kind of vapid vulgarity of 'there aint gonna be any war' – but because of the implied patrician contempt for 'them', and the absence of any hint of idealism.

Macmillan himself kept on referring to the saying, and never repented it: in an interview with *The Daily Mail* in January 1961 he insisted 'We've got it good. Let's keep it good. There is nothing to be ashamed of in that'. His whole tone was a world away from the austerity of his family's 'Christian Socialism'.

Let's face it – the temptations of comfort are not an argument in favour of poverty. I think people resent, and rightly, the Victorian reformer's attitude. Is it right that the rich man can go to the Savoy, but the poor man can't have a drink in the pub? Moral standards? Perhaps things, for the time being, have gone a bit too much the other way. I am concerned about it. But the British people don't like being preached at. And I am not pessimistic about the general outlook.

Again, in November 1961 he said at the Mansion House: 'One often regrets impromptu remarks but I do not regret that one. What I do regret is that time and time again other people have taken it out of its context. For I was not making a boast but giving a warning.'

But it *was* a boast, as the original context makes clear. For Macmillan, and others of his generation, it may have seemed like the realization of a long ambition, the triumph after the years of the slump. But for the younger generation, it was not a boast which gave any satisfaction. Certainly the association with 'you've never had it so good' was regretted in the years after the election by many of his colleagues. As Lord Kilmuir wrote:[5]

On a more general level we utterly failed in these years to find a popular non-materialistic policy for the party. . . . 'You never had it so good' was true and appropriate in the context of 1959, but . . . lost its impact. This new feeling was difficult to define. It was 'anti-Establishment' but not anarchic; it embraced no existing political philosophy; it could not be explained in class or in economic terms . . . we were absolutely baffled by it. The return of idealism to politics caught both parties off balance, and the Conservatives suffered worst.

NOTES

1. Samuel Brittan, *The Treasury Under the Tories, 1951–1964* (Harmondsworth: Penguin, 1964), p. 202
2. D. E. Butler and Richard Rose, *The British General Election of 1959* (London: Macmillan, 1960), p. 21
3. S. H. Beer, *Modern British Politics* (London: Faber & Faber, 1965), p. 302
4. William Rees-Mogg, 'Three Big Winners: Baldwin, Macmillan and Wilson', *The Sunday Times*, 3 April 1966
5. Viscount Kilmuir, *Political Adventure* (London: Weidenfeld & Nicolson, 1964), p. 321

11. The Peak of his Power

Power? It's like a dead sea fruit.
When you achieve it there's nothing there.
HAROLD MACMILLAN[1]

After the 1959 election, Macmillan was at the height of his power and reputation, at home and abroad. At home, he had led his party to victory, restored his colleagues' confidence, and demoralized the opposition. Abroad, he had zigzagged towards a summit, and emerged as a world statesman.

He was an unlikely leader to be carrying Britain into the 1960s, but he had captured the public imagination. He had succeeded in disguising the painful retreat from Empire, and the wobbly state of the British economy, with bold excursions abroad, with the maintenance of the H-bomb, and much talk of Britain's greatness. He had presented a modernized 'Tory democracy', with the same kind of panache as Disraeli or Lord Randolph Churchill, and the same confidence that the British people would prefer, in the end, the rule of patricians to plebs. While ten years before Britain seemed settled as a Socialist country, now it seemed unchangeably Conservative. In the age of new-found plenty, such as all Europe was discovering, he was able to appear as a special magician.

Acting suited his temperament. Behind the façade, he was an isolated man, with the detachment of a don, and of an actor. He was the most intellectual prime minister since Asquith, and when he retreated from the political fray, he retreated more contentedly into a world of books than into a world of friends:

it remained significant that he 'learnt books before people',[2] and he would talk about books, and hover around book-shelves, as if he still saw them as a refuge from people. He talked, too, with the detached wit and articulateness of a don: he talked superbly, at his best with a few people, or in a cosy collegiate atmosphere. His voice was soft and expressive, with the old-fashioned precise emphases on words like sys*tim*, sur-*plus*, air*port*, and old Scottish pronunciations like *wheren't* for *weren't*. He described people with a fondness for categories and parallels which seemed to emphasize his scholastic back-ground (Sir David Eccles, he once said, 'was the only Old Wykehamist you could possibly mistake for an Old Harro-vian'). He loved to relate anything that happened to some historical – preferably classical – precedent, and his view of Britain seemed a part of his view of earlier empires. As he put it to me in 1961:

> People often don't realize that the Victorian age was only an inter-ruption in British history. The hundred years of British domination which ended in 1914 was a very rare thing in history – an Antonine age which only happens about once in a thousand years – and we can't expect it to happen again. The trouble is that a lot of people look back to that time of stability and expect to be able to carry on with it. They talk a lot about the glories of the old Elizabethan Age, but they forget that that was a time when Britain was politically very insecure, between much greater empires. We only kept the country going then by taking tremendous risks and adventures. It's more like that today – it's exciting living on the edge of bankruptcy.

When he talked, he did not seem to mind, or even to notice, whom he talked to: he liked to catch questions or topics, and to soliloquize, with the kind of theatrical business which made him seem almost self-generating. He had always liked acting: he had loved the music-halls in his schooldays, and was always coming out with comic songs. Before the war, his friends teased him about his theatrical tricks ('Harold, the cuff-shoot-ing season hasn't begun yet', he was told when he was declaim-ing at one dinner party). But now he had a part in keeping with his grand style, and he made the most of it; as with Disraeli, the day-dreams of a lifetime seemed to be coming to the surface. As he grew older, and into the part, his gestures became more eccentric: the shake of the head, the dropping of the mouth, the baring of the teeth, the pulling-in of the cheeks, the wobbling of the hand, the comedian's sense of timing – the whole bag of tricks seemed in danger of taking over, so that his intellectual originality was constantly surprising. He had a series of set pieces in tragic roles which he would constantly repeat to his colleagues, often with tears in his eyes – the veteran of Passchendaele, the champion of Stockton's unemployed, the trustee of future generations of children and grandchildren.

He loved being prime minister. Few prime ministers ever willingly give up the job, but Macmillan, like Disraeli, seemed self-consciously revelling in it, as if constantly saying to himself, 'I am the prime minister'. Once he was being driven in a car through London, and heard some people cheering him in the street; he turned to a private secretary and said: 'If only they knew!' He looked happiest of all in clubland, with its aura of faded Victorian romance, where he might have been living out his young ambition. His style of talk – the raillery, the reminiscences, the tongue-in-cheek – suited exactly the clubroom atmosphere: it had the ideal stage.

He was able to change his roles with bewildering speed: Lord Longford has described how he visited Macmillan in 1957 to seek his support in having the Lane pictures returned to Dublin. 'Before I left his mood changed for a second time. He had been the West End clubman; then the shrewd Scottish business type. Now, for a few minutes, he became the visionary, almost the original crofter peering out through the Western mists. . . .'[3]

But it was not his theatrical business that impressed his colleagues and opponents; it was the sheer speed and clarity of his mind. Behind the actor, there was always the intellectual lurking, assessing, balancing, watching for weak points. In the House of Commons, he had full scope for histrionics, which he abused, and at question time, which he hated, he was often arrogant and rude; but he could surprise and demolish a questioner with an incisive retort. In cabinet, from many accounts, his manner was quite opposite from the grand generalizations of his speeches: he was always – at least until his last year – able to apprehend difficult problems, and to sum up the points of difference and of common agreement. 'It won't be until the cabinet minutes are published in thirty years' time that his real quality will appear,' said one of his colleagues: 'in spite of all his grand talk about destiny, it was really in committees that he was best: I think he was really a fox, who wanted to be a hedgehog.'*

He had lost a lot of his pre-war zeal for organizational problems; like Disraeli, he got bored with details and felt, as one colleague put it, that 'details shouldn't be brought into the front room'; he disliked scientific jargon and enjoyed regarding experts as superior servants, and phrases like: 'We've got a man who's very good at that kind of thing.' He liked to spark off ideas, and let others follow them through. But he could still, when he wanted to, apply his mind very effectively to organization and planning. He was much involved, for instance, in the reorganization of the cotton industry, and later with urging Peter Thorneycroft to reorganize the Ministry of Defence. In 1961 it was he, rather than the chancellor, Selwyn Lloyd, who instituted the new planning machinery of 'Neddy', which marked the come-back of planning into Tory respectability.

His relations with industrialists, which had been his *forte* before the war, were now less happy; his aloof and mandarin style did not appeal to the new generation of professional manager-tycoons. His touch was illustrated by the remark 'Exporting is fun', which was included in a speech to businessmen in 1960. In fact, he never actually used the phrase; when he came to that part of his speech, he left it out; but the Press reported the written phrase, not the spoken one, and the words stuck. Months later, in December 1961, at a lunch for the

---

* 'The fox knows many things, but the hedgehog knows one big thing': see Isaiah Berlin's study of Tolstoy, *The Hedgehog and the Fox*.

Export Council for Europe, he referred to the phrase, and apologized for it, and reminded his listeners that he had himself been an exporter: 'I have now been working for about forty-one years; fifteen of them I have wasted in the service of the Government, twenty-six of them I have been trying to sell books in every part of the world. . . .' But the role of the shrewd businessman, which he adopted in private, was not one which Macmillan now played publicly with much enthusiasm.

It is said of prime ministers that they have no friends, and it was often said of Macmillan. Certainly he was very aloof from his cabinet colleagues, and very few of them saw the inside of his house, Birch Grove. His closest confidant in the cabinet was probably Lord Mills, with whom he did not have very much in common but with whom, not being a political rival, he could talk very freely: Mills gave him a comforting, though rather misleading, impression of being in touch with industry. He had a few old friends from earlier days, but their numbers were depleted. Ronald Knox, his old tutor, with whom he kept in touch, died in 1957. Harry Crookshank was another old friend from Eton and the Guards; he was an old-fashioned Tory M.P. of whom Macmillan wrote, in an appreciation in *The Times*, after he died in 1961, that he was a 'true Grenadier'.

His only really close colleagues were his own entourage in 10 Downing Street – a fact which many politicians resented. Macmillan went much further than Eden or Attlee – though not as far as Churchill – in turning his own office into a private court, a miniature White House, or – as he referred to it – 'my Vatican City life'. The more power that devolved around the prime minister, the more important his own advisers became. For almost the whole of his premiership he had the same group of people round him, confided in them, trusted them completely and, when he went abroad, took them with him: when he resigned, they were knighted or ennobled. In their varied characters, they seemed to embody the different elements in his own personality.

The most important of them was the secretary of the cabinet

and head of the Home Civil Service, Sir Norman Brook. Brook had been secretary to the cabinet under Attlee, Churchill and Eden; but Macmillan turned him into his personal adviser as well – giving him a power unique amongst civil servants. Brook was a man of massive discretion, dedicated to secrecy and conditioned to all the whims of politicians: with his slow voice and his bloodhound look, following Macmillan round the world, he sometimes seemed like an austere and academic variant on his master. Second to Brook in seniority was Macmillan's personal private secretary – first Frederick Bishop, whom he inherited from Eden, and then – for five years – Timothy Bligh, an adventurous and unconventional Treasury man, on whom Macmillan increasingly relied: he had political sense on top of his civil-service background, and developed antennae through Whitehall. An important figure for Macmillan was his 'public relations adviser', Harold Evans, a discreet professional civil servant who was guardian of Macmillan's unflappable image, and who was with him throughout his premiership. Another key adviser was Philip de Zulueta, his private secretary from the Foreign Office, who worked in Downing Street altogether for nine years.

But the most surprising of the entourage was John Wyndham – later Lord Egremont – whose special relationship with the prime minister made No 10 seem much more like a private court, and which raised some eyebrows in the rest of Whitehall. Wyndham, a wealthy, eccentric millionaire, had developed a lasting admiration for Macmillan in Algiers during the war, and had later rejoined him as an unpaid civil servant, first in the Foreign Office, then in the Treasury, and now in Downing Street. Wyndham admired Macmillan's courage and intellect; Macmillan on his side was clearly fascinated by Wyndham's outspokenness and his manners of a Restoration lording: it was a relationship, it seemed, rather like Johnson's and Boswell's. Macmillan used often to go to Petworth, the vast house where Wyndham lived in Sussex, and obviously enjoyed his company and way of life.

As Macmillan grew older, and his premiership wore on, so

he seemed more interested in the company of aristocrats and the surroundings of country houses, and less keen on middle-class or intellectual company. After the election, and in a reshuffle in 1960, he brought still more aristocrats into positions in the Government, to the vexation of ambitious young M.P.s: the prevalence of peers, particularly earls, became exceptional even for Tory governments: 'There has been nothing like it in England since the days of the eighteenth-century Duke of Newcastle,' claimed Christopher Hollis, an ex-Tory M.P.: 'and the record is today unparalleled by any country in the world save only Laos, Saudi Arabia and perhaps the Yemen.'⁴ In October 1960 he appointed his nephew by marriage, the Duke of Devonshire, to be under-secretary at the Commonwealth Relations Office, and later to be Minister of State: it was a defensible appointment if only because the Commonwealth is impressed by dukes, but it laid Macmillan further open to the charge of – literally – nepotism. Another controversial appointment was the Marquess of Lansdowne – who was interrelated with the Devonshires and the Cecils – to be under secretary of the Foreign Office, where he played a much-criticized role in Katanga.

Macmillan's aristocratic appointments were partly balanced by his promotion of self-made men: in October 1959 he made Ernest Marples, the exuberant construction tycoon, Minister of Transport; he promoted Harold Watkinson, a technocratic ex-businessman and journalist, to be Minister of Defence; and in 1960 he brought Edward Heath into the Foreign Office as number two to the wholly aristocratic Earl of Home. But he seemed less interested in the solid centre of the party. 'He enjoys the self-made men like Mills or Marples,' said one of his cabinet colleagues: 'it's the middle-class intellectuals, like himself, that he's bored by.'

The exact nature of Macmillan's snobbery was a matter of much discussion among his colleagues: it was not that it was a rare Tory characteristic; it was more that it was so out of keeping with his intellect. 'I think it's a special Scottish kind of snobbery,' said one of his cabinet: 'The Scots seem to keep an unreal view of the English aristocrats.' Macmillan himself enjoyed mocking snobs: he complained about the current obsession with 'The Establishment', and he said once:

People go on writing about the Foreign Office or the banks as if they were still run by three or four Whig families. The gossip columns go on writing about leisured aristocrats and butlers as if they were the people who really mattered. It's like going to a play, where the stage is full of chambermaids and butlers: I suppose that must be the sort of thing that people like to hear about.

But he himself seemed to be taking part in that kind of play.

He insisted that he chose his Government on merit, and he remarked in 1958 that he thought his cabinet was 'probably more non-U than the Socialists were: I wouldn't think there were more than four of them who are gentlemen in the strict sense of the term.' But he was always (his colleagues observed) very aware of the gradations of aristocracy while he professed to mock them: he would refer to someone jokingly as 'his lordship', but he would never forget that he was a lord.

It seemed odd that a man of Macmillan's well-based background, who was in a position to make peers and see through them, should remain so fascinated with the apparatus of aristocracy. When he eventually resigned, he refused the traditional offer of an earldom, or even of the Garter – though the Queen pressed it, and Churchill had accepted it. Was it that he did not wish to confuse the grand old aristocracy with the tawdry new? Was it that he did not wish to be bracketed with the other ex-premier earls, like Avon and Attlee? Was it a kind of arrogance, that he who had been the puppet-master did not wish to look like a puppet? Or was it, in the end, the Scots crofter's grandson, the plain proud Mr Macmillan, that was most important?

*

While Macmillan was on his way back from Africa, in February 1960, there occurred an episode that was politically unimportant, but which demonstrated both his old buccaneering instinct and his lifelong nostalgia for Oxford. The chancellorship of Oxford – an honorific post with few duties but scope for patronage – had fallen vacant after the death of Lord Halifax; and in a crafty manoeuvre the Oxford historian Hugh Trevor-Roper invited Macmillan to stand for the job, to do down the orthodox candidate, Sir Oliver Franks, who was already supported by most Oxford heads of colleges. The invitation arrived while Macmillan was on the ship, together with an explanation from Trevor-Roper of how Macmillan might win. Few people took the invitation seriously; but Macmillan replied that there was nothing that he would like more than to be chancellor, that he was quite ready for a fight, but that he must not commit himself till his return. To the horror of many colleagues, including Sir Norman Brook and Heathcoat Amory, Macmillan went ahead and faced the battle with obvious relish: 'It's like a fox-hunt,' he remarked: 'It's not so much what you get, it's the chase that counts.' The stage was set for a caricature of an Oxford election, full of venomous intrigue and lobbying, and elaborate arguments as to which of the two candidates represented 'the Establishment'. Trevor-Roper managed to make out a case that the prime minister was really the anti-Establishment candidate, the old rebel pitting himself against the faceless bureaucrats.

The prime minister, not surprisingly, won. *Mauricius Haraldus Macmillan* became Chancellor of Oxford. In the House of Commons Anthony Wedgwood Benn, after questioning the prime minister, said: 'May I also congratulate him on having proved by his own tremendous victory in a ballot held in Latin, open for all to see, that the Establishment has nothing to learn from the Electrical Trades Union?' Macmillan replied: 'Except that on this occasion, I think, the Establishment was beaten.' He had always liked having things both ways.

He was duly installed on 1 May, wearing the chancellor's gown of brocaded black silk trimmed with gold lace, and a cap which he wore back to front. He made a speech half in English half in Latin, and said 'I have always loved Oxford with a true and deep affection. I can never repay the debt that I owe to my college and my university. *Hic mihi dies semper recordandus erit, hic candido calculo notandus* (This is a day I shall always remember – a red letter day).' He favourably compared his election with a political election – 'no election address, no canvassing, no speeches, no television', and spoke nostalgically about the Oxford of his own undergraduate days, when there was no industry except a marmalade factory.

The first fruits of patronage came in June, when the new chancellor was allowed to nominate fourteen people to receive honorary doctorates of law: apart from official dignitaries, like the Archbishop of York and the vice-chancellor, he chose Selwyn Lloyd and Lord Home; his old Eton friend Crookshank; the historian Sir Lewis Namier, whom he had had published and revered; Dame Evelyn Sharp, his permanent secretary at the Ministry of Housing. Macmillan praised his honorands in Latin, calling Selwyn Lloyd 'my friend through many vicissitudes of fortune', and that evening they all had dinner at a Gaudy at Christ Church, when Macmillan, totally in his element, made another speech. 'I rather enjoy patronage,' he said, 'at least it makes all those *years* of reading Trollope seem worth while.'

Even before he became chancellor, he often made excursions to Oxford: in December 1959 he was invited to the Oxford Union to see a bust of himself unveiled by Walter Monckton (who as president of the Union in 1913 had given Macmillan his first chance to speak). Speakers reminded him that at Oxford he had supported socialist motions, and he replied, 'I knew I was once a liberal but I'd forgotten I was a socialist.'

But after he became chancellor he spent more and more of his time at Oxford – either in his official capacity, or visiting his grandson at Balliol, or visiting his old prep school, Summer Fields: and Oxford dons were astonished by his habit of accepting invitations. He often seemed prouder of being chancellor than of being prime minister. When he spoke to the Oxford Society in July 1960, after he had become chancellor, he said that those who had not known Oxford before 1940 were like those who, as Talleyrand said, had never known '*la douceur de la vie*' before the French Revolution. He talked of the beauty, charm and grace he remembered and said, 'It has given us more than we can ever hope to repay.'

His obsession with Oxford, and its most nostalgic aspects, underlined what was worrying most of his younger colleagues: that at a time of rapid technological change and opportunity, he was showing increasing distaste for the future. And Oxford, too, underpinned his confidence. 'I've always thought that his decline can be traced to when he became chancellor,' said one young Tory M.P.: 'After he got that, he felt there was nothing he couldn't do.'

NOTES

1. *Queen*, 22 May 1963
2. Ibid.
3. Lord Longford, *Five Lives* (London: Hutchinson, 1964), p. 100
4. Christopher Hollis, *Political Quarterly*, July 1961, p. 220

12. Africa

There is a wind of nationalism and freedom blowing round the world.
STANLEY BALDWIN, 1934

The most urgent problem confronting Macmillan after the 1959 election was Africa – and particularly Central Africa. Macmillan was not himself emotionally involved in the problem. He had never actually been there. As for others of his generation, Africa was a continent that had always seemed secondary to Asia, cut off from the rest of the world, and which had erupted, suddenly and mysteriously, since the war. 'It's like a sleeping hippo in a pool,' he said once; 'suddenly it gets a prod from the white man and wakes up; and it won't go to sleep again.' He never seemed much at ease in African company and tended – as on other shy occasions – to react with an over-heartiness of manner, and jovial expressions like: 'My dear friend!' But Africa was the last stage of the evacuation from Empire, which could not be avoided, and it was becoming regarded as the crucial uncommitted corner of the cold war.

The Conservatives were in a muddle. The two strands of Tory policy in Africa – the traditional relationship with the white communities in the south and the new support for independent black States in the north – were increasingly in conflict, and caught between them was the Central African Federation. As soon as he became prime minister, Macmillan had had to grapple with the Federation, and in particular with

its prime minister, Sir Roy Welensky. The deteriorating relationship between Macmillan and Welensky was to provide a
constant drama over six years. Welensky, a square-shaped ex-
railway driver and heavyweight boxer, with a most persuasive
voice, was a man in a heroic pioneer mould: he was determined
to maintain the Federation, with a white government at the
head of it; and he enjoyed the support of a vocal sector of right-
wing Conservatives, and the hard core of the 'Rhodesia lobby',
including many who had helped to put Macmillan into power
in the first place. Welensky began by admiring the 'resolution, skill and courage' of Macmillan, and at the prime
ministers' conference of 1957 was much impressed by his
Churchillian qualities. But Macmillan soon came round to
the view that Welensky was an obstacle in his retreat from
Africa: and Welensky was to prove no match for Macmillan's
tactics – his most elaborate exercise in ambiguity.

The first crisis came in 1959 – a year which set the seal on
British colonial rule in Africa. In March, Africans began protesting and rioting in Nyasaland, Southern Rhodesia declared
a state of emergency and Northern Rhodesia banned the principal African party, led by Kenneth Kaunda. In Nyasaland, 851
Africans were detained, and the Government alleged that the
Africans were plotting a massacre. The Tories came under
heavy fire, and the Colonial Secretary Alan Lennox-Boyd –
who was presiding over his dwindling Empire with genial
pessimism – appointed an independent and quite Irish judge,
Sir Patrick Devlin, to investigate with three other commissioners. They produced a highly-charged report which stated,
sensationally, that 'Nyasaland is – no doubt temporarily – a
police state'.

The British Government rejected the report, and simultaneously published a contradictory report from the Governor of
Nyasaland. Macmillan seemed to be behaving, as he had after
Suez, as if nothing had happened: it was the low point of his
political morality. But he had become aware that the problems of Africa were inescapable, and in July, just before
the Devlin report was published, he announced that an advi-

sory committee would be set up which, he explained blandly, would 'dispel widespread ignorance of the purpose and working of federation'.

The white Rhodesians, from the beginning, were suspicious of the commission. Macmillan sent out first Lord Perth and then Lord Home to sound out Welensky, and gradually – 'as soothing as cream and as sharp as a razor', as Welensky put it – persuaded him to accept the idea of a commission. By September, Macmillan had suggested as chairman his old Balliol friend Lord Monckton, an urbane lawyer with a reputation for settling big cases out of court, whom Welensky accepted; and in the next months the other members, including five Africans, were with difficulty assembled.

The Labour party refused to take part, suspecting with some reason that the commission would be a white-wash; but Macmillan managed to persuade Lord Shawcross, an ex-Labour minister and a great friend of Monckton's, who agreed to join after a private assurance from Macmillan that no solution to the federation would be ruled out – not even secession. In the House of Commons Macmillan said that the commission would be free in practice to hear all points of view, but said nothing about the issue of secession. He reassured Welensky, however, that the British Government had no intention of making an extension of the commission's terms of reference to include secession. Thus began Macmillan's intricate diplomatic manoeuvre.

In the meantime came the general election, and Macmillan's triumphant return. The right wing, including Lord Hailsham, was less in evidence, and it was made clear that Macmillan's new Government intended to grapple with the new Africa.

The first sign of earnestness was spectacular: Macmillan decided to go out to Africa himself. Officially it was described as a continuation of the Commonwealth tour of two years before, but in fact it had a more special purpose.

The party began their tour at Accra, which was not exactly a success. Nkrumah was ebullient in public, but only spent two hours alone with Macmillan, and gave a noisy anti-colonialist tirade in the middle of the visit. Macmillan made a careful speech at a banquet, including a reference to a 'wind of change'; but hardly anyone noticed the phrase (which had, anyway, been used by Lord Home months before).

In Nigeria, his next stop, he was more enthusiastically received. In Ibadan he toured the university, unruffled by the sudden appearance of a procession of protesters proclaiming 'HAIL MCNATO' and 'LORD MALVERN IS AN ASS. TELL HIM SO.' Just before he left he was questioned by a fiery Nigerian journalist about his plans for Nyasaland and Northern Rhodesia, and in an unguarded moment he said that 'the people of the two territories will be given an opportunity to decide on whether the federation is beneficial to them'.

He arrived in Salisbury, the capital of the federation, to find a furore. His statement in Lagos had been heavily reported, and interpreted (not surprisingly) as allowing the territories the right to secede: and to make things worse the Rhodesians were incensed by a remark that Lord Shawcross had recently made in a television interview on *Face to Face*, implying that he would feel quite free to recommend the break-up of federation if necessary. Macmillan skilfully assuaged Welensky by explaining that his Lagos statement had been misreported (which it had not), and that 'it is certainly not the function of the Commission to destroy the Federation; on the contrary, it is to find means by which the Federation can go forward'. He made a long, careful speech, mixing praise of the Rhodesian pioneers and Lord Malvern with some sly reminders:

In much of the present controversy [he said] the origins of federation seem to have been forgotten or misrepresented. It was not a plan to enable one territory to obtain some advantage for itself. It was a plan to enable all, by co-operation to gain mutual advantages. . . .

Macmillan was asked by a group of reporters (of whom I was one) whether it was conceivable that the commission could recommend the break-up of federation. He shrugged his shoulders and said: 'Well, I suppose if they all agreed that nothing could be done, they might have to say so. It would be like that rhyme from Belloc:

They answered as they took their fees
"There is no cure for this disease".

But Welensky, as it turned out, was not assuaged for long: for, five days later, Dr Banda, in jail in Nyasaland, had a visit from his lawyer, Dingle Foot, which was secretly tape-recorded and relayed, two days later, to Welensky. Foot tried to persuade Banda to give evidence to the Monckton Commission. He told him that Macleod was very anxious to release him; and that Lord Monckton was 'certainly taking the line that he is not going to be restricted by the terms of reference'. Welensky having received the transcript of this interview, tried to ask Macmillan about Banda's release, but found him evasive, and complained that only after Macmillan had left was he told that Macmillan and Macleod had decided to release Banda. Welensky began to realize what he was up against.

In the meantime Macmillan had moved on to his terminus, South Africa. It was a tense visit. Macmillan had been under heavy fire in London for going to South Africa at all, and thus seeming to condone *apartheid*: he was not to be allowed to see any African leaders, and most of his tour had been carefully arranged beforehand, to take him to the showplaces of Dr Verwoerd's Government. He toured round a model African township, 'Meadowlands', and was entertained in the police station: he was taken to a new 'tribal university'; he was welcomed by tribal chiefs in Swaziland, and awkwardly brandished a *knopkierie* and shields. He seemed to enjoy the company of English South African businessmen, but with his Afrikaner hosts his relations were uneasy: he was coldly received by their foreign minister, Eric Louw, and had a brisk Press conference with Dr Verwoerd, where only one journalist dared ask questions. Among the Africans his visit was the object of great suspicion: a demonstrator shouted 'He's going to be like Montgomery!', and slogans were paraded saying 'WE'VE NEVER HAD IT SO BAD'.

In Cape Town he was the personal guest of Dr Verwoerd, in the prime minister's house, *Grote Schuur*, built by Cecil Rhodes. Verwoerd entertained him with gentle courtesy, and Macmillan was astonished by his host's biblical confidence, and by the Calvinist household. The climax of the visit was to be a speech by Macmillan to both Houses of the South African Parliament. It was expected to be a congratulatory one, on the golden wedding of the Union of South Africa (the streets were full of celebratory flags). No one was expecting that Macmillan had carried through Africa a speech outlining Britain's policy towards Africa. The speech had in fact been drafted two months before by Sir John Maud, who had visited London to advise Macmillan, had been rewritten by Macmillan and Sir Norman Brook, and touched up through the tour. Verwoerd had not been shown it, but he had been told the gist of it on the evening before.

I watched the speech being made, from the balcony of the crowded House of Assembly in Cape Town. It was a performance very unlike the usual noisy debating of the South African Parliament, and the members were at first dazed by the rhetoric and historical scope of the speech. It began with elaborate compliments to South Africa's progress and courage in war, and quietly led on to an exposition of African nationalism which Macmillan, with superb deftness, compared to Afrikaner nationalism:

The most striking of all the impressions I have formed since I left London a month ago is of the strength of this African national consciousness. In different places it may take different forms, but it is happening everywhere. The wind of change is blowing through the continent. Whether we like it or not, this growth of national consciousness is a political fact. We must all accept it as a fact. Our national policies must take account of it. Of course, you understand this as well as anyone. You are sprung from Europe, the home of nationalism. And here in Africa you have yourselves created a full nation – a new nation. Indeed, in the history of our times yours will be recorded as the first of the African nationalisms.

He went on to explain the importance of keeping the African

States away from the Communist *bloc* and then, with courtesy but firmness, came to the nub of the speech, the dissociation from South Africa's policies.

It is the basic principle for our modern Commonwealth that we respect each other's sovereignty in matters of internal policy. At the same time, we must recognize that, in this shrinking world in which we live today, the internal policies of one nation may have effects outside it. We may sometimes be tempted to say to each other, 'Mind your own business'. But in these days I would myself expand the old saying so that it runs, 'Mind your own business, but mind how it affects my business, too'.

Let me be very frank with you, my friends. What governments and parliaments in the United Kingdom have done since the war in according independence to India, Pakistan, Ceylon, Malaya and Ghana, and what they will do for Nigeria and the other countries now nearing independence – all this, though we take full and sole responsibility for it, we do in the belief that it is the only way to establish the future of the Commonwealth and of the free world on sound foundations.

All this, of course, is also of deep and close concern to you, for nothing we do in this small world can be done in a corner or remain hidden. What we do today in West, Central and East Africa becomes known to everyone in the Union, whatever his language, colour or tradition.

Let me assure you in all friendliness that we are well aware of this, and that we have acted and will act with full knowledge of the responsibility we have to you and to all our friends. Nevertheless, I am sure you will agree that in our own areas of responsibility we must each do what we think right. What we think right derives from long experience, both of failure and success in the management of our own affairs.

We have tried to learn and apply the lessons of both. Our judgement of right and wrong and of justice is rooted in the same soil as yours – in Christianity and in the rule of law as the basis of a free society.

This experience of our own explains why it has been our aim, in countries for which we have borne responsibility, not only to raise the material standards of living but to create a society which respects the rights of individuals – a society in which men are given the opportunity to grow to their full stature, and that must in our view include the opportunity to have an increasing share in political power and responsibility; a society in which individual merit, and individual merit alone, is the criterion for man's advancement whether political or economic.

Finally, in countries inhabited by several different races, it has been our aim to find the means by which the community can become more of a community, and fellowship can be fostered between its various parts. . . .

It may well be that in trying to do our duty as we see it, we shall sometimes make difficulties for you. If this proves to be so we shall regret it. But I know that even so, you would not ask us to flinch from doing our duty. You, too, will do your duty as you see it.

I am well aware of the peculiar nature of the problems with which you are faced here in the Union of South Africa. I know the differences between your situation and that of most of the other States in Africa. . . .

As a fellow member of the Commonwealth, it is our earnest desire to give South Africa our support and encouragement, but I hope you won't mind my saying frankly that there are some aspects of your policies which make it impossible for us to do this without being false to our own deep convictions about the political destinies of free men, to which in our own territories we are trying to give effect.

I think we ought as friends to face together – without seeking to apportion credit or blame – the fact that in the world of today this difference of outlook lies between us . . .

He then concluded – as if he had been saying nothing very much – with an attack on boycotts and some conventional sentiments about the Commonwealth. It was a speech of masterly construction and phrasing, beautifully spoken, combining a sweep of history with unambiguous political points. It was probably the finest of Macmillan's career.

The reaction to the speech in South Africa was a double-take. The House applauded it, Dr Verwoerd politely agreed to differ, and in the lobby afterwards the M.P.s were enthusiastic about the oratory: they seemed flattered to hear South Africa involved in this great historical survey. It was only after the London papers had interpreted the speech and headlined the 'Wind of Change' that its message became sharper. 'Although Mr Macmillan has acknowledged our special position,' wrote the nationalist *Die Burger*, 'he also made it clear that Britain could no longer afford to be seen in our company when certain of our affairs are broached.' 'He gave the African people some inspiration and hope,' said the banned African leader Albert Luthuli. But Macmillan's Edwardian manner and his Kiplingesque appearance, and the very fact that he had troubled to come to South Africa (the first British prime minister to do so), still made his presence reassuring to the whites; and when he drove through Cape Town to the ship that was to take him back to England, he was cheered by the white South Africans whom he had just diplomatically disowned.

The 'Wind of Change' speech was not in fact very original, and it was quite tactful. (Macmillan had wanted to quote Melbourne's dictum that 'Nobody ever did anything very foolish except from some high principle', but he thought better of it.) The dissociation from *apartheid* had been made before at the United Nations, and Britain's willingness to grant independence to black Africa was obvious. But it seemed to remove a large ambiguity about Britain's choice in the time of crisis: only a year before, Lord Home had said that Britain and South Africa were 'two countries on the same side in the essential task of securing the safety and liberty of the free peoples of the world'. Macmillan's speech made it clear that the two countries were not necessarily on the same side, and it was backed up – as Macmillan warned Verwoerd – by the withdrawal of British support at the United Nations.

As it turned out, the speech probably had more influence in encouraging African nationalists elsewhere than in changing the South African situation. In the next months much of it became outdated, and (as Kilmuir reported) 'neither Macmillan nor his colleagues had any conception of the mine he had unwittingly exploded'. Nineteen-sixty, which was to be 'the Year of Africa', generated 'winds of change' all over the continent and the phrase, never very original, soon became a cliché. Even while Macmillan was in South Africa, a conference in Brussels was deciding to give independence to the Congo in June; and Nigeria and Tanganyika were both due for independence. Macmillan soon seemed alarmed by the repercussions of his phrase. He said in a television broadcast on 16 March, illustrated by film shots of Africa: 'In Cape Town I spoke of the wind of change that was blowing through Africa. But that's not the same thing as a howling tempest which would blow away the whole of the new developing civilization. We must, at all costs, avoid that.'

And in South Africa, only two months after Macmillan's visit, there was a massacre of sixty-two Africans at Sharpeville which seemed likely, at the time, finally to isolate South Africa from the world. A state of emergency was proclaimed, 1,700 people were detained, Dr Verwoerd was shot and the value of South African shares dropped by £650 million. Most of the world protested. It seemed then that South Africa would never revert to a close relationship with Britain. But gradually a kind of normality returned, South Africa had first a recovery, then a boom. Investment surged back, and Britain's relationship was not at the end of it very different from before Macmillan's speech. The 'wind of change', as it turned out, blew everywhere *except* in South Africa.

In the meantime, throughout 1960, Macmillan's main problem was still Welensky: the Federation was much more dangerous in Westminster politics than South Africa. The new Colonial Secretary, Iain Macleod, set about with great ingenuity preparing new constitutions and 'fancy franchises' for Nyasaland and Northern Rhodesia, which would satisfy African demands without outraging the whites: it was an exercise which required all Macleod's bridge-playing skills; 'juggling,' as Welensky put it, 'with never fewer than three balls in the air'. Immense ingenuity was devoted to these relatively tiny populations of five million people; it was as if all the imperial experience of Britain over a hundred years was narrowed down to this small sector of Africa. Macleod's subtlety was added to Macmillan's. As Welensky complained:

I found Iain Macleod very difficult to understand. I doubt if we ever talked the same language. He seemed to believe that, as Secretary of State, he had a great and challenging mission, which he was ruthless in carrying out; and if resisted or criticized he tended to become bitterly angry. He was subtle and secretive; but in face of rational, firm opposition he could not always control his own feelings.[1]

Then, in September 1960, the Monckton report was completed. It was a remarkable document: twenty-three of the twenty-six members signed a report recommending, among many other things, that there should be a broader federal franchise, that Northern Rhodesia should have an African majority in the legislature and, most important, that the British Government should declare its intention to permit the secession of any territory after a trial period. Duncan Sandys flew out to see Welensky, in an electric atmosphere: 'We both knew,' said Welensky, 'that this terrible piece of high explosive, with a four-weeks' time-fuse attached to it, lay between us.' Welensky wrote to Macleod saying 'As I anticipated from the beginning, the report is a disaster', and also to Macmillan – who was about to leave for the United Nations – repudiating the references in the report to secession.

Macmillan and his ministers managed to restrain Welensky, who then wrote a sad note to Lord Home, whom he always regarded as his ally, saying 'I cannot escape the feeling that I have been pretty gullible over all this'. On 11 October the Monckton report was published, and immediately afterwards Welensky publicly protested that the commissioners had been allowed, against all promises and terms of reference, to discuss secession. *The Times* said that the commissioners had shown 'intelligence, knowledge, and vision'. *The Daily Express* said that the Government should have thrown the report on the fire.

In March 1961, at the Commonwealth conference in London, South Africa was about to become a republic, and the question of her membership of the Commonwealth came up again. Several African States were determined to force her out. Macmillan, who presided, was anxious for South Africa to remain in the Commonwealth, and used all his art to moderate both sides. Verwoerd was friendly, diplomatic, but eventually obdurate on a crucial point; he could not allow a black High Commissioner in Pretoria. There was a long silence, broken by the Nigerian High Commissioner, Balewa, who insisted that South Africa must agree, or leave the Commonwealth. South Africa left. Welensky commented: 'The way in which this decision was forced by the new members of the Commonwealth and calmly accepted by the old – with the exception of Australia – showed how far and how quickly we had travelled down the road to dissolution.'²

Macmillan was clearly gloomy: Kilmuir reported 'I have never seen Macmillan so utterly miserable and distressed'. In an eloquent speech introducing a debate on South Africa on 22 March, Macmillan said that he had always thought that there were good arguments for allowing South Africa to remain in the Commonwealth, while expressing strong disapproval of her racial policies; and he went on to explain that he was not satisfied that South Africa's exclusion from the Commonwealth 'would best help all those European people who do not accept the doctrine of *apartheid*, nor as far as I could see would it help the Africans . . . moreoever it seemed to me that there was a danger of falling into a somewhat Pharisaical attitude in this. In my view – and I am not ashamed to say so – it was better to hold out our hands and help than to avert our eyes and pass by on the other side.' 'I am convinced,' he went on, 'that had Dr Verwoerd shown the smallest move towards an understanding of the views of his Commonwealth colleagues, or made any concession, I still think the Conference would have looked beyond the immediate difficulties to the possibilities of the future.' But Verwoerd refused to relax 'the extreme rigidity of his dogma' and it became apparent that he must withdraw his application.

During the Commonwealth conference, Welensky had dinner alone with Macmillan at Admiralty House:

He was always one of the most accomplished actors in public life [recollected Welensky afterwards], and in the three hours I spent with him he put on a truly magnificent performance. As he spoke of his deep sympathy and understanding of us in Africa, his eyes were moist and shining and his voice vibrated with emotion. Paddling out into this tide of words, I mentioned recent happenings in Northern Rhodesia. The tears rolled down Macmillan's cheeks. 'Roy, do you really believe that I, who have seen the horror of two world wars, would have tolerated a situation in which Britishers would have been shooting down Britishers, their brothers, alongside whom they had fought on many a battlefield?'

'Before you go any further, Harold,' [Welensky replied (according to his own account)] 'you'd better understand that I sent a Canberra up to Nairobi last month. I know you were gathering aircraft and troops there. Where else in the world were you going to use them except against us?'

'But of course,' sighed Macmillan, 'of course, Roy, we all make mistakes. Those aircraft and those troops weren't to be used against you. We were collecting them in case you needed help, and we should have had them ready for you.'[3]

The long retreat from federation continued, with frequent digressions and complications, for the following two years: there was perpetual wrangling, but not only between London and Salisbury, but between Macleod and Sandys inside the cabinet, who disagreed about the pace of advance in Northern Rhodesia, and whose differences were repeatedly coming up in cabinet. Macleod seemed to be feeling the strain of his involvement with Africa, and Macmillan – his colleagues noticed – was often irritated by Macleod's passion. In October 1961, in a reshuffle, his place was taken by a much more phlegmatic Colonial Secretary, Reginald Maudling who, together with Sandys, continued the gradual and painful extrication.

It became steadily clearer that Macmillan's Government had one preoccupation with Africa – to get out of it. Welensky recorded a notorious lunch with Duncan Sandys on his visit to Salisbury in February 1962, at which Lord Alport and Julian Greenfield were also present. Welensky insisted that it would not be difficult to keep Nyasaland in the Federation: 'No, Roy,' replied Sandys: 'you see, we British have lost the will to govern.' Welensky's colleague Julian Greenfield snapped back

'But we haven't'. Welensky had migraine that night, and reported that Alport vomited.[4] Alport denied that he was taken ill, but said 'I was extremely angry. I realized that quite inadvertently Sandys had given to the Rhodesian critics of British policy an apparent justification for the myth that they were so busily creating to the effect that Britain was played out and spineless.'[5]

In February 1962 Maudling put forward a new constitution for Northern Rhodesia, which prepared the way for an African majority, and Welensky, in a fury, flew to London to see Macmillan. Welensky accused Macmillan of giving in to threats, and Macmillan replied with a lecture on the dangers of using force: 'It is too simple a reading of history to think that you can exercise control simply by the use of power.'[6]

After only five months in the job, Macmillan promoted Maudling to be Chancellor of the Exchequer, and to handle Central Africa he turned to the most ingenious negotiator of all, R. A. Butler, who now took charge of all Central African affairs, with firm briefing from Macmillan. Butler took on his disagreeable assignment with characteristic urbanity: he went out to Salisbury, got on well with Welensky, and reduced the diplomatic temperature by the use of boring detail: back in London, he encouraged investors to put money in the Federation, while privately dropping dark hints about a looser confederation, with no place for 'a Bismarck' (i.e. Welensky). Butler delayed and concealed the outcome as far as he could, but by 19 December he finally announced that Nyasaland could withdraw from the Federation: on the same day Welensky retorted (no doubt remembering his lunch with Sandys): 'I say that Britain has lost the will to govern in Africa and is utterly reckless of the fate of the inhabitants of the Federation. By contrast we in the Federation have neither lost faith in ourselves nor in our will to govern decently and fairly.'

The final break-up of the Federation followed next year: in March Welensky came to London for talks: Butler read him a draft statement saying 'any Territory must be allowed to secede if it so wishes', and Welensky promptly refused to go on to lunch with Macmillan. Butler and his officials went out to Victoria Falls in June, to preside over the funeral arrangements with deliberate dullness, submerging high emotions with mountains of facts. The difficult dismantling of the Federation began, creating the two new States of Malawi and Zambia. Welensky complained that 'The most hopeful and constructive experiment in racial partnership that Africa has seen in our time has been wantonly destroyed by the Government which only ten years earlier gave it its impetus': and he reflected that 'Harold Macmillan's mind was the most complicated I have encountered in my political life'.[7]

Welensky certainly seemed gullible, and he had (if his memoirs are to be taken at their face value) a capacity to be repeatedly astonished by British double-dealing which seems odd for one who was himself no mean hand at humbug. But certainly Macmillan was enormously evasive, made more so by his successive ministers, and sometimes unnecessarily so. They succeeded, again and again, in avoiding direct confrontations with Welensky, in blurring the issue with conflicting statements, and in delaying the final outcome until it seemed as if the Federation was destroying itself.

Macmillan's operation resembled, in miniature, de Gaulle's operation in Algiers; both leaders were put into power by their right wing, and then turned against it: and Macmillan's withdrawal from the Federation was the ironic end-game to his advocacy of the Suez war. Macmillan succeeded – as a Labour prime minister might not have succeeded – in avoiding a major clash, or a major division in Britain. Welensky, constantly hoodwinked by soothing diplomacy, was never able to muster an effective opposition inside the Tory party; and as the months and years passed, the British interest in the Federation gradually diminished.

But the hard core of the problem remained – the 250,000 white settlers in Southern Rhodesia: and that problem Macmillan never faced up to. The more his Government were seen to be withdrawing from the Federation, for reasons of expediency rather than moral disapproval, the more the settlers in Southern Rhodesia hardened their attitudes, confident that the British had 'lost the will to govern'. The United Nations took growing interest, and passed successive resolutions in debates in which Britain played no part: and Britain, while disallowing the United Nations' right to intervene, in what they regarded as a private affair, took no steps herself: as a radical Conservative M.P., Humphry Berkeley, protested in July 1962,

We find ourselves in the worst of all possible worlds. We are generally held to be responsible for what is going on. We have publicly, but to the outside world somewhat unconvincingly, established the fact that we are not responsible. At the same time, apparently, we feel inhibited from criticizing the actions of the Southern Rhodesia government.

The course was already set that would lead to Rhodesia declaring independence. This was the price of Macmillan's avoidance of confrontation, and his slow retreat from Federation: that it left in the middle of Africa a white community confident, with good reason, that Britain would not intervene.

NOTES

1. Roy Welensky, *4000 Days* (London: Collins, 1964), p. 187
2. Ibid., p. 304 3. Ibid., p. 305 4. Ibid., p. 319
5. Lord Alport, *The Sudden Assignment* (London: Hodder & Stoughton, 1965), p. 168
6. Roy Welensky, *4000 Days*, p. 323
7. Ibid., p. 361

13. The Purge

I think the Prime Minister has to be a butcher,
and know the joints. That is perhaps
where I have not been quite competent in knowing the ways
that you cut up a carcass.

LORD BUTLER[1]

On the home front, Macmillan's Government after the general election seemed for a time very secure. Throughout 1960, although there was discontent among young Tory M.P.s that Macmillan was doing nothing with his majority, the polls and by-elections were in the Tories' favour. The Labour party were preoccupied by their own bitter division about nuclear policy; and the summit, in spite of its failure, had distracted attention from the stagnation of Macmillan's domestic policies. Whitehall was becoming increasingly worried about Britain's economic future, coming round to the Common Market, and facing the 'Great Reappraisal'; but the British public were still basking in the mood of 'never had it so good'.

By 1961, however, the dangers of Macmillan's complacency were already becoming more apparent, and the course was set for his greatest crisis. Selwyn Lloyd, who had become chancellor in July 1960, followed Macmillan's inflationary policies, and was not much worried by the growing balance of payments deficit. In the fateful 1961 budget, he was still not much worried: he relaxed surtax, without making any attempt at taxing capital gains, thus proclaiming a 'rich man's budget'. ('How any set of politicians can be so hamfisted as to do one without the other and then introduce a wage pause three months later passes belief,' commented Samuel Brittan later.[2]) Soon afterwards, as wages galloped ahead, the Government were faced with a fully-fledged sterling crisis, made worse by the revaluation of the German mark in March and subsequent rumours of the devaluation of the pound.

The Treasury officials panicked, and Selwyn Lloyd had to introduce a 'little budget' in July, which put up the bank rate to seven per cent, increased consumer taxes and forced a much fiercer squeeze on Government spending and bank overdrafts. Most important, and most damaging to the Tories, Lloyd instituted the 'pay pause' to stop the spiralling wages. Though clumsily enforced, and very badly presented, it represented the first serious attempt towards an incomes policy, which five years later was to be far more widely accepted. But, accompanied by the inequality of the earlier budget, its effects on Tory popularity were disastrous. In the following winter, as unemployment rose, resentment grew. In the following March there were three fateful by-elections. At the first, Blackpool North, the Tory majority slumped by 15,000. At the second, Middlesbrough East, the Tory vote, upset by the arrival of a Liberal, went down by 12,000: in the third, at Orpington, the Tories lost nearly 10,000 votes and the Liberals took the seat from the Tories.

The shock of Orpington, and the other by-elections in the spring of 1962, finally broke the complacency of the Tory party. Macmillan had now been prime minister for five years, and the heroic days of the 1959 election and 'Supermac' were fading. The credit squeeze was biting. To many observers Orpington, with its trim suburban hedges, seemed to show the backwash of affluence – the disillusion and worry with mortgages and hire-purchase. Orpington itself turned out to be a freak, and has continued to be so ever since; but it broke the assumption of 'they've never had it so good' – that people who had come up in the world would turn to the Tories.

Macmillan seemed less shaken by the setbacks than many of his colleagues. The day after Orpington, he spoke to party workers, in carefully unflappable tones: 'We have lost a number of skirmishes, perhaps a battle, but not a campaign. In war it is a characteristic of our country to concentrate on winning the last battle, which we usually do.' He admitted that there was sense of disappointment and even shock, but said that 'It is not a time to lose our nerve, which I am sure you will not do'. It was he, in fact, who was to lose his nerve.

As the fortunes of the Conservatives began falling away, Macmillan realized that he must revitalize the party. The 'purge' which was to follow was to be a major trauma for the Tory party, and it is important to analyse Macmillan's thinking in some detail. He realized that if there were to be an election in the autumn – which seemed likely at the time – he would need younger men, who could project a new conservatism, who might even win the election but who, if they lost, would be prepared to fight in opposition. Macmillan discussed the changes with some of his colleagues; he let it be known that Kilmuir and Mills, both rising seventy, were quite ready to go; that Watkinson had mentioned that he'd like some time to go back into business; that David Eccles, too, wanted a change of job; and that John Maclay, the Secretary of State for Scotland, whose wife was ill, would like to retire. There was a faint sound of musical chairs, but no great sense of urgency.

But the central, and most embarrassing, problem was the chancellor – against whose policies, and particularly the pay pause, a good deal of the grumbling had been directed. Macmillan's relationship with Selwyn Lloyd, for nearly five years, had been exceptionally close. In the retreat from Suez, his loyalty to Lloyd had been dogged: politicians and Bernard Levin went on mocking Lloyd's nervous speeches, and anxious appearance, and his subservience to the prime minister ('Why do we attack the monkey,' said Aneurin Bevan, 'when the organ-grinder is here?'); but Macmillan kept him on and on, and behind his public diffidence Lloyd was, in fact, an able administrator. When Macmillan moved Lloyd to the Treasury in 1961, he suggested that he would stay there for two or three years; and there was even the hint that he might then become prime minister.

It was clear that Macmillan, and others in the cabinet, were not happy about Lloyd's handing of the Treasury. Lloyd had introduced many innovations – set up Macmillan's new planning council, Neddy, reorganized the nationalized industries, introduced 'regulators' to adjust spending between budgets – but he had (Macmillan believed with some reason) bungled the pay pause, been too influenced by Treasury gloom, and failed to put across his policies to the country. The prime minister seemed irritated by Lloyd's lack of grasp of economic affairs, and his reluctance to grapple with the problem of wages: so that Macmillan himself took over the setting-up of a national incomes commission, Nicky, which Lloyd had begun. Yet Macmillan continued to confide in him, was personally very kind to him, lent him Chequers at week-ends. After Lloyd's 'sweets-and-ice-cream' budget of April 1962 – which was much criticized for its feebleness – Macmillan actually congratulated Lloyd on his handling of it.

But there were growing complaints against Lloyd from the younger members of the cabinet who were impatient of his pessimism and caution: and meanwhile the gloom of the Tories was mounting. On Monday 9 July there were fresh intimations of disaster; the Conservative Central Office reported to Macmillan that the next by-election, at North-East Leicester, would show a new setback. On the following day Butler (Home Secretary) and Macleod (the chairman of the party) called on Macmillan to press for major government changes, including the replacement of Selwyn Lloyd by Maudling. Their warnings were strong, but did not go as far as an ultimatum. The chief whip, Martin Redmayne, went further. He was finding great difficulty in placating the party; and he insisted that the reshuffle must be drastic, including at least six cabinet ministers.

At this point, it is clear, Macmillan took fright. He had shown signs of extreme nervous strain many times before, but usually only in foreign crises – at Bermuda in 1957, at Moscow in 1959, at the summit in Paris in 1960. In domestic political matters, where he felt less personally involved, as with the 'little local difficulties' in 1957, he normally showed extraordinary *sang-froid*. But now he felt himself suddenly threatened: he suspected a plot, centring round Butler; and he was determined to fight back. Macmillan, in one of his recurring images, seemed to see himself single-handedly defeating his enemies, and gambling with ruin. He retreated into isolation; he seemed distrustful of other people's advice; and he was visibly worried.

On the Tuesday evening Macmillan saw Lady Kilmuir at a state banquet, and said to her: 'I have the most terrible problems on my mind.' On the next evening there was a meeting of a cabinet committee, after which Macmillan took Kilmuir aside: he said 'The government is breaking up,' and went on (as Kilmuir reported it) to murmur 'You don't mind going?' Kilmuir had told Macmillan before that he was quite prepared to go before an election, but he was startled by the sudden question, and said: 'You know my views.'[3]

Then, on Thursday morning, an explosive story appeared in *The Daily Mail*, predicting big cabinet changes, including the promotion of Butler, and the departure of Lloyd from the Treasury – a story which was immediately suspected, like other *Daily Mail* scoops, of emanating from Butler. This further alarmed Macmillan: he had in mind to announce the changes the following week, but by now he dreaded the prospect of a week-end of hectic speculation and counter-plotting. So he decided, quite alone, that he must act very quickly. That morning there was the usual cabinet meeting: Macmillan seemed very friendly to Lloyd, and after the cabinet Lloyd had lunch with John Hare (then Minister of Labour, later Lord Blakenham) and Oliver Poole (then vice-chairman of the party). None of them had an inkling of what was coming. It was clear that Macmillan was dreading his task; it was the obverse side of his detachment (as he showed again with Profumo) that he hated the kind of candid man-to-man encounters that Churchill or Attlee would have taken in their stride. He was still, under all his confidence, a very shy man. Embarrassed and pained by the need for ruthlessness, he did it in the clumsiest possible way.

There was little difficulty with the first one, Lord Mills: Macmillan told him on the Thursday afternoon, and he was quite ready to go. At four o'clock Macmillan's principal private secretary, Timothy Bligh, called on Selwyn Lloyd, warning him that Macmillan wanted to talk to him – about his resignation. Lloyd, totally surprised, went over to see Macmillan. The prime minister, in a state of obvious tension, explained the critical situation of the party, the need for new blood, and suggested that there was a plot against himself. Macmillan hoped that Lloyd would go into the City, and become a peer. He was taken aback when Lloyd made it clear that he would stay in the Commons, and stay in politics.

That evening at dinner at Lord Rothermere's, Lloyd told his friend John Hare, who had always been his supporter over the pay pause: Hare was shocked by this sudden development since lunchtime, and the two men talked late into the night. The next morning Hare called on Macmillan to protest, and to offer his own resignation: Macmillan had a great respect for Hare, who represented the deep landed roots of the party, and if Hare *had* resigned he might well have brought Macmillan down. Macmillan took pains to assuage Hare, and managed eventually to persuade him that the purge was for the good of the party, and that Lloyd's leaving did not mean a change of policy. At the same time Lloyd went to see Nigel Birch, the most coruscating of Macmillan's open critics, still an ardent deflationist who had skulked on the sidelines since he resigned in 1957. Birch, who saw Lloyd as another victim of Macmillan's inflationary mania, advised him to be sure that his letter of resignation was published (Macmillan had avoided publishing Thorneycroft's resignation letter four years before). Together they drafted a resignation letter, carefully stressing Lloyd's anxiety that 'the growth of public expenditure, so much of it highly desirable in itself, should not outstrip our resources'.

On the next morning (13 July) Macmillan saw Lord Kilmuir for three-quarters of an hour and told him that there would be an 'immediate and dramatic' reconstruction of the cabinet.

Kilmuir, astonished by this embarrassing haste, had the impression that Macmillan was extremely alarmed, and 'determined to eliminate any risk for himself by a massive change of government. It astonished me that a man who had kept his head under the most severe stress and strain should lose both nerve and judgement in this way':⁴ Kilmuir never forgave Macmillan for this undignified departure. In the rest of the day Macmillan saw the other victims, including four other cabinet ministers – Charles Hill, David Eccles, Harold Watkinson and John Maclay. When he saw Hill, the old 'Radio Doctor', he reminded him that he had said that he wanted to go eventually: and he suggested that now would be a good time. Hill, like Kilmuir, was taken aback to learn that it would be announced that same evening. Macmillan explained that 'it would be very damaging – even fatal – to the Government to postpone the announcement'. 'There are times,' commented Hill afterwards, 'when the way a thing is done is so much more important than what is actually done.'⁵

The reshuffle was announced on the B.B.C. news, on Friday the thirteenth. Butler became Deputy Prime Minister and First Secretary of State; Maudling became Chancellor; Brooke became Home Secretary; Manningham-Buller Lord Chancellor; Thorneycroft Minister of Defence. Seven new men came into the cabinet – Sir Edward Boyle (Education), Sir Keith Joseph (Housing), William Deedes (Information), Enoch Powell (Health), Peter Thorneycroft (Defence), Michael Noble (Scotland) and John Boyd Carpenter (Chief Secretary of the Treasury).

Then followed the expected furore. There was an ominous letter to *The Times* the following morning, from Nigel Birch:

Sir,
   For the second time the Prime Minister has got rid of a Chancellor of the Exchequer who tried to get expenditure under control.
   Once is more than enough.

Yours truly,
NIGEL BIRCH

When Lloyd took his seat on the back-benches on Tuesday he was cheered by the Tories, while Macmillan was greeted with silence. The next day Nigel Birch presided over a meeting of the Conservative back-bench finance committee, with more rumblings of revolt: Gerald Nabarro growled that Lloyd's treatment was 'shabby and disreputable', and that Westminster had 'been made to look like an abattoir'. The day after, Macmillan addressed the 1922 Committee, explaining in very emotional terms, the need for efficiency, in politics as in a regiment. There were continuing murmurs of revolt from the Tory right wing, urged on by Birch and Lambton. Even Lord Avon, after a long silence, made a speech at Leamington Spa on 21 July, saying, 'I feel that Mr Selwyn Lloyd has been harshly treated'. *The Times* renewed its puritanical campaign against Macmillan, complaining that he 'showed no awareness of the deeper causes for the present public disenchantment with his Administration', and insisting that 'the "you've never had it so good" philosophy has been rejected'. Jeremy Thorpe, the Liberal showman-politician, remarked 'greater love hath no man than this, that he lay down his friends for his life'.

But the mood of mutiny faded in the summer sun. None of the sacked ministers was prepared, or able, to lead a revolt, the rebellious M.P.s had no unified complaint against Macmillan, and there was no obvious contender in the cabinet. The censure debate on 25 July gave Macmillan a chance to vindicate himself. Gaitskell described the purge as the 'act of a desperate man in a desperate situation', but this was the kind of role that suited Macmillan, and he successfully rallied his party. He said with high eloquence: 'I have been accused of excessive loyalty to old friends and colleagues, and I have been accused of a detachment amounting almost to disdain. . . . These contradictory accusations do not move me.' (In fact, they were not contradictory.) He put forward a clutch of new policies – including the setting up of the National Incomes Commission, a Consumer Council, and a review of the law on monopolies and restrictive practices – which, though not at all earth-shaking, showed that the new cabinet meant business. By the time Parliament adjourned for the holidays, twenty-one days after the purge, Macmillan seemed quite well in command.

The changes, in fact, were in many ways just what the party needed. It was true that there were some odd appointments: Manningham-Buller was hardly an improvement on Kilmuir; Brooke, though a very decent man, had a smug image and a knack of losing votes; William Deedes, an ex-journalist, was not forceful enough with the Press. There were still just as many old Etonians – ten out of twenty-one in the cabinet. But the infusion of younger men into the social-service ministries, Boyle, Joseph and Powell, and later Rippon in the Ministry of Works – 'the beavers' as Macmillan called them – brought new energy and enterprise, and even some sense of purpose to the Tories: the atmosphere and cooperation seemed better than before. Macmillan was not obviously on the same wavelength as these young men, but he showed himself quite able to give opportunities to people, like Powell or Joseph, whom he did not necessarily like or understand.

But neither Macmillan nor his party ever fully recovered from the purge. With luck, the new cabinet might have regained confidence; but luck was against them, and a series of setbacks – Enahoro, Skybolt, de Gaulle and Profumo – was to keep them on the run. The spell of loyalty which had marked the last five-and-a-half years was now broken: and Lord Kilmuir reflected ruefully on a remark that he had made to me a few months before, that 'loyalty is the Tory's secret weapon': 'I doubt if it ever had to endure so severe a strain.' The retention of Selwyn Lloyd, through all the Suez clamour, was a kind of guarantee of loyalty; and it was one of the great ironies of politics, after all the demands for Lloyd's resignation, that when he did go the party was never the same again. The cult of loyalty had been Macmillan's special thing, and in the retreat from Suez it had been a key factor; but the cost of loyalty had been an accumulation of dead wood, growing complacency, and growing public impatience. When, eventually, Macmillan came to realize that a change must be made, he was forced to a sudden ruthlessness which shattered the cult; from then on, his colleagues were noticeably less loyal to him. Moreover, the unflappable mask had suddenly been let fall. Macmillan had been seen to panic, in the face of public opinion: the old disdain could never carry complete conviction again.

And Macmillan himself was never quite the same. He knew very soon afterwards, that he had bungled the purge: and the presence of Lloyd, still in the Commons, seemed to haunt him like a ghost. He knew that his credit of loyalty had been spent, and that it would take time to build up a new balance. He was left with very little room for manoeuvre; so that, when the Profumo affair burst upon him, he would not accept Profumo's resignation – a decision which brought disastrous results.

In the year following the purge, he felt himself much more isolated: he lacked close friends and advisers, and with Mills and Kilmuir gone, there was no one of his own age around. He was nine years older than the next oldest in the cabinet, and seventeen years older than the average age (fifty-one years). He was, like de Gaulle and Adenauer, an old man in a Government of young men; the ruthlessness of the purge had helped to put him more in the position of president than prime minister – with attendant advantages, but also great perils. Moreover he seemed to his colleagues less physically strong, less able to listen, and to be now showing his age.

Yet he could reflect, without too much difficulty, that he was indispensable, as Churchill had done nine years before. He was not (he reminded his colleagues) a beech tree, like Churchill, who overshadowed the saplings around him; he was more an oak tree, that allowed trees to grow up all round. He had given great opportunities to several men, who had each in turn been hailed as the future prime minister – Macleod, Lloyd, Hailsham, and now again Butler, as deputy prime minister; and yet they never quite seemed to measure up to his own stature. The ambitious young ministers lacked conviction or charisma; and though they complained, and even intrigued against Macmillan, they were like school prefects complaining against the headmaster: none of them seemed to carry the mantle of the old Tory party – the mantle of Churchill. Macmillan could never truly visualize any of them as his successor.

NOTES

1. *The Listener*, 28 June 1966 (interview with Kenneth Harris)
2. Samuel Brittan, *The Treasury under the Tories, 1951–1964* (Harmondsworth: Penguin, 1964), p. 236
3. Viscount Kilmuir, *Political Adventure* (London: Weidenfeld & Nicolson, 1964), p. 323
4. Ibid., p. 324
5. Charles Hill, *Both Sides of the Hill* (London: Heinemann, 1964), p. 247

14. Into Europe

*The slogan of the Macmillan era was 'interdependence',
but it was a word which meant different things at
different times. Only from 1960 onwards was it accepted
that interdependence included
a substantial abrogation of national sovereignty.*
C. M. WOODHOUSE[1]

In the meantime, as Britain's economic future looked gloomier, and the prospects of the Tory party seemed dimmer, Macmillan had been moving towards the most crucial decision of his career – the bid to join Europe. It was soon after the breakdown of the summit that Macmillan began to show serious interest in the possibility of Britain joining the Common Market. The summit fiasco baulked his Churchillian ambition to build the bridge between East and West: and the arrival of the young President Kennedy, as we shall note in the next chapter, made his services as a broker less necessary.

Several streams converged to generate a strong tide towards Europe, and it would have been hard for any prime minister to go against it. The Treasury, under Sir Frank Lee (who became joint permanent secretary in January 1960) had become more despondent about the performance of British industry, and more convinced of the need to join a larger market. The Foreign Office, in contrast to the time when Macmillan had been there, had begun to take the Common Market seriously: and in July 1960 Edward Heath came into the Foreign Office to reinforce Lord Home, with new enthusiasm for the European idea after seeing the economic evidence. The hope that the European Free Trade Area of 'the Seven', which Britain had established the year before, could negotiate a free trade area with the Six had dwindled. The big business interests, represented by the Federation of British Industries, were pressing more strongly for British entry. And early in 1960 the Economic Steering Committee, made up of senior civil servants under Sir Frank Lee, examined possible relations of Britain with Europe, and came to the conclusion that Britain, primarily for political reasons, should try to join the Six, with suitable modifications.[2] There was not much sign of a swing of public opinion, to match these mandarin movements; but the Press, led by *The Economist* and including even *The Daily Mirror*, was making loud noises in favour of joining Europe. While from outside the decision to try to go into Europe seemed abrupt and even dangerous, from the inside it seemed – to many people at least – inescapable.

Macmillan himself, during his previous years in power, had not – as we have seen – shown consistent enthusiasm for coming closer to Europe. He was more genuinely interested in Europe than Churchill, but he still clung to the outdated Churchillian concept of Britain being at the centre of the interlocking circles of America, the Commonwealth and Europe. As foreign secretary, Macmillan was sceptical, like nearly all British politicians, about the preparations for 'relaunching' Europe; and for most of his time as prime minister he was preoccupied with his relations with the Commonwealth and America. He shared the difficulties of other Englishmen, that, however much they agreed intellectually that Britain's new role should be within Europe, their emotional ties were in other directions. The establishment of EFTA occupied a good deal of the Government's time, and early in 1960 Macmillan seemed more concerned about the economic split in Europe, between EFTA and the Common Market, than about the prospects of Britain joining the Six.

But the Six were becoming steadily more convincing; and when Douglas Dillon, the American Under-Secretary of State, came to London in December 1959, he made it clear that his Government took the Six much more seriously than the Seven. In March 1960 on a visit to Washington, Macmillan had talks with Christian Herter and Douglas Dillon to try to dispel American coolness towards E F T A. A devastating leak appeared in *The Washington Post*, which had a Macmillanish sound: it was alleged that Macmillan had said that it was Britain's historical role to crush Napoleonic ambitions to integrate Europe, and if France and Western Germany continued on this road Britain would have no alternative but to lead another peripheral alliance against them. He was reported to have said, too, that he feared a revival of Nazism after Adenauer left, and recalled that at the time of Napoleon Britain allied herself with Russia to break the French ambitions. The leak was given great prominence in Europe, where it seemed to bear out traditional suspicions of British behaviour. The Foreign Office denied it, and the truth of the leak has never been established, but it sounded all too like Macmillan. 'Opposition leaders fancy they catch echoes of a familiar voice in the passage about "Britain's historic role",' said *The Times*'s political correspondent on 1 April: and reactions on the continent were violent. In Parliament when he returned, Macmillan emphasized (on 1 April) that Britain did not want to weaken the Six, but to prevent the gap within Europe from growing: 'We have seen over and over again how fatal that is: in my own lifetime I have seen it twice.'

In the course of 1960 the pressures towards a *rapprochement* with the Common Market became almost irresistible. Not only were British civil servants, businessmen and editors coming round to it – often with the uncritical zeal of the newly-converted – but after the collapse of the summit there was a need for some kind of Tory mission in foreign affairs, to show that Britain could have a new role in the world. Macmillan was advised, both by political colleagues and by the Tory Central Office, that entering Europe could be part of a new crusade.

He was slow to make up his mind. In August he was invited by Adenauer to Bad Godesberg, which he described as a historic meeting, and gained the impression – perhaps too strongly – that Adenauer would promote Britain's entry. In the course of the autumn Macmillan took soundings, through unofficial contacts in the Western European Union – the one body which included the Six *and* Britain. By the end of the year Macmillan had come round to the view that Britain should apply to join the Six.

It was the biggest decision of Macmillan's premiership. It was a risk, and there were big obstacles. In the cabinet, Hailsham, Maudling and Butler were all sceptical, if not opposed. The right wing of the Tory party, as well as the left wing of the Labour party, were highly suspicious of Europe. It was undeniably a very abrupt switch of policy. In the election manifesto of 1959 there was no mention of the Common Market. It was, as Gaitskell said, 'the end of a thousand years of history'.

Macmillan set about it with characteristic caution: he dreaded any abrupt confrontation. He began to edge his party into Europe, slowly and with plenty of diversions – in the same kind of way that he edged them out of Africa. It was a well-tried method; but this time with a serious snag. There would not be any rousing national crusade, and this was soon noticed by the Europeans who were unconvinced that Macmillan's changes of heart were serious. He was gambling, but gambling secretly. While he said to his colleagues 'we must play it high!', to the public he played it very low.

In the first half of 1961 Macmillan gradually prepared his cabinet for the shift of policy, while still blurring the question of whether Britain should join with the safer question of finding out how she *could* join – a confusion that was part of Macmillan's practised committeemanship. By 16 February he had come rather further into the open: in answer to a question in the House of Commons, he said 'If we were to receive an invitation from the six governments to take part in meetings with them for the purpose of political consultation we should certainly be disposed to accept it'. In March there was strong encouragement from the continent, in a speech by the French foreign minister, Couve de Murville.

In April Macmillan saw Kennedy in Washington, and discussed with him the question of Britain's entry. Macmillan had already decided before he saw the president; but Kennedy was unexpectedly sympathetic.

Kennedy fully understood the economic difficulties British entry would bring to the United States. But these were in his mind overborne by the political benefits. If Britain joined the Market, London could offset the eccentricities of policy in Paris and Bonn; moreover, Britain, with its world obligations, could keep the E.E.C. from becoming a high-tariff, inward-looking white man's club. Above all, with British membership, the Market could become the basis for a true political federation of Europe.[3]

By the time Macmillan returned from America, the Common Market was very much in the air, and a cabinet decision was soon expected. Gradual hints were dropped, and on 17 May Heath gave the first major sign of the change, in a speech to the Commons in which he recommended full membership of the Common Market. By 30 May Woodrow Wyatt was asking in the House: 'Is the Prime Minister aware that there is growing support in the country for the skilful and adroit way he is carefully edging his party to the acceptance of Britain going into the Common Market?'

Macmillan approached gingerly the problem of squaring the Commonwealth. Just after Heath's speech there was a meeting of Commonwealth economic experts in London, to discuss Britain and Europe; but Macmillan clearly wanted to avoid a full Commonwealth Conference. Instead, he sent three persuasive emissaries – Duncan Sandys, Peter Thorneycroft and John Hare – to reassure, without much success, the Commonwealth capitals.

In the meantime the foreign secretary, Lord Home, was already being rather bolder and more candid than Macmillan. First in Chicago, and then in the House of Lords, on 21 June, he made it clear that Britain had decided to apply for entry. He did not try to disguise the political implications; 'If we get the economic conditions right, I believe we can face the political consequences' – and in a later speech in August, he said,

'Let me admit at once that the Treaty of Rome would involve considerable derogation of sovereignty'.

By the end of July Macmillan was ready for the formal announcement: it was a safe time, just before the adjournment of Parliament and the August bank holiday, with no time for a serious counter-attack before the autumn. He made his statement on 31 July, in quite flat terms, emphasizing that the eventual decision could only be made by the House of Commons, in consultation with the Commonwealth, and stressing that the Commonwealth ties must remain.

In the debate two days later he played down the importance of the decision and the commitments involved:

I must remind the House that E.E.C. is an economic community, not a defence alliance, or a foreign policy community or a cultural community. It is an economic community and the region where collective decisions are taken is related to the sphere covered by the treaty, economic tariffs, markets and all the rest.

But he was more eloquent and emphatic about Britain's role:

. . . if there are little Europeans, and perhaps there are, is it not the duty of this country, with its world-wide ties, to lend its weight to the majority of Europeans who see the true perspective of events? I believe that our right place is in the vanguard of the movement towards the greater unity of the free world, and that we can lead from within rather than outside. At any rate, I am persuaded that we ought to try. . . . I think that most of us recognize that in a changing world, if we are not to be left behind and to drop out of the main stream of the world's life, we must be prepared to change and adapt our methods. All through history this has been one of the main sources of our strength.

The immediate reaction to the first statement was amazingly tame. One right-wing Tory, Anthony Fell, burst out: 'Is the prime minister aware that his quite shocking statement, full of double talk, has had the effect on one of his previous supporters, that he now thinks the prime minister a national disaster?' But this only helpfully emphasized the wildness of the opposition. After the thirteen-hour debate, between twenty and thirty Tories abstained, and Fell voted against the Government; but Macmillan was able to go for his holiday without signs of menacing opposition. 'Few other politicians in British history could have executed such a feat,' commented Nora Beloff: 'Macmillan was about to go back on much of what he had said and done in ten years of office, including five years in Downing Street, without losing the smallest Parliamentary Secretary or Junior Whip along the way.'[4]

And so, in the autumn of 1961, the long negotiations in Brussels began, with a formidable British team under the leadership of Edward Heath. The negotiations themselves were immensely complex, but they were made far harder by Macmillan's technique of speaking with two voices, one for European ears, one for British. Macmillan believed that he was well ahead – perhaps a year, or two years, or longer – of British public opinion; and so he played down at first the full implications. As a result, Heath's negotiations were much hampered by the need to carry with him a divided party and a divided cabinet. It was not until a year after the first statement, in the autumn of 1962, that Macmillan really came into the open about the consequences of joining the Six.

In Brussels Heath took a bold line about Britain's ambitions, and opened the negotiations in October 1961 with a masterly and enthusiastic speech, stressing that 'our destiny is intimately linked with yours'; while in England, at the Conservative party conference on 14 October, Macmillan tried to present the entry into Europe as a kind of challenge: 'It is a bracing cold shower we shall enter, not a Turkish bath . . . if through indecision, timidity or sheer political expediency we had allowed this opportunity to slip from us we should have failed to rise to events.' But in the following months Macmillan and the rest of the cabinet continued to suggest that nothing would be lost: for instance, in the autumn of 1961 he was still expounding the old Churchillian doctrine of three circles.

Heath began the negotiations by demanding that whatever the Commonwealth lost in trade should be made up by 'comparable outlets' within the Community – a position which could not be accepted by the Six – and then argued over a vast range of individual commodities, from cricket bats to coconuts. Certainly if Britain had taken up a less extreme position at the beginning, and had been more prepared to offend the Commonwealth, the negotiations would have been quicker and might have had more prospects of success. By the time the negotiations were adjourned for the summer holidays in August, the British delegation had only begun to make material concessions.

Macmillan, in the meantime, was trying to prepare the way politically and diplomatically. He had deployed his cabinet colleagues ingeniously: Maudling, still sceptical about the European adventure, was now in the Colonial Office; and Butler, another sceptic, was actually put in charge of the cabinet committee dealing with the negotiations. Duncan Sandys, who had always been a keen European but could also boast 'I am half a New Zealander', was in the Commonwealth Relations Office; and Christopher Soames, another discreet pro-Common Marketeer, was at the Ministry of Agriculture, to pacify the farmers. To a remarkable extent, the anti-marketeers, who two years ago seemed insuperable, were subdued.

Macmillan's next big hurdle was the Commonwealth Prime Ministers' conference on 10 September. Now, in his opening speech, he emphasized more strongly that the British could not ignore Europe. He stressed that the British market by itself could not absorb the growing production of the Commonwealth, and that, inside the Common Market, Britain could much more effectively influence the pattern of world trade. He was saying, in effect, that if Britain was broke she was no use to anybody.

It was a stormy conference. Macmillan's hopes that the meeting could be kept quiet and unemotional were soon dashed: delegations freely leaked their views and speeches to the Press. But at the end of the conference, they agreed on a communiqué which did not actually limit Britain's future negotiations at Brussels. In it, the Commonwealth 'freely acknowledged' that Britain had tried to safeguard Commonwealth interests, and 'took note that the negotiations in Brussels were incomplete, and that a number of important questions had still to be negotiated'. It was a chilly statement, but at least Macmillan could not be branded as the betrayer of the Commonwealth.

The next hurdle was the annual Tory conference in October. A week before it, at the Labour conference, Hugh Gaitskell had for the first time openly emerged as an opponent of Britain's entry into the Common Market. Macmillan was now preparing to make the move into Europe a major election issue, and Gaitskell's outburst encouraged his commitment. Before the Tory conference, Macmillan published a pamphlet called 'Britain, the Commonwealth and Europe' which put forward his arguments at the Commonwealth conference. It was one of Macmillan's major pronouncements, a kind of 'Wind of Change' speech on the European front. 'The present Conservative government,' he began, 'has taken what is perhaps the most fateful and forward-looking policy decision in our peacetime history': and it was probably true. He pointed to the great changes in the Commonwealth and Europe, and proclaimed that Britain inside the Common Market would not only 'gain a new stature in Europe, but also increase its standing and influence in the councils of the world'. He stressed that, within the Common Market, Britain could influence its development, but while outside 'We could be faced with a political solution in Europe which ran counter to our views and interests but which we could do nothing to influence'. Macmillan was now past the point of no return: he clearly implied that if the negotiations were to fail, Britain would be in peril.

The Tory Conference was Macmillan's last great triumph. The anti-Common Marketeers were muddled and ineffective, and Butler showed a sudden enthusiasm for Europe by his celebrated rejoinder to Gaitskell: 'For them a thousand years of history books. For us the future.' Macmillan made an effective speech, on 14 October, repeating the views of his pamphlet and at last admitting that 'going in must involve some pooling of national freedom of action'. He stressed the urgency: 'If we wait indefinitely it will be too late. Now is the opportunity and we must seize it.' He was applauded almost unanimously. *The Times*'s political correspondent commented on 15 October: 'In Cabinet, in the parliamentary party and in conference, Mr Macmillan's victory, for the time being, has been complete.' In spite of all his domestic difficulties – the aftermath of the purge, and the economic troubles – Macmillan at this time seemed at the top of his career: he had, in two years, switched his party's foreign policy almost a hundred and eighty degrees.

It was, as it turned out, the false dawn. In the next month the public-opinion polls swung rapidly against the Conservatives, and five by-elections showed losses for the Tories. And on the world front, Macmillan came up against the full difficulties of trying to be both pro-American and pro-European.

Macmillan's relations with de Gaulle had seemed in the summer of 1962 to be at least neutral. In June he had seen the general for the first time since the negotiations had begun, at the Château de Champs. It is still not clear how much the two leaders said, or how much they understood each other. They apparently avoided discussing the problems of nuclear defence which were crucial to de Gaulle. They were both already aware of their differences about the new shape of Europe. They both had the same habit of talking in lofty and cryptic generalities, without descending to specifics. Macmillan tried hard to persuade de Gaulle of Britain's seriousness in identifying herself with Europe, and of his own readiness to see changes in the relations with the Commonwealth and America; and de Gaulle appeared to be impressed and surprised by this change. Macmillan certainly came away from Champs feeling new confidence in success.

But it was clear from the general's Press conference just before the meeting, that de Gaulle was preoccupied with the question of the independence of Europe from America, and had continuing doubts about Britain's eventual loyalties. De Gaulle's suspicions were not allayed by President Kennedy's conception of a 'Grand Design', which he first propounded in a speech at Philadelphia on 4 July, in which he spoke again about 'Atlantic partnership' and a 'declaration of interdependence'. Kennedy's view of Europe fitted well with Macmillan's, who saw Britain's entry into Europe as a way of coming closer to America; but de Gaulle had no intention of confusing independence with interdependence. The one thing that de Gaulle wanted from America – nuclear know-how – could not be given. Without this, the idea of an Atlantic partnership to him was meaningless.

In the next months the gulf between Paris and Washington became wider. In September de Gaulle triumphantly visited Germany, and prepared a new programme of Franco-German cooperation. In October the Cuban crisis, in which Kennedy came to his showdown without consulting his allies, revealed the irrelevance of Europe in a major crisis. And in November came the French elections, in which de Gaulle won an absolute majority, and the opposition groups – nearly all in favour of Britain's entry – became still less effective. By the time Macmillan visited de Gaulle again, at Rambouillet in December, the situation was less hopeful than in June: and de Gaulle knew that Macmillan would soon afterwards be flying to Nassau to see Kennedy, to discuss the collapse of the American-made 'Skybolt' missiles, on which Britain had based her nuclear defence policy.

As at the earlier meeting, it is not clear how far the leaders understood each other. Macmillan unwisely insisted on talking in French, without interpreters, and there may have been confusion. He said afterwards (on 21 January) that he was completely candid: 'It has been suggested that by making the Polaris agreement with President Kennedy a few days after I had seen General de Gaulle himself at Rambouillet I did not treat him with absolute sincerity.' He went on:

On the contrary we discussed this question and I explained that if the Americans decided to abandon Skybolt as unlikely to prove satisfactory I would do my utmost at Nassau to obtain an effective alternative. I explained to him in some detail my views of the relations between interdependence and independence, and said that we must have a British deterrent available for independent use if need be.

I am sure he fully understood our position. This impression was confirmed through diplomatic contacts after the Nassau agreement had been announced.

When three years later, in the election campaign of 1966, Harold Wilson repeated the charge that Macmillan had misled de Gaulle, Macmillan again strongly denied it. But whatever was said or understood at Rambouillet, de Gaulle gave Macmillan no encouragement. He explained at some length his objections to Britain joining the Six. According to some French accounts, de Gaulle consoled Macmillan with the words of Edith Piaf's song: '*Ne pleurez plus, milord*'. Others say that de Gaulle did propose an Anglo-French nuclear deal.

Two days later, Macmillan saw Kennedy at Nassau. It was a critical encounter for the prime minister. He was threatened politically by the cancellation of the Skybolt missiles, which the Americans had abruptly written off, unaware of the consequences to Macmillan. ('He should have warned me of the dangers to him,' said Kennedy afterwards, 'we could have come up with a solution before publicity.'[5]) Macmillan insisted that Britain must have Polaris missiles instead, with freedom to use them in national emergencies, and used every argument, including the one – much resented by Americans later – that if this was refused there could well be a wave of Tory anti-Americanism. As Schlesinger described it: 'Instead of pleading that his Government would fall, he seemed to be saying that his party would accept anti-Americanism to keep itself in power. But this was not a threat; it was a lamentation. It was evidently a bravura performance.'[6]

Macmillan made his point, and Kennedy agreed to give Britain Polaris, with – which was more important – the right to use it in a purely British emergency. Advisers on both sides warned that Polaris might affect the Common Market negotiations, but Macmillan insisted that it had nothing to do with them. To try to placate de Gaulle, the same offer of Polaris was made to France: but there was no time to make the offer tactfully, since Macmillan insisted that he must be able to announce the deal immediately; and the French quickly pointed out that France had 'neither the submarines required for the Polaris missiles nor the warheads'.[7] Macmillan returned to Nassau with what he wanted; but to some observers, it seemed already clear that the price was exclusion from Europe.

In the meantime Heath was running into new troubles in Brussels. During the autumn there was apparent deadlock on several fronts, particularly over dairy products. The British Government were very vulnerable to the farmers – particularly with by-elections going against them – and the French were becoming more intransigent. But the other members of the Six also seemed often impatient of Britain's difficulties:

The 'Europeans' on the Continent tended to be rather contemptuous of the debate the British were carrying on with themselves about the implications of their changed circumstances, and they pointed out that no such pining after the past accompanied their own clear-eyed decisions on the Common Market.[8]

The year 1963 began ominously, with a New Year message from de Gaulle to the French people, referring to Europe 'ready to receive in the future a Britain which could and would join it without reservation and definitively'. French commentators were interpreting the Nassau agreement as a clear sign of Britain's bonds with America, and André Fontaine, the well-informed commentator of *Le Monde*, suggested that Nassau had made people in 'high places' believe that to allow Britain to enter the Common Market would risk allowing an American 'Trojan Horse'.

On 14 January, just after the Six had reassembled in Brussels, de Gaulle gave his fateful Press conference.

It might have been thought that our English friends, in proposing their entry, had agreed to transform themselves to the point where they could apply all the required conditions. The question today is whether they can accept coming inside a single tariff wall, renouncing all preferences for the Commonwealth, abandoning any privileges for their own farmers, and repudiating the pledges they made to their EFTA partners. This is the real question. It cannot be said that at the present time Britain is ready to do these things. Will she ever be? To that question only Britain can reply.

Dazed and temporarily united in anger, the five other members and Britain tried to continue negotiations in Brussels. I remember, in Brussels at the time, how impossible it was to believe that the general had actually said 'no'. For a time, Britain hoped that Adenauer would bring pressure on de Gaulle; but a week later Adenauer came to Paris to sign the Franco-German peace treaty, and did not press the point of Britain's entry. Britain was firmly shut out of Europe. In his last speech to the delegates, Heath concluded:

We in Britain are not going to turn our backs on the mainland of Europe or on the countries of the Community. We are a part of Europe: by geography, tradition, history, culture and civilization. We shall continue to work with all our friends in Europe for the true unity and strength of this continent.

The most emphatic commitment to Europe came when Britain had been emphatically shut out. Macmillan himself replied to de Gaulle, in his own fashion, in an outspoken broadcast on 30 January, after the negotiations had finally broken down, rather belatedly called 'Challenge Accepted'. 'What happened at Brussels yesterday was bad,' he began: 'bad for us, bad for Europe, bad for the whole free world.' He maintained (questionably) that the negotiations had broken down 'not because they were going to fail, but curiously enough because they were going to succeed'.

Macmillan was dispirited, tired and bewildered. He was much less exposed than Heath, who had staked his career on going in. But he was still very vulnerable. As *The Observer* later put it (13 October): 'Instead of seeming a far-sighted statesman, he suddenly seemed a gambler who had miscalculated the odds.' The following month, he visited Rome on a visit planned long beforehand, looking grey and wan: he was warmly welcomed, but inconsolable. At a meeting with Italian delegates, discussing the technicalities and tariffs, he suddenly burst out, with an emotion which astonished the Italians, to say that he was not interested in these details, that he wanted to make only one thing clear – that for him the events of the past week had been a complete disaster, and he did not know what to do next.

At what point was Britain's entry doomed, and when, if at all, could it have been saved? The questions have been endlessly asked. President Kennedy speculated to Schlesinger:[9] 'Could it have been the decision not to give France nuclear information in 1962? or the refusal to establish de Gaulle's tripartite NATO directorship in 1958? or the treatment of de Gaulle by Roosevelt and Churchill during the Second World War?' Schlesinger replied that de Gaulle's suspicions of Britain and America were deeply embedded.

Certainly de Gaulle's suspicions of the 'anglo-saxons' were deep, long-lived, and well-founded. But if Macmillan had been more emphatic, and swifter, in declaring for Europe, de Gaulle would have found it much harder to stop him – particularly before the November elections. Macmillan's 'backing into Europe' was in many ways a consummate political performance; as in his retreat from Africa, he executed a half-circle without a major showdown with his party. He avoided any single moment of choice, and indeed gave the impression that there was no real choice to be made: imperceptibly the question changed from discussing how Britain might get into the Common Market, to getting into the Common Market.

But these manoeuvres were watched, all too closely, on the Continent. Not only de Gaulle and the Gaullists, but more anglophile Europeans, observed this apparent lack of commitment; and the delegates who had been used to the burning dedication of the European idea found this British determination to have it all ways very dislikeable. If Macmillan had risked a straightforward crusade earlier, if he had staked his career on Europe from the beginning and faced up to political and defence implications, he might have failed more ignominiously. But he might have achieved a unique place in history as the prime minister who ended Britain's isolation.

Yet the negative part of his achievement did remain. The negotiations, and the new climate they produced, turned Britain more firmly towards Europe; and the Commonwealth never loomed so large again. The very act of applying for entry was a break with the past, an admission that Britain could not stand alone. The gloomy predictions that Macmillan and others had made about what would happen to Britain outside Europe were not, of course, re-stated after the breakdown; but they remained in people's minds. The cold shower had begun to trickle. Many critics still blame Macmillan for trying so late, and so cautiously; but in the complacent 'never had it so good' atmosphere of the time, which he had himself generated, it is doubtful whether any leader – on the right or the left – could have moved earlier. It was not till three years later, with the final breaking of the boom, that the British people became really aware of the limitations of Britain's isolation.

NOTES

1. C. M. Woodhouse, *Post-War Britain* (London: Bodley Head, 1966), p. 51
2. Miriam Camps, *Britain and the European Community, 1955–63* (Oxford: O.U.P., 1964), p. 281
3. Arthur M. Schlesinger Jr, *A Thousand Days* (Boston, Mass.: Houghton Mifflin, 1965; London: Deutsch), p. 720
4. Nora Beloff, *The General Says No* (Harmondsworth: Penguin, 1963), p. 110
5. Arthur M. Schlesinger Jr, *A Thousand Days*, p. 736
6. Ibid., p. 737 7. Ibid., p. 738
8. Miriam Camps, *Britain and the European Community, 1955–63*, p. 463
9. Arthur M. Schlesinger Jr, *A Thousand Days*, p. 740

15. Kennedy and Disarmament

Let both sides, for the first time, formulate serious and
precise proposals for the inspection
and control of arms, and bring the absolute power to destroy
other nations under the absolute control of all nations.
PRESIDENT KENNEDY, JANUARY 1961

When in November 1960 John F. Kennedy was elected President of the United States, Macmillan's role in the world was necessarily transformed. The days of White House inertia were numbered, and an ambitious intellectual team were about to move in. Macmillan was relieved that Kennedy had beaten Nixon; but a young and independent-minded young president might well give him much less scope as a world leader. In fact, Kennedy's election did mark the end of Macmillan's bold diplomatic mediation; but Macmillan, with remarkable ease, soon established a private relationship with the president which was closer than with Eisenhower, though publicly less so. And on disarmament, at least, it did produce a solid result.

Their first meeting, in the naval canteen at Key West in March, when Macmillan made a long detour from Trinidad, was disconcertingly brusque. It was soon clear that Kennedy would not need the services of a broker to arrange meetings with Khrushchev: by June 1961 he was flying to Vienna to meet Khrushchev alone. But on his way back from Vienna Kennedy stopped in London to have talks with Macmillan, and they got on well. As Arthur Schlesinger described it: 'The languid Edwardian, who looked back to the sun-lit years before the First World War as a lost paradise, feared that the brisk young American, nearly a quarter of a century his junior, would consider him a museum piece'; but Macmillan soon established an avuncular relationship, and their talk 'marked the beginning of what became Kennedy's closest relationship with a foreign leader'.[1] They soon, says Schlesinger

discovered, despite the difference of age, a considerable temperamental rapport. Kennedy, with his own fondness for the British political style, liked Macmillan's patrician approach to politics, his impatience with official ritual, his insouciance with professionals, his pose of nonchalance, even when most deeply committed. Macmillan, for his part, responded to Kennedy's courage, his ability to see events unfolding against the vast canvas of history, his contempt for cliché, his unfailing sense of the ridiculous.

Their personal bond was strengthened by Macmillan's appointment of David Ormsby-Gore, who had family links with both Macmillan and Kennedy, as Ambassador to Washington. Kennedy had asked for Ormsby-Gore to be sent as ambassador, and at some stages – as we shall see – the influence of Ormsby-Gore was greater than that of Macmillan. The closeness of Ormsby-Gore to Kennedy was carefully played down by the British Government, lest it might generate resentment with the French and German ambassadors. The relationship ensured the quick, informal exchange of views between the two capitals: it was a reversion to an older style of diplomacy, which both leaders clearly enjoyed. Kennedy said: 'I trust David as I would my own cabinet.'[2]

In the three years of their collaboration, the most fruitful subject of discussion between Macmillan and Kennedy was disarmament. It was this, rather than his more flamboyant diplomatic adventures, which constituted his major world achievement. It showed the more genuine and plodding side of Macmillan's character – the patient pursuit of a problem with real but controlled emotion. His eloquence and his memories of Passchendaele gave him authority; but results came from persistence. It was the fox in him, more than the hedgehog.

Disarmament, at this time, had a complex and melancholy history. In 1955, when Britain was developing her H-bomb, the British were not interested in the banning of tests, but when Macmillan became prime minister, fortified by the bomb, he pressed for an agreement; he told Marshal Bulganin in 1957 that this was the most important point that had been raised in their long correspondence. But the Americans were preoccupied with the dangers of surprise attack, while the Russians would not accept control and inspection: a disarmament sub-committee met in London for five months without agreement. In 1958, after Russia had temporarily suspended nuclear tests, the Conference of Experts met at Geneva, and Macmillan, behind the scenes, put all his weight behind a test-ban agreement, while keeping in close touch with the Americans. The British diplomats and scientists, still feeling the 'guilt of Hiroshima', had the same passionate interest in abolishing testing: and the Campaign for Nuclear Disarmament, though it was apparently mocked and ignored by the Government, showed the strength of public opinion, and was a useful argument to the Americans.

The Russians proposed that a test-ban treaty could be agreed separately from general disarmament, and the British persuaded the Americans to accept this. The Conference of Experts eventually agreed that with an extensive control system, all nuclear tests could be monitored, and in October 1958 a three-power test-ban conference opened in Geneva, hoping to draw up a treaty. Macmillan suspended British nuclear tests for a year, and Eisenhower did likewise, against the advice of 'some of his most trusted advisers', and, it seems, to his later regret.[3] The test-ban conference soon ran into difficulties, and the Americans were divided over the desirability of a treaty: Eisenhower was persuaded by experts, particularly by Edward Teller, that underground tests could be made in big caverns which could not be detected, and this view, as Eisenhower said 'threw a pall over the conference'.[4] The 'big hole' obsession, as it came to be called, continued to hang over the discussions.

Macmillan was determined to keep the meetings going, and the chief British negotiator at Geneva, Sir Michael Wright, believed that without his intervention negotiations would probably have broken down in early 1959.[5] Macmillan saw that it would not be possible to have inspection of all suspicious events, and developed the idea of an annual quota of inspections which could not be vetoed. The Americans resisted the idea, and asked Macmillan not to raise it with Khrushchev when he saw him in March 1959. But Macmillan did raise it, Khrushchev received it well, and in May put it forward himself in a proposal to the conference. Nine months later it became official American policy.

The American delegation at Geneva played a feeble part, but the discussions went on, the suspension of tests was continued, the disagreements became less, and a draft treaty was in sight. Macmillan was very hopeful, and looked forward to a final agreement at the Paris summit in May 1960: he said in his speech before the summit that an agreement would have a profound influence on the whole question of disarmament:

We hope that it may be the pioneer scheme. That is why I attach so much importance to it, why I have tried myself to do everything possible to further it, and why I tried to persuade some of our American friends to overcome some of the minor and indeed major difficulties.

Despite the collapse of the summit, the test-ban talks continued, but the Russians were now less prepared to accept international verification. The moment of common trust had passed, and Macmillan blamed the American obsession with the 'big hole', and their insistence on large numbers of inspections.[6] Eisenhower was under growing pressure to start testing again: 'I remember certainly two occasions on which I pleaded with . . . President Eisenhower,' recalled Macmillan afterwards, 'to hold his hand and to continue the voluntary unofficial moratorium when I am bound to say his advisers were taking a rather different attitude.'[7]

This was the gloomy position when Kennedy became president in January 1961. Kennedy was well aware of the need for a test ban, and before he became president discussed the problem at length with experts, including Ormsby-Gore.[8] In his inaugural address he eloquently proclaimed the need for control. But he was strongly pressed by his advisers, including Eisenhower,[9] to resume American tests, to keep pace with the Russians who were thought to be about to resume. Macmillan tried hard to persuade Kennedy to postpone more testing: 'During the deadlock which followed in 1960–61,' wrote Sir Michael Wright, 'the influence of Macmillan was again an important contributory factor in securing that the West should go to the last mile in negotiation before being the first to resume testing.'[10]

But in August 1961 the Russians not unexpectedly announced that they would resume tests, and in the next two months they carried out thirty of them, nearly all in the atmosphere, culminating with one of over fifty megatons on 30 October. Kennedy was already convinced of the need for American tests on Christmas Island in the Pacific – for which he needed British permission: and on 21 December he discussed the problem with Macmillan in Bermuda. Macmillan made an emotional speech to Kennedy; he said that the arms race was a 'rogue elephant' which could get out of control, and that he believed, having studied Russia carefully, that its position was changing. Kennedy was moved, and at this meeting, according to Ormsby-Gore, the relationship of the two leaders 'blossomed considerably'.[11] But the president said that he thought he would be compelled to resume tests. Macmillan went back to England and, in the New Year, wrote Kennedy a long and very personal letter, warning that if the Americans resumed the Russians would probably carry out a new series, that the arms race would proliferate, and that only a supreme effort could rescue the world from the deadlock. 'If this capacity for destruction ended up in the hands of dictators, reactionaries, revolutionaries, madmen around the world, then sooner or later, possibly at the end of the century, either by error or folly or insanity the great crime would be committed.'[12] He suggested once again a summit meeting of Kennedy, Khrushchev and himself, to take a new initiative in disarmament. There was much argument in Washington about how the letter should be answered, and one State Department officer complained, 'We can't let Macmillan practise this emotional blackmail on us'. Kennedy was impressed by the letter, and sent a careful, sympathetic reply. But having seen the analysis of the Soviet tests, he insisted that he must go ahead, and announced the new tests on TV on 2 March.

Macmillan was sad and embittered, believing that the decision 'would shatter the hopes of millions of people'. He said that the British Government viewed the decision 'with deep distress'. At Geneva there seemed to be no progress; the Russians still rejected international verification inside their country. Macmillan wrote a further letter to Khrushchev, trying to reassure him about verification, and warned the House of Commons on 10 April that unless the situation changed the American tests would have to go on: and on 25 April, three years after their last nuclear explosion, the Americans began a new series of tests on Christmas Island. Macmillan's efforts had come to nothing, and there was now the extra ignominy of having to agree to tests on British soil.

Then, in October 1962, came Cuba, which changed the whole atmosphere of East–West relations and, in Macmillan's view, was 'one of the great turning-points of history'.

The British Government had intimations of the crisis on Saturday 20 October, the day before they were officially told of the missiles which had been found in Cuba. Ormsby-Gore had guessed that the president's repeated warnings to the Russians meant that offensive weapons had probably already been found there, and he informed Macmillan of this guess. The British Government were thus the first to know of the crisis.[13]

The next day, Macmillan was officially informed about the missiles. Kennedy called Ormsby-Gore to the White House, and outlined the alternatives. Ormsby-Gore said that he supported quarantine measures and felt that Macmillan would do the same. Later that day Kennedy spoke directly to Macmillan explaining that he had had to make the decision on his own responsibility, but that from now on he would keep in closest touch.[14] Macmillan replied the next day that Britain would give her support in the U.N., but pointed out that European opinion would need attention, because, living always close to the threat of missiles, they might not see what the fuss was all about. He was worried, too, that Khrushchev might try to exchange Cuba for Berlin, and he appealed once again for a summit meeting on disarmament.[15] Kennedy reassured him by saying that the crisis was not merely over Cuba, but a major showdown with Khrushchev. Macmillan seemed reassured, but the British Press was apprehensive and angry over the first world crisis in which Britain apparently had no influence.

The speed of developments was such that Britain's main influence was now through Ormsby-Gore. Kennedy had dinner with the Ormsby-Gores the night after his speech, and talked alone with the ambassador, who asked him if he could not release aerial photographs of the missiles to reassure sceptics: Kennedy agreed, and they chose photographs together. Ormsby-Gore also suggested that the Russian ships should be intercepted closer to Cuba than was planned, to give Khrushchev more time to climb down; and Kennedy agreed to this, too. 'This decision,' recalls Schlesinger, 'was of vital importance in postponing the moment of irreversible action.'[16]

In London, Macmillan was embarrassed by his public inaction: in his statement to the Commons during the crisis, on 25 October, he said that he 'Would always be ready to take an initiative at the moment at which I thought it valuable and when it would serve a useful purpose. But I cannot do so merely for the sake of appearing to do something – rather I must do so in order to achieve something useful.' Five days later he said 'I should say that it is not true that we in this country played an inactive role in this great trial of strength'. Activity could take different forms: 'a febrile, excited nervosity which expresses itself in frantic demands that somebody ought to do something or other is not always the most useful contribution'. He insisted that in view of the rapidity of the crisis, the American Government had maintained 'the closest possible cooperation with their allies'. But Macmillan, in the end, felt compelled to write to Khrushchev: 'I thought it right after consultation with some of my colleagues . . . to make a public intervention'; and after Kennedy's letter to Khrushchev on 27 October, he wrote to Khrushchev saying that once the Cuba situation had been dealt with, the way would be open for a nuclear test-ban agreement: 'I therefore ask you to take the action necessary to make all this possible. This is an opportunity which we should seize.' It is likely that Macmillan would have intervened if the tension had continued. But just as the letter was being delivered, Khrushchev's climb-down to Kennedy was announced. The crisis was over. It was, said Macmillan afterwards, 'the week of most strain I can ever remember in my life'.[17]

After the Cuban crisis had subsided, there were new signs of a *détente* with Russia, accelerated both by this exposure of the limitation of their power, and by the widening split with China. Macmillan, in contrast to his mood after the summit fiasco, was now talking less about the Russians as barbarians, and renewing his old hopes that Russia, as she became a richer, more bourgeois power, would become more genuinely concerned with peace. He was very mindful of Arthur Balfour's remark, before the Russian revolution: 'The more Russia is made a European, rather than an Asiatic power, the better for everybody.'[18] With Kennedy at Bermuda in 1960, he had explained how 'after reading Russian novels and everything else he could find about Russia, he felt that they might come round. . . . The West thought of them as enormously different, but their economic and social structure was not that alien.'[19] He talked often about the civilizing process within Russia: 'I remember how much in 1912 we admired Russian civilization: how we read Tolstoy and Dostoevski,' he recalled after he had resigned: 'I could not think that it was right to go on regarding the Russians as though they were barbarians.'[20]

The fact is that since 1959 [he said in June 1963],[21] there has been a *détente* between East and West, not in treaties or documents but in tone. Neither side has pressed its case unreasonably . . . we have begun to grasp the idea that the Russians should become Europeans. It may take a generation or two. But even in the last ten years they have become a much more modern society – I suppose we would like to say a much more bourgeois society – and this is the sort of thing that inevitably leads to a slackening of tension, in spite of the cold war which goes on – the spy activities and so on.

He explained that one reason for a partial test ban would be because 'one actual agreement would symbolize the *détente* which everyone knows has taken place but which it is difficult for any of us to grasp until there has been one solid achievement'.

He was encouraged by the Sino-Soviet split, and in conversation with Khrushchev, compared the dispute with the dilemma of the early Christian Church:

The early Christians in the first century acted and preached in accordance with their belief that the end of the world and the Second Coming were imminent. Then after a century they had to recognize that the world was not about to come to an end, and that the Second Coming was not imminent. So they had to adapt their theology and start to build a Church which would last in a world that was not going to come to an end.[21]

Macmillan never lost sight of his ambition for a test-ban treaty, and Kennedy was much closer to him on this than Eisenhower had been. A month after the Cuba crisis, the disarmament conference resumed at Geneva, just as the Americans and Russians were finishing their series of nuclear tests in the atmosphere. There were signs that the Russians might compromise about inspections, and new technical discussions began in the New Year: but the two powers could not agree about the number of inspections – the Americans wanted eight, the Russians wanted three – and negotiations again failed.

Kennedy and Macmillan went on trying. In March and April 1963, after exchanging careful drafts, they wrote a joint letter to Khrushchev, suggesting that the quota of inspections might be spread over several years, and that very senior representatives might go to Moscow, to speak on their behalf to

Khrushchev – thus by-passing the embattled experts at Geneva. Khrushchev wrote a reply which was 'declamatory and rude', and Kennedy, after reading it said, 'I'm not hopeful, I'm not hopeful'.[22] But Ormsby-Gore picked out the last paragraph of Khrushchev's letter, in which he grudgingly said he was prepared to have a discussion with senior representatives in Moscow, and suggested that the Western reply should concentrate on this, and suggest a meeting. Kennedy and Macmillan agreed, and a reply went off. In early June, Khrushchev said he would accept the emissaries, though the result depended 'on what they brought in their baggage to Moscow'.

Macmillan still hankered after a summit meeting, but Kennedy thought that Macmillan's presence would annoy the French and West Germans.[23] Eventually Kennedy and Macmillan both proposed Averell Harriman, the veteran American Under-Secretary of State, ex-ambassador to Moscow, 'a most practised and able negotiator', as Macmillan described him: and as the British representative Macmillan chose Lord Hailsham, because he 'has exactly the complimentary qualities' (he told journalists that he sent Hailsham because he thought he might amuse Khrushchev). The choice of Hailsham for this delicate negotiation aroused a good deal of surprised comment, and foreshadowed Macmillan's private predilection for Hailsham as his successor. Kennedy, after talking with Hailsham and Macmillan when he was passing through London in June, was worried that Hailsham would be too keen to mediate between America and Russia, and to get a treaty at almost any cost: and Macmillan agreed that Harriman should lead the negotiations.[24]

The Western delegation saw Khrushchev on 15 July, and he immediately ruled out the possibility of a comprehensive ban, since he still considered inspection to be a pretext for espionage. So Harriman pressed for a ban excluding underground tests, which he thought could be agreed in a few days, and negotiations began with Gromyko. Harriman argued toughly, insisting among other things on a clause which allowed any power to withdraw from the treaty in the light of 'extraordinary events'. Hailsham was worried about Harriman's inflexibility, and reported his worries to Macmillan, who asked Ormsby-Gore to call on Kennedy. Soon afterwards Macmillan spoke to Kennedy on the telephone, 'with a certain elaborateness', saying that he had had to ask Ormsby-Gore to express his concern. Kennedy replied: 'Don't worry, David is right here. It's been worked out, and I've told them to go ahead.'[25]

On 25 July, the treaty was initialled in Moscow, and Macmillan told the House of Commons: 'The House will, I know, understand my own feelings at seeing at last the result of efforts made over many years and of hopes long deferred.' It was the fifth time that Macmillan had tried for a limited ban, and it had at last succeeded.

There were, of course, many other factors besides Macmillan's long efforts. The British diplomats and scientists had shown great patience, both with the Russians and the Americans, as the balance swung from one to the other. Kennedy had gone a long way in countering the objections of the experts and of the Senate. And the main reason for the treaty was that both the superpowers, for the first time simultaneously, had an interest in ending tests. But Macmillan had succeeded, through the years of distrust, in keeping the lines open, and keeping the object in sight; and he had argued the case passionately and effectively. The test-ban treaty was a magnificent achievement.

Ten weeks later, on 8 October, the treaty was ratified, and Kennedy wrote a private letter to Macmillan which, when he heard of Macmillan's illness, he suggested should be published.

Dear Friend,

This morning, as I signed the instrument of ratification of the Nuclear Test Ban Treaty, I could not but reflect on the extent to which your steadfastness of commitment and determined perseverance made this treaty possible. Thanks to your never flagging interest, we were ready with our views when the Soviets decided they were ready to negotiate.

If humanity is to be spared further radio-active contamination of the atmosphere, if the nuclear arms race is to be slowed down, if we are to make more rapid progress towards lasting stability in international affairs, it would be in no small measure due to your own deep concern and long labour.

History will eventually record your indispensable role in bringing about the limitation of nuclear testing; but I cannot let this moment pass without expressing to you my own keen appreciation of your signal contribution to world peace.

With warm regards,
Sincerely, JOHN F. KENNEDY

But Macmillan's moment of triumph came when the British public had other things to think about. When the treaty was signed, Britain was in the throes of the Profumo affair; and just after Kennedy's letter was published, Macmillan from his sickbed announced his resignation. His real achievements were apt to be unnoticed.

NOTES

1. Arthur M. Schlesinger Jr, *A Thousand Days* (Boston, Mass.: Houghton Mifflin, 1965; London: Deutsch), p. 340
2. Theodore Sorensen, *Kennedy* (New York: Harper & Row, 1965; London: Hodder & Stoughton), p. 559
3. Dwight D. Eisenhower, *Waging Peace* (New York: Doubleday, 1966; London: Heinemann), p. 482
4. Ibid., p. 479
5. Sir Michael Wright, *Disarm and Verify* (London: Chatto & Windus, 1964), p. 136
6. Arthur M. Schlesinger Jr, *A Thousand Days*, p. 401
7. House of Commons, 5 March 1962
8. Arthur M. Schlesinger Jr, *A Thousand Days*, p. 401
9. Dwight D. Eisenhower, *Waging Peace*, p. 481
10. Sir Michael Wright, *Disarm and Verify*, pp. 137-8
11. Arthur M. Schlesinger Jr, *A Thousand Days*, p. 430
12. Ibid., pp. 432-3
13. From Elie Abel, *The Missiles of October* (London: MacGibbon & Kee, 1966), p. 82
14. Arthur M. Schlesinger Jr, *A Thousand Days*, p. 697
15. Theodore Sorensen, *Kennedy*, p. 705
16. Arthur M. Schlesinger Jr, *A Thousand Days*, p. 699
17. House of Commons, 17 June 1963
18. Harold Macmillan, *Winds of Change*, vol. I (London: Macmillan, 1963), p. 13

19. Arthur M. Schlesinger Jr, *A Thousand Days*, p. 430
20. *The Sunday Times*, 9 February 1964
21. *The Daily Express*, 12 June 1963
22. Arthur M. Schlesinger Jr, *A Thousand Days*, p. 767
23. Theodore Sorensen, *Kennedy*, p. 735
24. Ibid., p. 734
25. Arthur M. Schlesinger Jr, *A Thousand Days*, p. 775

16. Departure

*We know of no spectacle more ridiculous as the British public
in one of its periodical fits of morality.*
MACAULAY

By the autumn of 1962, when the new purged cabinet reassembled, there was little left of the Tory election euphoria
of three years before. There were many signs that the mood of
the country had changed. The war nostalgia which marked the
post-Suez time had given way to a spate of national introspec-
tion and enquiry, epitomized by a succession of books and TV
programmes, and reaching a climax with a masochistic number of *Encounter* magazine, called 'Suicide of a Nation?'.
The phrase 'never had it so good' had gone sour since the pay
pause. Puritan critics, led by *The Times*, were encouraged by
the enormous and unpredicted proliferation of betting shops
and gambling clubs which followed the Betting Act of July
1960, and the relaxation of obscenity laws and film censorship.
The failure of the summit, and the success of the Common
Market, underlined Britain's weakened position in the world,
and the young American president could not but draw attention to the age of the British prime minister. A sudden upsurge
of satire, set off by the revue *Beyond the Fringe*, the magazine
Private Eye, and the B.B.C.'s *That Was The Week That Was*,
gave a new platform for the protests of youth, and undermined
the more pompous aspects of government; a parody of Macmillan's television style by Peter Cook in *Beyond the Fringe*
epitomized the new scepticism about the old 'Supermac'. The

public-opinion polls had shown a growing swing against the Tories. They had lost the 'middle ground' of which Macmillan had been so confident; and would never regain it.

Macmillan was well aware of the unpopularity, and belatedly tried to give a new stimulus to the Government: apart from the purge, there was a series of new royal commissions, on broadcasting, education, traffic and science. But Macmillan could not convey any sense of excitement or optimism for the future generation, for he did not feel it. Macmillan in 1959 seemed to fit in with the mood of the country; Macmillan in 1962 seemed left behind by the tide. The slogans Supermac and Macwonder were now totally inapposite.

At the party conference in October 1962 Macmillan rode the waves. There was little sign of anyone challenging his leadership. But he was facing a series of new troubles. In September the spy Vassall had been arrested and sentenced. The Press and the opposition, in full cry for another spy scandal, clamoured for a full enquiry, and the papers were full of wild stories involving the two admiralty ministers, Lord Carrington and Thomas Galbraith. As Macmillan himself later described it: 'Every now and then, of course, a wave of this kind of emotion sweeps over a large number of people and while it is in full flood it is almost irresistible.' The Press hounded Galbraith, Galbraith offered his resignation, and Macmillan felt bound to accept it: he told Galbraith that the resignation might, in the end, help him, Galbraith, but would not help himself.[1] The Press continued to clamour for Carrington's blood, and eventually, on 14 November, Macmillan announced an enquiry, led by Lord Radcliffe. The tribunal met the next month; the journalists summoned before it refused to reveal the sources of their allegations, and were sent to prison. Lord Radcliffe exonerated the ministers, Galbraith was reinstated, and the Press was humiliated. But it was a Pyrrhic victory for the Government; for it brought about a simmering resentment in the Press – all the way from *The Times* to *The News of the World* – which was to have its revenge soon afterwards.

Through the autumn the troubles mounted. The Common

Market negotiations approached an impasse. The Cuba crisis showed up Britain's irrelevance. The Americans cancelled Skybolt. Macmillan had his awkward encounter at Rambouillet. The winter was the coldest for nearly two centuries, and unemployment rose to a new peak of four per cent. And then, in February, the Common Market negotiations collapsed. By the beginning of March – with Britain still freezing – the Labour lead in the Gallup polls was the highest for seventeen years.

How could Macmillan survive? He had now been prime minister for over six years, a longer continuous stretch than anyone had had since Asquith. Enemies made over the years now had their opportunity. The Press were against him. *The Times* demanded his resignation as early as November, insisting that 'the country has moved near enough to a presidential form of government to mean that only a change of Prime Minister will persuade people that they are looking upon a new Ministry'. The opponents of the wind of change policy, the opponents of the Common Market policy, the opponents of the inflationary policy, the opponents of the purge, were all poised for the kill. There was a growing feeling – particularly after the election of Harold Wilson as leader of the Labour party in February at the age of forty-seven – that the Tories needed a younger man. In March, a Gallup poll showed that three out of five people in Britain thought that Macmillan should go. For later historians who look for the causes of the eclipse of the Tory party in the mid-sixties, the failure to oust Macmillan at this point must be a central element.

But he survived. The 'Mac must go' movement in Parliament, as Anthony Howard reported it on 23 February, 'seemed to be confined to a few Knights of the Shires, virtually the whole of the Chip-on-the-Shoulder Brigade and a large proportion of the seventy-two Tory M.P.s elected for the first time in 1959'. There was no seriously organized movement, because there was no single alternative leader.

And in cabinet, and in his private talks, Macmillan still kept his control. His colleagues found him less forceful, and

241

visibly aging; but he was still a master of committees, still adept at weighing and balancing; and the more anxious and apprehensive the party became, the more it favoured his air of Olympian detachment. By March, he was well aware of the resentments building up against him. He had talks with party leaders, and mentioned the possibility of retiring; but came to the conclusion that no one else could take over a united party, and that he should stay on. By 10 April, at the annual lunch of the 1922 Committee he spoke gaily about modernization and efficiency, and then cheerfully announced: 'I shall be leading you into the general election and I shall be with you in the new parliament.' Many Tory M.P.s were aghast. But Macmillan set about blandly preparing the party for an election, with the unlikely slogan 'modernize with Macmillan'.

In the meantime, from March until May, the arrest of Chief Enahoro, whose deportation for trial was demanded by the Nigerian Government, brought a new wave of resentment against the Government: Macmillan and Brooke, the home secretary, appeared dishonest and inhumane in their arguments.

And then, in June, when Macmillan was holidaying in Scotland, the Profumo scandal – which had been brewing up over the last six months – finally broke over his head. John Profumo, the Minister for War, wrote to the prime minister to say that he had lied to the House of Commons, and wished to resign his seat. To a prime minister already under heavy attack, this sudden announcement, which brought back the whole network of scandals and rumours that surrounded Profumo – seemed bound to be the final blow. For the scandal, when it first emerged – following hard on the Argyll divorce case – seemed to be a melodramatic caricature of the case against Macmillan's administration: the arrogant amateurism; the covering up; the casualness towards security; the fondness for aristocrats; the 'never had it so good'; and finally the complacent indifference of the prime minister himself. All these complaints burst out again, in a new flood of righteous indignation, when Profumo admitted his lie. The Press, still smarting under the Vassall affair, knew its moment had come, and *The Times* summed up the indictment with a celebrated editorial called 'It *is* a moral issue':

Eleven years of Conservative rule have brought the nation psychologically and spiritually to a low ebb. . . . The Prime Minister and his colleagues can cling together and be still there a year hence. They will have to do more than that to justify themselves.

The Gallup poll after Profumo's confession showed Labour with the highest lead it had recorded in twenty-five years – twenty per cent – and Macmillan with the lowest rating since Chamberlain.

As soon as Profumo confessed, it seemed to many people in both parties that Macmillan must be deeply implicated, that he must have known about it, and decided to hush it up, and it was this that gave real excitement to the attack. Between the confession and the reassembly of Parliament there was a fortnight for rumours to spread, undenied. In fact Macmillan was very vulnerable – to the charge of incompetence, not of complicity – but the more excited and hysterical the attack became, the safer was his position. For he had one major advantage over all his critics – that he alone knew the full story. By being able to confute most, if not all, the accusations and rumours, he could make his opponents look gullible and foolish; and in the aftermath of public shame that was bound to follow, his dignity could be restored. And, in another respect, the Profumo affair made his position more secure. It very soon became clear to his colleagues that the one thing that could not be allowed to happen was for the prime minister to be brought down, as he himself put it, 'by two tarts'. As Lord Hailsham, with well-timed anger, announced on television: 'A great party is not to be brought down because of a scandal by a woman of easy virtue and a proved liar.' And so, by great irony, the Profumo affair which looked as if it would be the means of ousting Macmillan, turned out to be the means of his survival.

On 9 June, after a week-end of frenzied attack from the Press – led by *The Sunday Telegraph* – Macmillan returned to

London, to face the storm. He arrived with apparent calm, and announced that Lord Hailsham would be going to Moscow, to negotiate a test-ban treaty. He met the party leaders, and summoned a cabinet, in which he partly reassured his colleagues, most notably Enoch Powell.

On 17 June the great debate came. Harold Wilson began by announcing that the disclosures had 'shocked the moral conscience of the nation'. But he carefully concentrated his attack on Macmillan's neglect of security:

After the Vassall case [he summed up], he felt that he could not stand another serious security case involving a ministerial resignation, and he gambled desperately and hoped that nothing would ever come out. For political reasons he was gambling with national security. I think that this is why he was at such pains to demonstrate to me his unflappability and his unconcern.

Macmillan, facing the great test of his career, made a speech of studied candour. He knew the advantage, in times of crisis, of frankness to the House of Commons. ('It is part of its tradition that, as in a school, Members admire a boy who owns up', he later wrote about Baldwin, and went on to quote a passage from Trollope: 'The fact is if you "own up" in a genial sort of way the House will forgive anything.'[2]) He began with high emotion:

On me, as head of the Administration, what has happened has inflicted a deep, bitter, and lasting wound . . . I find it difficult to tell the House what a blow it has been to me, for it seems to have undermined one of the very foundations upon which political life must be conducted.

He explained, with breathtaking frankness, why he had not himself questioned Profumo:

First, I thought he would have spoken more freely to the Chief Whip and the Law Officers than to me, his political chief. Secondly, for me personally to carry out an examination of this kind, in the probing detail necessary, would have made it difficult, if not impossible, for him to feel in future . . . that he enjoyed my confidence.

He went on:

I must confess frankly to the House that, in considering what I
should do, the Vassall case, and the effect which it had upon Mr Galbraith, was certainly in my mind. I have been reproached for accepting the resignation of my hon. Friend when I did, when rather similar
rumours were circulating. . . .

The admission of personal embarrassment revealed an extraordinary weakness in a prime minister. It showed – as the
clumsiness of the purge had showed – that behind all Macmillan's public panache, there still lurked the inhibited introvert:
it was a very human weakness, but it was the opposite of the
Tory image of 'robustness'. There were many who thought
that, if Macmillan had confronted Profumo himself, in a
worldly and sceptical way, the lie would never have happened,
and Profumo and the party would have been saved. The picture of Macmillan's detachment was increased when he explained why he accepted Profumo's statement that the letter
to Christine Keeler beginning 'Darling' was quite harmless: 'I
believe that that might be accepted – I do not live among young
people much myself.'[3]

The main gist of Macmillan's defence was, quite simply, that
he had not been told the full evidence: he had not been told
when Profumo had been first warned by Sir Norman Brook
about his association with Ivanov, two years before; he had
not been told the evidence that the security services had
received from Stephen Ward and others. He emphasized the
dangers of security services going too far. He ended, as he had
begun, with an emotional appeal:

My colleagues have been deceived, and I have been deceived, grossly
deceived – and the House has been deceived – but we have not been
parties to deception, and I claim that upon a fair view of the facts
as I have set them out I am entitled to the sympathetic understanding
and confidence of the House and of the country.

Macmillan's defence was not robust, but it was disarming;
and it took some of the wind out of the opposition's sails. The
debate which followed was fierce, but not lethal: the Labour

245

party had determined – rather hypocritically – to concentrate on the security risk, and that risk had not really been great. The most ferocious attack came from the Tory side, from the bitterest and cleverest of Macmillan's critics, Nigel Birch: he poured scorn on the prime minister's trust for Profumo, and ended with a demand for his resignation, and the words of Browning's 'The Lost Leader':

> . . . *let him never come back to us!*
> *There would be doubt, hesitation and pain.*
> *Forced praise on our part – the glimmer of twilight.*
> *Never glad confident morning again!*

The debate ended with a close shave: in the division, there were twenty-seven abstentions, from the left as well as the right of the party, including Nigel Birch, Aubrey Jones, Lord Lambton, Peter Kirk, Anthony Fell, Humphry Berkeley and Harry Legge-Bourke. Macmillan left the House looking bowed and dispirited.

For the next two weeks, Macmillan was on the brink. 'I had been astonished on the Monday of the debate,' recorded R. A. Butler afterwards, 'by the absolute rage of fire which worked through the Conservative party in favour of a younger man.'[4] To Macmillan's enemies, the affair and his speech summed up just what was wrong with him – his out-of-touchness, his self-absorption, his age. For a few days – as he described it afterwards – he himself considered 'chucking it all in';[5] he felt the traditions of Toryism had been betrayed by the Cliveden swimming-pool. But he knew that he could expect a wave of support from the constituencies; and the party leaders had decided that, for the time being at least, they needed him to stay. The Conservative whips tried to rally supporters by suggesting that if they supported Macmillan now, he would retire in a few months' time. That there was any kind of 'bargain' was hotly denied; but certainly there was an understanding. It was also suggested, in an implausible interpretation of the constitution, that if Macmillan was forced to resign now, the Queen might have to send for Harold Wilson to form a

Government. On the week-end after the debate Lord Poole warned Tory officials in a public speech:

If they throw out, or seem to have thrown out, the prime minister as a direct result of the Profumo affair, there will be such a revulsion of feeling in the country as a whole that they will not need to speculate much about the result of the next general election, or perhaps the one after that.

But Poole, like the whips, was careful not to commit himself as to how long Macmillan should stay. Then, a week later, Macmillan appeared in a television interview, in which he finally made clear his intention to continue: 'All being well, if I keep my health and strength, I hope to lead the party into the election . . . of course, I must have the support of the party, and I think I have it.' On the same week-end, underlining Macmillan's statesmanship, President Kennedy stopped at Birch Grove, and Macmillan told him that Britain could not accept a mixed-manned nuclear fleet for NATO.

For the time being he had got away with it. Once the excitement was over, the Gallup polls showed a less extreme Labour swing, dropping to fourteen-and-a-half per cent on 10 August. But there were great worries as to whether he could lead the party to an election, and sporadic sniping from rivals. R. A. Butler, on 8 July, said on television: 'I think I am pretty well aware that people want us to give a fresh impression of vigour and decision before the next election.' Maudling, at a fête in Cambridgeshire, said 'We have not been successful in obtaining the allegiance of the younger generation of voters, because we have not yet found a way of talking to them in language they understand or in terms of the ideals they cherish.' Macmillan knew that – as he put it – 'They may want to get rid of the old gentleman at the top'; but he knew too that the rivals for the succession, insofar that they existed, tended to cancel each other out. He was still very much in control of the cabinet; and when he met the 1922 Committee to justify himself on 25 July, he was able by a lucky chance to announce the initialling of the test-ban treaty. He told the backbenchers, 'My sole motive is to serve the party and the country – and when I go it will be after consultation with those people whose view I hold in the highest regard'. On 1 August, just before Parliament went on holiday, he appeared on TV again, and said that he wanted to continue as leader, to follow up the test-ban treaty, and to consolidate the party. He had recovered his position, to an extraordinary extent, since the debate; and he had kept the question of when he should go firmly in his own hands.

In the holiday, Macmillan began discussing again the possible successors. Once again there was his old rival of the thirties, Butler. By appointing Butler deputy prime minister, Macmillan had certainly made him *appear* as the crown prince. 'It can be argued that Macmillan did all he could during his seven years as Prime Minister to advance the fortunes of Butler,' wrote Randolph Churchill in his Macmillan-inspired account;[6] and Lord Swinton, who was Macmillan's confidant, concurs.[7] Macleod gave the opposite view: 'The truth is that at all times, from the first day of his premiership to the last, Macmillan was determined that Butler, though incomparably the best qualified of the contenders, should not succeed him.'[8] It seems clear, in the light of what happened, that Macmillan, while outwardly promoting Butler, was ensuring that he should not succeed; but for part of this, at least, Butler himself must be blamed, for it became clear later that Butler had virtually thrown in the sponge: 'I reached the conclusion in June of that year . . .,' he said afterwards, 'that it was almost inevitable that the Conservative party would choose a younger man.'[9]

Maudling, too, was clearly not favoured by Macmillan. He had made him Chancellor of the Exchequer and admired his ability, but he could not see him as leading the party to electoral victory: and the two men had very little liking for each other. With Heath, Macmillan had much closer bonds: he had always been his special protégé, and had shown his mettle at Brussels. But since the defeat at Brussels, Macmillan had callously allowed Heath to slide into obscurity, with no special signs of trust or responsibility: he was merely number two in the Foreign Office. Macmillan's failure to promote the man whom he had himself virtually discovered, and whom the party eventually chose for themselves, remains one of the paradoxes of his political legacy. The ambiguities of his character showed themselves in the contenders: the separate strands finally came apart, leaving only loose ends.

Considering all the successors, Macmillan eventually, and quite privately, made a truly astonishing choice – Lord Hailsham. He discussed the possibility with friends, and by the end of September had told Hailsham himself. In the past, Macmillan and Hailsham had been visibly at odds: their rivalry went back as far as 1938, when Macmillan spoke against Hailsham at the Oxford by-election, where Hailsham was the official Tory appeaser. During most of his premiership, Macmillan was irritated by Hailsham's emotionalism and rhetoric, and he was embarrassed by his flamboyant leadership of the party in the 1959 election. Hailsham was disappointed when, after the election, he was rewarded with the minuscule job of Minister of Science. He was unsympathetic to Macmillan's policies on the wind of change and on the Common Market, and was not entrusted with delicate missions. Macmillan and Hailsham, it is true, had points of background in common – American mothers, Etonian scholars, Disraelian attitudes; but Hailsham had little sympathy with Macmillan's aristocratic style and convoluted political methods.

Yet during 1963, Macmillan came round to the idea of Hailsham: an early warning of this was his sending of Hailsham to Moscow in June, to negotiate the test-ban treaty – a job for which he was not well suited. Macmillan evidently thought that Hailsham could rally the party to an election victory, and that, if the party didn't want himself, they had best have the opposite. Some colleagues went so far as to suspect that he had put up Hailsham in the knowledge that, faced with this bizarre alternative, the party would quickly turn back to the devil it knew. The reasoning of any dominating leader contemplating retirement is infinitely self-deceiving: in

Macmillan's case it was to prove disastrous. He found it difficult to imagine anyone as a satisfactory successor: and he seemed, in the end, to regard all his colleagues with some degree of contempt.

In any case Macmillan was undecided whether to stay on. On the week-end of 5 October – just before the annual Tory conference – he seemed inclined to resign, but was urged to stay by his son Maurice and his son-in-law, Julian Amery, and Lord Poole, who came over for lunch. He was persuaded that only he could achieve a further *détente* between America and Russia – much as Churchill had been persuaded nine years before. He had talks with the foreign secretary, Lord Home, who had just got back from Washington, and agreed that there was a good prospect of a summit in the spring. By Monday Macmillan had made up his mind to stay, and had written half his speech for the conference.

Then, on 8 October, the decision was taken out of his hands. He woke up in pain, and summoned the doctor, who diagnosed a blocked prostate gland, but thought an operation was not necessary. He presided over a three-hour cabinet, and told his colleagues that there would have to be a decision about the leadership at Blackpool, and that he would announce it. But that evening, Macmillan was told he must have an operation, and was taken to hospital. While the delegates to the conference were assembling at Blackpool, they were astonished to hear from the B.B.C. news that Macmillan would be absent from official duties for some weeks, and that the First Secretary, Butler, would – once again – be acting prime minister.

The next day, while Macmillan was being prepared for the operation in hospital, he finally decided that he must resign. Several factors pressed on him. He thought he was more ill than he in fact was (only a fortnight afterwards he was regretting his decision). He was conscious that there was no enthusiasm for him staying on, and that the chief whip in particular, Martin Redmayne – who had rallied the party during the Profumo debate – was clearly now anxious for him to go. And the next morning, as a *coup de grâce, The Times* had a strong leader which insisted that

It is necessary for the nation's future political health that the coming election finds both parties at their best and the battle be closely fought. Each leader has to have the capacity to be either a strenuous prime minister or energetic in opposition. Mr Macmillan has said more than once that he will do what is best for the nation and his party. His colleagues must be ready to do likewise.

Macmillan, for once, took *The Times*'s advice. He sent off a letter which he had dictated the previous night, to Lord Home, to announce to the conference; and that evening at Blackpool Home read out the message, in which Macmillan said, 'It is now clear that, whatever might have been my previous feelings, it will not be possible for me to carry the physical burden of leading the party at the next general election,' and hoped that, 'It will soon be possible for the customary processes of consultation to be carried on within the party about its future leadership'.

Thus followed the most extraordinary part of Macmillan's premiership – his leaving of it. It was the most chaotic interregnum for the Tory party since 1922. Not only was it faced with the prospect of operating the obscure customary processes in the full glare of the conference and TV publicity; but also, in the meantime, Macmillan's pervasive influence was still making itself felt from the sick-bed. The resulting intrigue and muddle was so thick that, after it, the customary processes were abandoned for ever.

Macmillan's active preference for Hailsham, which he had made known at the week-end, soon became known to the conference, through his confidants Amery, Soames and his son Maurice. Hailsham rashly threw his hat into the ring by announcing that he would disclaim his peerage. It seemed for a short while that the timing of Macmillan's resignation, in the midst of this emotional assembly, would favour Hailsham's rumbustious personality. Hailsham was visibly revelling in the blaze of publicity; he appeared exuberantly on television, posing with his baby and baby-food, and reacted boyishly to the cheering crowds, urged on by his small clique. But as Hailsham's popular following grew, so the opposition of his colleagues became more apparent: they were resentful of his barging ahead, and alarmed by his demagogy. Twenty-four hours after he had entered the ring, it was clear that there was a strong 'Stop Hailsham' movement.

The other contenders were all at a disadvantage: they could not, by the traditions of the party, proclaim their candidature too loudly. They were expected quietly to 'emerge'; but in this urgent and noisy atmosphere, they could not safely remain silent. Butler was obviously available: he had insisted on making the leader's speech at the end of the conference, and had moved into the suite booked for Macmillan. 'I certainly put my hat in the ring,' he said afterwards, 'and did my best to show that if I were wanted, I was available.'[10] But Butler did not put in his hat at all boldly, and neither did the other likely contenders, Maudling and Macleod. Butler maintains that he was unaware until the end of the week that there was a fifth contender – Lord Home:

The first I heard of Home getting the job was when I was sitting in one of those delightful hotel bedrooms at the party conference, and Alec Home, who is a very straightforward and decent man, came in to me and talked to me before the speech I made – on the afternoon of the Saturday. He said: 'I'm going to see my doctor on Tuesday', and I said 'Why?', and he said: 'Because I have been approached about the possibility of my becoming the Leader of the Conservative party.'[11]

In fact, as soon as it was clear that Hailsham could not command support, key figures in the party had veered towards Lord Home; and these included Major John Morrison, the chairman of the 1922 Committee, and Martin Redmayne, the chief whip. It was a choice which clearly showed a determination to avoid Butler. Yet Butler could easily have prevented it, by letting it be known that he would not serve under Home. By the Monday after the conference, Macmillan had recovered from his operation and, observing the chaos he had left from his hospital bed, determined to resolve it. He dictated a memorandum to his deputy, Butler, proposing that polls be taken of all the main elements of the party – cabinet, Commons, Lords and constituencies. Butler read the memorandum to the cabinet next day, who accepted it, and the polls were instituted. In the meantime Macmillan had visits from most of his cabinet, one by one, in his hospital room.

By Thursday, the critical day, the soundings were completed: Macmillan, from the matron's room, received the reports one by one. All four reports showed a preference for Home. Lord Dilhorne, the Lord Chancellor, had been taking the soundings, as Butler described it, 'like a large clumber spaniel sniffing the bottoms of the hedgerows': he reported a clear majority in the cabinet for Home. After lunch, Macmillan saw the pollsters again, this time together, and asked them to repeat to the others their advice: 'From their advice it became clear,' reported Randolph Churchill, 'that those who wanted Hailsham were violent against Butler and those who wanted Butler were equally violent against Hailsham. Everything pointed to Home.'

In the meantime, Macleod and Maudling, having heard rumours that Home was to be chosen, were determined to oppose it, claiming that they did not even know he was a contender: 'It is some measure of the tightness of the magic circle on this occasion,' wrote Macleod in a celebrated attack 'that neither the Chancellor of the Exchequer nor the Leader of the House of Commons had any inkling of what was happening.'[12] Macleod, Maudling and others met at midnight at Enoch Powell's house and planned to stop Home's election: they telephoned the chief whip, and asked him to report this alliance to Macmillan. The next morning Macleod organized a meeting between Butler, Maudling and Hailsham to confirm the 'Stop Home' movement.

But the next morning, when Macmillan had been told of this 'Stop Home' movement and had read the morning papers, he was determined to push ahead with Home's nomination.

When Home, on the telephone, seemed hesitant, he said 'Look, we can't change our view now. All the troops are on the starting line. Everything is arranged. It will just cause ghastly confusion if we delay.'[13] Just after 9.0 A.M. Macmillan sent his private secretary, Timothy Bligh, with his letter of resignation to the Queen. Two hours later, the Queen came to visit him in hospital. Macmillan read her a memorandum he had prepared, incorporating the four reports from the pollsters and recommending the choice of Lord Home. An hour later, it was announced that the Queen had invited Lord Home to try to form an administration.

And so Macmillan's premiership ended, on the most controversial note of all. It was not, of course, he alone who was responsible for putting in Lord Home; the old guard of the party were right behind him. But without Macmillan's intervention, it is very unlikely that Home would have got the job; and it was in keeping with Macmillan's style of government that he should leave the country, for the first time in the twentieth century, with a prime minister from the House of Lords.

NOTES

1. See Macmillan's speech on Profumo, 17 June 1963
2. Harold Macmillan, *Winds of Change*, vol. I (London: Macmillan, 1966), p. 409
3. Hansard [*sic*]
4. *The Listener*, 28 July 1966 (interview with Kenneth Harris)
5. *The Daily Express*, 12 July 1963
6. Randolph Churchill, *The Fight for the Tory Leadership* (London: Heinemann, 1964), p. 94
7. Lord Swinton, *Sixty Years of Power* (London: Hutchinson, 1966), p. 189
8. *The Spectator*, 17 January 1964
9. *The Listener*, 28 July 1966 (interview with Kenneth Harris)
10. Ibid. 11. Ibid.
12. *The Spectator*, 17 January 1964
13. Randolph Churchill, *The Fight for the Tory Leadership*, p. 137

17. Macmillan and his Age

If people want a sense of purpose they should get it from their archbishop. They should certainly not get it from their politicians.
HAROLD MACMILLAN TO HENRY FAIRLIE, 1963

What, in the end, was the achievement of Harold Macmillan? How far did he realize his own ambitions? How far did he alter the course of English history? The next generation of Tories who had been under his spell, and then found themselves out of office, were soon inclined to associate the name of Macmillan with deception and failure. Looking back on the great schemes, now, on which he spent so much eloquence and time, they add up to surprisingly little. The visit to Moscow didn't achieve much. The summit was a fiasco. The wind of change speech had a quite different result to that which was intended. The attempt to join the Common Market was abortive. While he constantly spoke of the need for an independent deterrent in 'the counsels of the world', the bomb added little to our world influence; and the worsening economic situation at home – made worse still by Macmillan's refusal to deflate or devalue – undermined Britain's influence abroad. Of his positive schemes only one – the test-ban treaty – was a triumph.

Looking back on his career as prime minister, it is hard to find consistent aims, and easy to find inconsistencies: the image of juggling five balls in the air, which he used to Lord Swinton of his political operations, was all too applicable to his statesmanship: he seemed confident that, by skilful juggling, he could dodge the real choices. He stuck to Churchill's old idea of Britain being at the centre of three interlocking circles, long after the geo-political realities had made this absurd. While trying to move closer to Europe he was trying still harder not to move away from America. In his attitude to Afro-Asians, he oscillated between being tough (as at Suez) and conciliating (as in the wind of change) – he could not decide whether he was a Baldwin or a Churchill. In his attitude to Russians, he seemed equally eloquent about them as a barbarian threat, and as a satisfied power.

How much of this confusion and ineffectiveness was an inevitable result of Britain's post-war dilemma, and how far could anyone else have done better? Certainly, in the first years of his rule, the problems were ugly, and Macmillan succeeded, as perhaps no one else could, in restoring confidence and self-respect. It is important to recall the anger and frustration of the pre-Suez time – even apart from the Suez crisis itself. It was the time when Britain, both on the Left and the Right, was finally becoming aware of her reduced role in the world: and this was not a message that any prime minister could afford to proclaim. As with de Gaulle, some measure of national deception seemed called for; and, however inconsequential the showmanship and panache of Macmillan may now look, it was very necessary in the late 1950s. It is doubtful whether any more straightforward prime minister – certainly not a Labour one – could have survived the retreat from Suez and Africa, without a jingo rebellion from both sides. There was a sense in which Macmillan in 1958 and 1959 exactly personified the state of the country. In that time of nostalgia, war memoirs and sudden affluence, he reassured the British that they were, above all, civilized: and even though they had lost influence and were living beyond their means, the special relationship to America made up for that. Macmillan's picture of Anglo-American relations, of 'being Greeks in their Roman Empire' was a consoling one for many: and it was displayed with a flourish in the extraordinary television duet of Macmillan and Eisenhower.

Macmillan's ambiguities undoubtedly succeeded, as de Gaulle's succeeded, in disarming the right wing. Like Disraeli and other Tory leaders, he provided the shadow of old-fashioned conservatism, without the substance, and this made him hard to attack and harder to outbid: two years after he had taken office, the attitudes of Lord Salisbury and his group already visibly belonged to a different age, and to a blind alley. He had succeeded in realigning the Tory party, and edging it towards the contemporary world, in a way that neither Churchill nor Eden had succeeded, or even really tried. And he had helped to hold together the Western alliance, and to modify American attitudes, at a time when the world seemed dangerously close to war.

If he had resigned in 1960 his record – at least in the eyes of his own party – would have been remarkable: he would certainly have been acknowledged as one of the great prime ministers of the century. But after the 1959 election the retreat was over, Suez and Salisbury were forgotten, and a new generation of Tory M.P.s and Tory voters looked for positive policies, a much more radical readjustment of Britain's role, and even for a crusade. The party had the biggest majority since the war, the opposition was demoralized and there was no sign of a rival leader. It was then that Macmillan had his greatest opportunity, and then that he showed his real inadequacy and age. With his juggling and conjuring, the lack of constructive political thinking became more apparent. Between 1960 and 1962 Britain became much more aware of slipping back in the World League, both economically and politically. Macmillan's aloof and disdainful style, which had had its uses when concealing un-Tory behaviour, now concealed only a defensiveness, and an apparent refusal to show leadership. 'They've never had it so good' rebounded and re-echoed through the Stock Exchange boom, the property bonanza, the take-over bids, the 'casino capitalism', and eventually the credit squeeze: and the prime minister's aloofness was caricatured, absurdly, but not inaptly, in the Profumo affair.

No doubt any prime minister at that time would have been

tempted to evasiveness and diversions; the retreat from Empire, and the return to a duller world of productivity and balance of payments, is not a stirring course. It was difficult to provide bold measures, because nothing much was happening to Britain – it was just quietly running down. Yet Macmillan's position was, at his peak, very strong and many of the apparent obstacles to realism were, in fact, of his own making. Such is the power of publicity and patronage of a modern prime minister that he can project, not just himself, but a whole stage. Macmillan, a consummate actor-manager, could impose his own scenery, his own style, his own subject-matter, and his own cast of characters, including his successor, on to Parliament and the nation; only when they departed was it apparent how much of this décor was Macmillan's, not Britain's. Macmillan's diversionary techniques, the art of government by camouflage, had served him very well in the past; but when it came to having to change the mood and direction of the country, as was needed above all in the entry into Europe, the technique was no longer applicable; it was then that open and total commitment was needed, a visible leadership, to convince not only Britain but Europe; but by then, it seemed, the disguise had become a habit, and the crusade never came.

What was it, in Macmillan's character, that prevented him in the end from grappling with Britain's real problems? He was, after all, a man of outstanding intellect and courage; and the qualities he showed before the war – his patient capacity to analyse economic problems, his passion for organization, his intellectual integrity, his determination to say what he thought – all these were precisely what were called for at the time he came to power. To many of those who had known him before the war, the fact of his becoming prime minister seemed almost too good to be true – to have, at last, an intellectual Tory, a man who had been right on the two great pre-war issues, and who had had the courage to speak up. To them he was a kind of philosopher-king: and even to *The New Statesman* in 1955, he was the keeper of the Tory conscience, who would therefore 'never head the Tory party'.

But between the pre-war and post-war Macmillans there was a great discrepancy, which puzzled many of his colleagues; when reading his own account of his pre-war career, in which he sounds apologetic and bored by his own radical past, the discrepancy increases. 'For so able a man to have come to seem so stuffy to the present generation,' wrote *The Economist*, 'for a man of such individual charm to seem so buttoned up (and to write now in so buttoned-up a way) these are matters of psychology that a biographer, one day, will have to unravel.' Was it the fascination of power, after so long and frustrating a time in the wilderness? Was it the element of personal loneliness in his life, which induced an increasingly pessimistic view of the world? Was it the political bitterness of seeing the Labour party come to power after the war? Was it the gigantic influence of Churchill, which blurred his radical, analytical instincts and generated romance and nostalgia? Or was it, more simply, that he had grown older, sadder and softer?

Probably all these elements contributed. Certainly he had, in his own life, taken a great buffeting. Certainly, too, he was unprepared to come to terms with the new problems of the 1960s: he was confused (as he often admitted) by the new affluence, and the problems of inflation; he could not stop thinking in terms of Stockton-on-Tees; and he readily identified Nasser with Hitler. He went on refighting old battles. Like many others, he transferred the two bogys of the 1930s, appeasement and unemployment, on which he had been so right, into the quite different conditions of the 1960s. On the most important question of the 1950s, the entry into Europe, he failed – as he has written – to press the case at the most crucial time.

But perhaps the most important source of inadequacy was the fact that the different elements in his character, which showed themselves early on, never quite came to terms with each other. The conflict which made him a fascinating personality made him, in the end, a disappointing prime minister. In his last years his various personalities – the literary, the military, the intellectual, the ducal – were never fully co-ordinated, and he would, more and more, take refuge from one in another. His colleagues were never sure which Macmillan might pop up at any one time – the intellectual of the 'middle way'; the soldier of Suez; the literary doyen of clubland; the patron of earls and marquesses. The whole was never greater than the sum of the parts.

Certainly the most important Macmillan was the one of his youth, the scholar, hard-working and deeply analytical. Like Disraeli, he came to politics from a world of books: and as with Disraeli, that gave him a detachment which was valuable, but also a romanticism which was dangerous; so that when he finally became prime minister, he seemed to be living the title-role in someone else's biography. It was the intellectual Macmillan, the 'gownsman', who gave the real contribution to government: but like many politicians, he wanted to be something else, and the 'swordsman' was always longing to get out. The combination was magnificently successful in wartime, but in the post-war situation it was much more dangerous. As prime minister he wanted – even more than other prime ministers – to be involved, not in workaday economic problems, but in the heroic epics of international affairs. But at that point of history it was the intellectual realist, above all, that the country needed.

How far is it fair for Conservatives to blame Macmillan – as many now do – for their party's subsequent decline and disarray? Certainly after twelve years, with mounting resentments, any prime minister would have found it hard to keep the voters excited, and the party united. Certainly Macmillan's Tory colleagues cannot claim that they offered vigorous pressure, or an organized alternative. Certainly it would have been hard for any single leader to span two periods so different in mood as the late fifties and the early sixties. Yet Macmillan must take the main blame for the fact that the Tories lost their hold on that 'middle ground' which, as he himself had so often emphasized, was the key to political survival. Once the Tories had lost it, and given the Labour party the chance to occupy it, the counter-attack was to become increasingly difficult: the party's posture, and Macmillan's, became essentially defensive, and the purge of 1962 appeared, as it was, a desperate bid for survival. In the efforts that followed, to revivify the party and revamp its policies, neither Macmillan nor his successor ever managed to establish the sense of confidence in the future, such as Harold Wilson so carefully cultivated. And once the Tories were defeated, their lack of unifying purpose became much more apparent, and it was to prove much harder to recapture the 'middle ground' than it was after the much greater landslide of 1945.

Yet what makes a prime minister's reputation is, in the end, as much luck as character: Disraeli, after all, had many of the limitations of Macmillan, but he was on a flood tide. Macmillan became prime minister at an awkward and ebbing time; and he had two major unpredictable setbacks. The first, the collapse of the summit in 1960, though it much affected Macmillan's morale, probably did not make much difference to the pattern of events: the *détente* was to happen anyway. But the second, the collapse of the Common Market negotiations in 1963, undermined Macmillan's whole policy, both foreign and economic. If the Common Market policy had succeeded, Macmillan's historical achievement would have been spectacular; he would have pulled his party out of Africa, and into Europe, both against their traditional prejudices. It is easy now to suggest that the entry into Europe was foredoomed; but it was far from obvious to critics at the time. With only a slightly different turn to events, Macmillan and the Tory party might have made Britain part of a new Europe, and even triumphed at the general election. His ambiguities would have been justified in the final unambiguous achievement.

MACMILLAN: THE ILLUSTRATIONS

THE SCHOOLBOY: At Summer Fields and at Eton (above), the young Macmillan was quiet and introverted, with big soulful eyes. He was clever, but not outstanding, and overshadowed by his elder brother.

THE SON-IN-LAW: The young captain (who then sported a monocle)
became engaged in 1920 to the duke's daughter, Lady Dorothy Cavendish.
A huge fashionable wedding followed, and much country-house life.

THE PARLIAMENTARY SECRETARY: At forty-six he had his first taste of office, under Herbert Morrison (left) – whom he admired – in the wartime Ministry of Supply. For the first time he could put theory into practice.

THE MINISTER: In 1942 came the 'big stuff,' when Churchill sent him as Minister to Algiers, with great political scope. He had personal dealings with Churchill, and was already in some rivalry with Eden.

IN OPPOSITION: After the war, with Labour in power, Macmillan seemed personally and politically depressed. He spoke enthusiastically about United Europe – as at the Hague – but could not follow it up.

THE MAN OF THE PEOPLE: As Minister of Housing, in 1951 Macmillan became for the first time a national figure, and a Tory hero: he launched the 'people's house' and sat in it uneasily at the Ideal Home Exhibition in 1953.

THE CHANCELLOR OF THE EXCHEQUER: At the height of the Suez crisis he was to be seen in Trafalgar Square, launching the Premium Bonds with the Dagenham Girl Pipers; but he was also deeply involved with Suez.

THE PRIME MINISTER: Two months later, he became premier, and had a celebratory dinner with Churchill; he saw himself as the heir to Churchill, in seeking a summit and re-establishing the relationship with America.

THE MAN OF THE COMMONWEALTH: On his tour of the East in 1958, he gained a new confidence and panache: he was garlanded and gratified by the friendly Indian veterans (above) and acclaimed by Australian crowds; he returned to London with an extraordinary new expansiveness (below).

THE GROUSE MOORS: Macmillan liked grouse-shooting, and liked being photographed on the moors: here he is setting off with the Duchess of Devonshire and Hugh Fraser. The aristocratic image did him well in his first years as prime minister, but it eventually turned sour against him.

THE PEACEMAKER: In February 1959 Macmillan went to Moscow in a blaze of showmanship, infuriating his allies and his opposition, and receiving some snubs; but he made progress towards test bans.

THE TELEVISION STATESMAN: The bizarre climax of Macmillan's TV career came conveniently just before the 1959 election, when he appeared in an after-dinner talk with Eisenhower, exchanging views on summitry.

THE PATRICIAN: Macmillan, although bored by many aristocratic pastimes – like racing (above) – enjoyed the pageantry and theatricality of social events; like Disraeli, he seemed to see himself as part of a fashionable play.

THE MAN OF AFRICA: After the general election, Macmillan was increasingly concerned about Africa, and particularly about Rhodesia. He had constant and ambiguous exchanges with Sir Roy Welensky (above) and repeatedly had to mediate between the two ministers most involved, Macleod (right) and Sandys.

THE CHANCELLOR OF OXFORD: Back from Africa, he astonished his colleagues by standing for the Chancellorship of Oxford University, and winning: he was installed in pomp—with his mortar-board back to front—and thenceforth became even more attached to Oxford, and to Balliol.

WITH KENNEDY: Macmillan soon established a close avuncular relationship, though with less influence than during the Eisenhower days: in
June 1963, Kennedy came to stay for the week-end at Birch Grove (above).

THE EX-PRIME MINISTER: After his resignation, he recuperated quite soon, and returned to be chairman of the family publishing house, which he had left twelve years before – and which he drastically reorganized.

Index

Butler, R. A. (cont.)
Minister, 203; Common Market views, 212, 216f.; in charge when Macmillan ill, 250, 253; in succession question 248, 252

Campaign for Nuclear Disarmament, 227
Carrington, Lord, 138, 240
Caserta Agreement 1944, 70
Catroux, General, 64
Cavendish family, 16ff.
Central African Federation, 181, 184f., 190f., 193f.; breaks up, 194
Chamberlain, Neville, 26f., 36, 46, 49ff., 52f.; finally goes, 56
Chetwynd, George, 76
Christian Socialist Movement, 3, 4
Churchill, Randolph, 76, 125, 248, 253
Churchill, Winston, 51, 77, 80, 89, 90, 95; as Chancellor, 24, 26f., 48; becomes Prime Minister of Coalition 1940, 57; sends Macmillan to French North Africa, 59ff.; Casablanca Conference and after, 63ff.; Italy, 67ff.; Greece, 71ff.; iron curtain speech, 84; launches United Europe Movement 1947, 86; in power 1951, 93, 98; resignation, 100f.; influence on Macmillan, 48, 73, 85, 119
Coalition Government formed, 57
Cole, G. D. H., 39, 43, 48
Collins, Norman, 164
Colman, Prentis and Varley in 1959 election campaign, 162
Committee of Liberation, 62, 64
Common Market, 88, 105ff., 197, 209ff.; Press in favour, 210; negotiations begin, 215; Commonwealth Conference on, 216ff.; the General says no, 221f.

Commonwealth conferences, 1957, 134, 182; 1961, 191; 1962, 216
Congo, 190
Congress of Europe, 86
Conservative Party Conferences: Blackpool 1946, 80; Brighton 1947, 82; Scarborough 1952, 96; Margate 1953, 97; 1960, 154; 1961, 215; 1962, 217
Cooper, Duff, 15, 23, 33, 66
Council of Europe, 86, 106
Cranborne, Lord, see Salisbury, Lord
Cripps, Sir Stafford, 83
Crookshank, Harry, 173, 178
Crossman, Richard, 60, 65, 77, 119, 163
Crowther, Geoffrey, 38
Cuba crisis, 152, 219, 230ff.
Cyprus, 105, 116, 131, 135ff.

Dalton, Hugh, 28, 31, 50f., 85, 87, 94ff.
Damaskinos, Archbishop, 72
Darlan, Admiral, 62
Dawson, Geoffrey, 56
Deedes, William, 203, 205
De Gaulle, General, later President: leader of Committee of (National) Liberation, 62, 63, 64, 65; admiration for Macmillan during war, 62f.; Casablanca Conference, 63f.; summit talks, 143, 146, 149ff.; threatens NATO, 152; Common Market, 205, 218ff.; says no, 221f.
De Murville, Couve, 147, 212
Depressed Areas Bill 1934, 37
Devlin, Sir Patrick, 182; Devlin report, 155, 164, 182
Devonshire family, 16ff., 175
Dewinck, General, 65
De Zulueta, Philip, 174
Dilhorne, Lord, 253
Dillon, Douglas, 210f.
Disarmament, 225ff.; Geneva con-